Corwin Phelps

An Ideal Republic - or way out of the Fog

Corwin Phelps

An Ideal Republic - or way out of the Fog

ISBN/EAN: 9783337023355

Printed in Europe, USA, Canada, Australia, Japan

Cover: Foto ©Andreas Hilbeck / pixelio.de

More available books at **www.hansebooks.com**

An Ideal Republic

OR

WAY OUT OF THE FOG

BY

CORWIN PHELPS.

———

CHICAGO, ILL.

W. L. Raynolds, Publisher, 267 South Lincoln Street.

1896.

PREFACE.

In no period of our history have the signs of the times been more ominous or portentous of evil than at the present. The wonderful strides made by organized capital in the last quarter of a century, and the consequent impoverishment of the masses with its evil effects upon industry and society, the gradual encroachments of concentrated wealth upon the rights of man to live, support his family and enjoy the fruits of his toil, have been so marked as to create universal apprehension and alarm. It is in consequence of this unrest that the author has been induced to make an effort to present a pen picture in an allegorical sketch of the causes leading up to our present financial distress and at the same time offer a simple common sense solution of the problems that now confront the American people, threatening the very existence and perpetuity of our civilization.

In resorting to romance to illustrate facts the writer has only followed in the footsteps of many prominent authors, and it will be remembered that even the wise and religious teachings of the lowly Nazarene were principally allegorical.

It has been said that "God worketh all things according to His own good pleasure," and it would now seem to an observing mind that evolution is the principle through which He worketh to the end that all may steadily progress both intellectually and spiritually toward better conditions.

In the last half century so wonderful has been the progress in the invention of labor-saving machinery that our whole social system has undergone an entire change. One man under present industrial systems can produce more of the comforts of life than could ten men half a century ago. And yet we are met by the stupendous fact that those who produce these things do not enjoy the fruits of their labor.

During this marvelous period of advancement in manufacture and production the science of government has not advanced; hence the whole human economy is thrown out of balance, and until the science of government is so improved as to bring about an equilibrium we may look for financial storms, commercial disaster and great suffering. But it is to be hoped that when the great corporations and money combinations go to pieces by their own weight, and through unlimited greed have forced starvation upon the masses, then men will begin to think, the light of reason will be turned upon government, its abuses exposed, new methods and laws adopted, and man will step out upon a higher plane of civilization.

Having served as a common soldier in our civil war, and shared the joys and sorrows of the great common people of our great Republic since that time, the writer feels that his experiences have been such as would enable him to give in story a better outline of the evolution of thought on religion, politics and kindred subjects; a better history of progressive events; a truer and more perfect view of every-day life as it has occurred from day to day through the most wonderful epoch known to the history of our race than usually falls to the lot of any man; and that through long and deep meditation he has been able to pierce the great mystery that enshrouds our land, has been able to give the simplest and most logical way out of our present distress and place ourselves upon that higher plane of civilization for which mankind so fondly yearns. Call it history, forecast, romance, a fiction of higher life, in fact call it what you will, the author sends out this book feeling doubly sure it will find a warm place in every true American heart and will be cherished by all who love their fellow-man and look forward with hope toward our country's future greatness. Respectfully dedicated to every liying soul who loves mankind.

CORWIN PHELPS.

AN IDEAL REPUBLIC

OR

WAY OUT OF THE FOG.

CHAPTER I.

GENERAL BUNDY had obtained a world-wide reputation for patriotism and bravery through his valuable services in the war of 1812. He was a man of broad views and much more than ordinary ability. He had descended from a family of Revolutionary Patriots and had taken advantage of every facility which the country afforded for obtaining a knowledge of the arts and sciences; he had also given attention to the study of government and political economy. He was a farmer by occupation, and owned one of the most picturesque and fertile tracts of land in Gurney county, in the state of Massachusetts. He had married the daughter of one of the most prominent farmers of the county and, of course, named his oldest son, George Washington.

As it is not the intention of the writer to give the history of Gen. Bundy, further than is necessary to properly introduce to the reader, his son, George, who will figure to some extent in our story, I will proceed to state, that in 1840, having by industry and economy accumulated a little surplus cash, he determined to make a visit to distant relatives in England and it was arranged that George should accompany him.

While in England, a circumstance occurred which will illustrate, to some extent, how deeply had been implanted in this young American, our peculiar views of humanity and government.

Upon the occasion mentioned, the father and son had the pleasure of seeing the Queen and her retinue pass along one of those grand drives of which London loves to boast.

What most attracted the attention of the young American, were the footmen accompanying the Queen's carriage team.

"Why," said he to his father, "why have all these footmen that I see dressed in livery, along with the team?"

"This," said his father, "is only a custom of Royalty, handed down from the past and the object, no doubt, is a display of power; it represents a condition of things growing out of barbarism."

"A government," said George, "that has to maintain its authority by a display like that, is certainly a government founded on something beside justice; it looks as if they were trying to exalt the Queen to a place which none but God should occupy, and to place the others on a level with the horses in the team; it looks like degrading one part of the human family, to make a show of the other part."

"True," said his father, "it looks that way to us, who are taught that the right to govern is derived from the consent of the governed. In this country, the people are divided into three classes, first, the Royal family, who hold the reins of government. Second, the Nobility, who are allowed titles and own a large portion of the land and other property. The people once owned the land but were robbed of it by William, the Conquerer, and he gave it out in such manner as would best enable him to form and maintain a dynasty sufficiently powerful to hold the people in subjection to his will. From that time on, the property has been kept in these particular families by inheritance laws. These families are called the Nobility, and their principal occupation is collecting rent from the common people."

"Do these nobles go as footmen with the Queen's carriage team?"

"No, they are next to the Royal family."

"Then I am glad some of the English people are

considered higher, better and nobler than animals, but am sorry that it is on account of their owning land."

"The bulk of the people form the next class. They are the workers and are brought in direct competition one with another. The weaker go to the wall and are often reduced to want, while the stronger, more unscrupulous and dishonest become bankers, and are fast building up a power that is greater and stronger than the monarchy itself, and is slowly but surely, octopus like, extending its tentacles to all parts of the earth, and it is greatly to be feared that what Britain lost by the sword in our country, will be finally recovered by the money power, through a well systematized plan of usury, gold speculation and legislative bribery."

It has been said that "eternal vigilance is the price of liberty." Nothing is truer, and it is well worth remembering.

After returning to the United States, Gen. Bundy gave his son the benefit of a good common school education, and on coming of age, he married Miss Crabtree, the daughter of a well-to-do farmer in the neighborhood. The union proved a happy one, and the year 1861 found George Washington Bundy on a farm of his own, six miles from the town of Bopeep,

His wife was a lady of more than ordinary intelligence, and one who had many friends. At this time they had three children—Frank, and two younger daughters.

At the first tap of the drum which called the American people "to arms," Mr. Bundy, after giving all needed instructions as to the management of his farm, went to town and enlisted. When the company was organized, he was elected Captain, and soon received his Commission. Army drilling soon commenced and the Regiment to which Captain Bundy was assigned was one of the first sent to the front.

Three times during the first year he received promotion for bravery, and in the fall of 1862 he lost his left arm. After this he returned to the field, as Colonel, in command of one of the best Regiments which Massachusetts furnished during the war.

During Col. Bundy's absence, the management of the farm fell upon Mrs. Bundy. Corn and potatoes had been partially cultivated, but a large hay crop was on hand. So many men had gone to the front that it was next to impossible to get help, and Mrs. Bundy was at her wits end. "Necessity is the mother of invention," and Mrs. Bundy was not long in getting things in motion. The mowing machine was brought from the shed, where Mr. Bundy had so carefully placed it the year before. With Frank's limited knowledge and his mother's superior judgment, the machine was soon ready for the field. It was an easy matter to cut five or six acres a day, but this was not all—the grass had to be stirred, raked into winrows and then put into cocks, to guard against possible showers.

Jane, the eldest daughter, was now thirteen years old. Her father had often allowed her to drive, so she soon learned to run the mowing machine, while Frank and his mother attended to the hay. After cutting for a day or two, they would haul the hay in, and by the time the work was finished, Frank, feeling the responsibility, had learned to assume the management, thereby materially aiding his mother.

This was a time of bustle and confusion—troops were being mustered, drilled, armed and equiped for the war. Regiments were being moved to the front, brigades and armies being formed, and soon the clash of arms was heard, and then came the news of the killed, the dying, the wounded and the missing. People gathered in little squads at the bulletin boards, coming from all parts of the country to learn the fate of their loved ones. Noble hearted women started for the scene of action to care for the sick and wounded and soothe the dying.

Prayer meetings were frequent in the town and all over the country. where all would meet and seek consolation in prayer. Every mail brought tidings of battles lost and battles won, long lists of killed and wounded; and how earnestly these lists were scanned, to see if a father, son, brother, husband or lover had been killed. Oh, such anxiety and expectation. Hope, fear and despair all came at once, to stir the depths of human feelings. The aged, the sick, women and children all hoped and some hoped against fate.

Thus time rolled on at Washington. The government was encompassed by enemies. Gold and silver had disappeard into the vaults of Wall Street. At the first tap of the drum bankers demanded of the government exorbitant interest, and the immortal Lincoln found himself confronted by a more formidable foe in Wall and Lombard Streets than even in the South. But in this sad dilemma, there was still a way. Abandon the use of gold and silver and coin money from paper only.

In its distress the Government did not stop to argue questions of finance with bankers, but simplv took advantage of its own right to make its own money, of whatever substance was cheapest and best and most convenient for use. Had our law makers shown as bold a front to the bankers as they did to the Confederates, gold would have lost its power and been valuable only as bullion and in trade with foreign countries, and even then only when balance of trade was against us.

But bankers, who, by sharp schemes, had succeeded in getting possession of all the gold, were too sharp to allow a policy like this to go into effect. To avert it they came together and lobbied a bill through Congress for an issue of bonds, with interest payable in coin. It appears strange that the paper money would buy corn, wheat, arms, ammunition, pay troops and labor, do, in fact, all the business of the country, but was not good enough to pay interest on bonds that had been purchased with greenbacks.

By this act of injustice the bondholders were made a special class, and the only class in the United States who could demand gold as money for any purpose, whatever; and the act was not passed by party vote. Just how it got through Congress, is not clear, but it was passed under the protest of our wisest statesmen; and in order to carry out its provisions, it became necessary for Government to actually repudiate its own money by refusing to take it for duty on imports. But notwithstanding this unfortunate, not to say dishonest legislation, the greenback went forth among the people, saved the country, and did its work nobly. It took the place of gold and the war moved on with unabated fury. Ships of war were being constructed, and fortifications being built; armies were moving to the front and more troops being called for. While this constant drain of the working people was going on, old men, women and children came nobly to the rescue. Farm machines, with good horses, came into play; girls ran the mowing machines, ran plows and cultivators, and farming went on with very little interruption.

During these long years of war Col. Bundy improved every opportunity to write home, and his pay was always placed in the keeping of his wife, and when the last man had surrendered, he returned to the family from whom he had been so long separated and who welcomed him with fond embraces.

CHAPTER II.

THE writer will now introduce Mr. Goldburg, who had moved to Bopeep three years previous to the beginning of the late war. Mr. Goldburg, though an English Jew, was very much American in appearance and style, but had all the cunning and greed of a Jew. He had just come from California, where he had given a man a small "grub stake" of ten dollars, and in that way had become interested in a mine which the man discovered and worked; then sold out for forty thousand dollars, making twenty thousand dollars each. Having settled in Bopeep, the first thing was to look around for a good investment Property was low, and business dull, owing to a scarcity of money. As the city was surrounded by a fertile country, the Jew could see no loss of money and invested in property at the beginning of the war, at the beggarly prices existing, and it was not long in getting noised abroad that Mr. Goldburg had a little money he could be induced to put into land at a very low figure. He would also loan money on good real estate security. Mr. Goldburg soon succeeded, by foreclosure of mortgage and direct purchase in converting his twenty thousand dollars into land and town property, at bedrock prices.

When greenbacks went into circulation, money became plenty. Every one had money. Everything brought a good price, and every one who had no land wanted to buy. As a consequence, land jumped at a single bound to twice its former value. He now began selling his land as fast as possible, and money being plentiful and every branch of industry quickened, he was not long in turning his land into greenbacks at twice their former value and even more. On settling up he found that in three years' double-deal, he had increased his capital to fifty thousand dollars above all living expenses.

Having this snug sum on hand, the Jew decided to invest in government bonds and retire from business, living on the interest. Acting on this plan he soon had his bonds snugly laid away in his safe "Now," said he to his wife, "we will have nothing to do but draw the interest in gold on these bonds and live at ease; the interest will amount to over three thousand dollars in gold and that will buy four thousand or five thousand dollars' worth of greenbacks. Gold is bound to go at a premium, for people must have it to pay duty on imports. This arrangement is one of the greatest things for the banks that could be conceived; in the first place, people will have to sell their greenbacks to the banks at the banker's price to get gold to pay their duty on imports; then the banks will take the greenbacks to buy more bonds and the government will pay the gold back to the bankers again as interest on the bonds. So you see the banks will be giving the gold out all the time for greenbacks, and getting it back for interest, and at the end of the year, the banks will have the identical gold that they commenced with, and still will have bought greenbacks at a big discount, over and over again, and as fast as the greenbacks accumulate, they can put them into government bonds and draw more gold interest.

"Talk about the dead-open-and-shut string game, gold-brick or three-card monte that we had in the mines, where there was no law; they fade into insignificance in comparison with this game that has become law at the nation's capital. And there is no doubt that these bankers will see to it that gold brings a good price, so I think we can safely count on our interest amounting to six or seven thousand a year in greenbacks. It is possible the people will send different representatives to the next Congress, and this kind of work be knocked in the head, but even so, we shall get $3,000 a year. We can live well on $1,000 here at home and can spend the remainder in luxury. In this easy way of living, we will be looked up to, more than is even the nobility of the old world monarchies.

"I never until of late began to comprehend the vast power there is in money. It seems strange how a nation of intelligent people will allow the money and wealth to concentrate in the hands of individuals without limit. I would as soon think of building and running a steam boiler without a safety valve, or build a reservoir without a flood gate, as to think of allowing money to accumulate in the hands of individuals without limit."

For several weeks time passed pleasantly at the Goldburg home; he had hired a man to go in his place to the war, and while others were facing all kinds of danger, disappointment and even death, Mr. Goldburg sat back in his easy chair and amused himself by reading accounts of other people's troubles. But this kind of an easy way of getting along was plainly too much for Mr. Goldburg; he soon began to feel the want of that excitement that invariably accompanies money getting, or as it might be more properly termed, gold gambling.

He often told his wife of this restless feeling and sometimes thought of keeping his bonds and borrowing money enough to start some small business, just to occupy his time and increase his income a little. "But," said he, "this paying interest I don't like. It is the wrong side of business. It is giving a certainty for an uncertainty. It is the very thing that makes paupers of many and millionaires of a few. In short it is something for nothing, and as the pistol is to the highwayman, so is interest to the banker, and is the very thing that enables one class to live off of another with perfect impunity."

For some time he was revolving this proposition in his mind but no action was taken until one day, in an excited manner, he called his wife who had been looking after household duties; as she entered the room he sprang to his feet and was clutching the morning paper nervously in his hands; as she approached he motioned her to a seat and gave her the paper as he pointed to an article that was headed "The Banking act in full, as it passed both houses, was signed by the President and has become a law."

"Read it," he said, "I am afraid I do not understand it right, there must be some mistake and I want to see what you make of it." But without his lady having time to read, he took the paper and read the important things aloud.

"Now," said he, "if I understand this right, the government proposes to take my bonds on deposit, keep and be responsible for them, pay me my interest in full and in gold every six months and in addition to this, government gives me ninety dollars out of every one hundred of my money back at one per cent interest to go to banking on; so you see that while I am drawing my interest from the government in gold I can loan the same money here and they will pay me a large interest again. So you see if the people are the government, as they claim to be, it is certainly very kind in them to pay me interest on $50,000 at Washington, and then give me $45,000 of my money back so I can lend it to them the second time and get another interest on the same money. Now I don't believe there is anything in it. I believe it is a lie got up by political shysters to injure the administration.

"I am surprised that the government don't suppress some of these papers, but it won't do to be too fast. The other legislation such as paying interest in gold and then in order to meet the demands for gold thus created, placing the exception clause on greenbacks, is equally as bad. And it begins to look as though our laws were made in Wall Street instead of Washington and it may turn out that way yet.

"But if this is a true bill, I will be able to make $10,000 a year right here in banking and draw my interest, amounting to $3,000, in gold beside, and there is no telling what that gold will be worth before the war is over, that is, if this class legislation is not repealed. Why, it is better than a gold mine; it will beat any pension and will be showing the class more favor, who get the benefit of it, than the nobility of

England. I shall start for New York in the morning and see if there be any truth in it."

That night Mr. Goldburg packed his valise, and in the morning started for New York. On arriving, he went to a hotel, and retired early, to dream of the possibility of being yet mistaken, concerning the true meaning of the law. He was afraid of being laughed at by his bankers if it should prove to be a burlesque.

"If it is possible that this law has passed Congress and my understanding of it is correct, it must certainly have been done by a conspiracy between the bankers and the party leaders in Congress, who have taken advantage of the terrible straits in which the government is placed to crowd the bill through when the attention of the Representatives was concentrated upon war measures which they considered of more importance; it is too bare-faced to last long, but I can take advantage of it while it lasts and while the Wall Street bankers are making millions, I can make a few thousands." His mind ran on in this way till nearly morning when he dropped into a restless sleep.

Long after day light he awoke, raised himself to a sitting posture, reached for the paper which was in his coat pocket and opening it he again read the U. S. Banking Act, for the ninety-ninth time. It was still there—not a dream, the golden god still continued to smile.

After breakfast Mr. Goldburg consulted his watch; it was only half past seven. "O horror," he said in his impatience, "the bank will not be open for two hours. These bankers are as autocratic as the Czar of Russia." At last, nine o'clock arrived and Mr. Goldburg dropped into the office of one of the largest banking firms in the city. It was a house where he had formerly done a good deal of business and he was recognized at once. On stating that he wanted to talk over business matters of importance, he was ushered into a private room and informed that the law had already gone into effect. It had cost a good deal of money to lobby it through Congress, but the bankers' association had put up all the money and would expect those taking advantage of the law, to reimburse them.

Everything being satisfactory, Mr. Goldburg laid before the bankers a proposition to organize a company to conduct a banking business at Bopeep; he dwelt extensively on the agricultural resources of the country, its grand water power and maufacturing probabilities, and being well pleased with the locality the bankers expressed a willingness to take one half of the stock. This being satisfactory they proposed to organize by making one of the New York bankers president and Mr. Goldburg cashier. A few days were then spent in organizing and completing details, the most important of which was to secure from the government $90,000 in cash at one per cent for twenty years, while government was paying them six per cent in gold on the same money. Mr. Goldburg said it was what Californians would call "double-shooting the turn."

At last, everything being arranged, Mr. Goldburg returned to Bopeep accompanied by Mr. Goldman, a representative of the New York bankers. A suitable room was soon secured and a large iron safe set in place, a few tables, chairs and screens were all that were necessary to start and run a business that in time would dominate all others and make more criminals than whiskey, more beggars than beer.

Mr. Goldman was an apostate Jew Americanized; his stock of general information was sadly deficient but he wore good clothes and had studied finance from boyhood. None knew better than he the different monetary systems and the value of money, bonds and stocks; he was not a capitalist and spent every dollar of his salary for dress and in gambling, and seemed to have no inclination to own property.

At the same time he seemed to have every faculty for making sharp turns on the money changer's tables and for years he had been in the employ of the same firm. Had he made his start, like some others, by some accident or chance, no doubt he would have been one of the most exacting and unscrupulous men on the earth, but as he had no means himself, he became a willing tool for others, to carry out their very laudable purpose of building up a money aristocracy, by the use of every possible scheme or device which could be invented for obtaining money from the people without giving anything in return. How they succeeded in getting millions of dollars from the people, for absolutely nothing, will be seen further on.

I say from the people, because as the people own everything, there is positively no other source from which men can obtain wealth.

I say they gave nothing in return, because they had nothing to give, and as they produced nothing, every dollar they obtained was obtained for nothing.

You may clothe the transaction in all the high-sounding language at your disposal; you may cover it up with a multitude of figures; you may talk about interest, discount and commission; but the facts remain the same, that there is not a millionaire who ever lived who has given the world or given the people value received for what he has; consequently it is legalized robbery, but in order to accommodate this book to the absurd teachings of our early education, I will call it speculation.

CHAPTER III.

WHEN Mr. Goldburg first landed in the little town of Bopeep he purchased a small piece of land for a nominal sum, on the outskirt of the town, and built a small cottage. His family consisted of his wife, one son, who was then eleven years old, and a daughter, Rebecca, thirteen years of age. Mr. Goldburg had married a California girl, at least her people had emigrated to that state from Ohio in an early day, and like a solitary plant in rich soil and genial climate, the girl, unfettered by religious dogmas or political bias, had grown into womanhood with a degree of self-reliance which few women of her day possessed.

Her love of money was only equal to the good that could be accomplished with the same. She had read about Jesus overturning the tables of the money changers, telling them that they had turned the house of the Lord into a den of thieves, his condemning usury, and she had learned to look upon a millionaire as a miser, as a brute. She disliked ostentation but taught her children to be plain, but neat and good.

Among her neighbors she was a real favorite but found little time to visit, as she and her children were kept pretty busy in the garden and in planting and cultivating shrubs to beautify their little home.

Her husband often wanted her to employ some one to do the work but she objected, saying that the more trouble a thing cost the more she appreciated it; besides it would keep the children out of mischief and furnish them good healthy employment and cultivate in them a taste for such things. In addition to this, she enjoyed arranging things as much as she did seeing them after they were arranged.

There was a good common school in the place and

Mrs. Goldburg never allowed work to interfere with her children going to school, but on the contrary, looked upon the work they were called to do around home as a kind of stepping-stone or preparation of their young minds, under her own guidance, for a higher development, through their studies in school and during school terms they were kept in constant attendance.

Both advanced rapidly in their studies and Rebecca was the favorite of the whole school. She seemed to have a magic influence that drew all toward her. While she was perfectly self-reliant, she had at the same time warm sympathies and ever kind words for her playmates, and they all loved her, all wanted to play with her, and the girl that occupied a desk with her was envied by all the others.

In the early married life of Mr. Goldburg he was poor and had to rustle in every conceivable way to make ends meet and he often found himself in debt; while this was the case his wife took a lively interest in his business and often took in odd jobs of sewing or mending for the miners in order to assist in supplying the family wants; but now having accumulated a large sum of money, what she considered a fortune, had retired from the gold mine, also from other business and made a safe investment of all their money in government bonds that was paying them an enormous interest, more in fact than was necessary to keep the family in luxury, she could see no necessity for her husband's going into this new venture. "But," said her husband, "there is no venture about it. All I have to do is to take the money that government gives me, amounting on my part to $45,000, and loan it out to the people here for whatever interest I choose to ask and I don't think we will be apt to let any go for less than eight per cent. Why, just think of it, $45,000 at eight per cent wil lgive me over $3,500 clear money; besides some are bound to have bad luck and fail to pay on time, then the bank will foreclose, buy in their property at forced sale for a great deal less than what it is worth, and in that way make a great deal of money. You see it is make, make everywhere."

"But suppose," said his wife, "the bank should lose some of this $45,000, would you not lose your bonds?"

"Of course it would seem that way, but we have this $45,000 for twenty years, and the gold interest on the bonds converted into greenbacks and compounded every six months, in twenty years will amount to over $100,000, so you see that even were I to lose every dollar of the $45,000, and then at the end of the twenty years lose the bonds, I would still be worth $100,000 or over, just from the interest paid me during that time."

"If the government lets you have $45,000 at one per cent, why don't they put $5,000 more to that and pay off the bonds and stop the interest and lend the money to the people at one per cent instead of letting you loan it at eight per cent?"

"Of course, if the legislation was all done for the benefit of the people, it would be a different thing. But the way it is, the people stay at home and let Congress do the legislating; but the bankers have a strong organization and they get a great many of their members elected to the House and often to the Senate, and then they send strong men to Washington with plenty of money and they generally manage to get the bills through for their own benefit."

"This present law," said he, "is all for the benefit of the bankers and if I don't take the benefit some one else will. In fact some one will have to, for as soon as the war is over the bankers will get an act passed withdrawing the greenbacks from circulation and then the people will be compelled to go to the banks for money, there will be no other way to get it, for it is law.

"And so far as our losing is concerned, it is out of the question; bankers never lose. If a bank breaks, it is the depositors that lose and not the bankers.

"Farmers' crops may fail, cattle die and floods carry off land improvements, but the land will remain to pay the banker."

"Well, I do not see," said Mrs. Goldburg, "what good there is in taking all this additional business upon yourself. The banking business is complicated and these men who are in it have been schooled in finance since childhood and you will be forced to study night and day to keep up."

"There is just where you are mistaken," said Mr. Goldburg, "it is right the reverse; it takes a smart man to run a peanut stand and make money, but any fool who has enough bonds, can get money of the government for nothing, loan it to the people and make money, have a lawyer make out the mortgage and make the man who borrows the money pay for it. The most difficult problem that a banker has to solve is how to keep the money on hand, beyond the reach of thieves, and the mechanics are helping him out on that by building iron safes and vaults that are perfectly impregnable."

"Well, my dear husband, don't you think that you could enjoy life better to let all this money making business go and turn your attention to studying science, in reading, traveling, and in fact anything to enjoy life and make time pass pleasantly? You see the interest on these bonds is more than enough to keep us all in luxury, and you will have nothing on your mind, but enjoy yourself in your own way; you can travel and enjoy everything that is going on in the whole country.

"It seems to me that all the money a man makes more than what he can use in a natural life time and give his children a good comfortable start in the world is a waste of energy. I can not see what good this surplus wealth can do you or anybody else. It looks like foolishness to waste time in trying to get some-thing that we do not need and really have no use for. Besides you say these laws are all made for the benefit of the banks, that they were lobbied through Congress when the attention of the people was absorbed in war. Now when the war is over I am afraid there will be a day of retribution."

Mr. Goldburg then explained that so far as retiring on the interest was concerned it would be more desirable by all-odds, but it was, under the present reign of things, perfectly impracticable.

"The money power has full control of all our financial legislation," said he, "and the laws are already so framed that a few unscrupulous men will gather the wealth of this country together so rapidly that the plutocratic world will look on with silent admiration. And men of small fortunes like ourselves will be swallowed up by stock and bond manipulation, squeezed out and forced to the wall, and in a short time this will be a government of millionaires and paupers, and as the choice between the two I prefer to be a millionaire. It is true the financial laws are all one-sided and in reality, this whole banking scheme is as much a robbery as was ever perpetrated by Joaquin or Robin Hood, but still it is law and has become a part of our government; and the American people are so patriotic that it will take a long time for them to be forced to acknowledge the fact, even after they know it is true. It is always easier to commit a wrong than it is to rectify one that has been committed.

"Besides, the banking law is the same in principle and effect that is now existing in Great Britain and it has prospered there for nearly two hundred years, and notwithstanding the Bank of England is nothing more or less than a private corporation, the same as our present bank, it has actually become stronger than the government itself and the whole people, even the nobility, are paying tribute to it.

"There is therefore no good reason to doubt but that the day will come when the Bank Association will name a candidate for President of each of the great political parties and thus having their own man at the helm, a strong navy, and an army recruited from the tramp element, would be able to control this government and these people.

"Joint stock companies will be organized to run the large papers and their stock put upon the market.

Bankers will buy it in and thus control the press, and by a system of advertising, will even force books into the schools that will start the young mind off in the right direction to believe that their only hope to live at all in this miserable world is in the gold base and national bank.

"An aristocracy will be built that will be as formidable in its proportions and exacting in its demands as that of Germany or Britain.

"Of course it will be hard for the American people to see their liberties curtailed and their property slipping away, but the newspapers that they look to for knowledge will give them a hundred different reasons for the hard times and demonstrate to them by figures enough to cover the whole side of a newspaper, that if it had not been for the National Banks keeping the people up, they would all have starved to death long ago, and in this way they will be led right on down and made slaves to their own ignorance.

"So I see but one safe way and that is to make all we can, take advantage of everything that comes in our favor, make thousands first, then millions if we can, for as sure as the sun rises and sets, there is no such thing as standing still in this day. If I do not rob some one, then some one will rob me; forty years from to-day, if we live, we will either be extremely rich or extremely poor."

Mrs. Goldburg had listened with a sad heart to this dreadful picture of her country's future, but having been already well posted as to how Mr. Goldburg had received his information, and also knowing that he had actually brought back from the treasury $45,000 to loan out among his neighbors, while his own money was every dollar of it invested in government bonds bearing an enormous interest, she felt that the facts were all against her and she was in no mood to differ with him in regard to our government in its distress falling a victim to the great money powers of Britain and the advisability of keeping on the safe side by taking advantage of every point that presented itself for increasing their financial importance and strength.

But Rebecca, who had breathed from infancy the free air of the Sierra Nevada, and whose constant association was with children whose fathers, brothers, uncles and cousins were offering up their lives to protect their homes and government, was as full of the patriotic spirit as the full blown rose is of perfume, and this dreadful picture was too much. Laying down the book she was idly reading during this long talk, in an instant, like the godess of Liberty with uplifted hands, she stood before her father and said, "Father, this cannot be, the noble hearted, brave men and boys of this country are in the army now, and thinking only of the loved ones and the foe, but while they are at the front, if a coil be thrown around the grand old Ship of State by these men who deal only in gold, they will no more stop its progress than the Indian who throws his noose over the flying locomotive. The one will be dragged to an ignominious death; the other will ride to his doom in a palace of state. Those who have tasted liberty will never die slaves."

Thus saying she left the room and in another apartment threw herself upon a lounge and burying her face in her hands gave herself up to silent grief.

The father and mother, as though by one impulse, arose to follow, and Mr. Goldburg, with a touch of remorse, said, "I never thought but I know now that I ought not to have said so much before our daughter, for her whole soul is filled with sentiments of American patriotism and she knows but little of man's true destiny." On reaching her side he tried hard to comfort her.

It was spring now. Nature was fast putting on her mantle of green; birds chirped merrily as they skipped from bough to bough; every breath of air seemed laden with rich perfume and all things were taking on new life, and the new National Bank had begun already to thrive.

Soldiers had been sending money home from the

army; products of all kinds brought a good price; wages were good and work plenty. All this helped to swell the deposits and a great deal of money had been loaned on good interest.

There was a vacant lot on the same square where the bank was now situated and Mr. Goldman, the clerk, in his usual business-like way, discovered that it belonged to a Mr. Stillwater, a well-to-do farmer, and that this same Mr. Stillwater had also $10,000 on deposit, so he suggested to Mr. Goldburg that it would be a good plan to induce Mr. Stillwater to build a first-class brick block and fit the corner up for the National Bank.

Being pleased with the proposition, Mr. Goldburg was not long in accidentally meeting Mr. Stillwater, and brought the suggestion of a building around in a very indifferent way by proposing to rent the corner at a good round figure, if he would put up a good building.

Mr. Stillwater said he had figured on the matter and found that it would cost $30,000 to put up the building and he could not raise that much; he had been offered $10,000 for the lot and he was now on a stand whether to sell the lot for $10,000, or borrow $20,000 which added to the $10,000 he now had in the bank would put up the building. He was, of course, informed that the bank would furnish what money was necessary and take a mortgage on the property. Mr. Stillwater said that he would think the matter over, and on the following day called at the bank and made arrangements for the $20,000. He then advertised for contract and in ten days had the building under way, the contract price being $30,000.

After Mr. Stillwater left the bank, Mr. Goldburg, addressing the clerk, said, "Mr. Goldman, do you not think that we have made a mistake in not buying the lot and erecting a building ourselves? The rent on the part of the building that we use will amount, I see, to as much as the interest on the $20,000."

"True," said Mr. Goldman, "but you see that as soon as this war is over the greenbacks will be withdrawn from circulation, money will become so scarce that this property will not sell for enough to pay the mortgage and the bank will then foreclose and bid it in at forced sale for less than one-half of its present cost."

"But," said Mr. Goldburg," is there any certainty of their being able to get the contraction act through?

"Knowing as you do," said Mr Goldman, "what has been already accomplished by way of legislation, can you for a moment doubt the ability of the money power to carry any act through Congress that will strengthen the position of the banks?"

CHAPTER IV.

WHEN Col. Bundy returned to the front with his regiment, it was decided that in order to send the children to school Mrs. Bundy should move to town. They therefore made arrangements with one of the neighbors to look after the farm during the winter; then they bought a small building in the suburbs of the town.

When snugly settled in their new home, Mrs. Bundy was not long in getting her children into school. Frank was given a desk on the extreme right of the room and after arranging his papers, books, etc., before commencing his studies, he cast his eyes about the room to take in the situation. From one to another of his neighbors his eyes passed with scarcely a reflection until directly opposite him they encountered another pair of eyes that held his own for an instant. It was a long, interested look. In fact they seemed to be looking right through his eyes down into his soul and reading his secret thoughts.

Their eyes seemed to meet by accident and separate as though some hidden power were controlling each in union.

Frank was soon buried in thought concerning his studies, but in spite of a strong effort to the contrary his mind wandered back to those lovely eyes, and he raised his eyes just in the right time to meet again the same long, interested look.

Frank was beginning to experience something he had never felt before; he knew what it meant, but resolved not to give up to his feelings. He came there to learn and he would let nothing divert his mind from his books, and if there was to be any love affair it must be after school was over. But with all these good resolutions his eyes would sometimes wander back to those of his fair enchantress.

When noon came Frank took his place at the foot of the spelling class. Miss Rebecca Goldburg, the banker's daughter, was the girl in whom he was so much interested and he noticed that she was next the head; it was not long before she was at the head and before they were done spelling Frank was at her side. She received him with a smile, but the class was not so well pleased. He was a new boy, and to go next to the head of the spelling class the first time was too much. Besides some of the boys thought Rebecca too well pleased.

In starting for home when school was out, Rebecca managed to walk with Frank's sister and when part way home they waited for Frank and all went home together. As they lived near each other they were soon well acquainted and fast friends.

On returning to school, Frank went to the ball grounds and took part in the play until school called and he was not long in discovering that he had aroused the jealousy of the whole class. At recess a boy about a year older than himself, who had been a kind of a bully among the others, grabbed his cap and began to soil it. Frank took it out of his hands and told him not to bother him any more; at this the boy began to abuse him and finally slapped him, but when Frank got the slap, as a sporting man would say, he let go his right in regular pugilistic style and landed square on the rib with such force that the big boy got away and said that he did not want to fight. After this little episode the boys were all Frank's friends.

As school progressed it was noticed that Frank was not only first in play but was also first in all his studies, and although not much larger than the average boy of his age it was plain to be seen that in strength and durability he had few equals.

In learning he was not slow but it required constant study to maintain his place at the head of his class, yet he never became so busily engaged in his studies but what Rebecca found a place in his thoughts and as the winter rolled by they were often together and growing constantly nearer and dearer to each other.

During the winter they had many an entertainment for the benefit of the boys in the army and Rebecca was often called upon to render patriotic pieces. It was in the rendition of these that she developed such an intense feeling for the American people and flag, that, coupled with her excellent delivery and pleasing manner, soon made her the favorite of the whole country, and especially of those whose friends were in the war. As her elocutionary powers developed, she was sent for from near and far and large sums of money were raised through exhibitions in which she played an important part. Through a regularly organized Relief corps, this money soon found its way to the Hospitals and did much to alleviate the sufferings of the sick and wounded soldiers.

At last the winter school closed and Mrs. Bundy, with her little family, returned to their country home. There was a feeling of sadness at parting with old friends and playmates, but it was overbalanced by the thought of again enjoying their old home; the horses, cows and chickens seemed like old friends, besides they were to mingle again with friends of other days who were dear to them. When again established everything seemed very natural and there was so much to do they were far from being lonesome.

Here and there a rail had been knocked from the fence; these had to be put in place, garden ground had to be cleared of its rubbish and made ready for planting; rose bushes and shrubbery had to be pruned, flower beds raked over, and it did Mrs. Bundy's heart good to see the enjoyment of the children in fixing up the place.

Frank had so far developed toward manhood that he was now able to do all kinds of work on the farm and with the superintendence of his mother, he soon had everything in running condition; the machinery was all put in order and soon plowing begun. No boy ever commenced his summer work with higher hopes and expectations than did he. The winter at school had been an enjoyable one and work passed lightly as he thought of many incidents in which Rebecca had played an important part and he looked forward to the time when he should become a man.

There was a nice farm in the neighborhood, which he hoped some day to own; he would change the fences to make it more convenient, would plant an orchard the first year and in his garden would have all the small fruits because they would come on quickly, he would tear down the old, dilapidated barn and replace it with a new one; the house, too, he would improve. He hoped to bring all these things about and to place Rebecca as the crowning jewel of all his hopes; as children, they had pledged eternal love and as a man, he felt that the greatest happiness which could fall to his lot would be to make her happy.

He thought much and often of these plans and they did not seem to him extravagant or overdrawn. The country was prosperous, work was plenty, there was an abundance of money, notwithstanding our country was carrying on war at the cost of more than a million dollars a day, there were good times, financially, all over the country, "Of course," said Frank, "if the country can prosper and carry on such a war, when the war ends and the expense is stopped and the thousands that are now in the army, both north and south return to their homes and go to building up and not tearing down, our productions will be doubled, our exports will be immense, and once at peace we will prosper beyond anything ever known.

"Our debt, they say, is a large part of it in greenbacks and bears no interest, besides it is needed to take the place of gold, as the bankers who have the gold have hidden it away until danger is over; the government will tell them to keep it now and we will have plenty of greenback money, and if they stay in circulation as long as the government lasts we will save interest enough in one hundred years to buy all the gold in New York."

This was the natural, common sense view of the situation entertained by the boy who knew nothing of the intrigues of the gold gamblers. Little did he think that even then there existed a conspiracy among the gold speculators looking to the withdrawal of the national currency as soon as the war was over, in order to make room for their gold to again circulate, it being now hoarded pending the uncertainty of war.

He did not know that the gold mongers had already lobbied a bill through Congress establishing National Banks to operate on the same general principle or plan upon which the Bank of England is organized and operates, and that under that system the Bank of England has from a very insignificant commencement become a power that in a wonderful degree controls the destiny of nations; and its oppressive hand has been felt in every civilized land.

One would think from the name, "Bank of England," the institution was strictly English, but it is not; it is simply an ulcer having fastened itself on the body politic of the English nation. And by careful investigation the reader will find it is strictly a Jewish scheme   In fact, instead of being what its name would indicate, it is nothing more nor less than a private corporation whose stock is owned principally by Jews, who could in all probability trace their ancestry back in an unbroken line to that remote period in history when Christ turned their parents, the money changers, out of the temple of God.

To realize the unfair advantage conferred upon the bank by the government we need only to take into consideration the fact that the government has become bankrupt while the bank has become the ruling power of the earth. And the government debt has become so large that they do not count on ever paying it, but will pay the interest throughout all time. Thus the English government pays tribute to a golden god of their own creation, and in order to make some excuse for allowing such a system to exist, the English statesmen have been forced to the sad extremity of proclaiming to the world the very dangerous doctrine, that a government debt is a government blessing. Shame, on the man who could make such an assertion.

After the Bundy family had been for some weeks upon the farm, they took a day to go to town and do some trading. The girls stopped at Mr. Goldburg's to visit while the mother and Frank went to the store to get such things as were needed in the family, and when they returned, Rebecca obtained permission to go with them and spend a week with Mrs. Bundy and family. Frank had no objection to this arrangement, in fact he was pleased with the plan.

The Bundy home was an ordinary frame building of seven rooms, built more for comfort than for beauty, but the arrangement of the flowers, trees and shrubs was artistic to a degree that is not always found among farmers. Such a variety of evergreens is seldom met with in a single grove as adorned their west yard, and the front and east of the yard was equally remarkable for the great variety of roses, flowers and shrubs. There was hardly a family in the whole country who had not contributed some small plant or flower to Mrs. Bundy's collection.

While Rebecca remained with the family, much of her time was spent working among the flowers and she declared it gave her great delight. After the morning work she would braid roses in her hair and at ten o'clock go with the other girls to take a lunch to Frank who was working in the field, and she would take it upon herself to open the basket and spread a nice white cloth upon the grass and then arrange the good things of which there was always quite, an abundance. Frank was quite used to little kindnesses, but this seemed to come from an angel's hand, and never did he seem to so enjoy the company of his little friend as here in his country home.

Rebecca, too, was of a light heart and felt a touch of joy in the country breeze; all was love to her and why should she not be happy, for love 'tis said, is happiness itself.

CHAPTER V.

IT is not our purpose to give a detailed account of all the loans made, debts collected and mortgages foreclosed by the First National Bank of Bopeep, but in order to get our story fully before the reader it will be necessary to draw your attention to a few of the secret workings.

After the bank had been running for several months, it was found that the deposits had largely exceeded the disbursements, and Mr. Goldman suggested to Mr. Goldburg that they make additional investments in bonds. Mr. Goldburg said it was impossible, as he had, in organizing the bank, put in all the capital he had and he did not consider it a safe proposition to invest so much of the deposits in bonds.

Mr. Goldman then explained that here was "the package of National Bank bills, $90,000, that the government so kindly gave us to bank on. They remain untouched; our loans have all been made out of the deposits so far, why not take $10,000 from our deposits and put with this package and buy another hundred thousand dollars' worth of bonds?"

Mr. Goldburg said the depositors might call for their money, and to take out $10,000 and invest in bonds would be liable to make them short of money.

Mr. Goldman replied it would not be so, for as soon as they got the bonds, they could increase the capital stock by depositing the bonds and getting $90,000 of bank bills "that will be just as good as this package; we will then have a capital in bonds of $200,000 and will be out only $10,000 on the last lot of bonds, and will draw a gold interest on the extra bonds amounting to several thousand a year; the nice thing about this banking act is, it was made for the bankers and not for the government, or the people, and is on the principle of 'now you see it and now you don't see it.' It is the only business in the world where a man draws interest on what he owes."

About this time a man registered at the leading hotel of the place of the name of Goldsmith. He was about thirty years old and the son of a rich man; he had grown up in the city of New York into a kind of hoodlum. By sheer compulsion he had received an education, and being connected with a family of millionaires, was kept in a position with very little to do and a big salary. Having plenty of money, he became a favorite with sluggers and gamblers. He had a native shrewdness which enabled him to hold his own among that class. His father had often tried to persuade him to drop his old associates and become interested in some paying business, but Mr. Goldsmith insisted that unless he could make lots of money, he wanted none. He came to Bopeep for the purpose of making a raise, and we shall see how well he succeeded.

There was lenty of water-power near Bopeep, plenty of timber and other valuable resources, and all it lacked was a railroad to make the country blossom as a rose. All were on tip-toe to see capital come in. Mr. Goldsmith, learning of the situation, determined to work up a scheme by which he would become a millionaire. He therefore informed his host that he represented unlimited capital and was looking up the railroad interest, and was of the opinion that if proper inducements were held out, he would build a road to Bopeep. He saw at once that he had struck a responsive chord; the landlord was elated and on the following day procured the best rig in the city and drove Mr. Goldsmith over the country to see its advantages, called a meeting of property owners to get an expression of feeling and pass such resolutions as would be appropriate for such a momentous occasion.

The next day the papers were ablaze with the wonderful news that a capitalist was in town looking up the Railroad interest.

Mr. Goldsmith, who it was understood was a large capitalist and financier of no ordinary ability, had agreed to take the matter under consideration and meet the people of Bopeep in a public meeting one week from that day. So a meeting was called.

During the next week Mr. Goldsmith was escorted in every direction, and no stone was left unturned to impress him with the wonderful resources of the country and the importance of such a road. Finally the week rolled by and the time came. Mr. Goldsmith had considered the matter well. That it was a good investment for a man that had money, there remained little doubt, but he had neither money nor reputation. In fact the only thing with which he was well supplied was, to use a quaint expression, gall. But he belonged to a wealthy family, was well posted on Wall Street methods or how millionaires make their money, and during the past week he had made the acquaintance of. Mr. Goldburg, the banker, and learned the name of every man that had money on deposit, and accompanied by Mr. Goldburg had visited these men and succeeded in getting them to sign for stock to the extent of $100,000.

At the meeting he gave a fine, account of the benefits to be derived from the road, and said if the city would vote $100,000 of six per cent ten-year bonds, and the county also vote $100,000 he would guarantee the building of the road just as fast as money would build it.

He said there could be no good reason why the county and city should not vote bonds, for the tax on the Railroad and other property that it would bring into the county would pay the bonds, interest and all in less than twenty years. This he demonstrated by actual figures, and before leaving town he called on each of the editors of city papers and dropped a small check by way of encouragement to puff the enterprise.

– He had also made fast friends with Mr. Goldburg and between him and that gentleman it was understood that as soon as bonds were voted, Messrs. Goldburg, Goldsmith and Goldman (using the latter for a cat's paw) would organize a Railroad Company and get a charter from the State.

After all this was arranged he returned to New York. One month from that day bonds were voted by a small majority after a red hot contest in which Mr. Goldburg's money played a very important part.

A charter was then procured and by the following spring the bonds were ready and the Company let a contract for construction. To meet the first payment of $100,000 Mr. Goldsmith's father loaned him $50,000 and Mr. Goldburg put up the other $50,000 out of the deposits of the bank. By the time the next payment fell due the $100,000 of private stock had been paid in. Soon after this the bonds were sold and things moved along lively for a time. Mr. Goldburg, who, being in the bank and knew just who had money, had been quite active and succeeded in selling among the citizens another $100,000 worth of stock.

But at last it all went. The road was not yet completed. Something had to be done. The money was all gone and they owed the contractor $150,000.

The Company was bankrupt. The citizens could raise no more money and the County and City would not, so they all said, "Let it sell." So the road was sold.

Messrs. Goldburg and Goldsmith bought it in for $150,000 and costs.

Then another company was organized in which Mr. Goldburg's banking partner in New York, became the third party.

The next meeting was to issue first mortgage bonds to the extent of $5,000,000. This it was estimated would complete the road and put on rolling stock. As the New York banker had millions of government money on hand without interest and money was plenty and loans slow, they were, of course, anxious to find investment and these first mortgage bonds went off at sight, and the work went on. The county, the city and the citizens were relieved of further anxiety. They had lost what they had invested, of course, but as there

was no help, they gave up their little wealth as cheerfully as though facing a six-shooter.

There were a few of the old school of Peter Cooper
and J. B. Weaver, greenback men, in the neighborhood
who went so far as to brand the whole thing as a base
fraud and declare that there should be some law to
protect the people against such bare-faced robbery.
But the company papers had made a little money out
of the affair, so they silenced these old greenbackers by
calling them anarchists, calamity-howlers, and accus-
ing them of being troubled with the greenback craze.

But with all this newspaper bombast, it was plain to
the people that they had lost half a million dollars of
their earnings, and county bonds that would have to
be paid by increased taxation.

Mr. Goldburg had become a Railroad magnate, and
would soon be, if not already, a millionaire, all from
the shrewdness of a man who had been considered a
New York hoodlum or black-leg. In less than one
year the road had been put in operation and had such
a large and profitable business, that although it had
cost about $5,000,000, the company decided to capi-
talize at $10,000,000 and arranged their fare and freight
so that the profit of the road would pay a dividend on
that amount of stock. Thus had Mr. Goldburg become
a millionaire at a bound.

It will be seen that Messrs. Goldburg and Goldsmith
paid $100,000, or $50,000 each; then the New York
Company put in $200,000 to pay for the road at
sheriff's sale; of this sum the New York bankers paid
$100,000. They were therefore out in the whole
transaction $100,000 each, all of which they were very
careful to take from the first dividend. They sold first
mortgage bonds to the extent of $5,000,000. This
built the road, and as it had no opposition, the freights
and fares were so adjusted as to pay a dividend on
$10,000,000. The road was therefore worth that
amount, and as they were out nothing and owed but
$5,000,000, they of course made $5,000,000 at the
expense of the people.

Many farmers and merchants about Bopeep lost from $1,000 to $10,000 in this transaction but it was legal. Had Mr. Goldsmith stolen $50 from these parties it would have been illegal and he would have been punished; in the former case it was legalized robbery.

At this time Mr. Goldburg received a letter from his old friend, Leland Sanford, of California, as follows:

MR. GOLDBURG; My Dear Sir: I hear, through our friend, Goldaker how you handled your little Railroad scheme; you can hardly imagine how it pleases me. When you went east I thought you were missing it, but I see now, no matter where a Californian goes, he is bound to "get there." The late war put so much money in circulation that it has brought about such activity in business as no country has ever seen, and by a little wire-pulling it can be gathered to the surface like cream; if we don't skim it some one else will. We must have millionaires and lots of them, otherwise the British bankers will own the whole thing. I suppose you have seen by the papers what a pull we made on the government—a franchise for a road, worth millions, money enough to build the road or nearly so, and land. You thought you were doing a big thing when you took advantage of the Banking Act, giving you the use of $45,000 at a nominal one per cent a month for twenty years. It was pretty good, of course. But think of the boost Uncle Sam gave us right here. Let me tell you, friend Goldburg, if the legislation continues favorable to us, there is no reason why you should not be worth $50,000,000 in twenty years.

We do not intend to pay the government one cent, as long as we can help it. We will stand Uncle Sam off, ship in Chinamen and with cheap labor extend our road just as far as we can find ground to build on. As we build with cheap labor and make our own prices, we will be able soon to not only control the California Legislature, but be well represented in Congress and the United States Senate.

The resources of this country are vast; population and wealth increasing rapidly, and under the present system of legislation millionaires will spring up like mushrooms. In fact, I think it a question of but a short time when the line of class will be as closely drawn in this country as in England, and even more people will be paying rent here than there.

Now in conclusion, let me tell you, or as the saying goes, let me give you a pointer; watch John Sherman and whatever he does, go thou and do likewise, and you'll not miss it. The first investment that I see for you out here, I will write you about.

Respectfully yours, LELAND SANFORD.

CHAPTER VI.

IN 1865 the Confederacy went to pieces and its armies surrendered. Col. Bundy returned with his regiment all covered with glory. They had been in many of the hardest fought battles of the war, many had been left in southern graves and those who returned bore marks of hard service.

They were not discharged until they reached Bopeep, and as they paraded the streets with battle-stained banners it would be hard to draw a picture that would do justice to the occasion. Mothers rushed forward to greet their boys; wives to embrace their husbands, even sweethearts could not restrain their feelings but rushed into a lover's arms. The Colonel was seized by admiring friends and borne along the street. The town was thronged with people and all went wild with joy. Long tables were set in the public square, people brought sweet-meats and emptied their baskets there and a more bountiful and joyous feast was probably never set in any land

The Colonel and wife stayed all night in the city with friends to enjoy the fireworks, and pronounced it a time long to be remembered, The city was illuminated from ground to garret; rockets went up from every corner, and boys played great havoc with the fire crackers. There was music and dancing in every hall, and services until twelve in every church with singing, praise and thanksgiving.

On the following day the family returned to their home in the country. The Colonel was overjoyed to have his little family around him once more, and it seemed that nature was joining in the general love feast that welcomed the loved ones, for never did the sun seem to shine so brightly or the birds sing so sweetly as then.

The young people of to-day have but little idea of

the warmth of feeling, self-forgetfulness and love that seemed to pervade the very atmosphere and make the American hearts beat when the boys came home from the army. Their hardships and sufferings had been terrible but the result glorious.

The Union had been preserved, slavery destroyed and the Goddess of Liberty stood erect, with torch in hand to enlighten the world. From east to west, from north to south, fathers, mothers, brothers, sisters, sweethearts, friends all joined in one fond embrace of love. All selfish thoughts and motives were for the moment lost.

The cheerful voice sounded only in accents of love and the great American heart beat with a warmth of affection that was broad as the universe and equal to all the nations of the earth.

Liberty for the time had been secured; our cause, which was believed to be just, was crowned with success; with one accord all offered up thanksgiving, and, now that slavery had been destroyed, they were ready to sacrifice everything but honor to reconcile the people of the South.

Such feeling of harmony, love and magnanimity but seldom permeates a whole people, as was found among the loyal legions of the United States, and in that we have a forecast of what a higher state of civilization will be when once attained.

But it appears that these feelings could not at that time last. Treason and conspiracy had already made their appearance in another locality. In the first place it was capital invested in slaves that brought about a war. Now it was the capital of Wall Street, Boston, Philadelphia and England invested in gold. In John Sherman they had found an able tool; how much they paid this unscrupulous knave for his services is not known to the public. But none who know his history doubt his debauchery, and to cover his damnable acts and keep himself and his confederates in power, the terrible wounds of the war had to be torn open anew at every election and kept constantly before the people. Thus while posing as a patriot with a reputation built largely upon his brother's noble record has he been enabled to wreck the great Republic, and start its patriotic citizens on the downward road toward a worse slavery or serfdom than ever existed in the South. How strange it is that a man with such brilliant opportunities will preter darkness rather than light.

For several weeks the old neighbors flocked to Col. Bundy's home; there was scarcely a day but some family of old friends dropped in, and they were all plain, honest people like the Bundys. Ladies, boys and girls all helped to do the work and in this way took the load from Mrs. Bundy's shoulders and also added very materially to their own opportunities of enjoyment.

Many hands make light work and the meals set up by Mrs. Bundy with the assistance of her friends were simply feasts and superior to many a royal repast. Never, perhaps, did time pass more joyously than during these reunions of old neighbors.

Col. Bundy had a good farm, house and lot in town, and savings from his salary while in service which had been carefully placed in the bank from time to time when it was received by Mrs. Bundy, amounted now to over $10,000. With this reserve he had no reason to worry about the future and felt quite at ease. But while the sheep are quietly slumbering in the shade the wolf is on his search for prey. So it was with Col. Bundy. While he was resting from his long ltfe of exposure, danger and fatigue, the gold speculators were carefully examining the books to see who had large deposits, and to figure out the best method of using an influence over the parties that would contribnte to their own net gain. Mr. Goldburg knew that Mr. Stillwater's building would soon be completed; that Mr. Stillwater owed the bank a large sum and in order to get payment promptly it would be well to assist him in renting the building as soon as possible.

He also knew that if he could persuade Col. Bundy to commence business there, he could make him a loan of at least $10,000 at a good round interest, and that all of the Colonel's property would be pledged for its

payment, and of course a $10,000 loan to a man own-
ing so much good property was no small object. In
view of all these facts Mr. Goldburg proposed to his
wife and daughter to visit Col. Bundy's home.

Nothing perhaps could have been more agreeable to
the ladies, so on the following Tuesday they were in
their carriage behind a span of black horses, with
silver-mounted harness; in fact there was no one else
in the place that could afford so fine a turnout.

As they drove along the quiet country road, nice
cosy cottages were constantly coming in view, orchards,
gardens, meadows, pastures, and fields of grain came
in by way of change; the meadow-lark, perched upon
the highest objects, warbled his short musical sounds,
which seemed to harmonize and blend beautifully with
the sweet notes of other singing birds. Even the hum
of insects seemed to add to the genial pleasure of the
ride, and the ladies were carried away in an ecstacy
of joy.

But Mr. Goldburg was too much interested in
another subject to pay much attention to the natural
beauty of the landscape by which he was surrounded.
Since he had become such a complete devotee and
worshipper of the golden calf, a greedy disposition
seemed to have taken possession of his whole nature
and flowers, birds, shady groves and happy homes were
all lost upon him.

On reaching the home of their friends they were met
at the gate and made welcome by the Colonel, his wife
and daughters. While the ladies returned to the
cottage, the Colonel and the Banker walked to the
barn, and after showing the coachman where to put
his horses, they joined the ladies. One of the girls
went to the fields to notify Frank, who turned his
horses in pasture and came to the house to welcome
the visitors and particularly his little schoolmate.

The visit was an enjoyable one. After dinner Mr.
Goldburg proposed a drive, and Frank and the girls
arranged for a stroll in the fields to gather berries and
wild flowers.

The afternoon was pleasant and the drive delightful

Home-like cottages dotted the country everywhere, bright children played along the road, fat cattle grazed on the rich grass, plowmen slowly followed their teams across the fields turning up the fresh black soil   The whole landscape in fact was a picture of prosperity. While the ladies talked of the general beauties of the drive, Mr. Goldburg inquired of the Colonel what business he thought of engaging in, remarking that the loss of his arm would rather unfit him for farming, and that the city would give him a better opportunity for educating his children,

The Colonel had made no definite arrangements for the future.   Mr. Goldburg then informed him that the Stillwater building was about completed and that there would be a fine chance for a store in it, and in his opinion, with the popularity the Colonel had, he could surely drive a thriving trade.   The Colonel said that he would think the matter over, and as they were nearing home the subject was dropped.

Before leaving Mr. Goldburg pressed upon the Colonel a warm invitation to come with his family and stay over night and they would talk over the store proposition, and if the Colonel needed any assistance he would see to it that there should be no lack of funds. Rebecca who was in the yard with the other children, was now called, and after an exchange of "Come and see me's" and a good bye shake with Mrs. Bundy and the Colonel, allowed Frank to help her into the carriage.

A few days after this the Colonel was in town and called at the bank.   Mr. Goldburg received him with cordiality and after a short conversation in which the banker brought up the store proposition and showed it up in its most favorable light, they took a walk for the purpose of seeing the building.

Mr. Goldburg had calculated on the amount of money that would be required to fill the room and accommodate the trade and estimated it $20,000.   He kindly offered to furnish the Colonel with what money he would need at a very reasonable interest,

"What interest will you expect?"

O, we usually get 10 per cent, but in your case of course we will make it light, and, well, we will say 8 per cent.

"That," said the Colonel, "will be $800 a year. What interest do you pay the government for this money?"

"O, the government charges us no interest, it is paying us interest in gold semi-annually on our whole investment. You see if a man is lucky enough to own bonds the government not only pays him his interest in gold, but of the $100,000 that we paid for the bonds it gives us $90,000 back to loan out among our neighbors."

"Then," said the Colonel, "when you have the whole $90,000 loaned at eight per cent you will realize on interest, on money that belongs to the government, some $7,200. This is clear gain, instead of the government taxing the banks it is the banks taxing the government on one hand and the people on the other. It seems to me that the government would do well to loan this money itself and save the interest; in the whole United States it would amount to enough to pension the soldiers both north and south."

But the banker did not care to continue this argument, so it was finally settled that the Colonel would take the matter of business under further consideration for a few days and that he would drop in again in a short time.

The question now came before the Bundy family, and as everything seemed to favor the proposition, the Colonel decided to commence at once. He took a lease on the building and employed an expert book-keeper and manager.

Mr. Goldburg accompanied them to the city and introduced the Colonel to some of the most prominent business men of New York.

The goods were soon ordered, and when they were on the shelves and everything nicely arranged, it was decided that it was the best and showiest store in the town.

The Colonel's cards were soon scattered among his

old friends and they began to drop in, and in a short time he was doing the best business in the city.

One year from this time, April 1, 1866, the Colonel took stock, balanced his books and found that his net gain for the year was over $3,000. This was indeed encouraging. His stock was all new, and in the best condition. Money was plenty and everybody busy. It is a coincidence well worth noting that never in the history of the United States have the people enjoyed such a wonderful degree of prosperity as at this time, when the iron chains by which Shylock held the people in financial bondage, had by the greed, cowardice and want of patriotism on the part of the bankers had been temporarily severed, and the government without Shylock's consent had become so bold as to issue an abundance of money that bankers could not entirely control. Hence the contraction act became a necessity to the nobility, and all the bankers and bondholders, aristocrats, money-changers and gold-gamblers of the civilized world united in one common brotherhood to rob the American people of the good conditions and the prosperity that evolution had brought about. As these fiends of hell, paupers, who had lived for years from the earnings of others, had by usury, trickery, bribery, class legislation and fraud secured possession of all the gold on earth, they wished through it to control the business of the world, as they had done for ages.

While the people of the United States had plenty of legal tender greenbacks that would pay debts, taxes, buy goods, in fact do anything that money can do, even buy gold if it was necessary, their gold would remain in the vaults uncalled for, hence it would become necessary to destroy the greenbacks and base all values on gold. Why base on gold? Because the Shylocks had all the gold stored up in their vaults and it would have remained out of use without legislation in its favor, and been valuable in the United States only as a commodity. And how base on gold? Simply by making gold a legal tender, destroying all other legal tender money, and make all debts, both public and private, payable only in gold and the job is done. Easy, is it not, and simple? Any man can understand that if he has to have gold to pay taxes, to pay notes, and to buy the necessaries of of life and Shylock owns the gold, that he has a one sided deal on hand, for gold he must have, the law demands it. Shylock then says that money is scarce; give me your wheat for fifty cents a bushel, your cotton for five cents a pound, and if you do not have money enough to pay your taxes and keep your family clothed, we will lend you money at a good round interest and take a mortgage on your farm. If you can't afford to pay your help good wages you can make them work for what they can eat, for eat they must.

They would have us believe that no one but a Sherman or a banker can understand these things, but we all know that when we had plenty of legal tender greenbacks we did not need gold, and as the bankers have the gold, why not let them keep it. We do not want it. We do not need it, and the sooner we demonetize gold the sooner we will destroy the money power and burst the shackles from 65,000,000 of financial slaves.

When there were plenty of legal tender greenbacks in circulation there were good times throughout the whole country; as fast as they were withdrawn, we returned to gold panics, bank failures, low prices, want and enforced idleness. And the wise statesman tells us that it is over production. What a fertile brain it must have taken to make such a discovery!

Think of it, people starving because crops are too good! (What a blessed thing it would be to have a famine), and people going poorly clad because there has been such an over-production of clothing—bosh.

While the wise men of the United States are giving the people taffy in the shape of over production, the wise men of Britain tell of the wonderful blessings that come from paying interest on a government debt, "A government debt is a government blessing."

While Col. Bundy was making up his yearly statement, the combined powers of darkness had their representatives at Washington backed by money unlimited. Their object was to destroy liberty and build up a class to destroy American money by redeeming it with interest bearing bonds and compel the American people to borrow gold from foreign syndicates to take the place of the greenbacks that were to be destroyed by act of Congress. April 12, 1866, marks the period when the work of this black and damnable conspiracy was consummated and culminated in the passage of the contraction act which kindled the fire to destroy the money. Just what it cost the gold power to get this act through Congress will never be known to the public, but the baneful effect it had upon the country can be attested by thousands of well to do farmers and business men who were squeezed out and forced into the street.

At the time of the passage of this act money was plenty; everyone found work and the outlook for the future had never been brighter; but the first year after the universal destruction of American money commenced, the American press was called upon to make record of 2,386 business failures, with an actual loss of $86,000,000.

For ten years this contraction continued, and the yearly failures increased until 1876, when $85,000,000 of the American money had been destroyed and the annual failures reached the enormous sum of 10,000, with an aggregate loss of $300,000,000. Search the annals of time if you will, but the finger of the past will point to no robbery of such magnitude being carried out by civil legislation; yet while it was going on politicians, urged on by the gold power, were crying, over-production, as an excuse for national distress and tearing open anew the wounds of the late war to detract public attention from the real danger.

During the first year of contraction goods throughout the United States decreased in value continually, and when Col. Bundy took stock at the end of the year he found that he had the same amount of goods on hand, but their value had decreased twenty per cent, which amounted to $4,000. This reduced cash value to $16,000; trade, in consequence of the destruction, had dropped off and his profits had barely covered his expenses.

The year before he had paid the bank $3,000. The debt it will be remembered was $10,000, interest $800, credit $3,000; balance due the bank $7,800. This year he could pay nothing, so he gave a note, as follows: Debt of last year $7,800, interest $624; total settled by note to bank $8,424.

The Colonel had listened to political talk about over-production that John Sherman had put into the mouths of his followers. He had read column after column of stupefying twaddle and far-fetched arguments dished up to order by and for a subsidized press, and it had not occurred to him that one of the grandest swindles that ever disgraced the annals of time was being daily and hourly systematically carried out.

As time passed on everything continued to fall in value and the country witnessed for the year, 2,608 business failures, representing a loss to creditors of $63,774,000 and $473,000,000 of money had been destroyed.

At the end of that year Col. Bundy found that his stock had been increased a little, but its cash value had actually gone down to $14,000, and being unable to settle his bank note he was forced to renew it, as follows: Old note $8,472, interest $674, new note to bank $9,089. The note was signed, and once more the Colonel hoped to succeed, but this year was only another of contraction, and again the books showed a loss on the same goods. The failures reached in the' United Staets 3,551. The contraction law continued to grind, and the following year produced 2,915 business failures, and still the following year 4,069.

The Colonel saw with a sad heart his goods constantly decreasing in value. He had been careful in his management of the stock, his trade had even been better than other merchants of the same city, he had done a cash business, but the trouble was, that to-day it would take double the amount of goods to pay his debts that it would four years ago. "No wonder," said he, "that there are over 4,000 business failures in the United States this year."

His own stock was to-day about the same in quality and quantity as when he commenced four years before; then it cost him cash $20,000, to-day it was worth less than $13,000. "This," said he, "is contraction. I will have to sell my entire stock to pay the bank, and if I let it run four more years and contraction continues it will take my store, farm, town property, and everything else to pay the $10,000 I borrowed from the bank, and still I paid $3,000 on it the first year. Several other merchants of the place have been forced into bankruptcy and I think it about time to call a halt."

After making up his mind fully what course it would be best for him to pursue he saw Mr. Goldburg, the banker, explained his situation and stated his fears for the future.

"You have," said the banker, "about $13,000 worth of goods in the store at present prices. Your note now amounts to something over $10,000, the goods can hardly be considered good security now for that amount, especially with constantly declining prices. We have been considering your case and are of the opinion that you will pull through all right, in fact it has been our intention from the first to pull you through. So far as I am concerned personally, your note would be good for any amount of money, but the bank has rules you see that must be observed, and when a man complies with the rules, it establishes confidence and his credit will be good and so capital. By giving a mortgage on your farm in addition to the store it will strengthen your credit beyond all question and with good credit you will be able to keep up your stock, and as others go out of business and fail, your business will be increased."

"Yes," said the Colonel, "but four year ago I was doing business on an investment of $20,000, and paying interest on one-half of my entire capital, while now I am doing business on a $13,000 capital, a declining market, and paying interest on over three-fourths of my entire capital. Had I four years ago taken my $10,000 of greenbacks and locked them up without interest, they would to-day come very near buying the same goods that I paid $20,000 for at that time. Had I at that time invested my $10,000 of greenbacks in government bonds, drawn my interest in gold every six months, converted the gold into greenbacks and again into bonds, I would have money enough to-day to buy the same amount of goods and a few thousand dollars to loan to my neighbors, But suppose I had done as bankers do, deposited my government bonds with the government and received in return ninety per cent in national bank notes; and loaned the ninety per cent out as you do at eight per cent, add the interest on the $9,000 to the gold interest, where would I be?

"To-day my bonds and interest would amount to $16,000, and during the same period with all the rush and push that I possess in an active business I have been compelled to witness my own little fortune, which was the hard earnings of four years' service upon the battle field and in the sickly swamps of the south, dwindle away and pass into the pockets and vaults of the men who deal in gold.

"What encouragement then to mortgage other property, this contraction law is still in force, its object has been plainly demonstrated. By destroying our American money the people are forced to borrow Wall Street or British gold to carry on business with and the interest which goes largely into the hands of foreign capitalists is eating up the profits and destroying every industry. As money becomes scarce everything decreases in value, and day by day our business men are forced out of business, over 4,000 failures in the last year. In fact I see no way, no hope, except to sell what I have, pay up and get out of business. It is hard to lose what I have invested but it will be worse to continue on in this way and lose my home."

"O," said the banker, "you should **not look** on the dark side of the subject, Colonel. We must hope for better times when resumption is reached." But the Colonel insisted that he could see no benefit to come from the resumption of specie payment except to the men who own the gold and silver.   Mr. Goldburg knew that if the store was closed out when times were so hard the goods would not pay the debt and he was a little doubtful about selling the Colonel's other property without injuring the reputation of the bank, so he offered the Colonel $1,000 and return his note. The Colonel would be losing about $2,000 on present invoice but still he felt that it was the best that he could do, for no one seemed to have any money but the bankers and money-changers. Mr. Goldburg wanted him to continue right on in charge of the store on a salary. As this proposition seemed better than bankruptcy it was accepted and Col. Bundy went out of business, another victim of British gold-bug legislation.

A few days after goods were transferred, suit was commenced against Mr. Stillwater and the building was finally ordered sold, but money was so extremely scarce that no bids were made and it was transferred to the bank to satisfy the mortgage. Mr. Stillwater had lost on the enterprise over $20,000 and was another victim to the same law, that with John Sherman's assistance had been lobbied through Congress in the interest of England and Wall Street bankers.

In justification of these unfortunate individuals in point of business capacity it might be here noted that during the ten years that contraction was doing its work of destroying American money, there were in the United States 4,617 business failures similar to that of Col. Bundy's and Mr. Stillwater's, and that a loss had been sustained by our people of not only millions but billions and even more.

CHAPTER VII.

AFTER Col. Bundy moved to the city, Frank, who was then in his nineteenth year, commenced going to school again; for three years he attended the city school preparatory to taking a collegiate course but on the decline of his father's financial affairs he determined to learn a trade, and being of powerful muscle he decided to work in iron and was not long in getting a place. The shop where he commenced work was at that time considered to be quite an extensive one, and Frank was so quick to learn that in a few months he was getting journeyman's wages.

He had during all this time continued to live at home and the warm friendship that so early sprang up between him aud Rebecca had ripened into love, and now that he was making a little money for himself they often talked of future plans and even had a place picked out where he would buy a lot and build a home. It was to be small, but neat, and the yard would be a garden of roses. All cost was carefully figured and was to come within Frank's earnings, for each had strong suspicions that Mr. Goldburg would oppose the match now that the boy was poor. In fact after Frank went to learn a trade Mr. Goldburg had treated him with marked indifference.

This finally became so marked that Rebecca preferred to meet her lover at his father's house. This continued for some time until about one year after Frank had commenced work in the shop, and soon after the Colonel had turned the store over to the bank, Mr. Goldburg summoned his daughter to his presence.

He was in his sitting room which was furnished in the height of elegance, and as Rebecca approached he motioned her to a seat.

"Rebecca," said he, speaking in a stern voice, "I am sorry to see this warm feeling that seems to exist between you and young Mr. Bundy. You certainly must know that it can never come to anything good so why persist in giving way to such a feeling?"

These last words were said in rather a pleading voice and touched Rebecca's feelings. She paused for a moment and then said, "Father, why are you so opposed to Mr. Bundy? You used to speak of him as one of the brightest and most promising boys in the whole country, why do you so dislike him now?"

"Mr. Bundy," said her father, "is bright enough of course, but he belongs to a different class from yours. There is a circle of society forming in this country which is as distinct from the lower class as are the noblemen of Britain. This now is a period of money getting. The moneyed men and bankers of this country are fully organized. Our society is well represented in the legislative halls of the country. The financiers of to-day are the greatest the world has ever known. By a single act of Congress they throw millions upon millions of dollars from the pockets of the masses to the vaults of the gold dominating class and make it appear quite smooth."

"What is a financier, papa?"

"A financier, daughter, is a man who gives his every thought and bends every effort of his nature and soul to the concentration of large capital and wealth in the hands of a few individuals by the use of money. The methods of doing this are various. Usury or interest is our grand factor; it is like a cancer, eats slowly but surely, is certain in its results and downs its victim with unerring precision. But men do not always take readily to borrowing money, it therefore becomes necessary to use compulsion and this is done by controlling legislation. By inducing the government to destroy the national money called greenbacks the people are compelled to borrow gold and silver from the banks to do business with. Then in the course of time, when all the banks have succeeded in getting all the gold in their vaults and the silver out among the people, they will bring a pressure to bear upon Congress through a subsidized press, bribery and a promise of support for office compel them to demonetize silver, and by this destroy its debt paying qualities, and thus compel the people to go to the banks and borrow gold.

"Of course anybody can understand these things. When properly explained it is as easy as a b c, but it requires a financier to explain it in such a way that the moneyed men will know it to be money in their pockets and the people will think it is the only thing on earth that will save them from everlasting ruin.

"He wants to be capable of mixing things up in such a way that no one can understand, in fact get it in such a tangle that with all his millions, all his great knowledge of finance he is forced to admit that the critical situation is actually beyond comprehension and he hardly knows what would be best for the working classes, and at the same time have every man he can influence in a quiet way, with money or not, crying out from street corners such old familiar chestnuts as, over-production, tariff, protect labor, reform, honest money, a government debt is a government blessing. Have every paper in the country paid for using these wonderful truths as headlines to column upon column of figures that would swamp an astronomer, and while all this clatter is going on, make the wonderful discovery that the whole trouble is caused by want of confidence, and this confidence must be restored by destroying government money, called greenbacks, and compel the people to borrow bank bills to do business with. Next comes the cry of over-production of silver and a want of confidence on the part of bankers. Of course confidence must be restored again and the only way to do that this time is to demonetize silver and compel people to borrow gold from the banks to take the place of the silver. Silver then goes down to nothing. Bankers buy it up, and when it is all in the hands of the money power, and the gold all loaned out, a false alarm is started about the over-production of gold, and gold is demonetized, as it was in 1850 by Belgium and Germany. When this occurs silver will be in the hands of the bankers, the mines all dead and people will have to borrow silver to pay their debts; all done to restore confidence. Gold like silver when it is demonetized will go down to nothing and bankers will buy it up for a mere song. You see this gold game beats the Louisiana lottery, for in the one case a man plays or not, just as he pleases, but in the other the whole country is robbed whether they will or not.

"So you see a financier must be a man without a conscience, with no scruples whatever; he must be capable of exacting the last farthing from the poor widow; he must be honest beyond doubt, and do everything he agrees to do, but never do anything that does not, in some way, redound to his own profit. He must also be worth millions, no matter how he gets it for it is an evidence of financial ability. But above all things and in short he must be master of the art of controlling the world by controlling its currency.

"It is generally admitted among bankers that John Sherman is the greatest financier that ever lived. In his natural organism he seems to have every requisite.

"Our mortgage system is one of the greatest methods of modern times. It is complete in its operation, and by it we are obtaining titles to land all over the United States. In fact it looks as though one-half the farmers would be paying rent by the time the greenbacks have all been destroyed, and we seem to obtain titles to these lands with hardly an effort.

"The joint incorporative system, too, is wonderful in its workings, and is being more thoroughly systematized every day. By its use we are enabled to own and operate all the business of the country and never leave our homes The men who operate the railroads do not own them. The men who own them, in many cases, never see them; and it is so with all kinds of business.

"In a few years the property will all be in the hands of a few, and all the business of the country will be done by joint stock incorporated companies.

"The poor will be given work, and will of course be contented. Some who have more ambition than others will be given places of more importance and greater responsibility. This will satisfy their ambition and they will be content to have opportunity and power to dominate their fellow men, and in this way we will own the whole mass. We will have slaves by the million without the trouble of caring for them. Our great republic, we believe, is destined to solve the problem as to how the few can rule the many without themselves being ruled by a king.

"The time is not far off when the nobility of the United States will materialize and in secret conventions assembled, take unto themselves titles, according to their wealth. A secret society will be formed duly protected by grips, signs, passwords, etc., and it will be known as the Noble Knights of America. Its members will be given titles according to their social position. The society will be divided into three degrees or chapters as follows: The first chapter will consist of all persons in the United States who wish to join, that are worth property to the extent of $100,000. The second chapter will consist of persons who are worth above $1,000,000. The third chapter to consist of persons who are worth above $10,000,000. All business of a political nature to be transacted in the first chapter. Members of the higher degrees will be also members of the first chapter.

"There will be a committee elected whose duty it shall be to receive correspondence from members in all parts of the country and report such as is considered important, to each regular meeting and it shall be through this committee that all money is to be distributed for election purposes and buying and suppressing such small newspapers as may be considered dangerous. As the owners of all the large papers will be members, their interest will be with the Nobility. It shall also be the duty of this committee to look to it that every convention is controlled to that end, that no person receives a nomination for any legislative office that is not a member, a tool or in sympathy with this society.

"Two months prior to each session of Congress there will be held a general legislative conference consisting of all the first chapter and representatives of the other two chapters to decide on what legislation is needed, appoint a committee to demand the same, and also to make an appropriation of money to secure this end.

"When this organization shall have been completed and fully installed we will have the strongest government on the face of earth. A solid republic with an aristocracy standing back of it that is the wealthiest that the world has ever known. The doctrine of self or popular government will have then reached its zenith, and the people will be contented under the wise administrations thus brought about. Besides the concentration of wealth in the hands of a society like this, and millions of poor to fill the army, will make nations tremble.

"The society will elect their own president, or control the one who is elected much easier than they do now. They will control the legislation, and with the army and navy, in this day of electricity, a successful revolution will be as impossible, as it would be in China or Japan, and our country will be ruled without a jar or discord. The poorer the people become the more submissive they will be.

"With all these prospects before us it would be sheer madness for you to marry one who has already taken his place among the lower classes. You have had opportunities of marrying millions; why should you make yourself a slave?

"That is all now, dearest, go and do what you will but banish all thoughts of this fellow from your mind."

As he said this he arose to leave the room.

"Wait one moment, father," said Rebecca with a voice full of emotion, "let me say one word."

"No," said her father turning half round as he passed out of the door, "we cannot argue this question, you must forget that man."

Rebecca saw the door shut with a heavy jar as her

father disappeared. She stood for a moment as one entranced, her hands clasped, her face turned upward, as if to implore the sympathy of angels, then sank heavily into a chair from which she had arisen.

This, the most terrible of all blows, had not come to Rebecca entirely unexpected. For days, weeks, even months she had thought, dreamed and dreaded this meeting, and now that it had passed she was left, as it were, standing for the time between hope and despair.

The love for her father was strong but had been weakened by his neglect, for in cultivating greed he had trampled love beneath his feet and become a stranger to its domain.

On the other hand her heart-strings had been kept at their greatest tension, by sweet words in accents mild, gentle smiles and such looks as love only knows and understands. She had walked, talked and listened to dreams of eternal love and happiness. She had wandered through gardens, gathered flowers, made bouquets to adorn the table of the one she loved and in each leaf that grew upon those stems she read their future fortunes. And now that the long looked for stroke had come, she was almost paralyze d. Thoughts crowded thick and fast, one upon another, and she at last gave away to weeping, but when these paroxysms of grief had passed away she arose as calm as a May morning, went to her chamber, knelt at her usual place and prayed as she had never prayed before.

"O, Thou great and ever living God, who holds the destiny of nations in thy hands; Thou who hath for centuries stored Thy great blessings on and in the earth for man's future consumption and good, gold, silver, iron, copper all contribute to man's wants. The earth's surface, too, at the touch of man's industry, blooms and blossoms as the rose and brings forth an abundance of life sustaining food. All these things hast Thou given for Thy children's greatest good and comfort, and wilt Thou not now look with Thy great pity and mercy upon one so sore distressed. Deep down in the heart hast Thou sown Thy seeds of love, and now that they have grown and blossomed, shall I pluck them out?

"O, God, I pray Thee to let this, the bitterest of all cups, pass; give me Thy love, give me Thy counsel that I may know the right path, and strength that I may remain true to my love, true to father and mother and true unto myself. Bless, too, O Father of all, I beseech Thee, the one who must also share with me this cup of the bitterest of all dregs. Strengthen him and keep him true to himself and true to Thee."

Thus, for hours Rebecca prayed, until at last, she retired, feeling that sweet consolation which is only found in deep and earnest prayer. As Rebecca felt a touch of Divine love, she also experienced a wonderful feeling of justification, and the determination to remain true to her love grew stronger and stronger.

CHAPTER VIII.

A SHORT time after the circumstance related at the close of the last chapter, while Mr. Goldburg was in New York on business connected with the store, Mrs. Goldburg and Rebecca spent an evening at Col. Bundy's, and while Mrs. Bundy's daughter and Rebecca were in the yard among the flowers, Mrs. Bundy and Mrs. Goldburg had a regular old fashioned visit to themselves, and Mrs. Bundy, who had fallen into the common error of thinking that unlimited wealth gave unlimited happiness, was not a little surprised at hearing the subject discussed from a different standpoint.

After Mrs. Bundy had told her how nicely they were getting along, how they had invested the little money they had left out of the financial wreck and how they were economizing, and trying to save a little each month out of the Colonel's salary and by careful management had been enabled to live quite comfortably on so small a sum; she continued by saying that notwithstanding they themselves were quite poor, she did not envy the happiness of those who had been more fortunate.

But Mrs. Goldburg soon assured her there was no occasion for being envious. Said she: "My experience is that it is not among the rich you need look for the greatest happiness. When we were poor my husband worked hard and came home nights tired, but his daily toil was over and he had nothing to do but to enjoy the blessings of home. I, too, by my little sewing for the miners, was enabled to contribute to some extent toward the expenses of living and I felt as though I really amounted to something, but now small matters are never counted.

"Mr. Goldburg comes home mentally tired from having pored over perplexing examples all day. He is always in deep thought about some business that is not going exactly as he would like. Some man does not suit and he has not, as yet been able to find a better one. There is some great scheme on hand to lobby a bill through Congress to make another big haul on the people and he has been assessed a large sum toward the fund to bribe officials. He is afraid the money will be misplaced and that he himself will be the one swindled at last, but he dare not refuse. All these big swindles are brought about in the same way and the money god is a tyrant and perfectly inexorable.

"He is always restless and nervous, often gets up late in the night and walks the floor for hours at a time in deep meditation. He never has time to talk; besides he does not seem to be interested in anything that we know anything about; in fact it seems as if his whole nature has undergone a change and I do not think it is age that has done it."

Pausing for a moment she continued:

"Do you know, Mrs. Bundy, I sometimes believe that money, when you get above a competency, is a curse. What benefit can we hope to derive from the millions that Mr. Goldburg is piling up?

"For the present it is only an annoyance, and when I look at the matter I fail to see where, when and how property in California and Oregon can benefit us here. True, we get the rent, but what of that, we do not need it, nor do we use it except to buy more land and have the trouble of collecting more rent. Just the interest alone that we get on bonds amounts to thousands and is more than enough to keep us in luxury. Then why run banks, railroads, factories and shops? It looks to me to be all trouble for nothing and it seems as though there ought to be some better way.

"The only thing that I can see in money above a competency is power. If power is used to oppress others then it certainly debases the one who uses it, and whoever knew a millionaire to use his power for any other purpose except to accumulate more, and that means oppression to some one.

"I see by some of the late papers that the doctors are beginning to treat drunkenness as a disease. I believe that they are right and that gambling is also a disease and that the man that gets to gambling in stocks with his millions, will finally contract the disease in such a malignant form as to become a burden to himself and all his friends, a blank in society and a curse to the human race."

This was all a new way of looking at things from what Mrs. Bundy had been accustomed to.

"It looks strange," said she, "that men should abandon all the walks of pleasure and usefulness to confine themselves in an office concocting all sorts of schemes to extort money from the people when they already have more than they can use even in luxurious living in a natural lifetime."

"Yes," said Mrs. Goldburg, "and since such is man's disposition I think the law should step in and prevent this suicidal course by saying when thou art gone thy effects shall revert back through the government to the place they naturally belong and from where they have been extorted by cunning tricks and usury."

"Looking at things from this standpoint," said Mrs. Bundy, "I think I ought to feel thankful for the family ties of love that have ever blest our home. Mr. Bundy through all our trials has been ever cheerful, and he treats me with as much care and solicitude as the day when we were married, and our children hardly know what it is to hear an unkind word. We may some time want for food but never for kindness and family love."

After tea when Mrs. Goldburg was about to depart, the girls insisted on Rebecca staying to spend the evening, to which she consented.

When Frank returned from the shop his two sisters were helping their mother in the kitchen and he found Rebecca alone in the parlor, The meeting was one of that class of lovers' meetings that is easier imagined than described. Rebecca laid all her father's objections before Frank with all the simplicity of a child. After a long silence Frank, in a serious and meditative voice, said:

"Rebecca, you do not know how dear you are to me, but I am afraid I am doing wrong in standing between you and your fortune which I can never hope to replace if it is taken from you."

"Love," said Rebecca, "is greater to me than all the gold that glitters."

He pressed her more closely to his heart and both stood motionless; language failed to give an expression in words to the thoughts that seemed to melt and mingle in every breath. At last supper was called and they joined the family. Nothing could have been more depressing than the circumstances under which these two were placed. Both sensitive, both intent on doing right, duty to parents was before them while duty to love and self claimed their consideration.

After supper Frank escorted Rebecca home but both felt too sad to talk and parted by simply pledging eternal love.

Soon after this Mr. Goldsmith, the New York gambler, who it will be remembered had worked up the railroad scheme in which he and Mr. Goldburg had both become millionaires, made his appearance in Bopeep and put up at the Palace hotel where he fell in with M. M. Taylor, an old acquaintance of his who was noted for his success in horse-racing and gambling on prize fights.

Mr. Goldsmith told his friend that he had a little deal on hand here that was good for a round million at least if he could make it work. On being pressed to give an outline of the scheme he said it was nothing more nor less than marrying the banker's daughter.

He said that he stood all right with the father, but although the girl had always treated him courteously, he was forced to confess that she was the hardest creature to approach he had ever met. He had called at the mansion several times on invitation intending to make advances and his heart had always failed him, but that he would take on a drink or two this time and put on a bold front, that a "faint heart never won fair lady," and that he intended to tackle the girl. His friend cautioned him not to be too fast, but he said "no, there is too much money at stake, I know the father is in favor of the match and I don't intend to put it off too long."

On the following evening he went to Mr. Goldburg's dressed in the height of dudish style, and on being announced, was received by Rebecca and ushered into the parlor where he was entertained by her and her mother in their most friendly manner. For an hour they chatted and Mr. Goldsmith made good his resolution by showing such a remarkable degree of boldness as to come near driving Rebecca from the room; but excusing rudeness on account of his being a millionaire, she managed to stand her ground.

On taking his leave he was so kind as to solicit her company to the theatre some evening She declined with a coldness that would have chilled the heart of a Polar bear. But Mr. Goldsmith had a determination which nothing but the love of money could have sustained and he was not to be frustrated, so he took his leave by informing the ladies he would call again in a day or two.

On returning home from the bank that evening Mr. Goldburg called his daughter into the room again and greeting her with a smile which was quite unusual, informed her that Mr. Goldsmith would spend the following evening with them and this would be a good time to make an impression.

As Mr. Goldsmith had made and now possessed more than two millions, his ability as a financier could hardly be doubted; and in addition to what he now had, on the death of his father he would fall heir to over ten millions. He ventured to remark to his daughter that he had heard Mr. Goldsmith speak in a very complimentary manner of her several times.

"Father," said Rebecca, in a very positive manner, "do you know that I hate that man?"

"What, what," said her father, "what did he ever do to make you hate him?"

"I hate him," said Rebecca, "because he is vulgar; because he has no fine feelings, because he never uttered a word in my presence that sounded as if he possessed a noble, manly heart. Father, I would rather be buried in the bottom of the sea and have the billows ebb and flow above me, than marry a man like that."

Mr. Goldburg was sorely disappointed in this state of affairs; he was so accustomed to have everything bend to his will on account of his money that it fairly staggered him to be confronted by his own daughter, a mere child as she appeared to him, and one who, as a rule, was willing to sacrifice everything in order that he might be pleased; and now that he was trying to secure her happiness it was the harder to bear, because he considered this as the great plan of his life which she was frustrating. But this disappointment was to teach him one valuable lesson—that even the power of gold is circumscribed.

Rebecca, on the other hand, recognized the importance her father attached to the affair. In fact she could not refrain from remarking to her mother that afternoon that it was the first time she had seen her father smile since he became a millionaire, and said she, "if my marrying that man is the only thing that will bring smiles to his face I am afraid he will never smile again."

On the following evening, true to his appointment Mr. Goldsmith accompanied the banker home.

It was Rebecca's first impulse to retire to her own room and report herself "not at home," but on second thought, her love and respect for her father prevented her carrying out a resolution that would have been so embarrassing to him; so preparing herself for the disagreeable task, she resolved to treat her guest with as much courtesy as possible, under the circumstances.

In spite of all her resolutions to the contrary, her reception of the millionaire was anything but what he would have desired. Her smiles were cold and comfortless and notwithstanding she seemed to treat him with courtesy, he could not shake off the feeling of self-abasement while in her presence. She seemed to look down into his very soul and read there the thoughts of a man in quest for gold.

This feeling came so strongly upon the great railroad magnate that when he was out of the house he felt like a bird set free and he hardly felt at ease until he had separated from Mr. Goldburg at the bank and joined his friend, the horse-race man, at the hotel. They retired at once to a private apartment and ordering a quantity of brandy and glasses, proceeded to drink freely. The millionaire then told his story and in conclusion said that, undoubtedly, the scheme had proved a failure, beyond all redemption. "The cause," he said, "was not clear, but that her mind was fully made up on the subject, would hardly admit of a doubt.

"I might," said he, "through the influence of money and intrigue with her father, who is as crazy after gold as a spring bird is for a worm, compel her to recognize my suit, but the world, in this enlightened age, could hardly produce a man who, in his right mind, would be willing to claim the hand of one who is possessed of such repelling force. I think it is the father's plan to marry her to some one who has or will have unlimited wealth; but if he don't have lots of trouble accomplishing that end, I shall miss my guess."

Mr. Goldburg on reaching the bank, went at once to his office and threw himself into a magnificent chair, took a cigar from a box of fine Havannas that cost not less than twenty-five dollars, and lighting it, in a somewhat nervous manner, threw himself back in his chair and gave himself up to very serious reflection.

The reception of Mr. Goldsmith by Rebecca had not met his hopes and expectations, by any means. That Frank Bundy yet occupied a place in her affections was plainly to be seen. But why Nature should implant such strong feelings in the hearts of the young, was something the banker could not understand; he could not blame the girl, it was Nature that was at fault. It seemed to him that the best part of life was spent in following fancies and notions before we learn to appreciate wealth and then it is often too late.

The fact that Rebecca was still young led him to think that if he could remove the cause, he might still accomplish his end; but how was this to be done?

In olden times the Priests, Rulers and men of wealth, had Trusties to put out of the way men who were objectionable, and even now the same methods are sometimes resorted to. He did not wish to resort to such extreme measures, still he felt it his imperative duty to protect his family against the disgrace of having his daughter marry a laboring man.

After preparing some business papers for the next mail, Mr. Goldburg locked up his private office and returned home fully determined to remove at once all obstacles to the marrying of his daughter to a man of her own class. He talked to Mrs. Goldburg about the matter, but finding that she entertained very different views upon the subject he resolved to act entirely upon his own judgment.'

A few days after this Mr. Goldburg made it a point to meet Frank as he was returning from work. As they met the banker stopped as if for a talk, which also brought Mr. Bundy to a standstill. After exchanging salutations the banker commenced:

"Mr. Bundy, I am sorry to see there is so much attachment existing between my daughter and yourself and feel it to be my duty as a father, to notify you that your meetings must be discontinued and all engagements which may exist be broken off."

"Why is this?" said Frank in an independent manner.

"You ought to know, sir," said Mr. Goldburg, "that as poor as you are, you could hardly expect to marry an heiress; but I will make you one condition, go to some great mining camp and prove yourself a man by bringing back $100,000 and she is yours."

"What," said Frank, in a sarcastic manner, "do you propose selling your own daughter?"

"No, sir," said the banker indignantly, "but I do not intend she shall marry a pauper."

This was too much; the boy did not stop to consider but acting on the impulse, in pugilistic style, struck the banker a blow in the eye which sent him sprawling in the mud, and without stopping to help him to his feet again, he walked on till he met a policeman, when he gave himself up.

The banker was assisted to his feet by bystanders and as soon as he recovered from his surprise, he hurried on and filed a complaint.

Frank gave bail, of course, and the trial was set for the following day.

Mr. Goldburg received the necessary medical attention and returned to his home. His wife and daughter were, of course, greatly alarmed by his appearance, but after satisfying themselves that he was not badly hurt, they were anxious to know the particulars. Mr. Goldburg, however, did not feel inclined to talk very freely but seemed to prefer to be alone; so they allowed him to rest quietly on the sofa.

During the trial of the case the court room was crowded with workingmen. It happened that the justice was an old soldier who had served under Col. Bundy, so Frank thought his chances for holding his own were pretty good. When court came to order, the statements of the banker and Frank were so nearly the same that further evidence was considered unnecessary and the case went to the court. Frank was fined five dollars and costs, which he proceeded to pay but was crowded back by the workingmen, while others paid the fine.

No trial in that city ever attracted such widespread attention as this, small as it was. The newspapers published a full account of the affair, with lengthy comments and it, like many differences passed, having done its part toward increasing the feeling between capital and labor, which is after all nothing more nor less than another name for the two classes—rich and poor.

Mr. Goldburg's sore head only made him the more determined and the next thing to be done was to throw Frank out of work. As he owned a large amount of stock in the business where Frank was working, beside furnishing them money through the bank to tide over rough places, it was no great trouble to have the young man discharged, and that without letters of recommendation. Frank was not surprised when he went to the shop at noon to find a request to call at the office. Of course, he knew what that meant, and after drawing his money, he went home to talk over the matter. On his way home he called at the other shops only to find his services were not needed. They would gladly have given him employment, but they were all, more or less, dependent on the bank for money. They knew this was a personal fight of the most powerful banker in the town against the boy and they were liable to lose favor if they had him in their employ.

Seeing plainly the situation, Frank decided at once what to do, in fact, there was but one thing to do, go beyond the reach of the banker's influence to try to get work. That night he related the whole affair to his father and mother, and after everything was fully explained his mother reported what Mrs. Goldburg had said, that there was but one use that could be made of money or property, above a competency, or what would keep a man and his family in luxury a long time, or while they lived, and that is its use to oppress others. She remembered Mr. Goldburg used to say the same thing before he became a millionaire, and said she: "I believe there should be some limit by law, to the amount of money or property a man may be allowed to own. Power is good, so much as will secure to us self-preservation, education, comfort and amusement; the next step is the power to oppress others, which some will use. Money is power, hence its acquisition should be limited to our needs.

"These views might appear radical to some, but all should at least agree, that the government is doing a great wrong when it gives the bankers millions of dollars to use to oppress their neighbors with, just because they happen to be rich enough to own government bonds. I should think if government has favors to bestow, the poor should receive the benefit, for the rich can take care of themselves. "

"Look out," said the Colonel, "you will be advocating woman suffrage next."

"Well," said Mrs. Bundy, "if we had woman suffrage it could not be much worse than now."

"They would make a fine lot of Congressmen, wouldn't they?" said Frank, in a jesting way.

"Congressmen," said his mother warming up to the subject, "if Congress had been composed of intelligent mothers how much British and Wall Street gold do you suppose it would have taken to put the Exception Clause upon the greenback or pass the United States Banking Act, or the act authorizing the selling of interest bearing bonds to take up a currency that bore no interest and was also needed in circulation? These acts are all such plain frauds that it becomes a question of honesty rather than ability, and if ever a woman gets into Congress by a majority vote of the people, her record will be so clean that no one will dare approach her with a bribe."

"It does look as if there must be something wrong," said Col. Bundy, "when a man of Mr. Goldburg's ability can become a millionaire in so short a time, and that, too, at a time when one-fourth of the best business men of the place have had to succumb to the terrible contraction of the currency and those who are still in business have lost money and are largely indebted to the banks. It is hard to conceive where this matter will end. The democratic party is rotten to the core, and the republican party seems to have been captured by the money power and has become the tool of great conspiracies to rob the people. Our only course, therefore, seems to be to worry along, make the best of it and see what evolution will bring forth next. Under the existing state of affairs, Mr. Goldburg, through his millions, in this place or community can crowd almost any man out of business that may in any manner stand in his way; that he can prevent Frank from getting work in any of the shops is quite enough to warrant this conclusion.

"But it only shows the power there is in money. If a half starved man were to come into the store and represent that he was working for some well known and responsible citizen and had a month's wages due him, which he could collect on the first of next month, buy a bill of goods, give an order on the man for the amount, and it would afterward be found that he was not working for the man, nor did he have any money due him; this would be obtaining money under false pretenses, which is a crime and can be punished as such. But Mr. Goldburg or any other millionaire, through moneyed influence, can force the people of this country to pay tithes to him, in the shape of interest and discount, to the extent of thousands of dollars each year; can drive a tradesman out of employ and virtually force him to leave the country or go to work at common labor.

"While these things are all wrong and rob the victim as effectually as in the other case, the law sees no crime and affords no relief; in fact, furnishes the money upon which bankers are allowed to collect interest.

"Politicians tell us the first duty of government is to protect property; it seems to me it would be better to make it the first duty of government to protect the citizen against the oppression of property owners.

"Mr. Goldburg has raked together millions of dollars here in the last four years. There is just the same property in the town now, that there was four years ago. Then the people owned it, now Mr. Goldburg and the bank own it. Had he taken it at the point of the bayonet or pistol, the result would have been the same—robbery pure and simple.

"That this sudden accumulation of wealth has been brought about by wicked and fraudulent legislation, there remains hardly room for a doubt, and an unproducing concern in the shape of a bank has been fastened upon the country, to which the people will be forced to pay tribute through all time to come, unless our present financial legislation undergoes an entire change. Although our form of government is quite a step in advance of the old world, it might be materially changed for the better."

The conversation now turned on Frank's departure. His mother wanted him to go back to their old place, but the farmers were all running behind and many who had been doing well while money was plenty had since the contraction of currency been forced to mortgage their farms to the bank to pay their taxes, which were still as high as they were before the contraction. Under the existing laws farming seemed to be a failure. The burning of greenbacks was still going on, and as they were disappearing from circulation, everything in the shape of property was falling to pieces and the bankers saw their notes and mortgages increasing in value.

CHAPTER IX.

THAT same evening, Mr. Goldburg came home with a handkerchief around his face and perfumed with liniment strong enough to perfume the whole house. Rebecca did everything possible to comfort her father and then busied herself with her own thoughts. She had just finished reading the account of the affair when her father entered, and she could not blame Frank for her father had no right to call him a pauper.

After Rebecca had retired, Mr. Goldburg proceeded to tell his wife what had happened during the day. After the trial was over he sent for the foreman of the shop and ordered him to discharge Frank at once, and said he was satisfied that the other shops, knowing the circumstances, would be afraid to employ him. In that event he would be compelled to leave the place, and as many of the shops were closed or running on half time, he would find it hard to secure a job and would probably be compelled to do as he had advised him at first—go to a mining locality, and in that case all trouble would end for a time, at least.

After a long pause, Mrs. Goldburg said, "My dear, don't you think you are doing wrong in persecuting Mr. Bundy in this way when he has never wronged you?"

"Never wronged me? Are not my eyes swelled larger than a washpan from the effects of his big fist, and has he not been trying to marry our daughter, who is heir to millions and he without a cent?"

"But," said Mrs. Goldburg, "you know he is a bright young man, of good habits and of a very respectable family; his grandfather was a General in the war of 1812, and his father came home from the late war covered with glory. He fought four long years and lost one arm in order to preserve this great nation."

"Yes," said the banker, "but that all amounts to nothing now. That glory, you see, was only transitory, only a shadow. They did preserve the country, it is true, but before the work was half completed the money power of London, New York, Boston and Philadelphia had combined and established their authority so firmly in Washington that the government by the people, became a government by the money power, whose mission is to own and control the people, the principle of self-government for which Col. Bundy fought, is now among the things of the past, and under the pressure of the money power the patriotic spirit of olden times is fast passing away. In a few more years that old stock of American patriots, of which Col. Bundy is a fair sample, will have disappeared, and will live only in history.

"There has not been a financial act passed in the United States since 1862 that was not dictated by the money power. The number of business failures brought about by class legislation can be numbered by the thousands and the loss to the people by shrinkage in value can be counted by millions upon millions; and the wealth of this country is being gathered into the hands of a few more easily than you could gather butter in a churn.

"The middle and lower classes are constantly being crowded out. Corporations are absorbing their business and driving private enterprise to the wall everywhere, and millionaires are springing up like mushrooms all along the line.

"Both the old political parties are subservient to the money power. We will therefore control the legislation. The sectional fight can be kept up until the money power becomes so thoroughly intrenched behind the financial and business interests of the country that they will control the destinies of the nation with the greatest ease.

"Even the people, as they see their property slipping away, will become discouraged, lose confidence in the government and patriotism will disappear. They already are beginning to recognize the fact that it is the dollars that make the man.

"Didn't you notice that when Gen. Grant was here last summer he came to my house, was escorted all over the country by me and in my carriage, and that he did not even call on Col. Bundy? And did not Gen. Sherman do the same thing? I tell you that it is the dollars that make the man now. These Generals both knew that I was not in the army. They knew that I was at home making every dollar I could from those who did go, and now I have the dollars and they have the experience.

"It was too good a time for me to make money to tie myself up in the army and take the chance of being killed. Of course they called us bad names sometimes but you will see before the century is out we will put one of our own men in the presidential chair and the brigadiers both north and south will take a back seat."

During this talk Mr. Goldburg composedly nursed his swollen face and talked as one in a dream. There could be no doubt that it came from his inmost soul, and although Mrs. Goldburg could not believe that God would ever permit this great liberty-loving people to pass helplessly under the rule of monetary despotism, she still felt that her husband was more to be pitied than blamed; that his love of an active business life increased in him a love for gold, and that the power given to gold by false legislation and superstition had actually led him on to an idolatrous worship of the golden calf. She could not oppose him but pray for him she would and long, long hours did she pray, but alas! the idols were uppermost in his mind and his desire was for gold as an inebriate's is for drink.

Mr. and Mrs. Goldburg retired late that night to court sleep with only trifling success. Mr. Goldburg would wake frequently only to complain of his bruised face, while Mrs. Goldburg was too full of feeling to sleep. She knew her daughter's heart trouble and

being in perfect sympathy they had filled her soul with
forebodings. She hoped and prayed and prayed and
hoped, and finally gave herself up to that infinite law
of love, entirely to spiritual guidance and found consolation in a christian hope.

But what shall we say of Rebecca. Those who have
had disappointments in love can realize her suffering.
With a sick and wounded heart she sought relief in
solitary prayer. She had been taught that Jesus could
be relied upon in the saddest case of disappointment,
and now that all her plans seemed blasted at a single
blow, she put her trust in Him and finally after half a
night of rolling, tossing, weeping and praying, she
passed into that gentle slumber, which brings peace
and rest to the troubled soul.

The slumbers of Frank, too, it may be supposed
were not of an unbroken nature. The bright picture of
the future which Rebecca and he had drawn, and all
their little arrangements and promises of love were
now to be realized far in the future, if at all. To
forego, in any degree the hope of realizing these things,
was to him like accepting life as a solitary blank.
There was but one course, and that was to seek employment and with nerve and muscle he would build
up a reputation and credit and some day get on his
feet again. As for Rebecca, he knew her feelings now,
but what effect his own feelings would have, he could
not tell, but at all events, he was powerless to act; he
could only go and hope, and in the hope he felt that
he could exert a superhuman strength. He had saved
about $300. He would go on this until he found work;
on the following morning he arose and penned the
following note:

HOME, BOPEEP, June 4th.

My Dear Rebecca: You know, doubtless, what has
transpired within the last few days. May God help
you to forget me, for I see nothing but disaster in the
near future. I am determined to go into the world and
do the best I can. Times are hard and men are out of
employment all over the country, but I shall hope for
the best. I shall love you as long is I continue to

breathe, but am, for the present, undone, and if you can forget me and marry some good man, I will forgive you. I go to-day. If I am successful, I will write to you, but if not, no one will ever hear from me.

God bless you, Darling. Good-bye.

FRANK.

At breakfast the family were all .sad. Frank tried hard to make his last meal at home an enjoyable one, but a feeling of sadness that lurked behind a smiling face, the anguish of heart which naturally follows so great a calamity, had shaken his nervous frame and he looked worn. His father and mother offered several plans by which they hoped to induce him to remain at home, "but gold is god," said Frank, "and if I remain here I will bring its power down on the whole family. If I go I may find something better; besides if I must forever remain poor it will be less galling to be among strangers than to be here among those who have known me under better circumstances. Mr. Goldburg would frustrate any plan I might adopt for making money here, and the power that is lodged in a man backed by millionaires is something to be dreaded. I have seen that slightly demonstrated already. No, I must go until I find a place where I can make money." So, finding all entreaties useless, his mother helped him to pack up, adding to his general stock of clothing, needles, thread, scissors and such things as only a mother could think of, and after taking an affectionate leave of his mother and two sisters he succeeded in reaching the depot in time to take the 10:40 train for New York; not forgetting to leave the little note he had written with his eldest sister to be delivered in person.

On reaching New York, after registering at a very common hotel where a great many mechanics and railroad men stopped, he soon fell in with other iron workers who were also seeking employment, and for three days he visited the different shops only to find that they had some men laid off and others working on half time.

Everyone said that there was a wonderful stagnation

in business, caused by a scarcity of money, and once in a while he would meet some of the old style greenback men kicking about the government withdrawing the greenbacks from circulation and issuing interest bearing bonds, thus compelling the people to pay interest on the bonds, and then pay interest on bank bills and gold to supply the circulation, but Frank paid very little attention to this because it was politics, and work was what he wanted.

At the hotel he met parties from Boston, Buffalo, Philadelphia and many other important points who said they had been laid off and had to come to New York to find work. Every paper brought news of more failures in different parts of the country. Some said that it was caused by contraction of the currency, others were not willing to give any reason, but all agreed that there was a scarcity of money.

Frank paid but little attention to politics but it looked like a plain case to him, that if the trouble was scarcity of money, and that must be true for everybody seemed to say no money, scarcity of money, and other statements of the same kind at almost every breath, and that the work of the contraction act was to withdraw the government money, greenback from circulation, then the contraction act must be the prime cause of the trouble, for it was plain the withdrawing money from circulation would make it scarce. But he was too much interested in finding work to give the subject much more than a passing thought, and it is presumed that the majority of the American people were under the same influences and governed by the same motives, and this accounts for their allowing themselves to be financially robbed by the money power in the way they were.

Seeing no possible chance for work in the city Frank made up his mind to go west. During his stay at the hotel he met an old schoolmate, now a conductor on one of the roads running west and offered to carry him over his run. Of course Frank took advantage of this proposition, and before the Conductor left the train he gave Frank letters that carried him through

to Chicago. He also gave him letters to other railroad
men in Chicago asking them to assist him in getting
work. On reaching that city the same difficulty confronted him; the same complaint among business men,
hard times, men out of employment, business failures
everywhere, everything falling in value, no money the
same old cry. Factories and shops running on half
time and hundreds of men laid off. After looking
through the shops Frank saw there was no chance for
him, so he presented his letters and found the railroad
men very kind but said it would be next to an impos-
sibility to get any kind of a job there at that time, but
if he wanted to go on through to California, he was
acquainted with many of the conductors on western
roads and would give him letters that would carry him
through. Frank had been thinking of California and
so he resolved to go and took the first train for Kansas
City. At that place he laid off for a day and was
happy to find money matters slightly improved.

Government had granted or given away large tracts
of government land to railroad corporations with the
understanding that the company was to build a road
through it. This was something of a departure from
the old system, which had been to grant a charter with
the understanding that the railroad company pay for
the right of way. Some people claimed that as the
right to build roads belonged to the people or to the
government, that railroad companies should have been
made to pay for their charter or franchise, and there
were many who seemed to doubt the wisdom and even
honesty of Congress in this wholesale giving away of
government land to private corporations, which was so
out of keeping with the former custom of retaining the
land for actual settlement, and as the same men that
passed the Banking and Contraction acts had also been
at the bottom of this giving away of public land, it
certainly looked bad, and to say the least, it was very
good for the railroad company, but very bad for the
people.

In order to obtain a title to these very valuable
lands the railroad company could well afford to turn

loose a little money in the way of building a road that
would pay a dividend as soon as completed and in
operation across a country where, for hundreds of
miles, the grading was of the lightest character. As
they advanced with their tracks, flaming circulars were
sent out setting forth the richness and quality of the
lands, and thousands of people in the east who had
been forced to mortgage their farms under the money
famine brought about by contraction, sold out for what
they could get, took their money and such stock as
they had not been forced to sell, in order to live, and
came to the new Eldorado to secure as soon as possible
a farm on the odd sections of government land that had
not been given away.

It was a great grain country and ready for the plow,
and those who had by bad legislation been robbed and
crowded out in the east, found themselves once more,
endowed by nature, with the greatest of all gifts—a
home.

Every ox, and even the cows, were yoked and the
prairies were overturned; great fields of wheat, corn
and barley took the place of the native grass; houses
and barns sprang up as if by magic, on every hand and
all was life and business.

But even here on these great prairies, these hardy
pioneers were destined not to escape the well laid
schemes of Shylock, for when their rich crop was
harvested they found the prices so low and cost of
shipping so high, that it would take half of their grain
to buy lumber to properly store the other half for
their own use.

As harvest time was near, Frank concluded to go to
the country, for the shops, even in Kansas City, were
well supplied with help; so he took the cars west, and
went to a small town situated in the midst of great
fields of grain, and hired to a farmer of the name of
Bradshaw, who was in town looking for hands, and
worked for him during harvest.

It was the year for State and Congressional elections
and politics ran high; three out of four were Republicans and voted the straight ticket, while at the same

time, feeling that something was going wrong at Washington; otherwise the country could never have drifted into such a terrible condition.

There were a few old Greenbackers in the neighborhood and they were constantly twitting the Republicans about the scarcity of money, hard times, and low prices and asserting that government had destroyed the money of the country when it was so much needed in circulation. For a long time these good, old, honest Republicans were at a loss for argument; it was hard to explain why there should be so much distress in the midst of plenty.

A great and extensive country, industrious people, good crops, a surplus of everything; gold and silver mines yielding millions of dollars monthly, at peace with the world, and in the midst of all these great blessings, small business men were being forced to the wall, farmers, after working from daylight till dark to mature a crop, after selling the same at beggarly prices, were forced to mortgage their land to the bank or money lenders, for enough money to carry them through the winter; thousands of men out of employment; farmers in Kansas burning corn for fuel, while people in the cities were starving for bread.

How to account for all this misery in the midst of plenty, without everlastingly condemning John Sherman and other political leaders and other good republicans, was a hard question to solve, but at last the solution came through the fertile brain of some good statesman and advocate of a gold standard, probably John Sherman.

The wisdom of these gold speculators is wonderful; they are like an oracle, there is nothing so absurd they cannot explain it, and in a way favorable to themselves. And this great statesman in his speech which the gold power has had printed in all their papers, proved himself master of the situation and declared to the world the prime cause of the very remarkable depression in business.

"It is over-production," said he, "yes, over-production."

Republicans had been looking for the solution of the question for a long time and it was a wonderful relief; the big papers kept it in head lines, the small papers had it spread all over their patent back, stump speakers spoke it, quiet people talked it; it was short, it was easy, and the good people who were fearful that the "Rebs." would get in power through the bad management of the Republicans, hailed it as a salvation cry; even children sang it as they came from school and it was considered a fair answer to any argument introduced or advanced by men, troubled with what at that time was called by the money power, the Greenback craze, and no people, perhaps, ever rode a more successful hobby.

While Frank was at this place he attended a farmers' meeting where the financial situation was under discussion. The meeting was non-partisan and everybody had a right to participate in the debate. The Democrats had very little to say. The Republicans insisted that all the ills had come from over-production, but could offer no remedy; when finally, an old-time greenbacker was called and said:

"Gentlemen, admitting that over-production is the cause of our great financial distress, where shall we look for a remedy? A few years ago we had an over-production of greenbacks. It hurt no one but the bankers and money lenders. It was very hard on them, so our law makers commenced destroying the greenbacks, and the times became better for the bond-holders, bankers, and gold men. They have made millions and are growing richer every day. Now we have an over-production of everything but money; we have worked too hard and produced too much grain, too many horses, too many cattle, in fact, there is nothing that will sell.

"There seems to be an over-production of men. Everyone knows that there are too many men; half of them cannot get work. If destroying the money would make such good times for the bankers and men who have gold to loan, the same remedy ought to apply now. It is a parallel case. Then it was an over-production of money.   To follow up the same plan in our case, we would have to insist upon the passing of an Act in Congress similar to that authorizing the destruction of the greenbacks.

"As there is an over-production of men, have a part of them destroyed; kill off all kinds of stock—cattle, hogs and horses—until you bring about an equilibrium between property and money.   You see there has been such an over-production of property and people, that the money which would be plentiful at one time, will not do now.

"So, gentlemen, it seems to me, it would be just as reasonable to destroy the people and property now, as it was to destroy the best money we had—the greenbacks.   I would suggest that government increase the circulation by issuing a new lot of greenbacks, buy up the government bonds and stop the interest; then, if the people complain of having too much money, I would suggest that they demonetize gold.

"The reason why we always have good times after a war, is not on account of the destruction, but because a large amount of money has been turned loose.   The reason we always have good times in a rich gold mining camp, is becuse the gold is so easily converted into money, that when a large quantity of gold is being taken out by the miners, a great deal of money goes into circulation and this, and nothing else, makes good times.

"The people of the United States to-day, are studying machinery and inventions of all kinds, and how to produce all the good things of life, and are leaving the management of the government to Shysters; these Shysters are controlled by money kings and they are all having their own way; but when this period of invention is past and the people turn their attention to government, those who live to see it will learn that hard times, unless caused by some natural calamity, comes from bad legislation, and when the causes are removed the unfavorable conditions will disappear.

"If any-man is in doubt that the present hard times are directly the result of class and dishonest money legislation, all he need do is to lay aside his political and party prejudice and investigate. The case will be found so clear that he will have no difficulty in arriving at a logical conclusion."

Mr. Bradshaw had two married sons who had taken land adjoining him. The family, like thousands of other families, had been crowded out in the east by the hard times and falling prices, which commenced with the destruction of the national money in the interest of gold, and continued until the stringency became so wide-spread and disastrous in its effects that even the great hobby of over-production, failed to satisfy.

Persons familiar with the history of the United States will remember that this destruction was the result of the Contraction Act passed by the Congress of 1865, and was pushed through by the same leaders who were afterward instrumental in giving away the government lands to private corporations. It is a notable fact, though not to be greatly wondered at, that many of these men are to-day very wealthy, and others are numbered among our millionaires.

Mr. Bradshaw had also two sons and two daughters living at home, unmarried. Frank was pleased to find the place so home-like, and when they found he was a son of Col. Bundy, they made him one of the family. It happened that the eldest son had known Col Bundy in the army, and had been with him in some of the most hotly contested battles of the late war and admired his noble character.

The harvest season passed off pleasantly, the tables were well supplied with good things; good beds were provided, and lunch brought regularly to the field by one of the girls. To make things more agreeable, the young people of the neighborhood would gather at Mr. Bradshaw's every Saturday night and dance till twelve o'clock. By the time harvesting and threshing were over, Frank had learned to love and appreciate the people of the whole neighborhood.

Mr. Bradshaw had hurried to market a large portion of his crop, in order to raise a little money to pay harvest hands, grocery bills and buy a little lumber to build a granary to store what was left. As the price of wheat was so low that he would be short of money, he decided to take the team and one of the boys and go over to where the Santa Fe railroad was building, and work on the road long enough to make what money would be necessary to pay grocery bills, buy a few clothes and schoolbooks; also pay taxes, which were no small item; in this way he could avoid putting a mortgage on his farm, as he had done to his sorrow, in Illinois.

"It looks rather hard," said Mr. Bradshaw, "for a man who owns as good a farm as I, with a surplus of corn, wheat, barley, with fat hogs and cattle, to be compelled to go from home to work for some rich corporation, in order to get money to live on and school my children, and in a free school at that; but such is contraction."

"I'll tell you what is a fact," said his oldest son, who was a well-read man, "these greenback men are right about the hard times; there is no shadow of doubt but what we are being robbed by the gold power, either through the ignorance or dishonesty of Congressmen; but the trouble is, if we leave the Republican party, then the Democrats and the South will get in power and we are liable to have another war; so it is hard to tell where this thing will end."

In accordance with Mr. Bradshaw's earnest solicitation, Frank decided to accompany him to the railroad and drive one of his teams. A couple of days took them to the work, and Frank was soon driving a scraper-team on a ten-foot fill. The work was hard and the hours long, but his team was a good one and everything worked well. A few teams on an adjoining job, which were owned by the Contractor, were badly worn out and he often saw the boss get among them with a shovel and beat them cruelly. It fairly made his blood boil to see such abuse of the dumb animals. He also noticed the accommodations about the camp were of the poorest kind and the bosses all seemed to be possessed of a very domineering spirit. The outfit also had two tent-saloons, supposed to belong to out-side parties, but really were owned by themselves.

· These saloons would always get back a large part of the money in a few days after the men were paid off; in fact, it appeared that at least one-third of their men simply worked for their board and a little whiskey.

Frank staid with the job several days, but it seemed to him the men were treated more like dogs than men and he could not help saying to Mr. Bradshaw, it seemed as if, under the present system of financial legislation, labor would become more dishonorable than slavery.

Late one afternoon, after Frank had been having a hard pull all day, up a steep bank, and his horses were very tired, as he reached the top of the bank, one of the bosses hit his near horse with a rock; Frank stopped the team, dropped the lines, sprang at the boss and knocked him off the bank and he fell into the pit, landing across the doubletree of another team. The men in the pit thought he was killed, but he soon recovered and crawled out and the work went on as usual. Frank expected to be discharged but was not; on the other hand, they discharged the boss and offered him the place. He decided to leave such a rough place and in one week was in Sacramento.

He arrived in the city on Sunday night and on Mon-day morning started out and, in the course of the day visited every shop in the city, only to find them crowded as in the east, and some of their men laying off; others on half time. At the hotel, he met parties from San Francisco, who reported the same condition of things there. He said to himself,· "such is the effect of contraction."

The newspapers, too, were full of accounts of business failures all over the country—from Plymouth Rock in the East to the Golden Gate in the West. There was not a single town or hamlet but felt the effect of the iron law, and many cursed John Sherman.

CHAPTER X.

FRANK at last resolved to look for work on a farm and made his arrangements at the hotel to leave his things till he came or sent for them. He started on foot into the country. The day was hot and he had a good introduction to California dust. There were houses and farms on each side of the street. Frank stopped at several of them, only to be treated more as an intruder than as a free-born citizen of America looking for work. If they talked to him at all, it was to tell him of the hard times and as this news did not interest him, he kept moving on till he came to a very neat cottage, with a small barn, a large, well-kept orchard near by, and he determined to stop and make some inquiries. In passing along the walk to the door of the cottage, he was struck with the beauty of the grounds. Flowers of many varieties, semi-tropical plants, gave the place a charming appearance to our young traveller. He knocked on the door and in repsonse a light footstep approached the door and it was opened, disclosing the face and form of one of California's belles. As her eyes met those of the stranger, she gave a dignified bow. Frank felt the peculiar coldness of her manner and at once inquired for the man of the house, and at the same time stated his business. When he had finished, instead of inviting him in, she simply told him to wait around till her father came from the field, then shut the door. Frank hesitated a moment and would have gone on his way if he had not just then discovered the father in the orchard, so off he started to talk with him.

The farmer told him he had plenty of work and needed help, but money was so scarce it was almost impossible to get enough together to pay a man. He could market almost anything by taking trade, but there seemed to be a money famine. If he would take a horse he would give him a job, but Frank wanted no horse. Finally, seeing the stranger was young and stout, he concluded to give him a job for a fews days and if he could raise the money he might keep him longer. As they were talking they had been quietly walking toward the house, and when they reached the barn the farmer asked, "Where are your blankets?" "Blankets," said Frank, thinking that the farmer must mean a trunk or a valise. "I have no blankets."

The farmer, seeing Frank's discomfiture, asked him how long he had been in California, and on learning that he had just arrived, informed him that it was not customary for employers to furnish beds in this country, but that laborers carried their blankets with them.

"But suppose a man is on foot, how is he to have his bed with him?"

"Pack it on his back," said the farmer.

"Do I really understand you to say, Mr. Hargrave—for this was the farmer's name—that men who work on farms in this country are forced to pack their beds upon their backs from place to place and sleep in barns, around haystacks and on the ground, along the leeward side of the fence?"

"That is the custom of this country," said Mr. Hargrave, "and it is one that cannot well be altered from the simple fact that a majority of the working men of this country are drunkards, vulgar, dirty and not fit to be taken into a family."

"I am astonished," said Frank, "and how men could be otherwise, when sleeping around haystacks and so completely isolated from society I cannot see."

Feeling the justice of Frank's remarks, Mr. Hargrave said that he had always allowed his men to sleep in the barn, but there were a great many men who would not on account of fire.

Mr. Hargrave was rather pleased with the young

man's independence and said that he would see the women and if they could make arrangements for him they would do so. So without inviting Frank into the house, he passed in himself to consult with the women as to the advisability of allowing a common working man to occupy one of their spare beds for a few days. Frank, full of indignation, started off, stopped, waited again, but the longer he waited the more indignant he became, until finally he walked off and a few hours' lively walk brought him to one of California's large ranches. He had been told that they employed a great many men and that he would be likely to get work. The house was back from the road and at the gate was posted in large letters the following: "No men wanted. Don't stop." This was a stunner, but Frank pushed on. Occasionally he met men with their blankets on their backs and he began to realize that what the farmer had told him was really true. He had noticed that they generally traveled in twos, and sometimes in threes. As there were thousands of men on the road, he soon met a couple. One was an Irishman and the other a Hoosier. On being hailed, they dropped their bedding and used the roll for a seat. They each had a fruit can which they used to make coffee in, and with a little coffee and a few crackers, there was no telling how far they could travel without other expense. They were covered with dust and sweat which made them look rough, but Frank fancied that back of all this dirt he could see an intelligence in each that spoke of better days.

"Where are you from?" said Pat.

"Kansas," said Frank.

"The divil take yez," said Pat, "there is so many Kansas men here that there is no work for anybody."

"What part of the country are you from?" said Frank.

"From every place but this," said Pat, "but we have been working around San Berdu and Los Angeles for the last couple of months and niver a bit of work will you get down there. The lower country is full of men that would steal a coat or anything to get in jail so as to get a bite to eat."

"Is there no work this side of there?"

"Not a bit of it."

"No work on the sections?"

"Sections?" said Pat, "sure and it is there that you'll find the Chinamen. There is no show for a white man this side of Arizona. The Railroad Companies have shipped in and are now working over five thousand Chinamen in California, and there are thousands of white men who can't get a job. Stanford, Crocker, and Huntington all ought to be hung."

Frank felt as though there was more or less justice in the remark. After chatting and resting awhile the party separated, each going his own way.

In the course of the evening Frank met a great many men, all carrying blankets, and all told the same story about work.

At last he came to another big ranch where there were many men at work putting up the fall crop of alfalfa hay. As it was growing late he made up his mind, if possible, to stay there all night, and on seeing the foreman he was agreeably disappointed at being kindly received, and the gentleman not only allowed him to stay but loaned him a pair of blankets and gave him permission to sleep in the stack. This seemed rather humiliating to Frank, but, thought he, "when you are in Rome you must do as Romans do."

On the following morning, seeing that Frank was stout and young, the foreman decided to give him a job through the balance of the haying; so he went to work and found the place run very much as the Railroad Company in Kansas, that is, on the same principle, only they had no saloons, but as for accommodations, he noticed that they put the horses in the stables and the men slept outside.

It might be here observed that this custom of compelling men to pack their beds with them in order to get work on farms continues in California to the present day. It originated in the peculiar way in which California was invaded by adventurers and gold-hunters in early days, who, by force of necessity carried their beds as they went out in search of gold, and its present degrading effect upon labor is plainly marked in this; a large per cent of the laboring men are drunkards. When a job is ended and they get their money, they go to the nearest saloon and drink as long as the money lasts, then start out "dead-broke" to hunt another job. They never speak to a woman, except to ask some farmer's wife for food, and the inside of a church would be as strange to one of them as an electric display to an Apache Indian.

This state of things exists to an alarming extent wherever blanket-packing is common, and to that condition it is largely due. The people of California should blush for shame for allowing such a degrading custom to exist in what should be the Paradise of America. If it cannot be stopped in any other way, the Legislature should pass a bill making it a crime to carry blankets upon the road, and employers for failing to provide good, clean, healthy sleeping apartments should be made amenable to the law.

Frank finished his work in this place in about a month and was offered a chance to drive an eight-mule team; but not considering himself competent for that, he went down to Fresno and Bakersfield. He could hear of no work but continually met men with their blankets, all miserable and dirty from sleeping outside; they all told the same old story of hard times and no work.

He tramped on down to Los Angeles and found reports had not been exaggerated. The sidewalks were lined with men seeking employment. He was astonished to find how many intelligent minds were hidden beneath frizzly hair and shaggy beards. "There is something morally wrong," said he to himself, "with the laws which control man's destiny; otherwise ignorance beneath silk hats would not be so common, nor intelligence among the outcasts."

He saw men standing on every corner, watching for a chance to go to work. If a farmer drove up a half dozen men would flock about him at once. Amid all this scramble for work he noticed several large Bulletin-boards on which were inscribed: "wanted," and then would follow a list like this: "Men for farm work, men for apiaries and men for many different kinds of work. Frank was puzzled to understand why men were looking for work, when so many men were wanted; so after looking about as long as he wished and not finding even the shadow of a chance to get a job, he went into an employment office. He found himself in a small, dirty looking room, with benches around the wall; adjoining this room was another; but an aperture was made in the wall to talk through.

A hungry looking crowd were sitting about on the benches when Frank entered, and after making a survey of the room to see that there was no immediate danger of being robbed, for the very atmosphere seemed to impress him that he was in a robber's roost, he presented himself at the hole in the wall and knocked; soon a man approached from the opposite side of the opening, and with an idiotic stare, waited for Frank to make known his business. The air of superiority which this man assumed, made Frank feel as if he had entered the office of a Vanderbilt or a Gould. He soon rallied, however, and in as few words as possible, explained that he wanted work.

"What kind of work do you want?" was asked.

"I am a boiler-maker."

"No work of that kind, but can give you a job of general work about machinery, if you will go to San Bernardino."

"What are your charges?"

"Two dollars."

Frank paid the money and received a card to Johnson & Co., for work at three dollars per day. He then went to the Depot, paid $2.50 for a ticket and the following morning presented himself to Johnson & Co. for work. The foreman of the shop looked at the paper and said in an indignant manner: "What does that Los Angeles man mean? I sent him an order for a man a month ago and you are the third man he has sent. I will notify him this very evening to send no more men. I would like to give every man employment, if I could, but I cannot." "You see," he said, sarcastically: "There has been an over-production of men."

"But how am I to get my money back," said Frank?

"Oh if you go back to the Office that sent you, they will not dare refuse to refund your money and you might be able to collect damages, if you are able to go to law. Justice has to be bought now; the men who buy a chance to go to work are not able to go into law, so the matter goes right on and nine men out of ten never go back to Los Angeles, simply because there is always a surplus of men there, and the railroad fare will amount to more than two dollars."

"It is, then," said Frank, "a kind of confidence scheme, legalized or, at least, not prohibited by the great State ot California and City of Los Angeles."

Taking in the situation as thousands had done before, rather than attempt to get his money back at ten times its cost, he resolved to go to Arizona.

At the hotel he fell in with a man who, in spite of his rough and weather-beaten appearance, seemed to be a gentleman. Frank soon learned that he belonged to that peculiar and shifty class of individuals who are to be found throughout the mining regions of the west, known as explorers or prospectors. They generally have a few burros, saddles and packing outfit and with a load of "grub," they go into the mountains to hunt for mines and stay until they run short of provisions; then with a collection of ore, they go to the nearest trading post for supplies. When they run out of money, they put their burros and outfit in a safe place, go to some mine that is running, and when they have replenished their pocket books, go back to the mountains and sometimes discover a rich mine of gold or silver, and as it takes money to work them, they are soon gobbled up by gold-mongers, who never expose themselves to rain and storm, but under our present system, reap all the benefits of these vast gold and silver regions.

The name of this man was Crosby. He told Frank he had been working on rock not far from there; that he had finished the job and was now going back to

Arizona to prospect. He had left his outfit at Yuma and would start that night.

"What is the fare to Yuma," asked Frank?

"Twenty dollars," said the man, "but I can get through in a box-car for two dollars, and if I can be lucky enough to strike an empty car, I can spread down my blankets and be very comfortable, and there is very little difference in time."

"I believe that would be a good way for me to go," said Frank.

"Why, of course, if you wish to go, stay with me and I will see you through all right."

"Another swindle," thought Frank, "but our whole social structure seems to be based on fraud, from Wall Street to the President, and from the President down. Why should a man have any scruples?"

After supper the men paid their bills, the prospector took his big roll of blankets and they started for the depot. It was quite dark when they reached the place. The freight train was about ready to start, and one of the brakemen was coming down the train, not only to see that the cars were all right, but more particularly to see if there was a chance to make a dollar.

"Hello, pard," said the prospector, as they met the brakeman, "what's the show for a ride?"

"Where do you want to go?"

"Yuma," was the reply.

"Got any stuff?"

"Well, to tell you the truth, pard, I've been on a h—l of a drunk and I'm all broke up and plum busted, but I guess my partner has got a little money."

"I'll take you both to Yuma for a V."

"Jerusalem," said Frank, who had been thoroughly posted before-hand, "we can't go on this train for that's more money than I've got."

"How much you got?" said the brakeman.

"Three dollars."

—"That won't do, must have four dollars."

After a short silence, the prospector said, "we'll have to wait for another train," and the two men started to walk off,

"Hold on," said the brakeman, 'I'll take you through. I always hate to leave a man."

So the three men went along up the train till they came to an empty car. The brakeman slipped the door to one side to let the two men pass in and then closed it again. The prospector was not long in spreading his blankets down at one end of the car and the two men were comfortably fixed for a long ride. As they stopped at night to take on water, the brakeman came to them, got his three dollars and told them he would let them know when they got to Yuma. On arriving there, they took breakfast at a Chinese restaurant. The prospector went to the outskirts of the town to see a Mexican with whom he had left his prospecting outfit. Finding everything all right, he bought a bill of provisions. Frank helped him to pack and they went outside of town and camped. The prospector, Mr. Wm. Crosby, insisted on Frank going with him on the trip and there being no additional expense, as Mr. Crosby had a complete outfit, he consented.

After buying an additional bill of goods they started for Errinsburg, which they reached in about five days. From there they went into the Permosa range of mountains where they found some good quartz, but water would have to be brought from Tisen's wells, a distance of ten miles, so they pushed on to the old Centennial Mill. This mill was a fine piece of machinery that must have cost from fifty to seventy-five thousand dollars. It was now standing desolate and alone on the desert.

"Why is it," said Frank, "that this fine machinery stands idle in this desolate spot?"

"I'll tell you," said Crosby, "there is a class of men that you will find through this whole mining region, called experts. They are generally self-made and sharp as a tack; they know how to test ore, have made a study of Geology and Mineralogy and have all the high sounding terms down pat; they can see through the earth and tell you all about it—dolomite, dilite, porphyry and granite—and show you exactly how they must be found in order to warrant the existence of rich deposit. In fact, take one of these experts who is well posted and convince him you have money in bank, that you want to invest in mines, and he will so completely befog your ideas by the use of high sounding words, that you will conclude there is but one way to become a successful mine operator and that is by the use of his peculiar knowledge. When these men hear of a new discovery, they go to it, and if it makes anything of a showing they take a bond on it, that is, they agree to pay so much on it in one year; providing they can make a sale, if not, they simply don't take it.

"They then make a map of the property, including several claims they themselves located, adjoining the discovery, go East to the Capitol of some State, or other prominent place, armed with letters of introduction and a pocket of gold nuggets or rich pieces of ore. They stop at the best hotel in the place and soon make the acquaintance of two or three enterprising bankers who become impressed with their wonderful knowledge of mining. The thing is to lay before the banker a plan to make some money, and he begins by presenting a map of the mines; 'here, you will observe, is the Silver Bullion; it is a regular fissure vein, has well defined walls and shows about six feet of vein matter; the ore is a lead carbonate with quite an amount of chloride of silver, in addition to silver product, it shows more or less free gold.

" 'The grade of the ore is not high, but that it will improve as we go down there can be but little doubt, in fact, the prospect is, that before we reach a depth of one hundred feet we will have a mine worth half a million of dollars.'

Here he reads over a list of some of the richest mines extant and explains that it is but a rare chance where they pay at the surface; he explains their present immense value, tells a few big stories and hauls from his pockets a handful of nuggets and rich specimens of ore and the bankers are elated.

" 'Here, you observe,' he continues, 'the map shows four other claims discovered and located by myself; a man of the name of Patterson discovered the Silver Bullion; he was dead busted and I gave him a grub stake to do a little work on it and it showed up fine, so I agreed to give him $1,000 for the claim, to be paid in one year; then I prospected the adjoining claim and I discovered and located the Silver Chief, the Gold Hunter, the Morning Glory and Polar Star, making a group of five claims. I consider it one of the most valuable properties in that country, but it will take capital to develop and work it.

" 'Now what I want is to organize a Company to develop this property and I shall need your assistance; of course I shall make it an object for you to take hold.

" 'My plan is to give you, gentlemen, a half interest with me in the property, with the understanding that you lend me your assistance in organizing a Company; you paying the expense of the same; then we will issue $300,000 of non-assessable stock, set aside $100,000 for developing purposes and to pay off the $1,000 that I owe upon the property; also for constructing roads, building mills, buying machinery, etc. Should this, when sold, not be sufficient to put the mine in paying condition, more stock can be sold to the extent of $200,000, the other $100,000 to be divided between us three, and should there remain, a sum unsold out of the $200,000, when the mine pays its first dividend, the same is to fall to us and, of course, be divided equally. Thus you see we shall be out but little and by careful management, be able to still hold a controlling interest.'

'Suppose,' said one of the bankers, 'we take a third party into the Company with the understanding that he puts up $500 to cover cost of printing, and lithographing stock?'

"The expert objects a little, of course, but soon consents, another man is called in and soon induced to put in the $500; so all the necessary papers are prepared and stock put on the market with flaming advertisements. The stock sells, the names of these influential individuals being sufficient recommendation, and the money rolls in.

"Some Dough-head who is related to some of the Company and belongs to the same church with others, and has been a failure all his life, is now chosen Superintendent and the Expert is made General Manager, and the two return to the town nearest the property and establish a Branch Office. They hire a few men whom they send out to work on the prospect. The Superintendent and General Manager board at a first-class hotel and hire a rig once a month to visit the mine and very often the salary and expenses of these men are more than the expense of work on the mine.

"The miners are anxious to have the job hold out, so they make a big pile of waste-rock, then gather together enough ore, if possible, to cover it up and at last they strike a good pocket; the work stops on that shaft and the men put to work on another claim; the Company is notified that the claim is proving wonderfully rich and a mill must be put up in order to handle the ore and get the work on a paying basis.

"A meeting of the Company is called at once; all hands are excited and count their wealth by millions; the stockholders, many of them, get on the cars and visit the property and of course see great piles of ore, enjoy their trip and see everything through a magnifying glass and they are not only fooled themselves, but they go home and deceive all their friends. They have seen the vein, with its great walls, the great piles of rich ore which, being full of pyrites, look brilliant to a man who comes prepared to see a rich mine and has no knowledge, whatever, of ore.

"How often have Generals, Statesmen and Journalists, been shown through the worthless mines and their silly questions laughed at by the miners, for months and even years afterward.

"When the bankers and stockholders find themselves at home again, everybody wants to see them and hear the truth about the matter and the stock finds ready sale. The expert goes back to attend to the purchase and shipment of the mill and takes good care while East to be pushed for money and compelled to sell a good share of his stock for cash; besides this, he has a good fat salary all this time and nothing to do; and now in building the mill he will make another haul and throw a good purse into the Superintendent's pocket just to keep him still.

"At last the mill is complete and in one way and another the money has been gotten away with and the mill that cost all the way from $25,000 to $100,000, starts up, runs ten or twenty days, then shuts down and never runs again; and today, scattered through the mountains all the way from British Columbia on the north, to Mexico on the south, you will find valuable machinery, often in the most inaccessible places, and the moving it in and setting up has alone cost fortunes upon fortunes. A great many have never run ten days and now lie rusting and only awaiting the ravages of a mountain fire."

After listening to the story Frank said, "Well, it is all new to me, but it seems quite in keeping with the general method into which we are fast drifting. In every department of business you find dishonesty, all men in public service from the street car driver to the Cabinet officers and even the President are all on the beat or make or knock down. The example seems to be set at Washington and is spreading like a contagion throughout the country. It will no doubt run its course and then be stopped suddenly, but in what way and by what force the monster will be grappled it would be hard to conjecture. Concentration of wealth in the hands of a few seems to be the result and the overthrow of the money power and destruction or reduction of all large estates."

There was a good well not far from the Centennial mill and a little adobe trading post where the men camped. On the following day a rain set in that lasted for three days. The whole country was deserted with the exception of a few mossbacks, who always stay around old mining camps and from year to year relocate old, abandoned prospects waiting for some one to come along and buy them.

They are a very peculiar class of men and by keeping up notices on everything that shows any signs of mineral they generally succeed in keeping prospectors out of the country, greatly retarding the growth of the camp. They generally live and die like coyotes, but occasionally one gets in another man's way and then sells for a snug sum.

After the storm had abated, Crosby determined to follow along the south side of the Harquihala range in a north-easterly direction, and as there was plenty of water in holes, or what Crosby called tanks, they were not likely to suffer from want of water as was often the case. Their first day's trip took them to an old mine called Yuma. It was a fine looking vein and several thousand dollars' worth of work had been done on it, but for some cause it had been abandoned and was entirely deserted. A notice showed that it had fallen into the hands of a mossback.

"This," said Crosby, "will show you how faulty are our mining laws. There has been a great deal of work done all through this country and a great many ledges that explorers would like to work on; but here you see the work of the mossback. He holds every prospect in the country, never does any work but, dog in the manger like, holds the country by relocation. There are monuments everywhere and if a prospector finds anything worth working for, he is liable to have some old location floated onto him.

"In Colorado the state law controls the matter and to a great extent does away with the mossback. Hence its mines are more prosperous than those of Arizona."

"From this," said Frank, "it would appear that it takes good laws to make a prosperous people."

Passing the old mine they camped at a small wet-weather spring about one mile from it, and on the following day came to water in the afternoon, and in what Mr. Crosby said was a fine place to prospect, so Frank took his first lesson in prospecting. He had already learned to camp in the desert without water, sleep on the ground and listen to the music of some stray rattle snake that had been disturbed by their presence, and to shake tarantulas from his blankets on getting up in the morning, but now he was to learn to hunt for gold.

"This is a very important trade," said Frank to Mr. Crosby, "for we must have gold; we might get along without bread; but whiskey and gold are two articles quite indispensable. We must have whiskey you see to control elections. It would be pretty hard for Americans to hold an election without it, and if we had no gold we could have no money; if we had no money we could have no bankers, we could have no aristocracy to look up to, so I can readily comprehend that the prosperity of the human family is entirely dependent on the success of the gold hunter."

Mr. Crosby appreciated this sarcasm and said, "Yes, gold is the thing that controls the world and a lack of it at one time might have been destruction, but thanks to the inventive genius of our wise men, they have discovered a method by which they can supply the world with honest money with very little gold. This they do by putting the little gold there is in the vaults and issuing promises to pay; of course millions of promises to pay can be issued and based on an infinitely small sum of gold, then all it wants is confidence to make it just as good as the gold itself."

They made their camp under some trees near the water and near at hand were several old dry trees that gave them plenty of wood. There was also plenty of grass near and they staked one burro and hobbled the other. After the camp was all arranged, Frank built a fire and they had what he called a boss meal.

"How long have you led this kind of a life," Frank asked his companion.

"O, I guess about fifteen years."

"For God's sake," said Frank, in surprise, "I have just been thinking that we ought to be able to find a mine in about a week."

"During the fifteen years," said Mr. Crosby, "I have made several finds but the most money I have ever made was selling a prospect not worth ten cents. I sold it on the strength of its being near another claim that was rich."

On the following morning they started up the mountain 'and every now and then, Crosby would pick up what he would call float; finally, he picked up a piece of copper ore, and after examining it carefully, said that it was a good piece of ore, and they must find the lead. Looking up the mountain, he said, "do you see that red streak yonder? That is possibly where this came from; we will go up that way." As they continued to ascend, they found other pieces of float of a similar character; finally when they reached the place, sure enough, the virgin copper was cropping out. After cleaning the ledge and examining if closely, Mr. Crosby said, "this mine would be worth a fortune to us both, if we had it in a good location; but here in this wild and remote region, it is liable to be useless for many years. Nothing but silver or gold will pay for working here, so we will look further."

That night when the men returned to camp they were completely worn out. They continued their prospecting about two weeks. They had found several leads and taken specimens of ore, and now that their supplies were getting rather low, and they wanted to test some of their ore, they decided to go on to Phoenix, Arizona, which they reached in four days; there they had, their ore tested and found it was not good enough to be worked at present, so Crosby wanted Frank to accompany him on a trip into a range of mountains across the river from Phoenix; as the winter rains came on they would push on toward the Mexican line. But Frank kept thinking of the fifteen years that Mr. Crosby had been prospecting and he decided it.was too much of an undertaking, so he walked to Maricopa and took the cars for Kansas City, thinking to try his hand once more at looking for work; on reaching that place he put up at a hotel where he would be likely to find shop-men.

CHAPTER XI.

PROPERLY presented to our readers, it becomes necessary at this time to introduce new scenes and new characters. In going back to the beginning of the great Rebellion, we find a young man of the name of Goulding. He was at that time about twenty-one years of age, was the son of a farmer and naturally possessed great financial ability, or in words better understood by common people, he was a natural-born scoundrel.

At first glance he regarded the commencement of war as his opportunity; while others of his age were enlisting by thousands, this cool-headed financier quietly hired out as teamster. After Fort Donaldson had succumbed to the hard fighting and superior numbers of Gen. Grant's force, John Goulding was left with a few wagons to haul supplies to a garrison on the Mississippi river; hauling wood and hay was the principal work and Mr. Goulding was not long in discovering that a contract might be made between the Quarter-master and himself that would be mutually profitable. Meeting the Quarter-master in town one day, he nudged him into a fine saloon, and after draining a couple of glasses of their contents—the best whiskey to be had—they passed into a little side room which was furnished with a table and chairs and arranged to suit the special convenience of gamblers and cut-throats, and it might be here added that no saloon in that day or even in this can be considered strictly first-class without a few just such rooms, where drunkards can be genteelly robbed and scoundrels or financiers sip their Tom and Jerry and concoct schemes of rascality that they would not dare even whisper in any other locality.

Taking seats at the table Mr. Goulding ordered more glasses and cigars, and after a few casual remarks the glasses were at hand and their contents quickly disappeared, then, after lighting their cigars, Mr. Goulding drew his chair a little nearer to his companion and in a low voice and a quiet, confidential way, he leisurely knocked the ashes from his cigar with his little finger, and said to the Lieutenant that he had a little scheme on hand through which he expected to make a few thousand dollars in a month or two. That in addition to what he had on hand he would require about two thousand dollars, if the Lieutenant could accommodate him to that much he could afford to pay a good round interest, besides would feel himself under great obligations for the favor.

The young Lieutenant, who had probably never in all his life seen so much money before coming into the service, was at first inclined to take the matter as a joke, but the quiet countenance of the teamster soon reassured him and he said, "Why, my man, I never in all my life had one-fourth part of that amount of money of my own."

"Is that so," said the teamster, in a slow, meditative way, and continuing, "if I were situated as you are I would look after my own interests and try and pick up a few honest dollars now and then."

"I have known men to get themselves into very serious trouble in making extra dollars," said the Quarter-master.

"O yes," said Mr. Goulding, "but it was their own fault, you want to do business on the square, that is, keep inside the law."

"Well," said the Lieutenant, beginning to get his eyes open a little, "if you can point out a way in which I can make a little money and do it honorably, I would be very glad to hear your plan."

This was exactly what Goulding wanted, it was his opportunity and he said:

"Now as to honorable methods. You must lay aside your baby notions and take into consideration the fact that some of our Congressmen and Senators get to be millionaires from their salaries and they are honorable men, and the more money they get the more honorable they are."

(Mr. Goulding had been hauling green wood into camp for two weeks just in order to work up this scheme.) "You are aware," said he, "that there has been a good deal of growling in camp about green wood, now I will see to it that the officers make a general protest, then you can advertise for a contract and of course mine will be the only bid and we will put it at a price so it will pay us both. Do you see?"

This plan was perfectly plain and practicable, so it was agreed to consider it farther.

The next thing to do for Goulding was to see the officers of the camp and tell them that if they insisted on having dry wood that he would take a contract and he would have it if he had to go to the Rocky Mountains for it. It would cost more than green wood but would be worth more. They of course all wanted dry wood and made out requisitions at once. So the Quarter-master went through the form of advertising and then gave Mr. Goulding the contract of furnishing wood at six dollars a cord.

Mr. Goulding paid one dollar for having it cut, hauled it with government team, gave the Quarter master two dollars per cord and had three dollars left for himself, and as the camp used several cords of wood a day, it was no bad job; besides he soon worked up a hay contract that paid him equally as well. So he was not long in getting money enough together to begin to make himself useful, and the next thing to do was to form an intrigue against the Sutler who was a kind of honest old farmer and not much of a financier. Consequently he was an easy victim and Mr. Goulding soon succeeded in having him dishonestly dismissed, and as to move the goods out would cost about all they were worth, the ex-Sutler was practically forced to sell for what he could get. As Goulding was the only buyer he naturally got the goods at his own price and made at least a thousand dollars on the turn. Six months before he was teaming at thirty dollars per

month and now, by rascality and sharp practice, he had
not only paved the way to future fortune but had also
established his reputation as a first-class financier.

When once settled down in the sutler business he
was in a position to make himself felt. He put in a
large stock on credit, borrowed money from every
officer and man where he could get it, and, by paying
promptly and borrowing every chance he got he soon
established a credit and reputation for honesty which
enabled him to do a thriving business.

We soon find him running branch stores and taking
large contracts for furnishing grain and all kinds of
supplies. Wherever it was possible to stand in with
an officer and rob the government he always took
advantage of it, and when the war was over went to
St. Louis with ill gotten gains amounting to over
$100,000.

The next big swindle we find him mixed up in was in
in Missouri. After making a trip through the State
and visiting a great many counties, and having talked
Railroad enough to know that the people were ripe for
a big fraud, he returned to St. Louis, and getting a
couple of other great financiers, he formed a Railroad
company and got a franchise from the State, employed
engineers and ran a preliminary line. The next thing
to do was to get counties along the line to vote bonds,
which was no difficult matter, and when they were all
voted, work was commenced at one end of the road
and kept up long enough to get the bonds and the
work was discontinued; the bonds sold for what they
would bring and the money invested in building lots in
Kansas City.

The work that had been done was sold to another
Company, and Goulding had once more proved his
ability as a first-class financier. When the bonds fell
due, they were protested and judgment rendered against
the county; the County Commissioner refused to levy
a tax to pay the bonds or interest and for ten years
they baffled the United States Marshal by holding their
meetings in secret.

There were some instances, however, when arrests

were made for contempt of court, and among these was the case of Col. Summerville, an old-time Missourian, who had emigrated to Kentucky in a very early day; his wife was a descendant of Daniel Boone; they had one son and one daughter and the whole family had a spotless reputation .

Col. Summerville had enlisted in the Confederate army in 1861 and had been promoted from time to time for bravery; he had fought till the last gun was fired, then surrendered and returned to the loving embrace of his family. He was one of that kind of men whom everybody loves. When any neighborhood difficulties arose, he was the first man called in to arbitrate; if any one was sick, Col. Summerville or his wife were always sent for and it was true of their house that "the latch-string was always out." No one in his neighborhood ever suffered for food. He never asked for office but always held one.

After the close of the war, his peaceful life was un-broken, until, while he was County Commissioner, he refused to levy a tax to pay the bonds that had been issued as subsidy for a road that was never built; he was arrested by a Marshal of the U. S. court for con-tempt, taken to Kansas City and incarcerated.

His wife, being quite old and feeble, soon died from the effect of the shock, his daughter was driven to insanity and died in an insane asylum.

His son Robert, now a boy of 18, was at this time in Texas, and as it was nearing spring, he decided to return home with a herd of cattle.

We will now look after the movements of Mr. Goulding who, having invested a large part of his money in town property which was almost certain to yield him large returns as the country developed, was quietly looking around for another opportunity to dis-play his genius as a financier. At this time it will be remembered, Texas was a vast region of grass land, covered with immense herds of cattle. In those days, cattle were rounded up in bunches by the stockmen, once or twice a year and the calves branded; the remainder of the year they were allowed to run at large on the broad plains undisturbed.

As the Railroad had now reached Kansas, a very profitable trade was springing up, that of driving cattle from Texas across the Indian Territory into Kansas and then shipping to the East. Mr. Goulding, with his usual financial foresight, took in the situation at a glance. He went to Texas and his first step was to hire a man who "knew all the ropes." He then bought two thousand head of cattle, divided them into five herds, put an outfit of men with each herd, and started across the State of Texas, and the Indian Territory, into Kansas. For two or three weeks the route took them through a cattle country and every day, small bunches of cattle would join their herds.

Robert Summerville was hired to drive one of the Goulding herds and while in camp the second night, Mr. Goulding called at each camp; he told the boys, if any one came to the herd to look for cattle, to "round up" and let them cut out whatever belonged to them; he also told them to let no cattle get into the herds, under any circumstances and wound up by saying, "I suppose a few will get in, in spite of us, and whatever stray cattle I have when I get to Kansas, I will cut out, take their brands, pay you boys two dollars per head for estray work, charge two dollars more for driving and selling and pay the money left over to the owner when I come back next spring.

The boys took little stock in his paying the owner for the cattle, but cattle were plentiful in Texas and if they were paid for their work, it mattered little to them what became of the rest of the money.

It was noticeable that the different droves were rapidly increasing in numbers.

As the reader may not be acquainted with the manner of handling these large herds, it might be well to explain that it takes from ten to sixteen men to drive two thousand head of cattle. They start up by working on the sides of the herd, thus pushing out the leaders, until the herd is forced into a string along the trail, nearly half a mile in length. The men who have good horses, ride along on each side to prevent the cattle from "bunching up;" two men work near the front to guide and three or four in the rear to "whoop up" the scallawags. The men are always well mounted and each carries a lariat and revolver, and an expert cattle man is expected to be able to catch a wild steer and tie him down in one minute.

When they commenced driving, Robert was placed on the side, but it was soon noticed that he turned all stray cattle away from the herd, so the Boss who was a typical "bad man" from Texas put him behind the herd, and another man took his place at the side. This created quite a little talk among the boys and from this time, Robert was made the butt of every jest.

The Boss was taking everything in and intended, when the boy was completely cowed, to make "grand bluff" and run him out of camp without pay; thereby gaining the applause of the other men and the hearty approval of the financier.

So things went on from bad to worse, until they had driven four days in the Indian Territory, which was at that time an unbroken wilderness, in that locality. When they halted for the night, four men remained with the cattle to keep them together, on good grass; the remainder, including Robert, went to the camp wagon, located under some cottonwood trees near by and on the bank of a small creek; the horses were all staked near camp.

The other droves belonging to Mr. Goulding, which had now increased to about two thousand head, making in all ten thousand, were some of them in sight, having camped at different points along the creek. That day the Boss had told the boys he intended to run the Missouri lad out of camp that night. All hands were rather pleased at this, as Robert had not been at all backward in saying that he thought Goulding was a regular cattle thief. The men were all expecting to get a two-dollar dividend, which was a big item, and they looked upon Robert as a kind of spy; they were all expecting some fun, for they were now on shooting ground and some of them had an idea the boy would fight.

Others said no, "he is a regular cur;" but the test was bound to come, and all hands had their ears open for whatever might turn up.

They staked their horses, spread out their blankets and all gathered at the wagon. . Robert had a clean towel of his own which he used in preference to the camp towel. The Boss, who was waiting for a chance to begin a row, noticed this and said:

"You are too nice to wipe with common people."

"Not that," said Robert, "I only prefer a clean towel to a dirty one."

"Well, I'll tell you," said the Boss, accompanying his words with oaths, "you're entirely too nice for this crowd; too honest, too; you ought to be back in Missouri with your mother, and I want to tell you that you've got to leave this camp and leave it before supper, too; you're too nice to eat with this crowd."

The allusion to Robert's mother had aroused the lion in him and he quickly responded:

"I will do no such thing."

The Boss had made his threat that he would run the boy out of camp and his reputation was at stake; to falter now, before this stripling of a Missourian, was to lose his prestige as "the bad man from Texas," so, little guessing the tornado he had set in motion, he went for his pistol; but the boy was too quick for him, he whipped out his pistol and fired. There was a flash, a puff of smoke, the sharp explosion, and the man's right arm was broken. He seized his pistol with the other hand but this took time and the boy's next shot buried a ball in a heavy-cased, silver watch, carried by the Boss: this gave him a little time and the two exchanged shots, fair and square, at the same time, and the Boss fell backward against a wagon-wheel and then to the ground.

The boy turned his pistol upon the crowd for a mo-ment but seeing no demonstration, he returned it to his belt. At this moment he saw Goulding approaching and went to meet him before he should get up to the crowd.

Goulding met him with an assumed grin; the boy

told him what he had done and demanded his money.

"What?" said Goulding, with assumed surprise, "you are not going to quit?"

"Of course I am," said the boy.

"Well," said Mr. Goulding, "of course you are your own master, but I would much rather you would stay and take care of the herd. I'll tell you what I will do, you go ahead and take care of that drove, take them through and I will furnish you all the extra riding-stock you need, giving you $125 a month, and I may have work for you by the year.

"No," said Robert, emphatically, "I don't like your style of doing business, I don't like this crowd and I want my money."

Seeing the boy was determined, Goulding gave him his money and before night he had found another herd, several miles ahead and secured employment at sixty dollars a month for the remaining part of the trip.

After a long summer drive across the plains, Mr. Goulding's cattle, about 10,000 in all, reached Abilene and after securing a camping place for all, about fifteen miles from town, Goulding left a few men with each herd and took the rest into the City. The next day a new outfit of men came and relieved the men with the cattle, and they were also ordered to town and the next day the cattle were started to Montana. Mr. Goulding was in Abilene four days before he could get money to pay his men; but he paid their expenses at a hotel, and on the fifth day he paid them and took their receipts; he promised to pay them an extra $16,000 on the cattle they had gobbled up on the road, but this he could not do for another week. When the week had expired, he put them off for another week, and so he continued to pacify them with promises. Suddenly the rumor was started that he had gone to St. Louis after money and would return in five days, but again the men were disappointed and, finally some of the men took a trip to the old camp, only to find the cattle had been gone more than two weeks and no one knew where. It was a debt they could not collect by law and that ended it.

Mr. Goulding proceeded to Montana, selected a splendid cattle ranch and in ten years, with what property he still owned in St. Louis and Kansas City, he had become a millionaire.

Reader, did it ever occur to you that every man who has become a millionaire, by the accumulations of a natural life-time, has made it by similar methods and is a scoundrel of dangerous power, and ought to be made the subject of special legislation?

If good, honest men ever became millionaires, they might be expected to accomplish great good. That class of men never make money so rapidly; therefore, it would seem, that in order to protect themselves against these monstrosities, or parasites in human form, it would be advisable for people to adopt a graduated income tax to limit incomes to an amount commensurate with human happiness.

CHAPTER XII.

ARRIVING at Abilene, Robert sold his horse and outfit and took the cars for Kansas City; there he secured a place to learn the trade of machinist. In a year he was transferred to a small city in Iowa and continued there until the following episode occurred; a long, dreary winter had passed, which was remarkable for its deep snow and hard weather in the mountains; it was followed by a long period of sunshine that swelled the streams to overflowing. During these high waters, one Sunday afternoon, after returning from church, Robert strolled down to the river bank to look at the high water as it rolled majestically by; as he cast his eyes up stream he noticed a small pleasure boat put off from shore; it was apparently half a mile away, but as the boat reached the center of the stream the strong current, in spite of the efforts of the oarsmen, carried it swiftly down the river and as it came nearer, Robert could see that there were four couples in the boat; from the swiftness of the current, they had evidently become alarmed for they were moving from side to side; at last, when a short distance from the railroad bridge, the boat capsized. The sight was appalling and soon a large crowd had gathered; at the first splash, all went out of sight, but soon reappeared.

One brave fellow who had been separated from his girl, seemed to fairly throw himself through the water in his herculean attempt to reach his companion and when he finally succeeded, the two sank in each other's arms and were never seen again; another, who seemed to be a powerful swimmer, was swimming slowly toward the shore; he had placed his lady's hand upon his shoulder and thus she was enabled to keep her head above water, while he pulled for life; another, in trying to save the life of one of the ladies, became strangled and the two went down together; the fourth abandoned his charge and struck boldly out for shore.

When Robert saw this, he rushed to the rescue and was soon midway of the railroad bridge. The lady was struggling in the strong current beneath and quick as thought he let himself down from the bridge; then, as straight as an arrow, shot into the water; for some seconds he was out of sight, then, coming to the surface, he shook the water from his face and beheld the frightened lady, not five feet away; a few strokes and he was at her side; as he approached he said in a quiet and assuring way: "Don't be frightened, but put your hand on my shonlder and I will take you out all right." The lady did as she was bid and displayed a confidence truly wonderful. Her escort who had deserted her so cruelly was now making good headway toward the shore and finally landed amid the jeers of the spectators.

As the swimmers floated down the stream, the crowd also kept moving. It was plain they were making some headway, but so slowly that it was doubtful if strength held out; minutes seemed like hours to those on shore, but there was no chance to render assistance; every boat in that part of town had been swept away by the high water and before another boat could be procured, it would be too late. At last a delivery wagon drove into the crowd; a young man sprang out and seizing a coil of rope that had been thrown out and looping one end about his head and shoulders, he sprang into the water and soon had it where the swimmers could get hold, and they were all rescued.

The scene which followed would be hard to describe; all were overjoyed and each gave vent to his feelings in his own peculiar way. The swimmers were assisted into the wagon and were driven to their homes.

The lady whose life Robert had so nobly saved, proved to be the daughter of a millionaire—Miss Sheppard—and the young man who had so cruelly left her to drown, was her lover, and he was the son of a millionaire.

When the wagon reached the mansion of Mr. Sheppard, Robert assisted the young lady to her door and on taking his leave, she gave him her hand and exacted a promise from him that he would call that very evening and let her know that he was well, and she added, "talk over the adventure."

After leaving the mansion they drove to the hotel where an account of the affair had preceded them and Robert received an ovation from the guests and many others, that had gathered to learn of the affair.

Late in the evening Robert, having fixed himself in proper shape, proceeded to fulfill his promise, but he had many misgivings. His self respect had been largely developed and he was both kind and courteous to a fault, but he had always had a kind of contempt for anything in the shape of aristocracy, snobocracy or plutocracy, and notwithstanding Minnie's smiles seemed to have a kind of gentle intoxication in them that was encouraging in the extreme, he could not help but feel a dread of the place where he might hope to receive them once more.

On reaching the mansion a ring at the bell brought a servant to the door who recognized him at once and ushered him into Minnie's apartments.

It would be a difficult matter to describe this young man's feelings on being admitted to her private parlor. The golden splendor of the richly decorated room was so far beyond and superior to the most extravagant picture of his imagination that the effect was truly dazzling; for a moment he was lost in bewilderment, but when their eyes met the magnetic glance lent inspiration to his soul, and he stepped gently across the room, over a soft carpet, rich and fine enough for even angels to tread upon, but neither the softness of the carpet nor the dazzling splendor of the room had any place in Robert's thoughts.

The form that reclined upon a lounge before him had filled his soul with, shall I call it admiration? not so, it is too tame a word. 'Twas love that filled the soul of the young man, and Minnie, too, pure as the falling snow, unutterable, unexpressible, indescribable, an inter-coming of two souls as one.

For one short moment our young friend stood by her side in silence, while eyes met and two fond hearts drank up each-other's thoughts. Then gently pressing the hand of the maiden that had been so confidently placed in his, he quietly sank into a chair. Now that those peculiar feelings, which we might call the blending of all the nobler impulses of man's nature, such as none but true lovers can ever know or understand, were over, a quick conversation commenced.

In response to his inquiry, the girl said in her sweetest tones that she did not feel so much exhausted until she reached home and then her strength seemed all at once to give way; she felt very weak and had been resting ever since, save while at supper. That she tried to get up and sit in the rocking-chair just before he came but was too weak; she felt better now, and as she made an effort to arise he took her hand and assisted her to a chair where she again expressed herself as being quite comfortable.

Then they talked over their adventure and Minnie said that as soon as she was with him all fear left her and she felt quite safe and only thought of paddling toward shore. She said she did not feel as though God would desert a man who had been so generous as to risk his own life to save another's.

Robert said he did not consider that he had done anything more than his duty or what any man ought to do under the same circumstances. That he had no thought whatever of drowning; he saw she would sink soon and only thought of bringing her safely to land. In this way they continued to chat and became more confidential until the conversation turned on love. They then talked of their own peculiar relations and Robert called her attention to the golden gulf that so -completely separated them, and how necessary it would be for each to make no vows which the power there is in gold might compel them to break.

All this had but little effect on Minnie who felt that

her life had been saved and her highest aspirations would be to crown his future happiness.

"I know," said she, that my father is an aristocrat; he has made great headway since the banking system was established, in accumulating wealth. He has constantly become more selfish as his wealth increased and it has been his highest hope that I would marry that young man that you saw desert me in the river to-day." After a pause she continued: "That is all past now and I will never let money have anything to do with making my choice. My feelings toward you are of so delicate a nature that I cannot express them fully, but I will say this much, that no money or want of money shall ever be a bar to our future happiness."

The evening soon passed. When Robert Summerville took his departure, Minnie accompanied him to the door and in spite of his resolution to the contrary, in bidding her good night with a promise to come again, he pressed her to his heart, and to a looker-on, the touch of lips could hardly have been considered accidental.

In leaving the house, Robert's soul was ablaze with the fire of love; but he knew too well the power there was in gold, and while he could face a desperado, whose murderous soul was full of hate, he knew that gold had always slunk away into its ever-ready hiding place and launched its poisoned missiles through a secret emissary; knowing all this and having so much at stake, he dared to be afraid.

On the following morning Robert went to work, as usual, and during the week, nothing of importance occurred except the finding of two bodies which had been washed ashore and lodged on a sand-bar several miles below. Robert's employer, knowing all the circumstances, refused to let him off so he could attend the funeral, giving as a reason that they could get no one to take his place. Robert knew this was a flimsy excuse, and as the millionaire, Sheppard, owned a large share of the stock in business, he fancied he could see in it the effect of special orders and that he had been spotted for discharge.

The following Sunday, according to agreement, he called the second time on Minnie and was not surprised to find her in tears, for he had heard a good deal and was prepared for almost anything. Minnie met him at the door and ushered him into the quiet parlor, where with great feeling she told him all that had happened and among other things that this must be his last visit to the mansion. The visit was short, necessarily, and they arranged to meet in one of the parks on the following Sunday. Time soon rolled away and they met again for an hour's talk, in which they promised to let time settle it and remain true till death.

On the following morning Robert was notified that his services would be dispensed with. He received his pay in full and after settling up his affairs, the remainder of the day was spent in visiting other shops; he hardly expected a job for it was well known that there was not a shop in the place that was not under obligations to Mr. Sheppard's National Bank. His little love affair had been so thoroughly ventilated by the press, that he knew that the influence would militate against him; beside, under the contraction of the currency, such a stringency in money matters had been produced, that nearly all the shops were running on half time.

On Tuesday he went to Kansas City where he fell in with a young man from Arizona, whom the reader will recognize as Frank Bundy. They were both looking for work in a shop, so they took in all the different places together, but they were not long in finding the chances were very poor and what was very discouraging was the constant report of business failures all over the country.

After satisfying themselves that there was no use of remaining in Kansas City, Frank proposed to go to New York, taking in all the intermediate points. Robert saw nothing better, and it was decided to go. Before starting they went to the jail to see Col. Summerville, Robert's father, who was still incarcerated by the United States court for refusing to issue a tax levy, while Judge of the County court, for the payment of bonds issued for the building of a Railroad that was never built. The parting between Robert and his father was affecting in the extreme. Mr. Summerville had been upright and honest all his life and was now in jail for so long a period that death would probably rob the cell of its victim.

The old gentleman had no complaints to make but deplored the condition into which our country had drifted. He said that greed ran rampant and National banks, lotteries, faro and other percentage games, were ruining the morals of the people and concentrating the wealth of the country—building up a moneyed class, that was, through the power of gold, controlling legislation and the protection of these classes, with their money-making games, schemes and systems, in their assumed property rights, had become the first duty of Government. The rights of honest citizens to live and enjoy the fruit of their toil was left entirely to chance; and legalized robbery was making more distress in the State of Missouri, to-day, than a thousand men like Jesse James. When it would end, he said, he could hardly guess; but nothing short of a thoroughly successful social and political revolution would efface the damnable effects of class legislation in the United States.

After bidding the father good-bye, they went to the depot and were soon on their way. They stopped off at Chicago, Fort Wayne, Toledo, Buffalo and other points; but in all these places it was the same old cry of hard times and at the same time, crops had never been better. The old greenback men said it was a money famine brought on by destroying the national money; but the wise statesmen said the people had produced too much or in other words, over-production. It was suggested that when these honorable, wise men met again, that they pass a law to prevent people from producing such immense crops; because, said they, there are thousands of families to-day hungry and half clad and if this enormous production continues for a few years more, half of the people will have to freeze for want of clothes or starve for want of proper food. A banker who had recently returned from a pleasure trip to Europe, which had cost him several thousand dollars, and was getting ready for a trip across the continent in a palace car, was asked his opinion as to what made such hard times. He said it was over-production and extravagance on the part of producers. Bankers, said he, get rich by being economical. This was quite clear, but the boys were too anxious, where any one had too much, to lose time in argument.

One morning when they were thoroughly discouraged, a man met them on North River wharf and asked if they would ship?

"What kind of men do you want?" said Frank.

"Firemen," was the reply, and you can ship to South Africa or Liverpool, as you please."

The boys were ready for anything and on the spur of the moment shipped for South Africa where they would try their luck in the mines.

No girl, perhaps, ever felt more deeply the departure of her lover than did Minnie Sheppard. She had a pure heart and a kind, loving disposition. Her love affair had been brief but purely mutual and without affectation. She felt that she was loved by one of God's noblest creatures, for the sake of herself and not her fortune. She knew too that Robert had been thrown out of his place on account of that love. Where he would go and what he would do was all a blank. Times were hard for those who had no capital and getting more so all the time.

She had read a great deal and heard her father talk about his banking schemes; while it seemed to her that this great country had been prepared by God himself for the express purpose of furnishing an asylum for the oppressed of the Old world to escape from the tyrannizing despotism of plutocracy, she at the same time knew, that the poor were growing poorer and the rich richer, and she also knew that such a state of affairs could only be brought about by the very wickedest class of legislation, and she feared that strong as her loved one was, the current of adverse circumstances might be even more difficult for him to contend with than that of the great river.

In early days her father had inherited a large amount of land and while times were flourishing, right after the war, he sold it at a good round price and bought government bonds bearing interest; after that, as Mr. Goldburg had done, he placed the bonds in the safe keeping of the government where he could draw his interest regularly. He then received from the government, under the banking act, 90 per cent of the money he had paid for the bonds, and through the bank he loaned that out to the farmers at an exorbitant interest, and as the circulation of money was contracted, by act of Congress soon after, prices of everything went down; the farmers were unable to pay and the bank got the land at half its real value. Exorbitant rents then followed and Mr. Sheppard had become a millionaire by a creation of law or in other words legalized robbery.

This sure way of getting money had made Mr. Sheppard selfish and arbitrary. Mr. Goldfinch, the young man who had left Minnie in the river to drown, was heir to a million and a half at least, and in order to unite that sum to what he proposed to give his daughter he had long looked forward to their marriage as an event greatly to be desired, and although Minnie had never shown any fondness for the young man, the decree had nevertheless gone forth and all that the contract lacked was her sanction.

Now that he had deserted her in such a cruel manner, she was outspoken in her determination never to marry him and her father was equally determined that she should. So the millionaire's ill gotten gains thwarted love and stood between Minnie and her highest hope of happiness.

CHAPTER XIII.

TIME flies. After a long, tiresome voyage, the boys, Frank and Robert, found themselves in a neat cottage with an American family of the name of Brown, having landed the day before on the coast of Africa. Mr. Brown was a fine specimen of an American, and while he possessed in a high degree that energy, thrift and in fact all the nobler elements of man's nature so peculiar to the American people, he was at the same time free from that pusillanimity so common to the American in foreign lands, and which is constantly being interpreted as meaning "I am greater than thou."

Mr. Brown's family consisted of wife and three small children. For several years he had been selling goods, making a specialty of miners' supplies and outfits. His house was situated on the outskirts of town, hid away among many trees of the most attractive variety and his immediate surroundings were so tastily ornamented with semi-tropical shrubs as to make the place a modern Eden.

In the immediate vicinity of his home was a large open grove where American missionaries pitched their tents, and his house had not only become the headquarters for Americans but it had also become a kind of home for foreigners in general. His tables were kept well supplied with newspapers in every tongue and the use of them was free.

After looking about the place for a day or two the boys concluded to buy an outfit and go to the mines. When the question of an outfit came up, Robert asked what they would want. Frank said that from his experience in prospecting in Arizona, he would say, a dozen canteens to keep from dying of thirst, and a hair rope to keep rattlesnakes out of their beds; but Mr. Brown assured them that neither would be necessary and a trade was soon arranged for five burros, three pack-saddles, with rope and accouterments, two riding saddles, a camp outfit and food enough for a month's trip. They each bought a good Winchester rifle, six-shooters, ammunition and prospecting tools.

On the following day they saddled and packed and were soon off. The animals worked admirably and showed good breeding by proving themselves quite gentle. After four days' travel they reached the foot-hills and then passed many abandoned mines and occasionally saw placer miners at work; but they pushed on until they reached some extensive quartz mines where a great many miners were employed.

They were kindly received at this place and the Superintendent showed them through the mine and after studying the formation for a few days, they concluded to take the course of the veins and look for other mines in the distant mountains.

They were informed that the country where they were going had not been looked over to any great extent, for several reasons; there were very few prospectors in the country and in that section the country was so infested with wild and dangerous animals that it was almost impossible to protect their burros; that several parties had attempted to explore, but had invariably lost their animals or narrowly escaped doing so; but our young friends being thoroughly armed, determined to try their luck, so they took leave of the camp where they had been so generously treated and pulled out for the mountains.

During the first day out they crossed a deep gorge or canon, then ascended to the summit of a ridge that seemed to run in the same direction they wished to travel. After following the ridge for several miles, through a dense forest, and passing an occasional jungle they came to a small valley of grass land where they found a growth of a kind of pea-vine which the animals seemed to like. This valley was but a few feet below the general surface of the country and on

the north side was a large quantity of dead timber
which had been broken down by the storms. It was
well on in the evening, and the boys considered the
matter of stopping for the night, and as they found a
small stream near the timber, it was decided to camp
there. In a few moments they had relieved the animals
of their burdens and picketed them in the pea-vines.
They then proceeded to throw some logs together, in
such a manner as to furnish very good protection for
themselves; and as a means of further protection they
built a few fires.

In following up the little stream, they found it came
from the solid rock, beneath the spreading branches of
friendly trees; ivy, too had crept among the branches
and opened its blossoms to add its mite to the dense
foliage that darkened every recess. Warbling birds
were merry-making in the tree tops and their thrilling
music blended with the rich perfumes of a million
blossoms, made it a place of enchantment.

For a long time these two Americans drank deeply
ot Nature's fountain and their souls went out in silent
meditation on earthly things and from Nature up to
Nature's God; their minds wandered to the days of old
when others shared their joys and sorrows; at last
Frank broke the silence by saying, "Rob, there is but
one thing lacking to make this spot a Paradise and to
make me the happiest man on earth."

"And what is that?"

"The presence of one whose name I do not care
to speak."

"That's the way the world goes," said Rob, "I was
on that train of thought myself; but it won't do to talk
about it, it's too serious. A fellow can't well express
himself, unless he plays the baby act, and I've made
up my mind to let by-gones be by-gones, and busy
myself on this dark continent, for it seems to me that
"what can't be cured, must be endured."

Here the conversation ended and the two were soon
engaged in preparing supper. Nothing transpired to
disturb their slumbers but the occasional cry of a
panther or the hooting of an inoffensive owl.

After breakfast, next morning, it was agreed that Robert should remain in camp to protect the burros and Frank, taking arms and a pick-axe for breaking rock, started for the hill.

An hour's walk took him to the crest of the mountain; he found on the slope what he took to be good country for mines, so he soon began picking up pieces of float and toward noon, stumbled onto a well defined vein of quartz and finding gold, he looked more closely; breaking up a quantity, he secured several pieces that looked well. He scratched around the lead for a couple of hours and being able to trace it for half a mile, was satisfied that it possessed considerable merit.

After eating his lunch, he spent the afternoon walking and hunting. He found a great deal of quartz but nothing more that he considered good. He returned to camp late in the evening, tired and hungry, but with several specimens of rock. Robert pounded it up and it proved to be rich, so they decided to remain there several days, locate the whole ledge, do some work on it, then extend their operations to take in the whole neighborhood; after this return to camp and try to make a sale.

Three weeks were spent in this way. No discoveries of importance were made, so they returned to the mining-camp, and in a few days the Superintendent went out to look at the claim and offered them $3,000, and they decided to sell.

They continued to prospect in that part of the country for several months but finding nothing, they returned to the coast and pitched their tent near Mr. Brown, who was glad to see them and hear of their success. Their only plan, as yet, was to rest for a short time. They were not satisfied to go home with no more than $1,500 each, so they must look further.

While they were encamped at Mr. Brown's, there arrived in the town a band of over one hundred natives bringing in ivory which they sold to Mr. Brown, spending several days picking out goods they wished to take back. They camped near, and the King soon became acquainted with the prospectors and, through

an interpreter, told them they lived a long way off;
they had been over a month on the road.   The Arabs,
they said, were invading their country, and robbing
indiscriminately and carrying many away into slavery.

"Why don't you fight them?" said Frank.

"O they all have guns and we have nothing but
spears, so they kill our people."

"Why don't you buy guns?"

We have nothing to buy guns with, besides we
don't know how to use them.   If you will go with us,
give us guns and teach us to use them, we will make
you King of the whole country and give you all the
wives you want."

That evening Frank and Robert talked the matter
over and the more they talked, the more interested
they became.   It seemed that a whole continent lay
bleeding before them, calling for help.   It seemed
plausible that what assistance they could render might
turn the tide and enable the natives to defend themselves successfully and also establish such lasting
friendship between them and the whites as to give
civilization an impetus in Africa that would be without
a parallel in history.   It was decided to arm and
equip the one hundred men, drill them in the use of
firearms, and they believed with that force, backed by
many spears, they could meet and destroy any band of
Arabs they would be likely to encounter.   This method
too would give them an opportunity to make explorations that could be reached in no other way.

Having each pledged his life to the enterprise and
the cause of humanity, the boys sought another interview with the King; two of his men had been raised at
the coast, spoke English fluently and were constantly
with the King.

Through their interpreter, another meeting was
arranged; the King and his aids met the young Americans at their tent and informed them that there were
five tribes and each tribe had several villages.   There
were many other Kings and they would make Frank
King over all if they would furnish arms, teach their
young men how to use them and then command them

so that they should destroy the Arab bands of robbers

Having made this the basis of their agreement, the men were brought up in line and made to promise allegiance to Frank as well as to Robert. That evening they purchased arms and on the following morning issued twenty guns, and taking ten men apiece, drilling commenced; both were highly pleased with their progress, and so great was the anxiety of the natives to learn, that as soon as they were dismissed they would turn around and drill each other.

After drilling three days they issued blank cartridges and firing commenced; in one month they had the whole company under complete control and when everything was in readiness they took up their line of march.

Never, perhaps, were mortals treated with more respect and kindness than were Frank and Robert.

Their route for many days, lay through an almost impenetrable forest; but the trail was well beaten.

The people seemed to have a profound respect for the King; but when they saw their own brave men handling fire-arms and maneuvering in perfect regularity, it was too much and they went fairly wild.

The men were, for the most part, very muscular and in perfect condition, physically. Their behavior toward the Americans was like that of a child toward a father in whom it had perfect confidence and for whom it cherished perfect love.

On reaching camp, they first put up their tent, then looked after their bedding, clothing, etc. Then their cooking received prompt attention, and everything was done which could add to their comfort.

Before starting, the boys had, with the assistance of Mr. Brown, provided themselves with supplies for a year's campaign, and rather than burden the natives, who had their own loads to carry, bought thirty additional burros. After traveling for six week, they reached the river Toboga, where an immense crowd had assembled to welcome them and assist them in crossing to the town of Koheka, which introduced them to the King's dominions, and there they camped.

The Prince of this province was a fair type of African nobility, and though he resembled neither Queen Victoria, King Leopold nor King William of Germany, in either language or color, yet the boys were of the opinion that he was a Royal Prince and made of the same flesh and blood as other Kings.

When King Kongo, for such was the name of the King under whom the boys had enlisted, had crossed the river, he was treated with marked respect by the nobility, but the people were too much interested in the new guns and the white men to care to participate in kingly feasts, and the adventurers were of the opinion that kingly pedigrees were, for the time being, forgotten.

The first night was devoted by the natives to all kinds of hilarity, a war dance being the principal feature, but the boys, being very weary, retired early. In a few days they started for the King's own home, Kiyongo, which they reached after having passed five large settlements and three important villages. The people whom they met seemed to have a mortal fear of the Arabs and were ready to abandon their villages at a moment's notice. The sight of guns in the hands of their own people, however, inspired them with courage and they were ready to go where they were needed. On arriving at Kiyongo, the King set men to work at once to construct a house for the two white men and in a very short time it was completed.

This village was beautifully situated on the banks of a lake three miles wide and more than one hundred miles long. The dominion of King Congo lay on the east side of this lake, while another powerful Chief occupied the opposite side; but the two tribes had been at peace for many years.

In a short time drilling was resumed and it was not long before the King from the opposite side of the lake sent an urgent appeal for help, stating that a band of Arabs, consisting of one hundred men, had taken and burned a village about fifty miles away; it was soon arranged that the white men should go with their little army. As they were to be among friends all the way, there was no necessity for extensive preparations and they were soon embarked in canoes carrying ten men each.

It was two days before they reached the village where they were to land, and when they arrived they were told that the town which had been taken. was ten miles further on, also that the Arabs had killed a great many and taken about thirty prisoners, fastened them to a slave chain and had moved that day to a spring five miles away where they were now camped and it was, no doubt, their intention to burn that town the next day.

As they had met with no resistance, they were camped carelessly at the edge of some tall grass near the spring. Being then the middle of the afternoon, the boys decided to make an attack upon the camp that night; the natives were scattered through the country and watching every movement of the Arabs, so the boys were kept thoroughly informed. At early night-fall, in a bright moonlight, they took up their line of march and reached the place about ten o'clock. On reconnoitering they found the whole camp was unprotected; a line was then formed and moved cautiously forward, and so carelessly was the camp guarded that they approached within sixty yards before an alarm was given. When the Arabs sprang to arms it was just in time to receive a death dealing volley; this was followed by a charge and the Arabs fled in consternation. The Chiefs of the band, with many others, had been killed and those who escaped generally left their arms in the excitement and were run down the next day by the natives. The affair could hardly be called a fight for the surprise had been so complete that the Arabs made no show of resistance and as soon as the little army had gained full possession of the camp, friends and relatives rushed in to sever the bonds and burst the slave chains.

This was a good commencement. One hundred stand of arms had been captured, with a large quantity of ammunition, over thirty prisoners had been released and one of the most desperate and cruel bands of robbers that infested the country had been destroyed.

CHAPTER XIV.

WE will now return to Bopeep and see what has been transpiring there. One evening in May, about two years after Frank had taken his departure, Mrs. Goldburg and her daughter were in their sitting room, and as Mr. Goldburg had gone to New York, the place seemed rather lonely. Rebecca had been very thoughtful all day, and though always good natured and assuming a cheerful manner, there was visible upon her face a look of sadness which elicited her mother's warmest sympathy. She had just finished a plaintive melody on the piano, and crossing the room to where her mother sat, she began: "Mother, why does father bring such senseless fellows to the house, for my company? Just think of that Mr. Foghorn."

"Why, your father told me he is the son of a millionaire and one of the most powerful ones in the United States."

"Well, I don't care whose son he is, I am sure he's not very intelligent; and there is Mr. Pinchback; I think the two would make fine companions—their whole conversation is on money, balls, clubs and actresses; speak to them of religion, poetry, history or science and you might as well talk to a monkey or a parrot. Mr. Foghorn told me his father paid more money toward getting the contraction act passed than any one man and that his profits therefrom could only be counted by millions. When I inquired if his father actually produced these vast sums by the workings of that law, he said, no, but it was transferred from the pockets of others into his, through the workings of that law, by very legitimate methods of business. He talked

about it as if it had never occurred to him that it was
pure, unvarnished robbery and the way he has been
brought up, I think he does not realize what a crime
it is to rob in this way.

"I cannot understand millionaires, mother; they
belong to churches, pray to God, help the poor; then
go out and rob them; this must be true, for what is it
but robberry to take what you don't earn?"

Mrs. Goldburg explained that these people had
become so accustomed to handling large sums of money,
that they do not realize that it is a crime to keep it
from the people; never having suffered themselves,
they do not appreciate the sufferings of others."

"Let me tell you what I think," said Rebecca, "I have
often heard you say, you believed when men handled
an amount of money above a competency, it is gambling;
men become blind to a sense of honor, when they use
money only to gratify a love for gain. I believe it
becomes an incurable disease, for it is the spiritual
man which is affected and the cause which makes its
existence possible should be removed. A law which
makes one man's condition better without injuring
another, must be a good law, so I believe the best law
that could be invented would be to prevent any one
man from owning more money or property than would
place him and his family above want. This would
save the millionaire the trouble of handling so much
money and would give others a chance to accumulate
enough to make themselves and their families comfortable."

"When our capital amounted to $100,000," said Mrs.
Goldburg, we could live in perfect splendor, have
everything the heart craved, and your father had a
little time to devote to comfort and enjoyment. I believe it was better."

"I agree with an article I read not long ago, that
every man is debased who makes or handles liquor in
any way; it seems the same to me about surplus wealth
when men have all the money they can use for comfort
or pleasure, they should turn their attention to bene-
fiting mankind; all gain above that is simply usurpa-

tion of power that should only belong to the government; it is all stolen goods and, like the liquor traffic, debases every man who indulges in it or engages in it. The tendency of a man, after he has accumulated wealth is to become hard-hearted and arbitrary.

"It may all be my imagination, but it seems to me that since father has become a millionaire, he has become cold toward his neighbors and has also changed his feelings toward us, so that love, if it exists at all, is in the background. This is not only so in our family, but in every family of my acquaintance; where ladies delight in show to the exclusion of all noble sentiments, they enjoy a measure of happiness, but it is small compared to the joy which comes from doing good. How any one can reconcile want, wealth and Christianity, is more than I can see.

"If you were to tell any of the Bankers of this town that the Bible is false, that Christ was an impostor, they would denounce you as they do Ingersoll and Tom Paine, and yet their actions are exactly the reverse of Christianity. To me it seems hypocrisy to profess Christianity and at the same time hoard up wealth, while children are going hungry and half-clad.

"They try to deceive God and man and their whole life is a fraud. In my father's case this love of gold has already become a disease, and I can trace its beginnings until now it has reached its climax. When he was in only moderate circumstances, my every wish was gratified, but now in order to establish something like a Family Dynasty, which will continue to wield a power to collect rents, take interest and oppress the poor for all time to come after he is gone, he would sacrifice all my feelings, all my affections and marry me to a man whose only recommendation is, he is the son of a millionaire.

"Mother, it makes me sad when I think of all these things, and when I see how cold father has become toward us, how he walks the floor at the dead hour of night, because some tenant of his in Oregon had failed to pay his rent, his excuse being, a flood had destroyed his crop. He walks the floor and worries; says he did not agree to keep down the river; because they lost their crop they want to beat him out of his rent. I believe he would even take their team but that by law, is exempt. I remember a time when he not only gave money himself to poor fellows who had been hurt in the mines, but went about and asked help of others. In those days he took more time to rest when he came from the store and his meals tasted better; now he casts a hurried look over the table, filled with good things, eats a cracker or two, then goes hurriedly to his office and spends the day poring over those horrid books. Such a condition is all wrong and no man could change so except by disease; that disease, too, is brought on by concentrating wealth, and if a government cannot be framed so as to prevent it then human government is a failure."

"O yes," said her mother, "it does seem as though there are a great many inconsistencies mixed up with money and religion, at least it looks so to me and when I talk with the most intelligent people that we have, upon this subject, they dodge the truth or acknowledge themselves as much in the fog as I am; but I have an abiding faith in Jesus and believe that as man continues to progress, the evils of which you complain will continue to grow worse, until they become such formidable enemies to human progress that the attention of the thinking world will be concentrated upon it, and then, and not until then will there be found a remedy. It will be a remedy, too, that will be as radical as the disease requires; but for the present we can only be patient and put our trust in Jesus."

At this juncture the conversation subsided for a while, then Rebecca said, "Mother, what do you suppose has become of Frank? I get to thinking about him sometimes and I fancy that he has become a drunkard and I sometimes imagine that someone has murdered him. I have always hoped that he would write to his mother, but he said he would never write or come back until he could command wealth enough to be independent of the millionaires."

"I feel sorry for his mother," said Mrs. Goldburg, "I called there a little while yesterday and she told me that she had been to see a lady medium or fortune-teller (something of that kind) and the lady pretended to go into a trance and told her that Frank was in Africa and that she would see him sometime."

Mrs. Goldburg little thought what an effect this strange message would have on Rebecca, for she herself had hardly given it a second thought, but to Rebecca it was like a love message from the lips of an angel. She knew not why she felt so; she had never believed in such things, but it seemed so strange and as the drowning man will grasp at a straw, so she hailed this as an omen of good luck and she often found herself thinking about Africa and scanning the news columns to see if some new light would not be thrown upon the subject.

That very evening, as soon as Mr. Goldburg left the room, Rebecca took a walk and called upon Mrs. Bundy who received her with more than ordinary cordiality and told her all about the queer message. Never had Mrs. Bundy shown so much feeling toward Rebecca as on this particular occasion. After they had talked confidentially for a while over the strange affair, Rebecca asked why she did not go again.

Mrs. Bundy said she had intended to do so but the minister told her it was the work of the devil and she had better not go, so she gave it up, but Rebecca was too much interested and had too much American spirit to be frightened by a devil or two, especially when the devil seemed only to have an existence in the fertile brain of a man who preached the Golden Rule on Sundays and spent the greater portion of his time through the week in collecting money and hoarding it up, while many little children were in want, and she insisted on going again the next day.

Mrs. Bundy being a woman of liberal views, but little persuasion was necessary and it was arranged to go again on the next Saturday, and when the time came they went, but the lady medium had left the city and so they had lost the opportunity of seeing her, but this did not hinder Rebecca from thinking about the story.

A few months after this Mrs. Goldburg and her daughter visited Saratoga for recreation and while there they made the acquaintance of a Mrs. Sheppard and her daughter Minnie. As the two families were similarly situated in life a warm friendship soon sprang up which was intensified between the two girls by the discovery, through conversation, that their love experience had been similar and that hope, fear and even despair often filled the heart of each, as they wandered through the pleasure grounds and enjoyed the refreshing scenes that met them on every hand; they plucked flowers and while enjoying their wonderful beauty and rich fragrance would pour into each other's ears the secrets of their love affairs.

In this way time passed on, days grew into weeks, weeks into months, but sweethearts never tire of talking about love and the loved ones. As day by day they wandered through groves, Nature bade them welcome through gentle zephyrs and the sweet songs of many birds, and while drinking deep of Nature's inspiring draughts, their loves and trials blended, friendship deepened and when the two families separated, each to return home, it was agreed between Minnie and Rebecca to continue their warm friendship through a correspondence, and from that time on the girls exchanged letters regularly and each hoped on the receipt of every letter that it would contain news that the writer had heard from the loved one, but years elapsed and nothing had been heard.

Often during this protracted correspondence the girls had occasion to sympathize with each other. Mr. Sheppard, like Mr. Goldburg, was anxious to see his daughter married to a millionaire and the girls were fully determined to wait for their first love's return.

CHAPTER XV.

WE will now return to the wilds of Africa to look after our adventurers.

Crowned with victory, the natives were anxious for more war with the Arabs and to destroy every band of slave-dealers. As other bands were known to exist, it was decided by our adventurers to lose no time in arming and drilling more men, and as the natives were bringing in an abundant supply of provisions, it was decided to remain where they were and drill until further developments. They were not destined to be kept long in waiting, for scarcely had they placed their troops under good control, before word came from the Eastern Coast, that a band of 200 Arabs was moving toward a town at the foot of the lake. It was agreed to embark from that place and on reaching their destination, the people were wild with joy. Provisions were furnished in the greatest abundance and everything was done to make them comfortable.

News of the approach of the Arabs was coming in every day and as there was a large town about forty miles away, the native King thought it would be destroyed. They decided to meet the robber band at that place. They therefore pushed forward and reached town in two days. There they learned that the Arabs were camped within ten miles and would come on the next day. They met men on the road and learned that the Arabs had 300 men, but the boys felt confident that the surprise in meeting fire-arms, backed by a country full of lancers, would make victory certain. The following morning they moved three miles to some

fallen timber that skirted a prairie; the trail passed
directly through this timber and could not be evaded
by the Arabs on account of the jungle.   After taking a
position behind this timber, they awaited the coming
of the Arabs.

In less than an hour a small squad of Arabs came up,
and seeing that the natives were making a stand, they
fell back a little.   The main body formed a line and
moved upon the natives with a bold step, but it was
evident they were not expecting to meet fire-ams.   Had
they known that 200 well trained and well armed men
lay behind the logs, that the country was full of lancers
ready to follow them in case of defeat and to assist in
case of a hard fight, that twenty men with fire-arms and
200 lancers had been sent out the night before by a
circuitous route, to occupy their old camp and cut off
all possibility of escape in case of defeat, they might
have been more cautious.

When within a few feet of the logs, the natives rose
and poured a deadly volley into their ranks, then
charged upon them with a yell and the whole line gave
way and were soon completely routed.

In their haste to get away, the Arabs, many of them,
had dropped their arms and fled; the large band who
had been sent to cut off their retreat, instead of cap-
turing them according to order, destroyed the whole
outfit.   Thus ended one of the most barbarous and
blood-thirsty bands of slave-hunters and ivory-thieves
that ever carried destruction to the heart of Africa.
The news of the extinction of so formidable a body of
cut-throats, by an inferior force of their own people
(for of course the little army under the white men
received the credit) was heralded to all parts of the
country and was soon known for a thousand miles away.

Tribal Kings came from all directions to make offer-
ings of friendship and establish a dynasty with the two
white men at their head.

Meanwhile the boys had not been idle; all the arms
had been brought from the battle-field and they found
they had captured over 300 stands of arms and a large
quantity of ammunition.

Three hundred more men were at once enlisted and drilled for future emergency, and in about a month the little army of 500 men returned to Kiyongo.

Abundant supplies were being brought in and when they were ready to start out, canoes for the transportation were freely given by the King.

When the fleet of canoes reached Kiyongo, they were met by an immense throng of people who had gathered from all parts of the country to receive them.

Thirty different tribal Kings had taken up quarters there to await their coming and make them Kings over the whole country.

On landing, they were received with barbarous eclat and feasted for three days with African ceremonies; then a council was held and their purpose made known, when the young men agreed upon the following stipulations:

We come not to destroy but to build up; we want to see, your burned towns rebuilt; you have a great, rich and glorious country and with peace, you will have happiness.

It is our purpose to have peace and so far as we can, we will destroy every band of robbers that comes within our reach; but as to your governments, we would not interfere with them.

We only ask that you should bring us food and such other things as we need and we will protect you; we will also have our friends come and live among you and teach you many things that will be of great benefit to you and we will live in peace together.

When this document was interpreted to the assembly, there was a general expression of satisfaction and the camp was in a tumult of joy. At this time there were no more bands operating through the country, though many more were liable to appear at any time; so they deemed it advisable to continue their military organizations and drilling. The destruction of these two bands had spread consternation among the others, so after a few months, Frank, being tired of this monotony and restless for adventure, formed a plan to go to the great range which lay west of them. It was therefore

arranged that Robert would remain in command of
their little army, while Frank took an outfit of ten men
and twenty burros and started on a tour of exploration.
For two months they traveled through a country which
equaled in fertility and natural advantages, Illinois or
Iowa, and reached the foot-hills of the range; a few
more days took them well up into the mountains. The
foot-hills of the range were covered with grass with
here and there a live-oak tree, but further on the
country became more abrupt and was covered with a
dense, pine forest; there were many ravines and each
had a stream of clear, cold water, the formation, so
far as he could judge, being slate, limestone porphyry
and granite.

The soil was of clay, very red, and he constantly
came across pieces of quartz, then a ledge showed up
here and there and every indication for gold was favorable. At last he camped in a ravine which seemed
good for placer gold.

The following morning he set some men to work
digging a hole on a bar near camp; after reaching a
depth of four feet they struck gravel and in eighteen
inches more they came to bed-rock and on trying the
dirt found it went from 25 to 50 to the pan in gold.

This was a discovery worth making and he determined to make the best of the find. On leaving
Kiyongo, anticipating the finding of gold, he had provided picks, shovels, pans, axes, whip-saws in fact
everything he was likely to need and being thoroughly
prepared he started the burro train back for supplies,
to a settlement he had passed, and with the remaining
men he commenced work on a ditch to bring water to
the bar; he also set two men at work with the whip-
saw to cut out lumber for sluices.

In one month after the ditch had been completed, a
tail race had been cut, sluices set and ground sluicing
commenced; mines were also opened in two other
places along the bar and when the loose dirt had been
washed down to the gravel, the sluice boxes were
raised, riffles put in and the gravel shoveled into the
sluices After a week's run a clean up was made that

showed a net yield of over twenty dollars per day to the hand or $1,100 for the week.

It seemed odd to the natives to do so much work for such a little bit of gold, but they saw that Frank set great store by it, so they worked cheerfully on; when asked by the interpreter what gold was good for, he was at a loss to know what to say. He knew that paper had been often used for money and when backed by the law of the country, was superior to gold as money. The uses of gold were so few that if it were not used for money it would be almost worthless. So in order to come as near the truth as possible, he was forced to acknowledge that it derived its value entirely from legislation and that such legislation was only tolerated through the superstition of civilized races; that as long as that superstition continued to hold the races in thralldom, gold would be considered valuable and the gold they were now digging could be traded for many valuable articles.

After they had been at work in the mines for about three months, messengers came into camp with a letter from Robert. It read as follows:

KIYONGO, October 4,—.

MY DEAR FRIEND: From natives, living at the foot of the Blue Range of mountains, I learned that you passed their village on your way to the mountains and was all right. I since learned that some of your men had been down to the village after food, had found gold and were at work, so I do not know when to look for you back and have concluded to make an effort to get a letter to you. Now I will start three as brave chaps as you ever saw to carry this to you.

About a month or six weeks ago I learned that a large body of men were burning the homes and butchering the inhabitants one after another in King Hooloo's county—you will remember him as being the one so inclined to be polite; had such a mild manner of speech. The word that came to me was that they were about one hundred miles above the King's home village, coming this way and destroying everything. My first thought was to send for you, but there was no time for that, so shouldering the responsibility, in less than ten hours after the messengers had arrived we were embarked on the lake. Our route took us fifty miles on the lake, then up a river for one hundred miles.

The men took turns in rowing and I think we made twenty-five or thirty miles a day; we were six days in going as far as we could by water, then we took to the land. I never saw a more willing lot of men. The fact that the whole country was looking to them for protection, seemed to develop in them a thought of their own importance and inspire them with both will and energy.

I think we made twenty miles a day on the trail and we were five days in reaching the King's village; he had been sending out men every day to meet us and let us know how things were and when we arrived at his village, the Arabs had destroyed a town within twenty-five miles, and were moving on the capitol or King's village. The inhabitants who could get away were coming in ahead of the Arabs and the road for twenty miles was lined with people; many had been killed, many captured and others taken to the bush.

Their object was ivory, slaves and subjugation, and they were about 1,000 strong and well armed.

Inferior as were our numbers, I determined to meet them on the road and trust to luck for position. The next day at day-break we were on the march and by 10 o'clock we passed into a canon that I saw, at a glance would give us every advantage; it was 300 feet wide with a wall twenty feet high and loose rock enough at the top to throw together for protection. My first move was to fell trees across the canon to serve as breast-works; I then placed 300 men on the bluffs and 200 behind the logs, which reached across the canon. In less than an hour everything was ready and every man in place. The Arabs marched in close order and made no halt until they discovered us. Then they formed a line across the canon with about 400 men, the rest were held in reserve, but the whole command was under the deadly range of the 300 men on the bluff.

It was a trying moment; they with 1,000 men as blood-thirsty as ever trod African soil, accustomed to blood-shed and bent on robbery and spoliation; we with a little force of 500 men unused to war, but they were defending their homes. Would the God of battle give them strength and courage or would they fail in this battle for life? These were vital questions, soon to find solution in actual combat.

The jungle was now full of natives armed with spears, battle-axes, clubs, etc., but they dared not face the deadly fire of the Arabs who began the battle by moving upon our log breast-works.

They advanced with bold and confident tread but when at close range, our men raised and poured a deadly volley into them; they halted and another volley sent them reeling back. The men on the bluff were at the same time pouring a shower of lead into the reserve and in ten minutes they were all on the retreat and closely pursued by our men; they soon became panic-stricken and fled like wild men. They were so scattered that they fell an easy prey to the native archers and spear-men and the small force that succeeded in getting back to their camp, were attacked that night by bushmen and entirely destroyed.

On the following day, I ordered all arms brought into camp and when all had been collected and counted, we had captured 900 stand of arms and a large quantity of ammunition, which I brought back to this village and have them safely stored for future emergencies.

Before we started back, twenty different Kings arrived in camp to offer thanks and proposed to make me King; but I answered them by simply having the statement read which we agreed upon at Kiyongo.

The country through which I have traveled is one immense farming region; it is a pity to have it laying idle while thousands of civilized people need it for homes. It is the opinion among the natives that this last victory will effectually stop the slave and ivory raids in this part, and it is thought that native Kings 3,000 miles away will be falling back on us for protection.

Hoping this will find you O. K., I am respectfully,
ROBERT SUMMERVILLE.

Until Frank received this letter he had been so
absorbed in mining that he had given but little thought
as to how Robert might be getting along, and now
when he learned what a time he had been having he
became anxious to see him.

During his stay in the mountains he had not only
pushed work rapidly on the mine, but he had pros-
pected several other ravines and found the whole
country to be very rich in gold. He had not only
found ravine and gulch digging equal in richness and
extent to Golden California, but he had also found
what afterwards proved to be the richest gold quartz
mines in the world. Now, being well satisfied with
his explorations, he determined to start for Kiyongo
at once, and after weighing his gold in small lots he
found that he had over $7,000, which was less than
twenty dollars a day to the man for the work done.

The natives did not seem to expect anything, or at
least no part of the gold; it seemed to have no charm
for them, but had they been slaves they could not have
been more subservient to the will of Frank, and he
only explained to them that he could buy many nice
things for the people with his gold.

After putting all their sluice boxes and tools away
where they would be safe from fire and flood they set
out for home, and being lighty loaded reached Kiyongo
in less than sixty days.

When the adventurers met they were overjoyed and
the first night after Frank's arrival they talked until
morning and it was acknowledged that neither had
ever known a similar circumstance.

In the morning they went to see Robert's little farm
and it was noted that he had more truck than the
whole native village. The King had built them a nice
residence and so far as land for cultivation was concerned it was co-extensive with the continent.

For two weeks they talked over everything and
finally decided that Frank should go to Mr. Brown's
trading post and get an outfit for a big expedition to
the mines. On informing the King they were greatly
pleased that he heartily approved of the plan and an

immense outfit of pack-animals was gathered and with
a large body of men Frank went to the coast, and as
he went, improved the trail where it was necessary.

The $7,000 in gold was deposited with Mr. Brown to
be placed on account in addition to what was left of
the $3,000.

An outfit of tools was then purchased and also several
horse teams and plows. Arrangements were made for
the pack trains to continue constantly on the road in
charge of a man who had been recommended by
Mr. Brown.

On reaching Kiyongo, the boys proceeded to dis-
tribute their beads, looking glasses, copper wire, cloth
and many other notions among the people. The
wives of all the soldiers were then called and received
alike fine presents.

The troops were called in line and told of the intention
to go to the mountains and dig for gold and that all
who went could take their families and all who wished
to remain at home could step out of the ranks. To the
surprise of Frank and Robert not a man stirred, but to
the contrary, all seemed anxious to go.

In a few days the outfit was ready and moved out.
It consisted of five hundred men, all armed, and being
accustomed to burdens they carried their own plunder,
two hundred burros loaded with tools and goods, such
as would be most attractive to the natives. This time
Frank went ahead with men and tools and as the
natives turned out from each village to assist, they
succeeded in making a very good road from village to
village, keeping ahead of the main body.

On reaching the mines, men and families were
selected for the different prospects along a gulch for
about two miles and each put up a small house of
poles, then a store was built which was to be headquarters.

Several whip-saws were started to keep the camp in
lumber and when the men were comfortably situated,
those who had been with Frank on his first trip were
detailed to teach the others to work.

At this time there was no place in this whole country

where there was anything going on except at this camp. The natives for years had been in constant dread of annihilation by a people who were superior to themselves only in the use of fire-arms, and in these two white men they had found a savior. Whenever a dispute arose their word was law, and as they were actuated by principles of justice, without a thought of self-aggrandizement or other selfish motive, they were unconsciously becoming the true missionaries of the gospel of Christ and taught the Golden Rule by precept in every day life. Their motto was, lots of practice and little prayer.

They believed that labor was the commencement of progress, and that a progressive state could be reached through no other channel, and in order to get the people into a progressive condition they arranged to have work for all, and that the people might be contented and happy they established a system of traffic with the villagers by which their comforts and wants were fully satisfied.

As there is a spirit in man's nature that is ever ready to progress when an opportunity is offered, so in this case, the better element in these tribes came to the standard of the unassuming chiefs. Some of course tired of work and went back to their villages, but the many became so accustomed to shifting the whole care of providing from their own shoulders by a little work that they greatly preferred the labor with plenty, to idleness with want.

Several large burro trains had been put upon the road by native chiefs or kings to keep the store supplied, great herds of goats, too, were constantly being brought up to the villages and driven to the mines and there exchanged for goods in the store, and every one was busy and all had plenty and were happy. The gold was constantly taken to the store and shipped to Kiyongo where the old King put it away in an old house, but by all it was regarded as the property of the white men, and at best, considered of but little consequence.

The growth of the camp was wonderful and in less

than one year other camps had been established; the mines were very rich and the country called New California.

At the end of the first year over 4,000 men were at work in the mines, and the gold that found its way into the store amounted at that time to the enormous sum of $6,000,000.

The second year an increase of population was noted, and also in the gold output, and notwithstanding that one million dollars had been shipped away for goods in the two years, there was still $12,000,000 in gold bars at Kiyongo.

At first glance this would seem to be an enormous sum but when we take into consideration the fact that the gold production of the United States of America has been given for the years 1849 and 1850 at $40,000,000 and $50,000,000, making in all $90,000,000 for the two years, and that nearly all this vast sum came from the gold mines of California, it will be seen that $12,000,000 pales into insignificance.

Up to this time Frank and Robert had worked with an eye singly to the good of the peculiar people among whom their sympathies had been enlisted, and now when they were contemplating their wonderful success, Frank said that he thought the time had come when they should get a few more white people into the country and form a government, then throw the country open to the world. "But," said he to Robert, "from what you have told me I think you should take what gold you want, and claim the hand of that Iowa girl."

"Yes," said Robert, "I have been thinking about that; but it occurs to me, you would do well to take some of that advice to yourself."

"Just so," said Frank, "but you see I have promised myself so often that I would do my level best to bring light into Africa, that I seem to be perfectly wedded to the cause that I believe will bring such good to mankind; beside it is dollars to cents that my girl has long ago been sacrificed to some millionaire; I would not have her know that I am alive for fear it would make her unhappy; so I have not written to her."

"Exactly right," said Robert, "and you will not be surprised to learn that I have dismissed the subject from my mind in the same manner and have determined to stay with our African propositions to the bitter end. If I fall, it will be while fighting for the good of mankind, and I am as anxious to carry out our plan of a civilized government in this country as I ever was."

"Right," said Frank, "we will shake on that," and the two young men clasped hands.

"Now," said Robert, "as we have agreed to stay with it, don't you think it will be well enough to formulate some plan for future operation?"

"Certainly," said Frank. After a while, Robert continued; "I have always let you have your way, not because I thought you were right, but because I admired your unassuming bravery and reckless, daredevil style of driving ahead; but I want to tell you now, you are as full of inconsistency as a Texas steer is of the devil."

"How so," said Frank. "Well, I will tell you," Robert continued: "in the first place, you have always claimed that gold has very little intrinsic value and should never have been used as a substance to make money of, simply because the amount of gold in the world is limited to its production and money should only be used to the necessities arising for its use. I have even heard you go so far as to say that the use of gold as money had produced more misery than any other cause, and still, as fast as possible, you are converting these people who know nothing about gold, into miners instead of teaching them to cultivate the earth to better advantage; you see that over in Kiyongo I raised more truck with three or four men than the whole village; now after talking as you always have, to turn around and make miners of all these people, is like a man preaching the religion of Christ, which is all based upon Justice and Charity, and at the same time hoarding up wealth, while others are suffering, or like standing in a million-dollar church and preaching humility." I am almost persuaded to propose abandoning this mining business, ship the gold out of the country and exchange it for something that would benefit the country and in future turn our attention to educating the people."

This little speech set Frank to solid thinking; he knew it to be half in jest, but he remembered that when a difference of opinion came up between them Robert had nine times out of ten given way to him; he therefore felt it his duty to make a sort of apology, so he said: "Robert, we are placed under very peculiar circumstances, and while I have tried to be entirely unselfish and governed by reason, I must admit that when I look back it seems as if I had been governed by what Orthodox Christians call intuition and Spiritualists would call Spirit control, I know not what it is; so long as the results are good, I care not.

"In the United States, millions of dollars have been collected, much of it among the poor, and missions established on the islands of the sea. The first thing to be done in these missions is generally to establish a trading-post and monopolize the trade; and although the trade is always for the people, it is quite often the case that these missions, like Congressmen, soon become rich. After trade is established, the next grand object to be attained is to persuade the natives to lay aside one superstition and take up another—for any belief without evidence is superstition—and until the savage is raised to that standard, intellectually, where he can comprehend the laws of divinity, and understand the development of natural law that proves the Divine teaching to be true to him they are only superstitions.

"In consequence of this, missions, the world over, have been failures as civilizers and only a partial success as a monetary scheme.

"Now unless we can adopt some new plan to civilize the people, our plan is a failure from the commencement. I have been reasoning over the matter in this way: Labor is the corner stone to all civilization; without labor there could be no such thing as civilization. To be busy is to be happy; to be idle is to be miserable and discontented. These are facts in man's nature; therefore the man who fosters labor, builds up civilization; and the man who controls labor through selfish motives, is an enemy to society, to Christianity and to God.

"These things being true, we must first teach these people to work and make themselves comfortable; we cannot educate them in art, science or religion in their present condition; it would be like resting a building upon its apex. We must not use force, force is wrong; love is law; therefore we must first show. these people the blessings to be derived from labor; then provide them with labor that is new to them and see to it that the result of that labor is improved condition; then the novelty of labor and its benefit combined, will attract these creatures and enlist their energy and when the first day's work is done and its fruit enjoyed, even though it be but a string of beads, if it satisfied the worker, a step in progress has been taken.

"Admitting these things to be correct, our line of procedure becomes plain. We must create a want— our stores all through the mines have done this by putting a variety of goods in sight that are both useful and attractive. Our next duty is to show these people a way by which they can obtain these goods. Our mines are peculiarly adapted to that end and although gold is a substance which receives its value entirely from legislation of other countries, it still answers our purpose in many ways; the work is easily learned and suited to the condition and the gold, too, is ready sale in foreign countries and can be exchanged for such goods as we want.

"Beside this, it furnishes work for pack trains which come here from all parts of the country. When more white men come into the country and we organize a government, their superstition in favor of using gold as money will be so strong that they will probably insist on using the twelve millions of gold on hand to make coin of, and when a shortage of gold occurs they will want to issue interest-bearing bonds and trade them for gold in London; should they succeed in carrying out this plan, the history of the United States of America would be repeated and in a few years London would have all our gold and silver, even our railroads, our bonds, and a large share of our business; our land, too, would eventually pass into their hands, but what we must try to do, is to make our own money of paper, based upon the wealth of the country and stability of the government and its ability to enforce its own laws.   Then we can have this gold to ship as a commodity for the purchase of railroad iron and machinery, and when we add to it our yearly product, we will soon have Steamships and Railroads of our own and no bonds, no interest no foreign capital.

"The gold that we have has cost nothing, for you see the people set no value on gold, but are well satisfied with their improved condition.   The gold we have is not ours but a means that God or nature has entrusted to our keeping, for the benefit of mankind.   If we hoard it up or use it to enslave or to control labor, to satisfy a greedy disposition in ourselves, then we are recreant to the trust; but as long as we can furnish and control labor in the interest of the people and civilization we are the true followers of Christ."

Robert had been listening to all this with an appreciative interest; they were his own sentiments photographed, but he had never heard them so plainly expressed before, and being in a good natured mood, he said, "Frank, you certainly are an enigma."

"Why so?"

"Simply because whenever you think you have established a good principle, you base it upon Christianity; and yet you are so entirely different from the people I know who call themselves Christians, that you are about the last piece of material I would have selected had I wanted to make a Christian.   I have known you for a long time and have never discovered any Bible, Hymn or Prayer book lying around loose, nor have I ever caught you praying and singing psalms or trying to persuade anyone else to."

"Psalms and loud prayers," said Frank, "are for those who need them, but my experience has been so serious and trying in its nature that what little devil there was

in my nature has all been driven out by the refining
influences of combined love and persecution and my
soul goes out to good intuitively, naturally; every
breath is an inspiration, every action in business is a
prayer for the cause I have espoused—that of liberating
mankind from the thralldom of ignorance and superstition. The birds in the trees sing psalms to me and
my Bible is the love of all mortals; is short and easily
understood; my Christianity is not one of creeds,
forms and ceremonies but it is the Christianity of love,
truth, justice—this is what Christ taught, hence is
Christianity."

"Well," said Robert," if this is Christianity just
count me in. I have always considered myself an
infidel after the Ingersoll type and am indebted to you
for a knowledge of the name I should rightly assume,
and in fact I am rather glad to know that after all I
am a Christian."

CHAPTER XVI.

AT THIS time there were several stores in the mines in charge of men who had been sent out by Mr. Brown at different times. The trail from the coast to the mines had been shortened somewhat and missed Kiyongo by about twenty-five miles and in consequence that place was quite dead, but in case they succeeded in making a government they had decided to make it the capitol, and now it was thought advisable to make a move in that direction. It was also thought best to consult the wishes of the people. So they were called together and asked if they would prefer going back to their homes and abandoning the mines, but all were unanimous in wishing to stay. They had good, comfortable homes, little gardens, and by their work could get many things at the store which they would never see in the country.

It was therefore arranged that Robert should remain in charge of the camps and keep the mines running in full blast. The camp from the first had been carefully managed in every way to improve the condition of the working men. They were constantly encouraged to bring their families, to raise gardens and keep goats, both for milk and mutton. The boys were highly gratified at the result of their labor in the way of civilizing the negro and while Robert was to continue the good work, Frank was to go to Kiyongo, assemble the Kings, talk up the advisability of bringing more white men into the country and organizing a strong government that would not only protect the people, but also civilize them and teach them many things.

The camp was now notified of their intention, and when Frank assembled his little band of soldiers to start for Kiyongo, they came in from all the mines to

see him off, and their peculiar ways of expressing
regrets at parting was not only impressive, but their
simplicity and honesty even moved these strong young
men to tears.

The trip to Kiyongo was long and tiresome, but
Frank was young and in the height of his glory; he
was married to the cause of progress and no millionaire
stood in his way.   Thus he soliloquized and pushed on.

When he arrived at Kiyongo, after resting, he held
a long consultation with the King, who entered into
his plan with childish interest.   The wonderful change
for the better that had been brought about by these
young men in checking the terrible onslaught of the
murderous Arabs had completely won his esteem, confidence and affection.   He readily consented to call a
meeting of all the Kings who could be reached, and
during the interval which would elapse, Frank would
explore a route through to the great river that was said
to lay east of them, and also find a better way of getting
goods.

Now as everything had been arranged with the King,
he was soon embarked on the lake with a small escort
in two canoes, and after a few days' rowing on one of
the most enchanting lakes imaginable he reached a
town at the foot of the lake where he had formerly
landed with his army.   When it had become known
that he had arrived, the natives gathered from every
direction to give him a welcome and the King of the
place offered his own service as guide.

As soon as it was possible they were off; including
the King's party their company was now large and as
they had plenty of tools Frank made it a point to
improve the road as they went.   The distance to the
river proved to be about one hundred miles.   At the
place where they camped two great rivers formed a
junction.   The country around was smooth but undu-
lating and apparently the farming land was vast in
extent with strips of timber and grass land, ready for
the plow.

A large island stood in the center of the stream which
at this point seemed to widen to a lake several

miles in length; and on being sounded for several miles proved to be navigable for the largest ocean steamers, and at the mouth of the river was a beautiful harbor. Frank conceived the idea that at no distant day there would be a grand city at the place of their encampment and named the place Summerville, in honor of his companion.

Everywhere along the great river they found ruins of large villages which were said to have been destroyed by Arabs; he was told that those who escaped death had moved to other settlements. They found many canoes along the bank, and natives from the interior villages were camped there, fishing. These canoes were used in sounding the river, and after seeing all that he thought was necessary of this region, they took a different route to return, by ascending the river several miles then crossing the country to the foot of the lake.

On Frank's return to Kiyongo, he expressed himself to the King as being highly gratified with his trip and stated that the time was not far distant when they would have a railroad from Kiyongo to the coast, The King's knowledge of railroads was, of course, very limited; this was perhaps fortunate, for had he known how the railroad companies in the United States had first robbed the government, then the people, oppressed their employes, and created general distress by their exorbitant rates, levied to produce interest or dividends on watered stock, their unwarrantable discrimination for or against cities, towns, villages and territories, he would certainly have held up his hands in holy horror and said keep out the railroads, for the slavish conditions that they bring about is even worse than being murdered and destroyed by heartless Arabs.

The time for the convention was now near at hand and Frank improved the time in making preparations for a trip to Mr. Brown's.

At the appointed time the Kings, to a man, came in obedience to the summons and their greatest curiosity was to know what he would do with so much gold; to them it was like lead and they supposed it would be

used for bullets to shoot squirrels, but Frank explained
that when a government was formed they would trade
the gold for railroad iron, machinery steam ships and
many other things that would be needed by civilized
people. He explained to them that a government was
nothing more nor less than an organized society of
civilized people formed for the purpose of protecting
every individual in his ability to live and enjoy perfect
liberty of action so long as he does nothing to interfere
with the rights of others. That in human nature there
has always cropped out a disposition on the part of a
few dishonest, greedy and unscrupulous men to rob and
deceive the others and take to themselves all the
property and all the good things of earth and prevent
the others from enjoying them; in civilized governments crafty and dishonest men have preyed upon
the credulity of honest men by inventing all kinds
of gambling percentage games to rob the people; these
games are generally called lotteries or banks. The Faro
Bank is quite common, but the most stupendous
swindle known to modern times is the National Bank.
He explained to them that gold had no value of any
consequence except as it was used by foreign nations
for money, and as its use was only made possible by
these swindling monopolies appealing to the superstitions of the people, it was liable to lose its value any
time through the natural progressive spread of light
and education, therefore it should be their policy to
ship all our gold and exchange it for more valuable
commodities as fast as possible.

He told them that the whole people would constitute
the government, and as the gold was one of the natural
products of the country, it would be used to put a good
and strong government into operation, that is if it was
agreeable to their wishes, and as they did not know the
damnable effects that a civilized government had produced with the natives or Indians of the United States,
they readily consented to his plans and authorized
him to go ahead, and it was agreed that the seat of
government should be on the lake near Kiyongo.

It was also agreed that in forming a government each King should continue to rule his own tribe as now, and each should be represented in the national council. That Frank should go to the coast and bring back good white men to take part in organizing the government, and when he returned they were to be once more called together for the purpose of framing a constitution by which they would all be governed.

To all of this the great Kings agreed and the pow wow wound up with a great feast.

As arrangements had already been made for a large pack outfit and one hundred men, Frank started for the coast. Six weeks from that time they camped on Mr. Brown's old camp ground and he noticed that there were a great many others camping there and was pleased to learn that they were Americans.

On reaching the place the camp was hardly arranged before Mr. and Mrs. Brown were on the spot to extend to Frank the warm hand of friendship and take him to their home, and while Mr. Brown and Frank enjoyed a glass of wine, Mrs. Brown prepared such a lunch as Frank had not tasted for many a day.

All had plenty to talk about. Mr. and Mrs. Brown wanted to know all about Frank and his many experiences and Frank was anxious to hear the news from the civilized world. It was late the next day before they could even begin to talk about business. . Mr. Brown told him that the gold he had sent was reported as having come from one of the camps near the coast. This he had no doubt done for the purpose of controlling the trade, out of which he had already made a comfortable fortune, but it suited Frank's purpose very well, so it was agreed for the present to keep everything quiet about the gold, and this matter over, it was decided that Frank should retire to his room which had been kindly furnished him by Mr. Brown and decorated with flowers for his special use.

On retiring to his room, Frank was soon busily engaged in poring over the late papers and was not at all disappointed to find that the great journals still found plenty of business in recording strikes, lockouts, railroad accidents, new trusts forming, great business outlooks, money to loan in all the banks on good real estate security, the greenback party dead, John L. Sullivan traveling the country as champion of the world, the pugilistic business having a regular boom, wonderful evidence of prosperity; such as mortgages, bonds and immense sale of whiskey. All the breweries bought by an English syndicate, all rag money destroyed and an honest gold dollar in circulation which would buy more wheat or cotton than any other dollar that was ever made.

While Frank was contemplating all these wonderful evidences of unparalleled prosperity, a gentleman was ushered into the room by Mrs. Brown and introduced as Mr. Gibbs, an American missionary, who, after a few complimentary remarks had been passed, proceeded to explain that he had come to Africa for the purpose of preaching and teaching Christianity and learning from Mr. Brown that Frank was operating in the interior, sought an interview for the purpose of gaining some knowledge of the country and people which might guide him in establishing a mission.

Frank treated Mr. Gibbs with kindness and gave him all the information at his command, and followed his remarks by saying that if they were prepared and desired to instruct the people in the rudiments of knowledge that he and all others of the same class would be very welcome visitors or residents.

Mr. Gibbs then stated that there were twelve gentlemen and seven ladies camped in the grove, all missionaries from different denominations, but one in Christ, and if he would appoint a time when he would address them, they would all be glad to be in attendance, so they were immediately summoned, and as their method of teaching was satisfactory, Frank closed his remarks by explaining that it was a long and tiresome trip and perhaps too much of an undertaking for ladies, but that the field was open and such as felt themselves equal to the task would receive perfect protection and every facility for travel that was at his command.

The ladies with one voice informed Mr. Bundy that they felt themselves equal to any emergency and all that they asked was protection and they would not be found wanting; everything being satisfactory, it was arranged that all should accompany the expedition. As they had their complete outfits they would accept nothing from Frank but a few riding animals for the ladies and they were to be prepared to start in one week.

That same evening as Frank was sitting quietly in his room musing over the situation, Mrs. Brown announced two gentlemen as desirous of an interview; they were admitted at once. The gentleman in advance, a tall, lean man, introduced himself as Hesikia Lincoln from Kansas, U. S. A.; his companion as Thomas Jefferson of the U. S. These gentlemen afterwards expressed their surprise at finding so young a man and described Frank as being a man of fine form, light complexion, terribly tanned, round smooth face, brown hair, slightly inclined to curl, large blue eyes with a dreamy expression. Honesty of purpose and motive backed by a strong will power seemed to be his leading points.

As the two men entered the room, he met and gave them a hearty shake, then all were seated and Mr. Lincoln proceeded to inform him that Mr. Jefferson and himself had first met at that place. They had come to Africa for the purpose of bettering their condition, but had found things, so far, quite dull and they had sought an interview with him to find out if he could point them to anything in the way of business or employment.

Frank at once recognized the fact that these were men of brains and he felt his own insignificance, but the quiet, unassuming manner of Mr. Lincoln reassured him as he proceeded to relate that he, Mr. Lincoln, had been a farmer in Kansas, but after the withdrawal of greenbacks was commenced, money became so scarce that he was compelled to borrow from the bank, and when the mortgage became bigger than the farm, he sold for what he could get and sought new fields,

The experience of Mr. Jefferson had been similar, only he had been engaged in a different branch of business, and what he most desired at present was more money or some means by which he could obtain that very necessary article.

Frank explained the condition of things in the interior briefly, then informed them of the desire of the people to form a strong central government. When he came to this part of his narration he saw the face of Mr. Lincoln brighten up and Mr. Jefferson draw his chair a little nearer, and after a few moments pause, Mr. Lincoln asked what kind of government have you thought of forming. The gentlemen had misgivings upon this point, no doubt, for the selfishness and ambition of most men would naturally lead them to form a kingdom and place himself at the head.

Frank hesitated for a moment, then said: "I think I know the kind of a government we want, and yet I do not know; we certainly want one that will give equal justice to all; we want every man to have equal rights well defined and we want a government strong enough to protect every individual in those rights, but just what kind or government will accomplish these things in the best manner, is what I do not know."

Should we accompany you to the interior, Mr. Bundy, could you give us any assurance of being able to provide the necessaries of life while this new government is in embryo?"

"Certainly," said Frank, "you will be provided with the best the country affords, and I will furnish you with all the pack and saddle animals you need and give you protection and care to the extent of my ability." So it was arranged that both with their families should accompany the expedition.

On the following day three young men called on Mr. Bundy and he observed that they were all about his own age. The first introduced himself as William Saunders, an Englishman, the others as Thomas Coy and Charles Baxter, both Americans. They were all good looking, smart and intelligent, and their language and manners bespoke men of education. They were all adventurers and wished to learn something of the interior.

Frank gave them a pretty fair description of the country but did not encourage them in going; in fact he was not favorably impressed with them. After a long talk they retired but came again the next day and asked his permission to accompany the expedition at their own expense.

It was too much for Frank to refuse when the parties were entire strangers and he could not tell why it was that he disliked them, so it was also arranged for them to accompany the expedition.

On the road it was noticed that they had a good many boxes of ammunition, and as Mr. Lincoln was noticing the boxes, Baxter remarked that he was afraid they had more ammunition than they would need, "but these boxes," said he, "contain surveying tools for I am an engineer."

The matter passed without farther thought on the part of Mr. Lincoln, but could he have seen the contents of the boxes he surely would have thought something more concerning it.

The facts were that Mr. Saunders had been a confidential employe in a bank in England and had managed to get away with $120,000 in gold; he had reached South Africa, where he expected to remain until a compromise could be effected by his friends; Mr. Coy was a bank defaulter from Chicago who was in Africa under almost the same circumstances, with a swag of $100,000; Baxter was a personal friend of Coy's who had been his accomplice, and as he had not been known as such it was intended that some day he would return and fix up a compromise for Coy, by returning a large part of the money. But now that a new government was to be established, the spirit of speculation with them ran high.

In a few days goods had been purchased, animals packed the expedition organized and on the move.

CHAPTER XVII.

WE again go back to Bopeep. Mr. Goldburg had united his vast wealth with that of Mr. Goldaker, a millionaire of Boston, and with their combined capital they had associated themselves with an English syndicate or banking firm. When greenbacks were withdrawn from circulation money became very scarce and farmers and business men were forced to borrow gold to do business with and take the place of the greenbacks, and while contraction was going on, this English syndicate, through agents, had loaned out millions of dollars on mortgages which were invariably made payable after harvest, and it was now arranged that the English bankers were to demand immediate payment on their mortgages and stop all farther loans; this would make such a stringency in money matters as to force wheat to its lowest possible price. Then Mr. Goldburg would step in, buy up the surplus crop at half its real value. After this, extensive loans would again be made and wheat go up; in this way they were successfully fleecing the farmers on one hand and consumers on the other.

The old Greenbackers, followers of Cooper and Weaver, were constantly exposing the scheme, but they were denounced as cranks by a subsidized press, and the game went merrily on, the people continuing to grow poor and lose their land, while these gold gamblers piled up their millions.

Mr. Goldburg's associate in Boston, Mr. Goldaker, had a son about twenty-five years of age, and Mr. Goldburg conceived the plan of a marriage between this young man and Rebecca, thereby consolidating the two estates which would add materially to their power as a monetary dynasty.

Mr. Goldburg had been baffled so often in his plans of marrying his daughter to some man where it would add to his own-power, by enabling him to control more millions, that he now determined to go at things in a business like way; so after making all the necessary arrangements with and having his plan approved by the father and son, he proceeded to bring about a meeting by taking the young man home with him, where he met for the first time Rebecca and her mother.

After a visit of several days, Mr. Goldaker returned to his home in Boston, highly elated over his visit. Miss Rebecca had treated him with great respect; true, he could not help feeling that she considered him her father's guest, but he was confident that when the ice was broken by her father and the great advantage that would follow the consolidation of the two estates fully explained, all would be well and the conquest would be an easy one.

On Saturday evening, after the departure of Mr. Goldaker, instead of going into his home office as he usually did and poring over his books until bed-time, Mr. Goldburg waited in the drawing room until his wife appeared.

The millionaire, in managing so large a business, had cultivated a habit of using just as few words as possible and be understood; he had not probably spoken half a dozen words to his wife or daughter in six months that was not strictly business. He had in fact become just the kind of a man that it takes to pile up millions—cold, selfish, and always busy—if not working, always thinking, not about science, nor religion, but about gold; after a vast estate has been accumulated, and invested in stocks, bonds, and securities, it will run itself and a man with very little brains or energy can draw the interest; but the first building up of these great dynasties make two things indispensable—favorable legislation and a man of very peculiar character.　Mr. Goldburg it seems turned out to be that kind of a man.　As his wife entered the room, he motioned her to a chair and in a very business like way said:　"I thought I would speak to you about an arrangement I have made with Mr. Goldaker, the father of the young man you have had as a guest.

"It is the same banker with whom I have been associated and he is called one of the richest millionaires in the United States; he is getting quite old and if a marriage can be effected between young Mr. Goldaker and Rebecca, he will put his whole estate under my management.

"The good that will be derived from such an arrangement can hardly be conceived by a person not conversant with the methods of handling aggregated capital.　As an illustration, with these two estates consolidated, I can buy up legislators, control the legislatures, conventions and elections; can lobby bills through Congress to advance my personal gain, without asking the odds of other capitalists and when the consolidated bankers carry a bill through Congress to scoop the people, I will be prepared to take advantage of it and increase my holdings all over the United States.

"I am sorry to see that Rebecca has so stubbornly rejected all propositions of marriage heretofore and I hope you will give her an outline of my plan.　I shall depend upon you to assist in bringing the very strongest influences to bear to insure a consummation of this plan.　I think it will be best for you to explain first and I will try to see her myself in the course of a few days and shall hope not to be compelled to use coercion."　Thus saying, without giving his wife a chance to reply, he left the room.

It so happened that the Goldburg family had some years before taken a small black boy to raise, who was now about ten years old; he was extremely bright but very rougish and had learned to love Rebecca with that love that is only begotten by kindness.　This boy was in the room during the whole conversation, and little did Mr. Goldburg think how interested he had been. As soon as the millionaire left the room, Fred, for that was his name, slipped unnoticed from the room and a moment later a rap was heard on Rebecca's door. Rebecca recognizing the tap as being that of her pet black boy, opened the door at once and the little fellow rushed in, his face shining black with excitement.

"O Missus Becca!" he said, "does you like, that ar dude from Boston?"

"Who are you calling dude?" said Rebecca. "O dat ar man dat talks about theatres, clubs and prize fights."

"O you naughty boy, you must not talk that way about Mr. Goldaker."

"I say Missus Becca, do you like Mr. Goldaker?"

"Of course I do, child, but why do you ask?"

"Cuz your pa said you must marry him and he would get a big lot of money solidated." "Who did he tell?"

"He told your ma, deed he did, Missus."

"Where is mama? Come, I must see her."

The boy led the way to Mrs. Goldburg, and when they entered the room her mother guessed what had transpired and proceeded to relate the whole talk.

Rebecca was not surprised for she had expected something of this kind sooner or later, but now that it had come she was all unnerved and she said in a pitiful, childish manner, "Mama, it seems awful to think that papa would be willing to sacrifice all my hope of happiness for gold when he already has more of the precious metal than he can ever use; it seems as though all that Satan offered Jesus would not be enough for him."

"I know what the matter of him is," said Fred, "he'es got goldoramus."

"What do you mean, you little scamp?" said Rebecca. "I will shut you up in the kitchen if you say another word."

At this the boy went back to his hiding place, behind a large chair, and the thought of a pan of doughnuts' that he saw the cook put away that day, flashed across his mind as he contemplated Rebecca's awful sentence and a broad grin spread over his face.

Turning to her mother, Rebecca said, "Who would think that Fred would remember my talk of the plutocrats having goldoramus. I never would have thought of it again. There is no accounting for the memory of children."

"He will probably remember that when other things of much more importance have long been forgotten," said her mother.

"It did not sound so badly," said Rebecca, "when I said it, but to hear it repeated makes me feel so small."

"You have spoiled the boy," said Mrs. Goldburg, "you treat him more as a pet than as a servant."

Rebecca made no reply to this but after a moment's pause said to her mother, "What do you think of this whole affair; don't you consider Mr. Goldaker rather presuming to want to marry a girl who has no thought of him whatever?"

"Of course," said her mother, "it looks strange, but with millionaires it seems that there is but one consideration in life and that is gain; gain beyond competency means power to control and oppress others. It is the religion of the devil and its devotees are just as much in earnest as are the followers of Christ's noblest teachings."

"Well, I won't like the man and I will never encourage him."

Then the little black boy jumped out from behind the chair where he had been quietly sitting and coming up to Rebecca, said, "I don't like him either," and Rebecca having forgotten her little fit of anger at the boy, said, "why, Fred, why don't you like Mr. Goldaker?" "Cuz," said Fred, "cuz he's got goldoramus." Seeing the look that came upon Rebecca's face, he quickly returned to his hiding place.

To say that Rebecca was provoked, would be to put it too mildly, but it was not in her heart to punish the boy, and as both ladies were too sad to talk they retired to their separate apartments.

There had, perhaps, been no time in Rebecca's life when she had been more sorely tried than now and she sought consolation in prayer. Oh! how she longed for Frank's strong arm to lean upon; she would rather go with him into a shanty and live upon the earnings of a poor wage-worker than be made a slave to her father's lust for gold; in her anguish she prayed that the gold might be sunk in the bottom of the sea. Why, oh, why, did not Frank come back? She prayed that God might send an angel to tell her when he would come back. At last she cried herself to sleep and in her dreams she seemed to see Frank in an office in a beautiful city, in a wild country and among a strange people; when he saw her he clasped her to his bosom and said, "O, how glad you have made me, I felt sure you had been sacrificed to some millionaire long before this."

The dream was so real that on awaking she could hardly realize it was but a dream, and when she awoke in the morning she was happy in spite of her trouble. After making her preparations for breakfast she consulted her watch and finding she had some time to spare, went into the garden. The sun had just risen, to shed its golden light on nature's broad expanse; the birds in drooping branches were warbling sweet notes of welcome; the morning glory and sunflower had already turned their faces eastward to welcome the coming day; the dew sparkled on every leaf and flower; the roses drooped in rich magnificence and pansies seemed to vie with them for beauty's palm; the pink verbena and even hollyhock seemed to look their very best, and Rebecca stood for a long time entranced by this wonderful display of God's great goodness; finally her heart overflowed and she sank to the earth and thanked God for his wonderful goodness.

After breakfast Mr. Goldburg went as usual to his office. There was no rest for him; Sunday was often his busiest day.

Rebecca and her mother went to church and the subject was, "Suffering in this world that we may inherit glory hereafter." The ideas presented by their new pastor interested them very much, for he was a man far in advance of his creed.

On reaching home the place seemed to be enshrouded in gloom. A family storm was imminent. Mrs. Goldburg had watched the effect of wealth on her husband's disposition too closely not to recognize in his words the day before a determination to enforce complete submission to his will. Rebecca had disregarded his wishes in rejecting proposals of marriage from several prominent millionaires and it was now evident he would use extreme measures. She knew Rebecca would resist these measures to the bitter end and would never submit to be forced into marriage with one she did not love. As a kind mother, she felt it her duty to shield her daughter from her father's arbitrary power, even though it brought about a separation, which she felt it was sure to do. From threatening remarks of her husband she had long feared something of this kind and she felt that opposition now would lead him to carry out his threat.

They were not long in the house before a servant handed Mrs. Goldburg a note from her husband, stating he had been called to Boston by telegraph and might be gone a month.

On Monday, Mrs. Goldburg's attention was called to a case of destitution on the outskirts of the city, a widow and her only daughter. Rebecca, taking with her the colored boy, visited them and found the girl suffering from a slight attack of biliousness; she gave them money and promised to send them medicine. On returning home, she found a letter awaiting her, post-marked Boston. She had great misgivings in opening it and as she suspected, it was from her would-be suitor. It was loving in the extreme. Feeling provoked at the situation, she went to her desk and replied, stating that she had regarded him simply as her father's guest and as such, he would be always welcome, but anything further, he must banish from his mind forever

Having finished the letter, she placed it in an envelope, directed it and laid it aside.

Taking another sheet of paper she wrote to the sick girl as follows:

My Dear; Take five pills at bedtime; after that one each day until you are all right, then come and see me.

· Rebecca.

This she put in an envelope, also, laid it on the

desk and set a box of pills beside it to be sent by the black boy to the sick girl on the following day; this done, she set a copy for the boy, as was her custom, called him in and set him to writing. She had already taught him to write quite well, but she kept him practicing, as she said, to keep him out of mischief; as soon as he was at work, she went to the drawing room to receive some callers.

No sooner had Rebecca gone, than the black boy dropped his pen, took the two letters out of the envelopes and after reading both, the thought struck him to play a gook joke on the Dude, as he called Mr. Goldaker, by changing the letters in the envelopes; to make it of more force, he added to Rebecca's letter to the girl—copying the hand as near as possible—"you have goldoramus; this will cure it." Then putting this in the envelope addressed to the Dude. This done he put the two letters back in the exact place he had found them.

When the company were gone Rebecca ran into the room, picked up the letters, examined the addresses to see that everything was correct, then sealing them, gave Mr. Goldaker's letter to the boy and sent him to post it at once.

When the letter had been laid on Mr. Goldaker's table, he was delighted at its early coming and hailed it as a good omen; he opened it with perfect confidence of having his love returned; but what must have been his surprise when he read:

My Dear; Take five pills at bedtime; after that one each day until you are all right, then come and see me; you have goldoramus, this will cure it. Rebecca.

As he had boasted about the letter that he would receive from Bopeep, from the heiress there, his two companions in the office, were watching him and expected he would read to them extracts, at least, of its expressions of love; but on the contrary, he hastily put it out of sight, and not a word or thought did he divulge.

That night, when alone in his room, he re-read the letter, studying it carefully; then resolved to do a little nice detective work. The first thing to be ascertained was the meaning of goldoramus; he could not find the word and concluded she must have a vocabulary of her own. As luck would have it there was a woman at this time cooking in the Goldburg household that had worked in his father's family for many years, so he wrote to her as follows:

MY DEAR MRS. STRAW: Please burn this letter and keep it all a secret. What I want you to do is to find out what is the meaning of the word goldoramus and let me know. See what dictionary the folks use and then find the word.   ————————

As soon as Mrs. Straw read the word it occurred to her that she had heard the black boy use it often, so she called him and asked what he meant by goldoramus?

"Don't you know what dat means?" said the boy.

'No," said the woman, "do you?"

"To be cors' I doz. Missus Becca says when a man wants all de gole das in de world, and den wants to lend it to de people to use for money and den wants a mortgage on all de property dar is on de earth, den wants people to pay him ten per cent intrust and den in ten years heel have all his gold back and close all de mortgages and take all de property, den wants de people to borrow de gole again to pay rent wid and so on, and so on, and so on, den Missus Becca says dat man hab got a disease and it am called goldoramus cause its caused by gold and is bery hard to cure. '

This was lucky and Mrs. Straw took down the statement, word for word, and sent it to the millionaire.

Mr. Goldaker had hoped that it might be that some one had sent the letter to him for a trick, but on receipt of this he gave that theory up. He was not yet willing however to give up the hope of getting hold of so large an estate, so he resolved to await developments.

CHAPTER XVIII.

THE expedition from Mr. Brown's attracted great attention in the villages they passed through, and being with Frank, whose name had been handed from tongue to tongue throughout the whole country, they were made to feel welcome everywhere, and on reaching Kiyongo the natives turned out enmasse to give them welcome.

The King offered them quarters in the village, but as they were well provided with tents it was decided to continue on to the old military post and there establish a permanent camp.

On arriving at the place they were soon comfortably fixed and Mr. Baxter's skill soon came in play in laying off the grounds. The greatest activity prevailed but Baxter, Coy and Saunders were not so busy but what they found time to lay plans for future operations.

Mr. Coy who had been thoroughly schooled in the way the bankers and money sharks had robbed the American people and gobbled up the property of a vast continent in a very few years, said to his two companions, Baxter and Saunders, "the first thing to do is to run a few base lines, map the country and try and get a grant; now is the time to get it, before these people learn its value."

It might be well to mention here that Frank had never confided in any one concerning his plans except Mr. Lincoln and Mr. Jefferson, and as he had by this time learned to talk the native language there was no interpreter with the expedition except those under his immediate control and they were not allowed to give any information in regard to the mines or to the gold. He had daily conference with the King, also with Lincoln and Jefferson, in whom he had learned to have implicit confidence, and it was finally decided to call a convention of the Kings to be assembled two months from that time, and that during the interval they were to secure the services of Mr. Baxter to look out a route for a railroad to the great river. Mr. Lincoln was to go in charge of the expedition, and Frank and Mr. Jefferson were to remain behind and put up a building. It was decided also that the missionaries should remain in camp until the Kings assembled, when it was believed that arrangements could be made for all.

When Mr. Baxter's services were solicited as engineer to look out and make a preliminary survey of a route for a railroad to the great river, he entered into the work with the greatest enthusiasm and said that all the pay he would ask was to be comfortably furnished with suitable escorts and assistance and he would make one map for Mr. Bundy and one for himself and that a copy of all notes made should be turned over for future reference; so the expedition embarked at once, consisting of Mr. Lincoln, Baxter, Saunders and Coy, and also two of the missionaries who had volunteered their services. They were furnished with an escort of ten men, and as they shipped in canoes to the foot of the lake, an order on the King of that time was given them for provisions and pack animals; they were also furnished with an interpreter.

After this expedition had started messengers were dispatched in every direction to summon the Kings to a council to be held two months from that time.

Now that this business had been attended to, Frank was left to a consideration of home affairs. Some of the Missionaries had already called his attention to the great beauties of the place where their camp was situated and said they had been talking up the possibilities of establishing a large mission there and making it the headquarters of the whole Missionary work. It being situated on the lake would make easy communication with the different tribal kingdoms.

Frank encouraged their plans and as one of the Missionaries was a civil engineer and had an instrument along, it was arranged to lay off a town, and when the

survey was completed Frank made it known that he
intended to take a party of natives with whip saws,
crosscuts and axes and go up the river to the pineries
and get out lumber for a building and raft it down.
This idea seemed to strike a sympathetic chord among
the missionaries and they at once decided to accompany
him and, as there were plenty of canoes and men to
man them, the expedition was soon on its way.

The Missionaries were not drones but the reverse of
this; they were generally men of nerve, men of muscle
and men of brains, and now that they were out from
the thralldom of church discipline their minds were
beginning to expand, and as they were often found
reading the teachings of Christ, Frank had strong
hopes that they would eventually accept those teachings in their simplicity, in their purity, unobscured by
church creed and musty dogmas. They had enlisted
to carry Christianity to the heart of Africa, at a sacrifice of even life, if it became necessary, and if they
could be induced to lay aside their dogmas and creeds
and teach truth and justice he felt they would be a
power.

The ladies were mild, lovable, but courageous in the
work they had undertaken and ready to do anything in
their power to further the interests of their mission,
and a trip to the great forests for the purpose of
securing the much needed lumber, to them seemed
eminently proper. When once encamped among the
great pines they would breathe nature's pure, inspiring
atmosphere laden with the rich perfumes, common to
those woodlands, hold their meetings of worship at
night and assist during the day in making the camp
comfortable for those who were so busily engaged in
getting lumber to put up two buildings, one for the
new government and one for the mission school.

As soon as they returned with the lumber it was
stacked up for drying. A large tent was stretched and
put in readiness for the coming convention. A part of
the lumber came in good play for tables, benches, etc.,
and while the men were attending to the preliminaries
the ladies had not been idle; beneath the boughs of a

great live oak they had set a table and formed a class of boys and girls, among whom were the two interpreters, and teaching of the rudiments of the English language was commenced. In this school the natives made such rapid progress in mastering English that in less than one month fifty native families had moved to the town to give their children a chance to attend the school. The natives had never seen as yet anything of the whites but kindness, justice and protection and they had learned to look on them as a species of good spirit.

A few days before the appointed time for the convention the Kings began to drop in; some came in canoes, others with burros, and the surveyors' expedition also returned on time, having gathered information from which a very accurate map of that part of the country could be made, and it was found that the most practicable route for a railroad from the river to the lake would be about one hundred miles.

When the time arrived for the convention there were thirty of the Kings on the ground and it was agreed that they, with all the whites were to have equal voice in the convention; the assistance of the ladies was solicited but they all declined.

On the day appointed, the convention came to order by calling Mr. Bundy to the chair and Mr. Lincoln as secretary. The object of the meeting was then stated and after prayer by Mr. Taylor, one of the missionaries, the convention was declared ready for business.

On motion of Mr. Jefferson, a committee of three was appointed by the chair, as follows: Mr. Jefferson, Kemp and Coy to draft articles which might be debated and afterward used as a guide to frame a constitution.

An hour was then spent in hearing remarks from different members, after which the convention adjourned until nine o'clock the next day.

On the following day the convention was called to order promptly at nine o'clock, Mr. Bundy in the chair; after roll call the report of the committee was called for and Mr. Jefferson responded, stating that the committee had failed to agree, but that he had formu-

lated a few thoughts as they suggested themselves
which he would bring before the convention and such
points as appeared objectionable could be stricken out;
he then proceeded to read as follows:

RIGHTS OF MAN.

That all mankind are created free and equal, endowed
with certain inherent rights; that of worshiping God
according to the dictates of his or her own conscience,
of life, liberty and the pursuit of happiness; that by
nature all are equally entitled to the products of nature,
which are the gifts of God.

That governments are formed for the purpose of
protecting each member in all these things, and while
a solitary citizen, man, woman or child, is living
hungry or half clad, government is a failure.

That poverty, ignorance and want are more formidable enemies than invading armies, and that the greatest
object to be attained by forming government is to
prevent poverty and want and to overcome ignorance,
by wholesome education and protect life commensurate
with human happiness.

That the right to make laws belongs to the people
and should never be delegated to any man or set of
men, and no act should become law until passed by
two houses and voted upon by the people.

That air, land and water are the lawful inheritance
of all and should in no case be monopolized by any
man or set of men, individual or incorporation to the
exclusion of others except so far as may be necessary
for their own individual use, and that whenever the
use of land is discontinued for two years it shall revert
to government and become public domain.

That the right of property must ever remain sacred,
and be protected by such inheritance laws as will forever prevent an aggregation of property or wealth in
the hands of a few, and the strong arm of the Republic
should be thrown around the family and its home.

- That to secure the right of property among the people
it is hereby declared to be one of the fundamental
principles of this government that no man, woman,
child or association shall in any way inherit more than

$100,000 of money or property, and if any man, woman or child sell or transfer property to one of his lawful heirs, at the death of the giver, the same amount shall be considered an inheritance and all above $100,000 shall revert to the government.

That the experience of nations has demonstrated beyond doubt that wealth is power, and when concentrated in the hands of a few becomes dangerous to the existence of good government, and it is therefore declared to be the policy of our people to levy an income tax that will prevent any man's income from exceeding $10,000 per year.

That all property or money belonging to any man, woman or association above $100,000 shall be considered a surplus and his or their right to hold the same shall only exist during the life of the holder, and then in default of heirs revert to the government.

That history teaches from time immemorial, clans and sects have been a prominent factor in the way of human progress; that political parties being in a direct line of descent from these clans are looked upon as being dangerous to the honest exercise of good government, and it is the policy of this government that they be prohibited by law.

That the competition in the civilized world and particularly in the United States between joint stock companies and private enterprise has proved beyond all question or doubt that incorporated joint stock companies thoroughly and systematically organized are the strongest and most economic method of doing business, yet developed. It is therefore declared to be the policy of this government that all business where a working capital of over $100,000 is required may be done by an incorporated company, organized after the form herein prescribed.

That it is the sense of this convention that the constitution of the United States of America contains the best formulated rules and principles for the guidance of good government yet invented and that it should be consulted extensively in framing our constitution.

That money is not property but a means of transferring property, that its value consists in the ability of the holder to exchange it for property; it is a note of credit with the government at its back; it represents the confidence of the people in the ability of the government to perform its functions, and as the people are the government it represents the confidence we have in ourselves.

That silver may be used for coins ranging from ten cents to one dollar, their weight regulated for convenience without regard to cost of material.

That to make money of gold or any other substance, where the value of the substance is liable to fluctuate and where the amount in existence is limited to the chance of finding, is an error of the past simply because money should only be limited to the necessities arising for its use. It is therefore declared to be the policy of this government in order to foster and encourage mining, that all surplus gold, silver, copper and lead be bought up, run into bars convenient for handling and kept for future use or foreign trade.

That in order to supply the people with money and a safe place of deposit, government should provide sub-treasuries where the business of the place will warrant it.

That in organizing our government it should have a department for the purpose of organizing and controlling joint stock companies. This department should be sub-divided as follows: Railroad and transportation department; Telegraph and news gathering department; Ship building department; Steamboat and navigation department; Commercial department; Manufacturing department; Mining department, and so on throughout every branch of business.

METHOD OF ORGANIZING COMPANIES.

In any town or village where a wholesale store becomes necessary, requiring a capital of $100,000 or over, a mass meeting may be called and resolutions adopted setting forth the necessities of such an institution; the report of this meeting should be published in all local papers for at least one month prior to election and then be voted on.

The officers necessary to run a wholesale store of this kind should consist of president, secretary and general manager; suitable persons to fill these places should be elected and anybody become a candidate by publishing a card to that effect. The persons elected as officers should lay a report of all the proceedings before the chief of department, who would lay the same before Congress, and when approved by that body, it would be returned to the chief of department, who would grant commissions to the officers and cause stock on the company to be struck in ten dollar shares, to the amount of the capital required; the same amount in full legal tender money of the government, together with the stock, be sent to the sub-treasury nearest the place of business, the money to be subject to the order of the president of the company and the stock kept on sale. All joint stock companies should be organized in the same or similar manner.

Railroads, steamboat lines, telegraphs, manufactories, in fact, every enterprise where $100,000 or over is required, should be organized and operated on the same general principle; the government furnishes the money and the people do the work; keeping it in mind, that money is only a means to facilitate business transactions.

That money is not capital—labor is capital; and money is a measure that enables capital to operate. We have a whole continent of fertile land; it is not capital. We have great mountains, no doubt contain-ing rich mines; that is not capital. A London banker would not give ten cents for this whole continent without labor; therefore we conclude that labor is capital and money a means—nothing more—and for a government to fail to provide a sufficient amount of money to keep every man at work, is a crime against man and a crime against God.

All large business being run on the same general principle, it naturally follows that the sub-treasury will be constantly well supplied with stock of all kinds and all the savings of the country will pass back into the treasury in exchange for stock.

The officers of a company are elected by the people but receive their commissions from the chief of the department, who may at any time remove them for cause, and appoint others, subject to the approval of the Senate.

Railroads being built on the same general plan—for increase of road—an increase of stock should also be issued and kept on sale.

All joint stock business should be so regulated that it will pay seven per cent on stock; five per cent of this to be paid to the stockholder and the remainder retained by the government to create a fund, from which a full dividend and arrearages will be paid on all stock of companies that have run behind; the balance to be turned into the treasury.

Should there be found a fund in the treasury increasing from this and other sources that threatens to so far contract the currency as to depress business, then fares and freights may be reduced and public work commenced that will keep the money in circulation.

Newspapers, publishing houses, and colleges may be run on the same general, joint stock plan.

That it shall be the business of every sub-treasury to keep stock constantly on hand and exchange the same for money or buy stock at its face value at any and all times.

That it shall be the duty of Congress to fix the rate of all wages for all joint-stock companies and it should be fixed, as nearly as possible, after the following plan: Take the price of good board and lodging for one day and multiply by four; that should constitute a days's wages.

Should it occur at any time that there are more men in the country than can get work, government should commence public work at once that will furnish employment for every man and passes should be given over all the roads to the work.

- That government should have a detective system, with representatives in every city, town and hamlet and all branches of business be so thoroughly and systematically guarded as to remove all possibility of a practice of the famous knock-down system so common in the United States of America.

When Mr. Jefferson finished, a profound silence reigned; the natives occupied seats on one side of the hall, the whites on the other; it was evident from the commencement of reading that the articles would find but little favor among the white members outside of Lincoln, Jefferson and Bundy; but these men felt that a force was about to be put in motion that no hand could stay or control; and its effect, good or bad, upon the progress of mankind, would depend largely upon what kind of force it was.

"The human family," said Mr. Jefferson, "are constantly looking for a guiding star. Our government must be that star; its brilliancy will depend upon its power for the good of all. As we approach a higher plane of civilization, man's brilliancy must depend upon intellect and honesty of purpose and not, as now, upon wealth, chicanery and show. Classes must fade and pass away; creeds and dogmas be forever destroyed; religion simplified to the Commandments and Golden Rule. These are now covered up in the fog of creeds, dogmas and superstitions. Churches must be shorn of their money making practices by destroying the power of gold, and God's blessing be meted out to all and His holy light shine upon mankind in all its brilliancy and splendor."

The reader will remember that Coy and Saunders were bank defaulters and had their gold buried, as gold always is when most needed, only waiting for legislation to give it value. They had been schooled in the methods by which great countries had been and were being controlled by bankers through the use of gold. Mr. Baxter was to them a willing tool and would share largely in their profits, if favorable legislation could be secured; at present the only value their gold had was in the superstitious idea of the white men that its use as money was among the fixed principles of government which could not be altered.

They had talked the matter over the night before and formulated a plan to start a National Bank, and as they had all the money in the country, they would keep it in reserve and loan the new government $600,000 of good, sound, paper money, based on their $200,000 in gold.

For this $600,000 loan to the new government they would take bonds with interest payable semi-annually; then they would deposit these bonds and be allowed by law, to issue ninety per cent of the amount in good, honest paper money, secured by the bonds, and loan it to the people; when that money was all gone, they could get a law passed, allowing them to deposit their notes and securities and issue another ninety per cent on them, and so keep on, and not only supply the government with all the money needed, but keep the people well supplied and at a very reasonable interest. "This plan," said Saunders, "is based upon true principles of banking, and any one familiar with banks and banking, will know it is not unreasonable. We have the gold to base our money on and of course it will be sound currency; should any man doubt our ability to furnish all the money required for the whole country, let him look at the Bank of England; it started less than two centuries ago, with a handful of gold and a few government securities and upon this same plan, it has loaned money to the government until the government debt became so great, that the thought of ever paying it, has long since been abandoned and the people have settled down to the idea that they must pay interest as long as the government lasts. So-called wise statesmen are proclaiming the doctrine that a government debt is a government blessing."

Mr. Coy said, "the United States had established the same system of banking and under its bracing influence, the country is prospering immensely; millionaires are springing up all over the country and the wealthy classes would soon be as permanently recognized as in England."

The course pursued by these men will not cause surprise when the reader remembers the fact that the bankers of other countries fought the plan of govern-

ment issuing and controlling the money in the interest
of the people. Having this grand money making
scheme already planned, they were prepared to bring it
before the great convention.

The Missionaries, as has been stated, were men of
brains but their reasoning faculties had been dulled by
swallowing dogmas; now that they had mastered the
art of believing the most absurd theories, without
evidence, they were satisfied to simply teach and
preach and left others to do the work. They looked
upon bankers as a peculiar kind of being whom God
had, for some mysterious reason, designed to be
millionaires and then forgot to mention it in His book;
that they were endowed with the special faculty of
understanding finances; so much so, that even Congressmen allowed them to dictate laws, and Presidents
made them their first counselors. To form a government and run it without bankers, was something
unprecedented, and when they learned that Coy and
Saunders were not only bankers, schooled in the art,
but that they actually had the gold in hand to base
their business upon, they felt sure God had sent them
there for the express purpose of furnishing the new
government with money; they looked upon Mr. Jefferson as a kind of political heretic and were likely to
oppose his extreme measures.

President Bundy had watched the course of things
and being fully impressed with the importance of
discussions in such matters, stated that the document
was before the house and must be disposed of.

A motion was then made by Mr. Coy to lay it on the
table and that a copy of the Constitution of the United
States be taken up by sections, and adopted or rejected
by vote. Mr. Coy spoke in favor of the motion and
branded the articles as a mass of absurdities and its
author as a political fanatic or an escaped Kansas-
calamity-howler; when he had finished, Mr. Jefferson
explained at some length that concentrated wealth had
been the oppressor of mankind from time immemorial;
rivers of blood had been poured out to satisfy man's
greed; it was not confined to any particular country or

people, but in all countries and in every age, the concentration of wealth had often become a power stronger than government itself. In the United States, said he, unbridled greed has concentrated property so rapidly, that the most intelligent, the most industrious people the world has ever produced, are being reduced to a state of penury, if not into absolute slavery.

"No good," said he, "ever came to the masses from the concentration of wealth. Wherever millionaires exist, paupers must also be found. Suppose the average wealth per capita is $500; it will take two thousand paupers to make one millionaire; or in other words, a man will have to rob two thousand men to become a millionaire, for it is a demonstrated fact that no man can begin with $500 and by legitimate business become a millionaire in a natural lifetime; therefore every man who accumulates $1,000,000 in his lifetime is as much a robber as a Younger or a James.

"But suppose a man accumulates $100,000,000, how many men has he robbed, and how many families have lost their homes? Two thousand paupers for each million would reach the immense sum of 200,000 men made poor and their families turned into the street or forced to pay rent, with no home to beautify, no place to call their own, and what have we gained by this wholesale devastation? Simply this, the right of one man to domineer over others and make a display of his ill gotten gains. Is this right? The American who thinks so should kiss his half-starved wife and babies on election morning, give them a picture of the millionaire in his castle, with his liveried servants, his palace car, his yacht, his coach and four, and gold galore; yes, give her this beautiful picture cut from a goldbug paper, and tell her how rich and prosperous our country is; then go to the polls and vote for these good old parties and politicians who have by their legislation brought about this state of things.

"A few short years ago, nature's God presented the American people with a whole continent of virgin soil and mountains containing mines of every description. The people who were living under the oppressive laws

of monetary despotism in the old world, escaped from
their thralldom and went to the United States for
homes. After the close of the war, so large a quantity
of money had been turned loose that the people fairly
jumped for joy. Vast forests were cleared; prairies
were broken up, new homes made and old ones
beautified. Laborers came and went, singing, "Uncle
Sam is rich enough to give us all a farm." The great
continent belonged to the people and all they asked
was a market for their surplus production—such as
corn, wheat, barley, bacon, rice, cotton, tobacco; we
had immense forests of valuable timber, and twelve
states and territories producing fabulous amounts of
gold, silver and copper.

"The people owned all this vast wealth at this time
and every man and woman found profitable employment
according to their strength and ability. All were happy
and life was a pleasure.

"Take a present look at that vast country—who
owns it and what gave they for its wealth?

"Have the farmers produced a surplus? Yes.
It can only be estimated by billions. What was done
with it? Sold to foreign countries. The farmers must
be getting rich! No, they are getting poorer all the
time. Where have all these billions of surplus products
gone? The great statesmen say it was over-production
that made this disastrous condition of affairs. Was the
surplus destroyed? No, it was sold. Where is the
money? Don't know. Millionaires have sprung up
on every hand, but their transactions are all legal, then
they must be getting the benefit of the farmer's toil
legally. That makes the farmer a slave.

"But how about the gold and silver miners? They
must have millions piled up. No, there is not enough
gold in the country to pay the interest on the entire
indebtedness to foreign countries for ten years. What
has become of the vast product of gold, silver and
copper? Gone to England, I presume. Then England
must owe the United States a large sum. No, the
United States owes England. What has England
given the United States for this vast quantity of gold

and silver and other productions? The only thing I can think of is interest and confidence. Their interest is always due and when they want an act of Congress passed in their behalf, they lose confidence, and in order to gain that confidence, the exception was put on the greenback; as time rolled on they lost confidence again, and to regain it the strengthening act had to be passed, by which the national debt was doubled at one foul stroke. But even this did not fully restore confidence, and in order to complete the job the national money had to be withdrawn and burned to increase the interest bearing debt and compel the people to borrow British gold to do business with.

"All this was done for confidence. If some of our great mathematicians would figure this out and show just how much it has cost the American people to buy British confidence, it would form an interesting chapter in political economy.

"Now in all candor I would ask where is this vein of unbridled accumulation to end? Millionaires have already become so powerful that they control the law-making power, and as greed has no limit, they will continue their legal robbery until the many will be even worse off than slaves and the few will be wasting property in vain display. Is this government by the people, of the people, and for the people? If so, then we might well say, God pity the people.

"Here we have a vast continent similar to that of the United States; when it is known that there is protection here and homes for all, the most intelligent and industrious people of that country will rush from there by the millions to secure those homes. Will bankers come? Not one. They would not give you ten cents for all these rich farming lands until people come here and want them. Then they will send their money here and buy up extensive tracts of land and let them lie idle, fenced by statute law. Is it right for a man to control the good things of earth and neither use them himself nor let others use them? No one will assert that an act of this kind is for the good of the masses.

"It has been shown that to make one millionaire, you must take the whole property of two thousand people. The man who makes the million gives nothing in return but poverty; if he did, he would not have made that amount but simply traded for it. It therefore follows that for every million dollars which Gould, the Astors, Vanderbilts or any other man has made in the United States since the war, two thousand men have been robbed of all they had. Will any one tell me that laws that make this possible are for the good of the people?

"We are now about to organize a government that will control the destinies of millions; shall it be a monarchy or republic? Laying aside all rules, I want every man favoring a republic to hold up his hand."

All looked at Mr. Bundy and as they thought of the power he wielded among the natives, all held up their hands simultaneously.

"A Republic it shall be, and the question arises, what kind of Republic? Do we want a repetition of what has occurred in the United States in the matter of concentrating wealth in the hands of a few?"

The missionaries all said, no.

"Shall our legislation be for the many or the few?"

All said, for the many.

"Then what I want is for some man to suggest a law that will hold land beyond the reach of bankers, gold-gamblers and speculators. I have given you the best thought I had on that subject. As soon as our government is formed it will own all the land except such as is reserved for the different tribes. Whenever the government commences selling land, the door will be open to money-sharks, land speculators, and mortgage-fiends. I know of but one way to prevent land from passing into the hands of speculators and that is, for government to make no sale of it at all.

"The land should ever remain the property of the government and its use should be given to the people by a law similar to the pre-emption law of the United States, allowing a man the privilege of going on to any piece of vacant land and by filing on the same, hold it as long as he keeps it in use, with the privilege of selling his possessory title or, at his death, leave it to such of his heirs as choose to occupy it; but when abandoned for two years, to revert to government.

"Our money should be made by the government, a full legal tender, its value regulated without regard to cost of material of which it is made, and as land is the most valuable and substantial of all property it alone should form the base for our circulating medium. Gold should never be used for money; because when it wears out the people who issued it through their government will lose the full per cent of the wear; it costs too much; it is limited in quantity and the government could not regulate the volume of currency with a limited amount of material. Silver should be used as money, coined in sums of from ten cents to one dollar; its weight, also size, regulated for convenience without regard to cost of material; if it is worth as much for bullion as for money, it is liable to be used by individuals, thus taking it from circulation, to the injury of trade.

"It may be said that a man could not raise money on his land by mortgaging it on a possessory title, but that is just what we want to prevent. The mortgage system has been one of the prime factors in building up in the United States a powerful land monopoly, and the law embraced in these propositions is intended to dispense with the cause which makes borrowing necessary, by having enough money in circulation to permit the doing of business on a spot cash system and abolish all, laws for the collection of debt, except for labor performed. That there are well defined causes for men running in debt is apparent; principal among these is scarcity of money and scarcity of work. Under the system proposed, these two wants are overcome; by limiting money—not to the chance of production of gold, but to the amount necessary to supply every demand. As the stock representing the business of the country will soon be absorbed by the savings of the people, it can be turned into money whenever a stringency occurs; and as government will be compelled to give every idle man employment, in order to keep the money in circulation and prevent it from accumulating in the treasury from the income tax and the twenty per cent returned on all business stock, as it now does in the great money centers of Britain and the United States, it necessarily follows that any man can get work; hence there will be no occasion for borrowing.

"There never has been nor ever will be a time when there is no public work that can be done to improve and beautify a country, and now that machinery has displaced so many men, they should be given work at building roads, reservoirs, and canals, reclaiming deserts, draining swamps, terracing mountains and making room for coming population. No one will question that the system proposed in these articles will so flood the money into the treasury as not only to remove all necessity for collecting taxes, but that the government will be actually compelled to carry on extensive works in order to keep its money in circulation. Even this is not the only benefit to be derived; our financial and banking system will be so simplified that a school boy can understand it. There will be but one kind of money and the business of the subtreasury will be to pay out money for stock, and exchange stock for money, but in no case make loans.

"When the stock shall have been all absorbed, then deposits may be received, the money to lay in the treasury until called for. In a short time the average amount of money laying in the vaults from this source, will be known and will be taken into consideration in making appropriations for public works.

"To make gold the base of all money, is an absurdity; because its value must fluctuate according to chance of production. To make money of two different substances, gold and silver, to be made and kept at the same intrinsic value, is simply impossible; because the value of each is constantly changing, by the wear of the coin and by the amount of production; therefore when a public man advocates giving money an intrinsic value, his motive should be closely scrutinized.

"With no law for the collection of debt, and abstract

titles being done away with, the business in these departments of law will be largely reduced.

"I will now say one word about inheritance and accumulation of wealth. If we would protect ourselves and leave a heritage for posterity, we should throw such safeguards around our government as will prevent all danger of its being in the future obstructed in its work by a power greater than itself.

The right of governments to regulate inheritance has never been disputed and has been exercised in all civilized countries; it therefore only becomes a question of the good of the whole people. Let us honestly and candidly try to see what will be best for the whole people.

"A good way to prevent theft, we believe, would be to prevent the man who would steal, from keeping, selling or controlling the goods after they were stolen; if this could be done, theft would become a thing of the past. If we can prevent individuals from keeping and controlling goods above a competency, then the sharp practice by which unscrupulous men obtain possession of these goods would not come in play and honest men would avoid the danger of being robbed by some money making scheme to which they are entire strangers. That there should be a limit to man's control of property is plain. Fire in a wooden house without a stove or other safeguard would be no more destructive to the goods of the house than is unlimited control of wealth by a single individual to the good results of a government. That the possession of money or property above your need is power, no one will deny, and in bad hands becomes an enemy to society.

"As government puts all its surplus into public improvements for the benefit of all, its accumulations are limited. Therefore if a man by chicanery and sharp practice that evades the law, succeeds in getting possession of a large amount of wealth, that no more belongs to him than if stolen, it will roll on from son to son, constantly increasing and drawing unto itself, until it absorbs every interest, turns families from their homes and finally becomes stronger than government,

controls legislation in its own behalf, making good
government impossible.

"Would it not be well while we limit our own accumulation as a whole in government, that we give that
government a fair chance for its life by limiting the
holdings of individuals to their need also? When
property is fairly distributed the people will take care
of themselves, but when property is concentrated in
the hands of heartless syndicates and corporations it
becomes an enemy to man and requires armies to
defend it.   As it is universally conceded that all governments have a right to regulate inheritance it becomes
only a question of policy on the part of the government and justice to every citizen of that government.
Then who would suffer by it? Very few, if any; there
are very few men we must remember, who inherit over
$100,000.   Did any of you gentlemen ever inherit that
amount?   Did any of your friends ever?   If so they
ceased to be your friend, no doubt, soon after.   The
men who inherit over $100,000 are very few, I take it,
in comparison to the masses.   But few as they are,
would even they suffer? $100,000 at five per cent
interest gives a man the net sum of $5,000 per year.
Suppose a man could hardly make a living; would that
small sum help him out any?   But suppose he was a
man of average intelligence, would not he make
$300,000 of that in the course of a life time?   Figure
on it and see if you don't think you could support a
family and give all your children a good start in the
world.   If a man were of any account and his children
a fair average could they not live in luxury?

"True they would not have ten, fifteen or twenty
thousand dollars to bet on every prize-fight or horse-
race, nor could they form syndicates and control legislation, but they would be the prosperous people of the
land and in point of intellect, religion and good morals
they would be far superior to our present aristocracy
and far more numerous.   Then how can you make it
appear that these men suffer?   You take not one thing
from them, you only deprive them of the power of
getting what they never earned and does not belong to

them. If a man at death has more than $100,000 for each of his heirs you can depend upon it he did not get it by any fair means; it has been drawn from the people in some underhanded way and should be returned to them through the government and so prevent danger of further accumulation. Now who suffers and who is wronged by this law?

"We see that a family is a government on a small scale. The Astor family have adopted this same system by leaving a competency to the majority and the bulk of the property to one. The Vanderbilts have followed up the same plan and so did J. Gould; they have given the world an example in inheritance worthy of consideration. England gives all to the oldest son.

"Did these men commit a wrong toward their own children by putting the majority off with a competency? If not then why does not the government step in and say these heirs shall share equally and the residue be inherited by the government which has protected their property and made it possible to accumulate so large a sum, and thus say to the magnate, the remainder of your vast property shall go back among the people from whom it has been drawn by extortion and sharp practice. Would such a law as this be good for the whole people? If so it is what our government by the people and for the people, implies.

"These truths seem to me to be self evident, that when a people organize themselves into a government and limit the power to accumulate wealth, and at the same time allow individuals and corporations to increase their holdings without check or limit, the result must surely follow that individual and corporate power will eventually predominate and the people and government be reduced to poverty and want.

"No long hours and hard work can fill their larder when one-third of the people are employed by syndicates and bankers in collecting rents and interest, the other one-third in protecting their vast estates and the government poverty-stricken, in debt and become a willing tool of oppression; we have history in the United States proving these conclusions not only to be logical, but true principles of philosophy, as unerring as the needle to the Mariner.

"Our system of doing all the heavy business of the country by stock companies has been so thoroughly tried in the United States and other countries, that there remains no doubt of its efficacy; but the control of the companies by government, when the stock is in the hands of banks and syndicates, has been an absolute failure; they over-run all law.

"By the proposed method the company is entirely under control of the government and the stock will be among the people; every working girl can invest her small earnings in stock and it will form a sort of floating paper, representing every large interest in the whole country and its good effects in absorbing the savings of the country can hardly be estimated; while the mild working of the inheritance law will prevent its being centralized.

"The next thing in our propositions is an article prohibiting the formation of political parties; of course it will be left to the law to define what political parties are. What we wish to prevent is a consolidated organization, with its representatives in every town, county and precinct, who work for the party for pay and promise of spoils, with newspapers to slander, falsify and misrepresent, in order to keep up animosity among neighbors and control the party vote. The principal agitators in these elections are generally well paid and backed up by concentrated party wealth which is being constantly augmented by bribe money and tax levied upon those in office.

"How often have we seen men, and even whole communities, worked into fever heat of passion, ready to cut each other's throat, and all over a political sham battle between parties. One day after the election all would be as quiet as a May morning. I find no language to express my contempt for this abominable system. It ought to be abolished.

"Under this order of things a method of selecting proper persons for office would certainly be necessary;

but it seems to me that the good sense of the people, if not deceived by party falsehood, or controlled by party discipline, would be equal to the emergency; and it would also appear that under our new business system, money and property would be so well distributed, newspapers become so numerous, and circulation of news so very cheap, with government control and unlimited capital, that a knowledge of our leading men would be as common as that of our next door neighbor. We believe that any man should have the privilege of bringing his name or that of a friend before the people, for any office, by simply publishing a card, and if conventions are held for nominating candidates they should be called from the people, no permanent organization maintained.

"When a man seeks an office on the strength of party service or of having belonged to some party for forty years, it too often happens that he has no other merit. While I regard this plan as something of an experiment, I believe that permanent parties can and should be abolished.

"We come now to the sub-treasury taking the place of the national bank. We have many very good reasons for making this change. In looking over the financial history of England and the United States, we find that the gold gamblers have many different methods of plying their gold game and this national banking system is the hub of the great wheel that rolls on to the tune of the 'gamblers win and the gentlemen lose,' and as we are to do away with the game, we will not need the wheel. We find that for honest business purposes the treasury answers every purpose; beside, it will give employment to a few men and thus help to keep the money, which will be so constantly flowing into the treasury from the income tax and two per cent on government business stock, in circulation. It is invested with every power that a bank could have, except to break and rob the depositors; of course it will be a failure on that point, but we should be willing to forego some of these blessings in order to expel from the land these two great political or financial ghosts known in the United States as want of confidence and over-production.

"For some years these monsters have run rampant in the United States, carried every election, impoverished the people, robbed families of their homes and made countless millions mourn.

"While we find great warehouses bursting with grain, others with manufactured goods, the people cry out for bread and clothes, but the cruel specter, over-production, says no. Then the people cry for money or for work and the other ghost looms up and says, your money is all buried; 'tis want of confidence. 'O consistency thou art a jewel.'

"One other thing I will call your attention to, then I am done; that is the detective system; it too has been tried in the United States where it has been demonstrated to be a wonderful power for good but it, like the corporations has also demonstrated that such power should be in the hands of government, not individuals.

"I shall now leave the matter with you, believing the good sense of those interested will vote down the proposition to table these articles."

As no one seemed inclined to discuss the matter further, it came to a vote and strange to say, with the exception of Lincoln and Jefferson, the whites were unanimously in favor of tabling the propositions and adopting the constitution of the United States, pure and simple, but the natives voted solid the other way, which defeated the motion.

A motion was made and carried to adjourn till next day; this motion was made by Coy in order that the gold men might work up some new scheme to defeat the propositions.

After the adjournment, Saunders, Coy and Baxter retired to their tent which they had isolated from the others as men who seek to control and enslave others by the use of gold, generally do. Saunders was first to break the silence. "Gentlemen," said he, "is that not enough to break a man all up? If I believed in a God I would think He was at work among these black devils; only think of it, they understood not one word still they voted solid."

"I wish I had the powers of hell for a little while," said Coy, "I would teach the black devils some sense; but 'tis no use, we have to work according to our strength. It looks pretty hard to risk life and liberty for a little gold and then when you get into a safe place, beyond all danger and reach of law, with the finest chance in the world to become a millionaire, to have your plans all thwarted by an old Kansas calamity-howler, especially when he has all the white men on his own side. I am not going to stand it without a fight; I would like to have a shot at that old crank with my Winchester; I think the talk about paper money would soon be settled."

"Well, I'll tell you," said Saunders, "I don't care how much paper money they have; in fact I rather like the plan, but we must have it based on gold."

"If they would only do with us," said Coy, "as the United States government did with Stanford, Huntington & Co., give us, for instance, half of the land on a strip of eighty miles wide clear across the continent, then guarantee bonds enough to build the road; as soon as this government is formed and a great continent like this thrown open to the world, we could get money on the bonds. This would work fine. I know just how Stanford and Huntington worked it and they came out millionaires, and Uncle Sam got left."

"Yes," said Saunders, "that would be pretty good, but what we want is a National Bank. You see if we get the bank we will have money to work the government with, and we can soon secure legislation and get hold of all kinds of securities, sell them in London, and if we don't beat the record of such men as Stanford, Huntington, Gould, and in fact all the millionaires of the United States with our $200,000, then we are no good. I think we are perfectly safe in loaning the government our paper to the extent of $600,000 and more, if they want it, all at a good round interest; after that it won't take long to get a Banking act passed and deposit our bonds and loan another lot of paper money; then we can lend our paper money to the government, loan the government money to the people, and after a while we will lose confidence and have them pass a Strengthening act paying the bonds all in gold. But then it is no use to speculate until the bloody plan this man has drawn up has been knocked out. If it goes we will have to sell our gold, or have it shipped back to the states for goods, when it would probably furnish some fly detective a very nice clue—no, we must silence this fanatic."

Then they discussed the plan of assassination but it was objected to on the ground of danger from the vengeance of the president, and to assassinate the two would raise the natives and they would all be killed. It had been reported that Gen. Summerville was on his way back and would arrive next day; he was an entire stranger to the whole party, but they resolved to see him before he met Bundy, Lincoln and Jefferson and get him interested in a National banking scheme and thereby secure his influence in opposition to what they denounced as fanaticism.

After supper they all went up town and there learned that Gen. Summerville was encamped within seven miles of town and would come on the next morning. They decided to meet him in camp and accordingly ordered their animals saddled and rode out, reaching the camp before night. Gen. Summervlile received them with great warmth; it had been a long time since he had seen a white man and he felt sincerely glad to see them, and felt complimented at receiving so much courtesy.

After a general round of conversation, Mr. Saunders informed the General of what had been done in the convention and great as was the opportunity of accomplishing so much, it seemed about to be lost by the obstinacy of a political crank. He further informed the General that he and his companions represented great wealth; that they were bankers and had brought with them an immense sum of gold coin for the express purpose of supplying the new government with the sinews of war. "Unless the Republic is organized on

true and tried principles," said he, "our assistance will
be lost; unless we have confidence, we can not let
money loose. We are ready to assist the enterprise by
furnishing all the money that will be needed, but we
must have confidence, and the only way the movers in
this enterprise can gain our confidence is to plant
their government on true principles of law—the banking law of the United States or that of Britain, has
been tried and proved. If that system is adopted we
can furnish all the money necessary but all notes,
bonds and obligations must be made payable in gold
and whenever a constitution like that of the United
States is adopted, banking laws passed and a warranted
title to land property, then we stand ready to furnish
this government with our bank notes, redeemable on
sight, to the extent of $600,000 at 7 per cent, and we
will keep $200,000 in gold constantly on hand for the
redemption of these notes; there will be no trouble
about money if we only have confidence.

"Another thing, if we give good titles to land and
have an approved banking system it will induce
emigration and create such confidence among the money
kings of England, that they will have a money-loan
office in every town and village; of course we will have
good times, but we must have confidence. In addition
to all this, as soon as we are organized and an act
passed granting us lands and guaranteeing bonds we
build a railroad from the great river to the lake and
create a regular boom; we can give a mortgage on the
land for money in England and exchange the bonds in
the same way; thus build the road and let the sale of
the land pay the debt. This is no idle dream; it is a
style of doing business invented in the United States
and you know how it worked. Look at the Goulds,
the Vanderbilts, Astors, Stanford, Crocker and a host
of other millionaires made by these and other similar
methods, and the people there know all about it, still
they seem to stand it all right and of course it will
work here in the same way, under the same law."

The general received their communication in a
friendly manner and said he had not given the matter

much thought, not knowing the circumstances, but he would certainly do everything in his power to have the government planted on true principles of justice, as he understood them.

Mr. Saunders then stated that they had been to a good deal of expense, risk and trouble, to bring money there for the benefit of humanity, and in order to prevent anything like failure, they had all agreed, in order to secure his services in getting a constitution and laws passed, similar to those of the United States, they would give him $20,000 in gold, either English or American coin, the same to be paid over as soon as the proper legislation was secured.

To this the General only replied, "well, the fee looks to me rather large for a man who has no profession."

"True," said Coy, "but it has been claimed that a man received $500,000 for the demonetization of silver in the United States, and that he did the whole thing by a trick."

The conversation then turned on other topics and the gold men took their leave.

It was long after night when the men reached their tent and they were not feeling over-sanguine of success; the General had received all their propositions kindly but had in no way committed himself; they admitted his coolness and felt confident his influence would settle it either way, but they were not sure as to what course he would pursue; all felt shaky, but Saunders said that $20,000 would buy men of wealth in the American legislative halls and he saw no good reason why a poor devil like this, out here in the wilds of Africa, should refuse such a tempting bait and he didn't believe he would.

The following morning, the General rode into town just in time to meet Mr. Bundy, Mr. Lincoln and Mr. Jefferson on their way to the hall, and alighting, the greeting was cordial all round.

The General informed Mr. Bundy that a pack-train was on the way with over $3,000,000 in gold, the output of the mines for the last three months.

"The native workers in the mines," said he, "are

steadily increasing in numbers and the output as well.
A large proportion of those who come have families
and are making themselves comfortable homes, the
mines are equaling those of California in '49. The
coast trail to Mr. Brown's is alive with pack-trains,
arrangements for a better means of transportation will
soon be necessary and I have come down to look after
this matter."

Pres. Bundy and his companions were highly elated
at all this good news and also congratulated themselves
that the General had arrived just in time to vote upon
the adoption of the proposed plan of organization.

Mr. Jefferson handed him the document and asked
him to go with him to his room where they would not
be disturbed; they would postpone voting on it until
he could be present, as they regarded his advice and
co-operation of the utmost importance. The General
took the document and promised to be on hand but
disclaimed being entitled to any such compliment.

In consequence of the arrival they postponed coming
to order for two hours. Mr. Jefferson, before this,
felt quite certain of the adoption of his proposition,
but what stand the General would take was as much of
a sealed book to him and his colleagues as it was to
the other side of the house. The proposition embraced
new ideas that had not been thought of, much less discussed, and feeling that each and all was of the utmost
importance, they were all filled with anxiety; each felt,
too, that it would be dishonorable to try to influence
the General outside of the convention before the other
side was heard.

In this may be seen one of the grand causes of
reform coming so slowly to the front. Reforms, it may
be remembered, work always for the good of all, and
when man becomes an earnest worker in reform he
rises so high above the selfish plane that he would
disdain to use methods to carry a point which a selfish
gold-pirate would embrace and consider it a mark of
statesmanship or splendid financiering.

Soon after the convention came to order, the General
put in an appearance. After this the ball was opened

by Mr. Jefferson with a motion that the proposition be adopted; this was seconded by a native king, anxious to show his legislative ability.

It was declared to be before the house as follows: Gentlemen of the convention, you have heard the propositions; to say they are of the highest importance would, in my estimation, be too tame. I would say to you, my fellow members, that in voting upon them you are called upon to settle one of the most important questions that have ever been decided by a body of men.

It is not only a question that will decide the fate of millions who will flee from the tyrannizing, plutocratic rule of corruption and injustice in the United States and other countries, and seek homes in this great continent; but 'tis the adoption of a system of government that will in due time spread throughout the civilized world, crush the power of gold and bring joy and comfort to all mankind.

We have seen that the United States, like this country, belonged at one time to the people; the labor of those people made it vastly more valuable to man. But to-day they do not own it; you all know who does, but you don't know exactly how they got it; it is evident, however, that they gave nothing in return, for many of them had nothing to give. We all know that gold, the National Bank and speculation in land have been the prime factors in robbing the people of the United States, building up a class of aristocrats and wrecking the great Republic.

The same people, with their families, will rush into this country in solid phalanx in search of homes; with their presence and labor they will make it a vast empire of wealth. Shall they in one hundred years find the lands which they have improved belonging to unscrupulous bankers or money-sharks? Or shall the property of the country forever remain in the hands of the people who created it? These are the questions you are called upon to decide; they are now before you.

As the President took his seat, Mr. Saunders took the floor and stated that the matter had been pretty thoroughly discussed but he would like very much to hear from Gen. Summerville upon the subject. This proposition was received with general applause, and when the General came forward his reception was something grand.

Before commencing, the General cast an interested look about the hall. As he stood there, a picture of robust health, perhaps his fine figure never showed to better advantage. As the importance of his decision was plainly marked on every face, so his form and features showed that he felt himself fully equal for the occasion, and he spoke as follows:

"Mr. President and gentlemen of the convention— Oft times while camping in the forests of this vast, wild region, far away from the comforts of civilized life, living on wild meat and such vegetable food as could be gathered, sleeping on the ground, facing every storm and battling with the deadly Arabs to protect the lives of these good people; yes, often amid these trials have I felt that my fate was hard, but it pales into insignificance in comparison with what I now enjoy, in having an opportunity of voting for the adoption of a system of government that is to hold all the millions of miles of rich farming land throughout this vast continent in reserve for the sole use of man and beyond the reach of cruel land-sharks. A government that will fence by its laws against the encroachments of the money-power. A government that will build our railroads, run them and leave the money among the people. Gentlemen, vote as you will, it will be the proudest moment of my life when I cast my vote for this proposition."

This was too much for Mr. Jefferson, Lincoln and Bundy; they left their seats and in turn clasped the hand of the speaker. The Missionaries followed, and for a time the house was in a tumult of joy; the enthusiasm was so great that even the gold-gamblers were forced to come forward and acknowledge their defeat. After the feeling had partially subsided, the house once more came to order and a vote was taken in which all voted for adoption, except the three gold men, and they refrained from voting.

The proposition being disposed of, the General offered the following, which he reduced to writing:

That Secretary Lincoln be sent to New York and instructed to buy one first-class battle-ship to be used on the great river. The same to be furnished with a full crew for the year's service.

That he also order the building of one battle-ship and four cruisers, also buy six large size ocean steamers, man them and load with material and machinery for the construction of railroads, and offer such inducements for immigration as would load all the steamers with as many as they could easily and comfortably carry, in addition to freight.

That he also establish an emigrant aid society in Chicago, St. Louis and Kansas City for the purpose of assisting poor but respectable families to reach New York in time to meet our steamers as they are kept regularly running; the fare to be $100 each, but to bring them at reduced rates when they are too poor to pay that amount.

That he bring four river steamers to be used on the great river, the fleet to land as soon as possible, at some point on the shore of the great river near the terminus of the proposed railroad.

The motion being seconded, Mr. Saunders took the floor and said that the motion sounded like a burlesque. It would be impossible to buy these things without money and he knew of but one way for government to get money and that was to issue bonds and sell them to the people who had money; when it became known the kind of government to be formed, the bond would not sell for enough to pay for the printing.

This brought things to a stand still.

The General walked over to the President, talked in a low tone for a moment; then Mr. Lincoln was called and consulted, after which the General again took the floor and said:

"It now becomes necessary that I explain that the want of money will be no obstacle in the way of carrying out the provisions of this proposition. If this country was full of money, it would not be good in a foreign country; even if our money were made of gold, it would have to be sold by weight as a commodity; our stamp would add nothing to its value. It simply becomes a question as to whether we have anything to ship that is ready sale; fortunately we have about $15,000,000 of gold. It is of no earthly value to us and the sooner we exchange it for something that is, the better it will be."

This was a stunner, but the motion soon passed and the meeting adjourned till the following day.

After adjournment it was evident that the presence of so much gold had thrown the white men into a perfect frenzy of excitement; the President, Secretary, General and Mr. Jefferson had retired to their quarters. The remainder of the white population gathered around their usual loafing places and the whole talk was about that gold.

The world probably never had a better illustration of the force of early education.

The child who is raised to believe in Mohammed will have no other religion; if raised a Jew, he will forever be a Jew; if Catholicism is taught him, 'the man or woman will confess their sins to a priest and rest upon his power to save; and since all civilized nations have kept gold stored in vaults for ages, stood outside themselves and implored its possessor for bread, for work and for money. Nations have crumbled and gone to decay; we have also observed the property of a great country like the United States, with its republican form of government, vast mining resources, and great agricultural and manufacturing industries in the hands of the masses, drift into the hands of a few in the short space of twenty years, all done through the power of gold. Is it to be wondered that people fall down and worship the power no man can stay?

I say a power that no man can stay, for it is true. If Baron Rothschild would to-morrow order his holdings all collected into money and returned to those he has robbed, through that deadly law called interest, they would have him either killed or in a mad-house inside of forty-eight hours, and the laws of usury would roll right along, crushing millions.

The power of gold is mysterious. You might as well try to comprehend the mystical power of the Veiled Prophet, or the Chinese Joss, as to try to fathom the depths of the power of gold.

Both are kept hidden from mortal sight; the former behind the veil, but gold in vaults or behind screens and thus it becomes an imaginary God at whose shrine whole nations fall down and worship. He who gets it within his vaults or can make people believe he has, is clothed with a power that ancient devils would have been proud of. Such are clothed with purple robes and fine linen and stand like a wall of fire between nature and nature's God. Thus the miser puts fetters upon intellect, tramples reason beneath his feet and will clog the wheels of progress until evolution destroys the idol; then man will step out upon a higher plane of civilization and reason be our guide.

Saunders approached the boy interpreter and asked if he knew anything about the gold.

"Yes sah," said the boy, "it is all piled up in an old house up at the village."

"What!" said Saunders, "piled up in an old house? People must be very honest around here."

"Why?" said the boy.

"Because gold is rather valuable to be laying around."

"What is it good for?" said the boy.

"Good for!" said Saunders, why 'tis good for money."

"But," said the boy, "suppose you don't use it for money, then what is it good for?"

This was a hard question and Saunders changed the subject by asking if they could see it.

"Ob course," said the boy, "you can all see it for what I know." So it was not long till every man had his pony saddled and-were off for the village, the boy in the lead. When they reached their destination, the King met them in front of his house and on learning the object of their visit, with a good deal of surprise, led them out back of his residence where stood an old house with one room and a few poles leaned across the door-way to keep the goats out; removing these they stepped inside and found the place piled full of boxes that had been especially designed for packing on burros. The King took down one of the top boxes and with a screwdriver soon succeeded in taking off the cover—sure enough! there lay the glittering metal, two bars, seventy-five pounds each.

The whites gazed upon them in amazement. They asked if there was gold in all the boxes; on being answerd in the affirmative, they lifted several to satisfy themselves that they were not dreaming and the King was finally forced to open several boxes before they could believe, and when they went away all agreed they had never before seen gold piled up like sacks of wheat. There seemed to be a prevailing opinion that there should be a vault dug in the solid earth to store it in, and a company of soldiers kept constantly on guard.

To see their idol brought down to a level with turnips, cabbage and potatoes, was too much. It looked to them like sacrilege and no doubt if they could, they would have tried the men who caused it, for heresy.

That night Saunders, Coy and Baxter had a little caucus of their own, and after discussing the situation thoroughly, they came to the conclusion that the mines must be immensely rich and the way to manage would be to stand right in with the fanatics.

Said Saunders, "they are nothing but fanatics, unless they are playing a nice game to get the gold out of the country, but I don't believe that, for the natives do not know the value of gold, and they could have had it all out of the country long before this, and been independent, but no; they are regular fanatics and they think they will do something wonderful.

"They want to fix it so there will be no poor, but if they read history they will find there has never been a time when there were not both rich and poor, and of course there never will be. You might divide the property and gold equally to-day and one week from to-day it would be in the hands of a few. There are many people who only care for a good living and leisure for enjoyment, and of course the more enter-prising will make the money.

"Look at the United States. There nature placed in the hands of the people a vast continent; they held it about ninety years and then the bankers got in their work on the greenback and have been concentrating the wealth of the country ever since, until to-day one-half of the people are little better than paupers, and millionaires come into existence like mushrooms. The people have done millions of dollars' worth of work only to find that while they were working others had been legislating, and the job had been so well done that the men who opened farms and built houses did not own them, but they now belong to the men in Wall and Lombard streets, who sit at their desks and make gold do their work. This shows the power there is in gold, and if these men think they can break this power they are wrong. Christ tried that and failed, for to-day most Christians worship gold six days and God only one.

"When immigration comes into the country the very men they are trying to help and protect will go right to work and organize parties with such names as they have been used to; sharpers will get in control of those parties and government; repeal all the laws they are making, make new ones and run things in the good old way.

"They will have millionaires, even if they have to make them, the same as in the United States, by giving land, then money to build a railroad and let them keep the whole thing."

"I believe you are right," said Coy. "It would seem the proper thing to stand in and await our time. After the steamers arrive with passengers and railroad mate-rial we will see how things move. They will of course sell all the gold as a commodity. I think it a shame to let all that gold go out of the country; we could just as well have issued interest-bearing bonds, sold them and kept that gold in this country; but they will issue paper money and build the road.

"People will take it because government will retain

all these valuable farming lands as a pledge for the honesty of the money. The same people who use the lands will not object to using the money; besides, the way they have it arranged, they can turn right around and invest all their savings in railroad stock; then cash the railroad stock again whenever they need money or if they want to leave the country, go to the treasury and buy gold. Rest assured, people will not object to that kind of money and gold will be a commodity and nothing else. It will knock banking and railroad schemes higher than a kite.

"When the railroad is built and a goodly amount of money in circulation, we can take maps of the country and descriptions, showing vast mineral deposits, go to England and lay the matter before the bankers there. If this gold is shipped, and such shipments continue for any length of time, it will knock the bottom out of gold; the banks of England holding the bulk of that metal will suffer heavy loss by this extraordinary production. This being the case they will probably stand in with any proposition that is likely to crush this new plan, put the gold in circulation here and save their country, also the United States, from being flooded with our gold.

"To effect this I have two plans in view: the first is, to take with me a list of all the men here, also a sample of all money issued; have fine counterfeits struck, put two or three thousand dollars in an envelope and send to each man, and the country will be so flooded with paper money that they will all cry out for gold. The paper money will then be considered a failure. This is the plan by which the English destroyed our Continental money during the Revolutionary war; it worked then, it will work now. Should this fail, my next plan would be to await our time, get up a conspiracy and overthrow the government, or at least the present system. This would probably be no difficult matter after the country begins to fill up."

On the following day the convention again assembled and Mr. Jefferson explained that there could be but little more work done until immigrants and material arrived. He then proceeded to outline a course of procedure that would redound to the good of all.

It was after this arranged that a party be organized to complete a railroad survey from the great river to the foot of the lake. This would enable them to furnish work for all as soon as landed.

Next in the line of business, Mr. Summerville was granted a commission as General-in-Chief of the army now at the mines. Mr. Bundy and Lincoln were installed as President and Secretary for a term of one year, when another Congress would be convened to perfect their government.

Mr. Broinly was appointed to make the survey. Mr. Jefferson received instruction and was to be sent to London and the United States to dispose of the gold and purchase steamers, railroad material, farming machinery and such other things as were thought necessary. To let contracts for the building of war vessels and deposit balance of gold in the Bank of England. It was also arranged that pack trains sufficient to carry all the gold to the coast be employed and loaded on their return trip with goods for the mines.

The business of the convention being over President Bundy and Gen. Summerville turned their attention to locating the different missionaries among the Kings. When each had been assigned, every preparation possible was made to assist them in their laudable purpose.

While these gentlemen were looking after the missionary work, Mr. Baxter had organized his expedition and was now only waiting to see the gold train off before taking his own leave.

An escort of one hundred men had been organized, the train too was now in readiness. On loading the gold Mr. Baxter was very much interested and declared he did not suppose there was so much gold in existence and he could not have imagined that $15,000,000 would make such a load.

The night before Mr. Jefferson was to start for the coast, he and the other three, Bundy, Lincoln and

Summerville were together in the President's office. In discussing the question of money, it was agreed to have the very best plates and paper that could be made and to use every precaution against counterfeits.

The General related the circumstance of Saunders, Coy and Baxter having met him on the road and their generous offer of $20,000 for his influence in making gold the base of all values. The President and Mr. Lincoln then called to mind the extraordinary amount of ammunition boxes, and they remembered that the boxes had long ago disappeared.

It was suggested that they were probably bank defaulters and it would be well to keep them in mind.

Mr. Lincoln referred to the methods used by the English to destroy our Continental money and said they would be likely to try the same plan, but he thought any attempt of that kind could be easily forestalled.

It is possible too that after the immigrants arrive they will try to work upon their superstitions in favor of using money made of gold and incite them to revolution, and in order to prevent this it was decided to have the passengers coming on government steamers, well posted on our financial system and also have them take the oath of allegience before receiving passage.

On the following day, Mr. Jefferson took leave of his associates and joined the pack train which was already under way. After a long, hard trip of six weeks they reached Mr. Brown's place just in time to take a steamer for Liverpool. Having transferred the boxes from the train to the steamer, Mr. Jefferson ordered the train loaded with goods for the mines and then went on board.

CHAPTER XIX.

THAT the reader may have a clear insight into the character of our millionaire, Mr. Goldburg, the writer feels it a duty to mention briefly his actions toward his son. Henry Goldburg had an exceptionally good character; his mother and sister, Rebecca, were proud of the boy, but owing to his constant attendance at school and college, they had but very little of his society. At the age of 21, having completed his course, he returned home and was given a place in the bank at $150 a month. Mr. Goldburg made a great effort to interest his son in some of his great railroad schemes and banking speculations; but Henry being of a literary turn of mind seemed to have but little taste for such things. One verse from Shakespeare, Bacon, Byron, Burns or Scott furnished him more food for reflection than all the railroad schemes his father ever heard of. He had already written several fine articles and his reputation was such that as a writer he bid fair to stand high. Mr. Goldburg seeing that the boy took no interest in his schemes, failed to see in him any other talent; in fact was himself blinded to any other merit and began to look upon the boy as a kind of "lunk-head."

In consequence of this, his only hope of perpetuating the great monetary dynasty he had so firmly established in the great American Republic, was to marry his daughter to some millionaire who had already commenced his record as a financier. This was one of his strongest reasons for favoring the suit of Mr. Goldaker.

At the age of 21 Henry married a Miss Bradley, daughter of a millionaire of Lowell. Miss Bradley was in every way a kind, sweet and pretty girl; while in her childish simplicity she was lovable, she was in no way calculated to be any great assistance to the young man in deciding his future course. They commenced married life at a first-class hotel and soon discovered that in this way of living his modest salary would be barely sufficient. The Bradleys had fitted the girl out with several thousand dollars' worth of jewelry and finery, and expected Mr. Goldburg would give his son a start, as became a millionaire; therefore gave the matter no further attention.

Henry soon realized that something must be done, and feeling it would be wrong to bring care to his young wife by discussing business matters so early in their honey-moon, worried over the matter for a time and then resolved, as any sensible young man would have done, to consult his mother. Before this thought was carried out, however, the young man met with assistance from a very different source from what he had expected.

Mr. Goldman, the bank clerk, who had been in the bank ever since it was founded, and who had furnished the brains for carrying out nearly every big financial steal that Mr. Goldburg had been in since their present relation commenced, was not slow to take in the situation.

Having great friendship and respect for Henry, he approached the matter with a warmth of feeling which was to him quite uncommon. Henry was pleased to see that his father's old trusty was taking so much interest in his welfare and was glad to take advantage of any counsel this experienced friend might offer.

"I know your feelings," said Mr. Goldman, "you want to make a start but you do not like to ask for money, and your chances for getting it are none too good. I would like to know what business you prefer."

"I have no particular choice," said Henry, "but I know I can do nothing without money."

"That is true," said Mr. Goldman, "in all ordinary business. In the banking business, however, it is very different. The House and Senate of the United States under the direction of English and American syndicates are remarkable for one thing at least, ; they have created a god and that god is coin. To commence business with limited capital is to invite failure. The laws are so completely on the side of the banker that it is only an accident when a man finds an opportunity of commencing business on a small capital with the slightest hope of success; the manipulation of Congress by the money power, has established in the United States a financial system which is destined to concentrate the property of the country in a very short time, in the hands of a few individuals, and men of small capital, under the system must encounter many obstacles. In fact it seems there is but one chance in a thousand for anything beyond a living; and that is secured only by one party swallowing up the other in regular fish style, by some sharp and fraudulent deal. As you are inclined to be liberal, you would soon go to the wall, just as thousands of others are constantly doing. Therefore the thought of any small deal should be abandoned. You could no doubt borrow money to commence on, but what is the use?"

After some little thought the financier quietly knocked the ashes from his cigar and in a sympathetic, confidential manner asked Henry how he would like the banking business.

"I have made a mistake, I fear, in not studying finance, which leaves me entirely unfit to take charge of a bank and in consequence of this my father would hardly let me have any money, besides banking necessarily takes a large capital."

"What your father would do, I cannot say, but in everything else you are wrong," said the expert, "for the truth is, while bankers mix things up in such a way as to befog the people outside, when you get behind the screens there is no business so simple. You have in reality been doing the most difficult work in your father's bank. There is really nothing in banking, under our present system, but drawing interest on government bonds, loaning money on real estate and collecting the interest. When it comes down to a nicety, that is all there is to it. All this talk you hear about ten thousand different causes that bring panics and financial distress is mere sophistry. It is thrown out to confuse the mind and hide the real cause, which is invariably some gigantic fraud practiced on the people. There is plenty of business in the western part of the city and if you will let stock gambling alone it will be less complicated than running a candy shop. Of course in making loans, you will have to be careful to have good security; keep the whip always in your own hands and don't be timid about using it.

"Now while your father would not be willing to lend you the necessary money, he would probably be willing to sign a check for the amount in 60 days."

"But," said Henry, "how am I to pay the money back in 60 days and continue business?"

"O," said the clerk, "after you are once started you can do business on the strength of your bonds and make loans from your deposits."

"But," said Henry, "suppose the depositors should close on me?"

"This they are not likely to do. The name, Goldburg, is worth a good deal; but if they do you can borrow money to tide you over or you can close your doors and the depositors are the ones who will lose."

"Henry hesitated a moment, then said, "If I have to borrow money the interest will eat me up, as it does others."

"Not so, said the clerk, "you only have to borrow for a day or two, in case of a scare; when you have paid your depositors off confidence will have been restored and in less than a week the money will all come back. Bankers generally accommodate each other in that way, so you see it is a very easy matter to use the same money in three or four different banks except in case of a general panic; but a man who has no more personal ambition for getting rich than you, can always keep enough of his deposits on hand to avert all danger and still make all the money he cares for. Banking, you see, is not strictly a business; but rather a game, and a very one sided game at that. It is what gamblers would call a dead open and shut percentage game. The principal percentage is in drawing interest on bonds they do not own, and also drawing interest on money they owe to their depositors by loaning it to another party.

"Now Henry," continued Mr. Goldman, "if you will do as I say I think you can make a start in banking on a letter of credit from your father and return his letter or check inside of 60 days and still have your business established as solid as a rock backed by a big income from interest on government bonds."

Henry was astonished, but he knew the ability of Mr. Goldman was unquestioned; he knew also how his father had piled up millions, while all his neighbors were losing money. He did not believe that loss on one side and gain on the other could be the result of honest methods; he had not yet discovered that the whole banking system was governed by laws carefully prepared by millionaires for the express purpose of legally robbing the people.

Having a young wife, he was anxious to take advantage of any advice his friend might give, in order to make a respectable start in life. As bankers seemed to be the only men in the country who were making money, he resolved to trust the whole matter to the superior judgment of his friend.

At this time Mr. Goldburg was in Chicago looking after some of his western interests, and Mr. Goldman informed Henry that it would be two months before his return, but as his instructions gave him full and unlimited power, it would not be necessary to await Mr. Goldburg's return. He further said that he would prepare the papers that evening for organizing a banking company and would let him use his name as one of the company. On the following day they went to the west part of the city, secured a room, ordered it fitted up, then called upon and secured the names of some of the most prominent men of that part of the city to be used in organizing a company. This done, they went to New York, where Mr. Goldman introduced Henry as the son of his employer, the millionaire of Bopeep, having already given him a check for $100,000 on 60 days' time with his father's name affixed by Cashier Goldman. In accordance with Goldman's instructions,

Henry stated to the banker that he desired a loan of $100,000 for a few days. As Mr. Goldman was well known to the bankers the money was forthcoming at once, and a charge of only $200 was made for the favor. Taking his $100,000 in greenbacks, Henry and his friend proceeded to invest it in Government bonds drawing 5 per cent interest, which would give Henry an annual income of $5,000. The next step was to apply for and secure a charter, according to law; with the charter Henry received $90,000 of his money back from the Government—not in greenbacks, but in National Bank notes, which was money to all intents and purposes. Mr. Goldman then gave Henry a check of $10,000 on 60 days' time; this was also signed by Mr. Goldman, Cashier for the millionaire. They then dropped into another bank where Goldman was well known, and had it cashed; the bank where they had borrowed the $100,000 was the next place visited and Henry returned to them their $100,000; this took the $90,000 received from Government and the $10,000 received on Goldburg's check on 60 days, signed by the Cashier of the bank at Bopeep. Henry then paid the $200 out of his pocket money and the two returned to Bopeep where Henry, with a clerk whom Goldburg recommended, opened a new National Bank.

The boy had pocket money enough to fit up a room and as he was the son of a millionaire and had secured the names of some of the most prominent men in New York to form his company, he at once had the confidence of the entire community and deposits soon filled his vaults. Acting on Mr. Goldman's advice, in a few weeks he paid the check of $10,000 out of his deposits and had established a business that would probably pay him $10,000 a year, beside the interest on $100,000 bonds which he never owned.

Everything was running so smoothly that Henry could hardly comprehend what had transpired, the change was so sudden; he felt as if he had been hypnotized and robbed some one; when he had a little leisure, he dropped in on his friend Goldman who seemed more than usually sociable. After seating themselves com-

posedly and lighting their cigars, Henry reported the
condition of the new Bank and added, that he could
hardly realize the change for, said he, "I really started
with nothing and am already growing into wealth, in
spite of my ignorance of finance, and that too, at a
time when business failures throughout the country
are more numerous than ever before."

"Your ignorance of finance," said Mr. Goldman, "is
the very thing which makes it look so strange; but
when you take the fact into consideration that all our
banking laws are made in London or Wall Street by
men who are schooled in the use of money to control
men, and have used their intellect to make the laws for
the express purpose of building up their own interests,
to the loss of all others, it is not so wonderful after all."

After a rambling conversation, Mr. Goldman said,
"you now have a business established (if banking can
be called a business), which by careful management,
will pay you from $10,000 to $20,000 annually; it
looks to me as if the proper thing for you to do, would
be to make a sinking fund of the interest on those
bonds; all they have really cost you is $10,000; that
you will, of course, have to pay from your deposits
and will eventually have to be paid back to the depositors.　As they have cost you so little you can afford to
set that money one side, keep it on interest constantly,
and give it to your oldest boy."

Henry flushed a little at this and in order to pass it
over lightly, at the same time display his rapidity at
figures, picked up a pencil and calculated the compound
interest of the bonds.　After a few minutes' lively work
he exclaimed, "my God, at the expiration of the bonds
in twenty years, beside having furnished me a basis to
do business on, they will have netted me in interest
over $250,000."　Pausing in deep thought for a few
moments, still examining the paper, he continued,
"but then it will be difficult to keep it on interest constantly."　"Not at all," said Mr. Goldman, "the bankers
have long since pushed a law through Congress to
withdraw the greenback from circulation.　The people
must have money to do business with and will thus be

compelled to go to the bank and borrow; there is no other way for them to get it. By making a special deal on this interest at 5 per cent you can have it com-pounded every six months; you were figuring on com-pounding every year, so you will have even more than your figures call for."

"Well, for the Lord's sake," said Henry, "is it pos-sible that all the National Banks in the country are drawing money out of the Government treasury in this way?" "Possible," said Goldman, "not only possible, but an actual fact."

"No wonder then," said Henry, "some men make millions while the people in general are losing money and fast becoming bankrupt; it could not be otherwise, and I now wonder what will be the outcome of all this and whither is our country drifting. In a little while, refinement, knowledge and virtue will all count for nothing and worth will be counted by dollars and cents; the masses will become so poor that they will barter their souls for cash."

"That," said Mr. Goldman, "will undoubtedly be the result and then classes will rule as in Europe, while the people are growing poorer, patriotism and courage will disappear."

"Why don't the newspapers blow up Congress for passing such laws?" said Henry.

"Many of the large papers are owned, or partially so, by bankers; the small ones, like the people, are gener-ally hard up and have to borrow money from the banks, therefore the press is as completely throttled in this country as in Russia."

"Why don't the people make a general remonstrance against such laws?"

"Because they read the papers and are led astray; if I were to stump the State and tell the whole truth, the papers would denounce and the people would not believe me, but would call me a crank. You have been reading our great dailies for several years, you have leisure and education, have established yourself in business at the expense of the Government and you hardly believe it."

"That is a fact," said Henry, "I will have to give it up. But since I come to think, it is not so strange after all; we are told that many deductive facts are the reverse of what they seem. The world seems to be flat but it is round. The American press would seem to be the guardian of justice but the rule holds good in regard to it and by carefully examining the matter we would find it to be exactly the reverse. If this is so, the same people who learned that the world is round, will find out in time that the press is only a deception."

Thanking his friend, Henry took his departure.

On returning from Chicago, the millionaire found his boy firmly planted in business, backed by the deposit of bonds in the sum of $100,000 and the question at once came to his mind as to how the young man procured the money. His first suspicions fell upon Mr. Goldman and he ordered a general overhauling of the books; finding the books balanced, he interviewed the New York bankers and found that his name had been used on checks which had all been paid. A detective was then employed and it was learned that Mr. Goldman had worked the whole thing. The boy had been started in business with an annual interest coming from bonds, amounting to $5,000 per year and a business that would make him a millionaire in course of a lifetime. This too had all been done and no crime could be attached to it, nor had one dollar of Mr. Goldburg's money been touched.

When Mr. Goldburg became fully acquainted with the transaction it gave him renewed confidence in his son and he notified Mr. Goldman to give him unlimited favor. Henry, however, was too honest and large hearted to ever become a millionaire; he contented himself with the ordinary resources of the bank and bonds; became rich but not a millionaire.

The writer would feel himself recreant to an important duty were he to close this chapter without calling the attention of the reader to the fact that there is no method by which a man engaged in any other branch of business could start in a similar way and continue in business six months.

CHAPTER XX.

AFTER a very agreeable voyage, Mr. Jefferson reached Liverpool. In the great cities of England he felt like a caged bird—the red tape and formalities were so common as to be almost beyond endurance. There were officers everywhere and the people constantly on the move. Life in all its different phases, from the oldest to the youngest, from the richest to the poorest were all striving, striving, striving; some for bread, some for wealth and a very few sought knowledge; but all strove according to their own peculiar desires and tastes.

"Why all this?" said Mr. Jefferson. "Why do men seek happiness in superfluous wealth and vain display while others are in want? If man has an immortal soul, then this wrong will surely react upon his future self. If we have no immortal part, why strive for more than we can use? It would be infinitely better to call a halt and enjoy what we already have."

After turning about $5,000,000 of gold over to the officials of the mint, Mr. Jefferson took in the city for a few days and did not lack attention; being of a retiring nature he managed to pass much of his time alone which better enabled him to consider and profit by the many instructive lessons which a great city affords.

His first step in business was to purchase:

4 Ocean Steamers.......................	$2,000,000
4 River Steamers at $200,000...........	800,000
Railroad Iron for 100 miles.............	400,000
4 Locomotives..........................	34,000
Flat, Freight and Passr. Cars...........	200,000
Tools and hardware....................	466,000
Supplies, voyage and colony...........	400,000
Total amount....................	$4,300,000

Having manned and loaded the four River Steamers and one large Steamer, also having taken on 2,000 immigrants, he dispatched them for Africa.

With the other three steamers partially loaded with railroad iron, he went to New York and proceeded to buy as follows:

Printing office fixtures, including press and all necessary machinery for running a first-class office, together with lythographing outfit for use of the treasury department in making money, and sundries, amounting in all to.............	$1,000,000
100 head cows, 100 work cattle, 100 horses	17,000
General supplies—groceries, dry goods.	500,000
10 saw mills—hardware and tools.........	400,000
Total...........................	$1,917,000
Amount paid out in London.......	4,300,000
Total paid out including 1 war ship	1,000,000
· Grand total..........	$7,217,000

The gold in all had minted $15,500,000, so it will therefore be seen that there was remaining in the bank to the credit of the Republic $8,283,000.

There had been collected from passengers in all $250,000; this Mr. Jefferson retained as an incidental fund. Before leaving New York he had made every possible effort to secure the service of the very best lithographers and engravers to accompany him and had been quite successful.

On the arrival of the first fleet on the great river, they were met by President Bundy who had already selected a landing; a town had also been surveyed and as a large part of the immigrants were composed of families and had tents, they selected lots and fixed up comfortable homes.

Some of them moved upon farming lands near the city, which had been surveyed in forty acre lots. A reservation of four miles square had been kept for the use of the city; then the next two miles from that had been run off into forty acre tracts; then twenty-two miles more in eighty acre lots, after that in 160 acre lots, all subject to squatter rights.

The cattle driven in by the natives were bought, tamed, put to work, and in two weeks from that time planting had commenced.

When Mr. Jefferson arrived he found railroad material and stores all landed; the families all nicely located in tents; store tents had been put up and filled with goods; a market place established where natives brought meat, eggs, fowls, fruits and vegetables to sell. It was wonderful how quickly they learned the use of money and it pleased the whites to see what friendly people they had found.

The small boats had been up the river with exploring parties and found an extensive forest of pine over 200 miles above; they had also passed through an immense hardwood country, and now that the machinery was on hand, it was decided to send two of the mills up at once. In a few days one was sent to the pinery to cut lumber for the buildings, the other to the hardwoods to cut lumber for wagon and ship timber. This mill was provided with machinery to make spokes, felloes and staves.

The Ocean steamers were sent to Liverpool for railroad iron; to proceed to the United States for work-horses and cattle, hogs and poultry; also passengers and goods.

Two weeks after the vessels took their departure, an enterprising individual from Texas, sailed into the harbor with a ship load of cattle and horses; he came on the strength of what he had learned in New York; the animals found ready sale with the immigrants and soon were employed in building railroad or putting in crops.

A sub-treasury had been established, money and stock had been printed and five companies had been organized—a steamship and navigation company, with a capital stock of $10,000,000; railroad transportation company, with a capital stock of $10,000,000; lumber and milling company, with a capital stock of $6,000,000; building company, with a capital stock of $4,000,000; commercial company, with a capital stock of $6,000,000;

mining company, with a capital stock of $2,000,000.

All the personal interest of the government in property was turned over to these companies, except the war vessel.

Now that the treasury could be drawn on for money, as work progressed, a remarkable activity commenced.

Scraper outfits were sent to the grade on the railroad, rock men were put to work, mines were being opened, mills were running and vast quantities of lumber were being landed at Summerville, the city which had sprung into existence at the landing on the great river.

Buildings were everywhere going up, bricks being moulded and stone quarries opened; coal was also being mined and would soon find its way to the coast for the use of steamers.

All this was being done without one word of complaint about money. Why should they complain? The money they had would buy anything that was to be had; it was good at the stores and gold coin was at a discount of 50 per cent, caused by a law of the country. Even California in her palmiest days, when gold was being made into money by the millions, never experienced more thrift than did this new Republic.

It will be remembered that when the United States issued so much greenback money to carry on the great war of the Rebellion, business of all kinds was quickened and notwithstanding the dreadful ravages of war, such a degree of prosperity has been seldom, if ever seen, outside of countries where new discoveries of great mineral wealth has accidentally placed a large amount of money in circulation.

From this it would seem that in all cases where money is plenty among the people, business is brisk; and as soon as the money comes under the control of a few individuals, it is to the injury of the whole. Just in the proportion that it is controlled, in the same proportion is business paralyzed.

In six months from the commencement of the work the railroad had been completed to the lake. Previous to this a colony of ship builders had been located on a beautiful town site that had been surveyed by government at the foot of the lake. These families had managed to get in lumber enough on wagons to construct comfortable houses, and now that the ship building material could be had over the railroad, a boat building company was formed, work on dock commenced at once, and soon the construction of lake boats was under way.

After the work on the railroad had been completed, the men and teams had been moved to the capital, Kiyongo, and work begun on a road to the mine.

One hundred miles from Kiyongo, in a low range of hills along the route of the new railroad, had been found a deposit of iron equal to those worked in the United States. Coal, lead and zinc had also been found. With the exception of some fifty miles of country where these mines were located, the entire route was through a farming region equal in fertility and general advantages to that of Illinois.

Several parties had been for months running section lines on a strip of ten miles wide on each side of the road and immigration was now coming in so rapidly that the settlement of this strip kept pace with the advance of the road, while other extensive tracts were also being surveyed and taken up.

A large part of the farmers who came were from the United States; a majority were men who had owned valuble lands and farms there, and during the war when money was plenty, had become involved, generally from improving their property or buying new machinery to facilitate labor; but in consequence of sickness, fire, flood, storm or other unforeseen circumstances were unable to meet the full obligation when due, and before another opportunity was offered the circulating medium was withdrawn through the enforcement of the contraction act and their productions went down in price to such an extent as to make the payment of debt and interest impossible. They were therefore forced by circumstances which they could not control to sell their homes for what they could get, and their losses went into the coffers to swell the fund that produced the present crop of millionaires.

A great many of these people on reaching Africa had money enough left to buy such teams and machinery as would be needed in opening a new farm.

Many of them when their crops had been planted, sent their teams to the grading camps to earn a little money and in this way the farming communities were kept alive without the sad alternative of going to the bank; others, who had no teams, went upon land and worked for their neighbors until they had money to buy teams with; others took land, worked for their neighbors who in turn came on with their teams and a crop was soon under way. There were still others who located their families upon land, and went themselves to the public works and there soon made money to procure the necessary team and implements to go on with their farming.

Aged persons, who in youth took part in the settlement of Indiana, Illinois, Mississippi, Wisconsin and other states will recognize in this a repetition of the history of that period, and they will remember how greed, selfishness and crime have increased among the people during the concentration of wealth under the unerring work of our financial legislation since that time. That the day will come when the mask will be torn aside, by means of which this wicked legislation has been so successfully hid for many years, there can be but little doubt, and then the American people will recognize the fact that the whole fabric is based upon gold and the national bank is only a machine for the successful playing of a confidence game. Its object, which already marks the period of its existence, is simply nothing more nor less than to rob the public in favor of a class, and thus concentrate wealth.

When the large immigration reached Kiyongo, soon after the railroad had been completed to the lake, they found the government in a most prosperous condition.

A man of the name of Pomroy—Brick Pomroy—was Secretary of the Treasury. He was an American, whether he was any relation to the great greenback leader has not been revealed to the author, but sure it is that he possessed some sterling qualities, otherwise

President Bundy would not have felt called upon in his appointment to express a belief that he was about the only man in the community who had so far overcome his superstitious worship of gold, that he could without a shudder, ship all the precious metal out of the country and have no fear of the idol's ghost or be overcome by pangs of remorse.

During the past year there had been money enough paid out for work by the different companies to supply plenty of the circulating medium. There had been enough gold coin brought into the country to cover the cattle, horses, hogs, poultry and farm implements imported. Merchants in sending for goods had always changed money at the treasury for check on New York or London and thus gold became unnecessary.

During the year $12,000,000 of gold bars had been received from the mines and now lay in the treasury awaiting shipment. It was the surplus of gold output for the year, the balance having been sent to Mr. Brown from time to time to be used in supplying the mines with dry goods and notions.

It might be here noted that as yet there had been but little change in the mines. Gen. Summerville was still there and the stores were all under his control. In them he had many white men employed but the mining was nearly all done by the natives.

After the government issued paper money, $12,000,-000 was sent to the mines and had been paid out for gold; this made money plentiful there, of course, just the same as money was plentiful in California in 1849 and 1850; the only difference was that in the one place it was gold dollars, the other it was paper.

A great deal of this money found its way back to Kiyongo, and when the railroad brought retail merchants in from Summerville on the great river, they had a lively trade with the natives and many became wealthy.

During the year a government had been perfected at Kiyongo in strict accordance with Mr. Jefferson's ideas as embraced in the rights of man.

Mr. Bundy was now President, Mr. Lincoln Secre-

tary of State, and Mr. Jefferson had long since been
sent on a foreign mission to look after the interests of
the Republic, secure desirable immigration, provide
for the sale of gold, and purchase and ship to the
Republic such articles as were found necessary.

A few months prior to the organization of Government a very intelligent individual located in Kiyongo
who, it was said, had a hobby; that hobby was called
squatter sovereignty and the man's name was Stephen
A. Douglas. It seems that President Bundy recognized in this man not a hobby but true business tact
and the very grandest of patriotic sentiments. He also
believed that he saw in him a peculiar fitness for
handling the Land Department in such a manner as to
secure every man in his right of possession of a home,
and at the same time prevent all possibility of lands
being monopolized or kept out of use for speculation;
he therefore appointed him Secretary of the Interior.

The most peculiar feature of the convention which
gave form to the new Government was the fact that
several ladies took part in its deliberations, and to their
zeal and wisdom was largely due the complete overthrow of such selfish dogmas and superstitions as
intrinsic value of money, honest dollar, national banks,
interest, discount, strengthening acts and confidence
games of all kinds as played by the gold power; tariff,
over-production, and a thousand and one other hobbies,
made to frighten the unwary and control their votes.

The Commercial company that had been organized
at Summerville now had a large wholesale house at
that place; one at Mango, that being the name of the
town at the foot of the lake, and another at Kiyongo.
They had a buyer in New York, who, acting under the
instructions of Mr. Jefferson, made all their purchases.
Being an extensive buyer, and having unlimited capital, he was enabled to get bottom prices; and as the
Company was limited to 7 per cent profit on original
investment, they were able to furnish the retail merchants with goods cheaper than they would have been
furnished by any other system, and the retail business
being open to competition, goods were quite reasonable.

Along the shores of the great river were hundreds of miles of fine farming land, almost equal to the great Mississippi Valley, and into this immense belt the immigrants were pouring in from the United States by thousands. These people were of all classes. Some had been merchants of large capital but on account of the contraction of the currency in favor of the money lenders, their goods had so lost in value as to place them entirely at the mercy of their creditors; they were therefore forced to die a slow but sure business death from being eaten up by that great financial cancer, called interest.

Others had been working for men who had been forced to suspend business from the same cause.

Then there were others who had been working where machinery in the hands of great corporations had come in competition with, and forced their employers out of business.

President Bundy, in visiting and looking to the welfare of these people, was surprised to find how few there were who knew the real cause of hard times in the United States. There had been no failure of crops, the mines were producing great quantities of gold and silver, yet many of them said it was hard to get work enough to buy food and clothes. When asked the cause of this, nine out of ten would say, over-production.

Sometimes they would get into discussions about it, and use the same old political gags, hobbies or absurdities as rag baby, honest dollar, sound money, supply and demand, tariff, protect labor, free trade but never a word about the exception clause on the greenback, the strengthening act, control of money by national banks, demonetization of silver in favor of money lenders and creditor class, the contraction or any of the giant swindles that had been pulled through Congress to rob the American people of not only millions but billions of dollars.

"These people," said the President, "do not seem to comprehend the fact that when there is plenty of money in a country there can be no such thing as over-production."

CHAPTER XXI

SOON after the railroad had been completed to the iron mines, 100 miles from Kiyongo, a gentleman made his appearance at that place and after looking about for a few days, visited the mine where a company of men were prospecting and taking out the ore. After spending several days making surveys, diagrams and plans, he returned to Kiyongo and called at the office of the Mining Department which was under the control, care and keeping of a lady who had distinguished herself in the convention by taking a lively part in formulating a constitution and laws for the new government. On approaching this lady, he found her perfectly at ease under the stress of business imposed upon that high office during this progressive period. The gentleman mentioned was an Englishman of rank and culture; as an engineer and manufacturer of steel, he had few superiors. For years he had been in charge of a large manufacturing concern in England, where the workman received $2.00 per day and he received $5,000 per year for carrying a cane. but at last one of those gold panics, so common to metal-money countries, came along and the work shut down. He was now looking for a chance to make a few millions, just as thousands of men have done in the United States by working the gold, national bank confidence-game.

After introducing himself in due form he presented his report on the mines and explained: "There is no question in regard to the vast extent of the deposit; the ore is of good quality; coal is near at hand; water is plenty and convenient; in short, it is equal to the great mines of Pennsylvania or Missouri and all that is needed is capital; without capital these properties are valueless. This valuable mineral has lain for ages buried up in the earth. Miners can find mines but it takes capital to work them. Your country here is poor, of course, because it is new. You have every-thing but capital and everything you have is worthless until you have capital to take hold.

"Our country is old and although it is but an island, it is the richest country in the world; in fact, all the gold which has been taken out of the mines in the United States is to-day safely stored in the vaults of the Bank of England and if moneyed men had as much confidence in this Republic as they have in the United States, you would see the gold pour into this country by the millions.

"If I can get a good title to a few hundred acres of these iron and coal lands, I can organize a company, issue stock and with my indorsement, I can sell that stock in England at a very small discount and can put a force of men at work inside of a year. Your land is perfectly valueless now and by giving me a deed it will bring millions of dollars of wealth into your country and will do more to secure the confidence of these great moneyed men, than anything you will have an opportunity of doing for ten years to come. Just think of having your steel rails made at home."

The lady saw at once that he had not posted himself on the laws of the Republic and said: "Sir, are you not aware that English money would not be good in this country?"

"Good," said the Englishman, setting himself back on his dignity, "gold is good in any country; its intrinsic value makes it good the world over."

"If England and the United States were to demone-tize gold to-morrow, what would it then be worth?" was asked.

"O," said the gentleman, "that is hardly a supposa-ble case; the world has always used gold for money and always will; it is believed God gave us gold for money, as he gave us coal to burn."

"I am aware," said the lady, "that the people in by-gone ages have believed this; they have had many other superstitions; for instance, they believed that God appointed their rulers. This myth, like many others, is about dead, and the days of the gold myth are already numbered. It is true that as far as we can see in the dark and bloody past, man has been a slave to his own superstitions; but the day of intellectual enlightenment has now come, and the people themselves have assumed the right to think.

"One of the fundamental principles of this Republic is to make and use our own money; we sell our own gold and ivory because we have no present use for either. If I ever encourage any people to borrow, it will not be money, but a bite to eat; and so far as English confidence is concerned the people of the United States can take it all, we don't want it."

She then handed him a primer, saying, "here, sir, is one of our law books; you can easily understand it and you will not need a lawyer. It contains all the laws governing the organization of joint stock companies." She then explained that if he wished to organize a company he would need to become a citizen and then the Government would issue all the money that would be required.

"But," said he, "I am told that you have been issuing money to all these big companies that are operating so extensively, and you may rest assured the day of inflation will come some day, and then your money will not be worth the paper it is printed on."

This was too much for the patriotic little woman; she arose slowly to her feet and the color came to her face as she quietly, but firmly said: "Sir, you are ignorant of our laws; I will therefore explain to you that the stock which you propose to sell in London will be kept in the treasury here, and when people get more money than they need in business, they will invest it in this stock. If you examine our laws, you will find that for every dollar of money that has been issued, a dollar of stock is kept in the treasury in ten dollar shares, so until that stock has all been sold an inflated money market will find relief in the purchase of this stock and when the stock has all been sold, the money will all be back in the treasury.

"Thus you see it will require vast expenditures on the part of the Government to prevent the money from continually finding its way back to the treasury; a stringency therefore is the thing to be feared, not inflation, and a stringency under our system can alway be avoided by liberal appropriation. When you examine our monetary system, which is very simple, you will find that while the Government exists the value of our money can never be impaired. The land, you will learn, is always public domain; not one foot of it will ever be sold to any man. Government, you will observe, lets the people use this land free from rent or taxes. The money is also public money; it belongs to the Government and is furnished to the people without interest. Its value is based upon the land which is already in the hands of the people. Do you suppose that people will discredit money when they hold the security in their own hands? Never. When I say to you that Government furnishes money to the people without interest, do not misconstrue my meaning.

"The Government of the United States withdrew their greenback money from circulation and issued interest-bearing bonds, for the people must have money; there was but one way to get it, and that was to borrow it and pay interest. The people of the United States, by legislation, are compelled to pay interest to the gold power and the bank for their circulating medium and it is under the working of that system that its Government has become one of the debtor countries of the globe. Please do not understand that we scatter our money broadcast for men to get an arm full, but the reverse of this; we confine all transactions to strictly business principles and are as careful to guard the interests of the country in handling our money, as the bankers in the United States and England are to guard the interests of the combined money power. Never a dollar of money goes out of our treasury until it is earned by the one who is to receive it, and then it bears no interest; never a dollar lays idle in our vaults while men are wanting work. We will terrace the hills and make homes for men upon the rugged mountain sides, ere one man who wants work shall be out of employment."

"In case I were to organize a company for the manufacture of steel with a cash capital of $3,000,000, what salary would I receive for management?" asked Mr. Davis, for that was the gentleman's name.

"General managers of companies," said the lady, "get $1,500.00 a year; men who work over fire and hot metal get $5.00 a day; the next grade of workmen get $4.00 and common hands $3.50."

"Then you put a gentleman on the same roll with working men?"

"Certainly," said the lady, "we employ none but gentlemen and our prices are fixed by law. For handling this Department of the Government I receive $1,500.00 a year. If I were to resign there would be many equally good, if not better qualified, who would apply for the situation."

The gentleman seemed restless and rising to his feet as he adjusted his glove, said: "I would consider myself disgracing a long line of noble ancestors were I to engage on such terms. If I could get a title to the property and handle it to my own profit I would engage, otherwise it may lay there till Gabriel blows his trumpet." Thus saying he left the room with a lofty air.

That afternoon 300 iron workers and a lot of carpenters and masons arrived from the United States. It was evident from their appearance that they all belonged to the working class; many had families and were a very intelligent company. Every man had a primer in his pocket and had evidently studied the laws of the country thoroughly;, they showed by every action, however, that they were filled with anxiety. They had spent their money to get to the country; they were workers of iron and not a smelter was running in the country. Mr. Jefferson had promised plenty of money. So far everything had looked all right, but the important question now was, would the Government make good these promises? Everything was at stake; they had come thousands of miles into a strange land at an expense of a million dollars, and what money they had left would hardly build comfortable homes, to say nothing of smelting works.

Some were impatient and went so far as to say they believed the whole thing was a scheme to get their passage money. They had not long to wait, however, for a deputation of three men was chosen to visit the office at once and learn the facts.

The three men chosen were representative Amiercan mechanics. On entering the office they presented credentials from Mr. Jefferson, whereupon they were greeted as old friends. After a little friendly intercourse the lady gave them passes over the road for as many as wished and desired them to visit the mines and report as to what would be needed.. "Then," said she, "an organization can be formed at once." She further informed them that in anticipation of this, Mr. Jefferson had shipped some months ago, a complete outfit of machinery, which had been received in good order and would be in readiness when required.

The result of this interview brought happiness to the little band of toilers.

That evening the lady chief of the Manufacturing Department visited the ladies of the party and welcomed all with cheerful greeting.

The anxiety of these people had been put to such a strain that the committee determined to take the cars that night; in the morning they found themselves at the camp. Two or three hours were all that were necessary to examine the location, so in the evening they returned to Kiyongo, and on the following day an organization was effected with a capital stock of $1,000,000; sub-treasury established at the mines, the money and stock forwarded to the same; the money to be used by the company as needed, the stock kept on sale. After this work went on lively. The Lumber company had already put a large quantity of lumber on the ground which was received by the new company, giving a check for the same, and in turn sold it to the workmen to build houses. The town site had been elegantly laid off and the buildings were constructed very tastefully. As soon as this was done grading commenced, then a building went up, the machinery was put in place and furnace arranged.

By this time merchants had erected buildings and brought in an abundance of supplies. Two more companies had been organized to do business in the same town; one to manufacture steel rails, the other to manufacture tools and hardware of all kinds. In less than six months more than two thousand of the toiling masses of the United States had reached the place and found work. All working men were receiving good wages and a city was springing into existence like magic; in fact the place was enjoying what might be called a veritable boom.

Brick yards were running, houses going up on every hand, streets were being graded and pipes laid. Every man found something to do and prosperity reigned, but no gold or national bank.

A sub-treasury had been established and it was found that many of the toilers invested their savings in stock; in this way a large part of the money paid out by the companies found its way back into the treasury. It has since been learned that in less than ten years the entire stock of that company had been absorbed by the savings of the people of the town and county; in addition to this, they all had comfortable homes.

By way of contrast it may be well to mention here that in the United States the stock would have been taken to some great money center, sold at a discount, beyond the reach of the people, then a savings bank established, run until its coffers were full, then burst, but finally pay off a little gold and a good deal of confidence; then make a big blow in the newspapers, start up again and play the same old game; then, in order to make the thing more interesting, reduce the wages and have a strike and lock-out; import pauper labor, take mortgage on homes while the men are idle, and thus scoop the town.

This is no calamity-howl; it is only what every American has seen over and over again and knows it to be a fact. It is what some call legalized robbery; others call it legitimate business and shrewd financiering. Call it what you will the result is just the same. The banker gets rich and toilers go hungry.

CHAPTER XXII.

WE must now drop this historical sketch to look after the gold men, or bank defaulters, Coy and Saunders. They had built themselves a cabin, buried their gold under the floor, and loafed about town while a city grew up around them. Not half a dozen blocks from their door three great manufacturing concerns had been started and were running full blast. One of these made wagons, another plows and the third manufactured fire-arms for the Government, to be stored for use in case of emergency. These companies were all run on the joint stock plan and employed 2,000 men. All this without gold and not a millionaire in the place.

Every lot about them had been built upon and they were now in the heart of a city. They could have sold their gold, invested the money in stock and their yearly dividend would have been over $5,000 each. But this was so far short of their expectations that they treated it with contempt, and were content to sell a few thousand dollars' worth of gold, erect a stone building, with secret rooms and vaults that would have been suitable for either a burglar or a banker. They then decided to wait for inflation or some other imaginary ghost to come along and give them a chance, as Coy said, to get in their work.

It will be remembered that Mr. Baxter undertook the survey of the railroad, and being by nature a nervous and industrious sort of man, he soon became interested in the work, which he pushed without interruption.

When immigrants arrived and the work of construc-

tion commenced at Summerville, other engineers took
the field; Mr. Baxter then moved on to Kiyongo and
continued in the work until the railroad reached the
mines.

About this time Coy and Saunders concluded to go
to the mines, and Baxter accompanied them. They
were not long in finding gold, and were soon located
on a small mountain creek; a cabin was the first thing
constructed, then a ditch was dug to bring water on the
bar; a mine was then opened which proved to be a
good one. They tried to hire natives, but they were
superstitious, and because the men had opposed their
chief, in the convention a few years before, they had
the idea that they represented the evil spirit, and even
the men who assisted Baxter in the survey, would not
work for them now; they thought some of going after
white men, but if they did, it might be the means of
bringing a crowd into the gulch and they would lose a
part of their ground. Stimulated by a greed for gold
and the hope of some day striking an inexhaustable
pile, they commenced operations.

Not one in the crowd had ever worked before, but
the hope of finding a million dollars in a pile, stimulated them; after working hard for two years, under
most extraordinary circumstances, they weighed their
gold and found they had $100,000, a little more than
$30,000 each, and they began to consider.

"Well," said Coy, "you can all do as you please, but
for my part, I am done with the work. Look at the
situation; we found an enormously rich gold mine,
worked it in the best possible manner, have done all
our own work, put in long hours and what have we
made? Thirty-three thousand apiece! Only yesterday
I saw an account of J. Gould and Jim Fisk having
gone from nothing up into the millions in about the
same time, and they didn't work as we have, either.
what is the use to work? We have been wearing ourselves out like a lot of chumps; and while we have
been here millions of dollars have been handled by
this Government and everybody is getting a whack at
it but us; we are a regular set of chumps."

"That is a fact," said Saunders, "I have been thinking the matter all over and have made up my mind to make you, gentlemen, a proposition."

"Hold on," said Baxter, "I object to the term gentlemen, on general principles. I don't think any man can be a gentleman and work as we have; until we do something, that we may be distinguished from this ignorant herd, I object to the name."

"I believe you are about right on that point," said Saunders, "but the proposition that I was about to make is, that we sell this claim for what we can get, return to Kiyongo, get such books as seem necessary, and open an office of some kind. Of course there is no chance to make any money at present; the Government is so thoroughly organized that everything is limited, and if it is allowed to run for ten years more, these principles of inheritance limit will become so thoroughly fixed in the minds of the people that all the gold in Christendom would not move them; beside, gold surely has lost its power."

"Yes," said Baxter, "I have learned one thing about gold; I used to think gold was King on account of its intrinsic value, but I find it all depends upon the laws. If the laws of the United States were to demonetize gold to-morrow it would be several thousand dollars out of our pockets; and if England should demonetize the next day we would not have enough to get home on."

"Yes," said Saunders, "but there is no danger of that; nothing short of revolutions would demonetize gold in the United States. The banks there are too strong. If John Sherman had been at the convention here in place of Jefferson, and some of his friends in place of Bundy and Lincoln, we would have had banks all over this country now; as it is we seem to have no chance; a worse lot of fanatics, I never saw.

"The conditions here now are of the worst possible character; there never was a country where there was so much money in general circulation as here. But when you try to get a corner on it, you find yourself hampered in every conceivable way.

"If you were to succeed in getting a corner on money

and cut the price of everything down, and start the cry of over-production, what is there to hinder Congress from coming together, issuing more money to take the place of that which you have in your vaults, and start men to grading wagon roads all over the country? You see people would go to work and earn money and their surplus production could lay in the warehouse and hurt no one; then people would learn that over-production is only a ghost; unless money is based on some substance like gold, you can have no over-production, you can have no interest, you can have no mortgage, you can have no banks, you can have no millionaires, you can have no slaves.

"When you strike down gold you destroy all inherent right and the possibility of perpetuating our great monetary dynasties will cease to exist. In such a state of things there will be but two ways of gaining honor, power and distinction. The first would be intellectual superiority; this would require a life time of hard study and you would have no time to display your power as a prince of wealth. The next, and only means that I can see, would be to excel in helping others, though often you would meet with unthankfulness, yet your name would go down to history all right.

"These are both hard roads to travel. If we wish to succeed we must protect the wealthy class, as their power lies in controlling the money in the world, through the limited amount in existence, and as there is but one way of limiting money, and that is to insist on its being made of a limited product, like gold, we must stay with the gold power. If we can establish a gold standard here, the money power of the world will assist us; as we dare not go to any other country with our gold, we must destroy this Government and establish one based on gold; we may even yet have our chains of national banks and make these fanatical people bow to our dictum."

"I only see one drawback to that," said Baxter, "and that is the mines; they will turn off gold so fast that it will be hard to control the currency even then."

"Not at all," said Coy, "look at the United States.

They have the richest gold mines in the world; where is the gold to-day? All in the vaults, and the people are not only paying interest to the money power on all the money they use, but are paying an annual interest on five times that amount of other debts and selling wheat at fifty cents a bushel to pay it. No, no I have no apprehension of danger from these mines; all I ask is for this Government to establish a gold standard and all the rest will be easy enough. Of course we can't make it all; we will have to stand in with England's money lords, as a few men stood in with them and became millionaires through their money schemes in the United States."

"I agree with you perfectly," said Saunders, "we must have these English syndicates at our backs; no doubt but they will get away with the lion's share, yet they cannot get along without us any more than we can without them. When the power is once established, we shall be independent. The harder they press us the harder we shall press the people. But I must return to my proposition; the two great forces through which the wealth of the United States has been so thoroughly concentrated in a few years, are the two great political parties. What we want here is two great parties; so far the law has discouraged such organizations, but there is really no statute law against it; all it wants is a few good organizers and I believe it can soon be effected.

"The two parties should be called Democratic and Republican. Thus we would get the benefit of their old prejudices. We can do nothing without having the people organized and we must also have them divided; we must get up strife of some kind. The tariff dodge has been used quite successfully in the United States and it might work here; a rag-baby song too would help out."

"Yes," said Baxter, "there is no doubting the importance of organization, but our people are mostly American and have been humbuged so much by political parties and shysters that I am not astonished at the unpopularity of such organizations. They will hardly

talk of such a thing.   When they get here, from under
the influence of party and a subsidized press, they look
back, see how that country has been robbed, and it
makes them sick.

"We might possibly organize a secret society and
afterward drift it into politics; but even that I am
afraid would be difficult.   They are all doing so much
better than they ever did before that even this might
fail.   Things, too, are growing constantly worse.   I see
by the late papers that over half of the railroad stock
has passed into the hands of the people already, and
there are probably very few persons who own over
$10,000 worth; when you see them all buying railroad
stock, even to the hired girls, it is a poor time to get
any marked changes in the Government."

"O, I don't know about that," said Coy, "John Sherman got the contraction act through Congress when
there was no possible excuse for it and the people were
in the very height of prosperity."

"That is so," said Saunders, "but you must remember they had no initiative then; the Sherman act
worked all right in the United States, but it won't
do here."

"Let mé offer a suggestion," said Baxter. · "Suppose
we go to the coast, to Summerville or some other good
location, buy property and go into business; trade there
is brisk.   New manufacturing plants are constantly
being started all over the country and business everywhere is booming.   I see there is now a ship building
company at Summerville that works more men than
any other yard in the world.   The navigation company
that was organized when we were there, now has thirty-
six ocean and ten river steamers; the stock of that
company, like the railroad stock, is now largely in the
hands of the people.

"Money was never more plentiful in any country than
it is here and that accounts for so few people coming
to these mines.   Of course it is all rag money, but we
can sell our gold, and if other people can get along
with it, I don't see why we can't, and then mercantile
business is always considered respectable."

"That is all right," said Coy, "but what is a merchant? I have seen too many merchants beg favors of bankers to think of that, and I am happy to say that my ambition carries my thoughts a little higher than waiting on the public. I would prefer having it just the other way; have them wait on me. The money power controls the world. A banker makes all men bow to his mandate. Gold is the foundation of the whole system and to secure enough of the precious metal to give me a start, I sacrificed every thing—love, honor, family, friends, everything for gold—and am I now, after outwitting the Nabobs of earth, to be baffled by a lot of Kansas fanatics? I never, never will submit. I know that to overthrow this Government all the gold power of the earth will be at my back, and I will murder every man, woman and child in the Capitol but that I will place myself in a position to exercise the power that belongs to this batch of gold.

"They have destroyed the whole system of banking by their fanatic legislation; I will fight it and stay with the contest until I have laws in my favor; destroy the Government or it destroys me. I hope I may never be forced into bloodshed, but the fundamental principles of this government must be changed; we should have gone at it long ago for I see it has grown stronger and stronger, day by day. I thought inflation would destroy the system long before this, but I see the money comes back into the treasury through the sale of stock faster than it goes out and in order to keep the money in circulation, Government has been compelled to raise the wages all over the country. I learn they tried first to start public work but found the men were all employed, so the last Congress was forced to raise wages and that raised the price of everything. The natural result of this constant employment of every man in the country is, that our exports exceed our imports and all the gold that comes from the mines and is brought into the country by immigration, goes into the treasury and then it does no one any good.

"I see by the last paper they are about passing a bill to come before the people at the coming election,

to ship the gold all to the United States and exchange
it for bonds, railroad stock or other good security.
The excuse for this law being the possibility of other
Governments demonetizing gold; and in that case it
would become almost worthless. I apprehend no danger of this; nothing short of a revolution could do it,
for the gold power is too strong. They control every
government on earth to-day, but this. If we go at it
right we can eventually have them controlling this,
and then our gold will have some value. I hate a
country that is doing business with rags."

Saunders then said, "I believe that a party can be
started on the whiskey question. I have noticed that
whiskey has been a prominent factor in American
politics."

"Yes," said Baxter, "but there they have us hedged
in again. In the United States they have a genteel
saloon-keeper on every corner, with barrels of whiskey,
boxes of cigars, bottles of rum and a well filled purse
to control votes. Here liquor is sold all over the
country by the same firm; their business houses are in
the most public place that can be found, with no
back door, and is only kept open six hours in a day,
and they sell only by the quart or gallon. They have
here halls of pleasure which take the place of saloons;
everybody visits them and they are a grand institution;
with these great halls, and women voting there is no
use to talk about making a fight on whiskey."

"That is all true," said Coy, "but we can look into
the matter a little and if there is no show, then I am
in for a revolution. Get together a few good men,
burn the capitol, destroy all the papers, seize the arse-
nal and prevent the people from getting arms, organize
a new government, compel every man belonging to the
old to adopt and swear allegiance to the new; hang
every man that refuses, and give an enormous salary
to every man who submits.

"Make but few radical changes at first; throttle the
press by buying up the editor, tell the people that you
know what you are doing is wrong, but you are doing
it to prevent something worse. (That is what John

Sherman told the people about the Sherman law.)

"Among the most important things to be eliminated from the constitution and laws, is woman suffrage; we can never control their votes with whiskey. We must have saloons to control votes and we can never have them established here until we drive woman from the polls. After this is done we must do away with paper money; denounce it as a rag-baby failure and buy or borrow all the gold, then have it made legal tender, and the measure of all values. Abolish the present whiskey laws and establish fashionable saloons; then give us national banks, English land and inheritance laws, and if we don't have half the people paying us rent and interest inside of ten years, then history is not worth reading. Look at what has been done in the United States in the last fifteen years."

"This would all look fine on paper," said Baxter, "but it would take one thousand well armed men in the capitol to carry out this program and I don't think we could get fifty."

Mr. Saunders now said: "No matter what we do in the way of enthroning gold, we would have to depend upon outside force; the vast amount of machinery coming into use in the United States and Britain, together with scarcity of money, has thrown millions of men out of work. Many of them are to-day starving; so according to English-American logic there is clearly an over-production of men. If we get the gold power at our backs, they can bring a body of men here as immigrants and when enough have arrived to do the work, we will arm and turn them loose. I believe the plan can be carried out, but we must get the banks and gold power at our backs."

This kind of talk was too much for Baxter and he replied: "Now I want to tell you, gentlemen, that I have watched the work of the gold power for years; I know its history well and I want to say to you that when it comes to fight you need not count on the bankers; they never will risk a dollar on a fight, unless they know before hand just how it is going to end. If they could get the British Government or any other into it they would. You can bet everything you have, they will always be playing on a dead sure thing. Gold has always been a power, but it has always stood behind the throne. As a dog is to his master, so the Government is to this great power. The dog makes all the noise and does all the fighting; the master looks on and makes all he can out of it; if his dog gets licked he stands in with the other dog. Bankers as a rule are not men, they are monstrosities, a kind of half breed, as it were, between the devil and a hog. Now, so far as I am concerned, honesty has never hurt me and I believe that I have some of the devil's and a good share of the hog's qualities about me; enough to make a very good banker.

"We have gold here to commence with and if we could get the same legislation that the gold men have in the United States, I see no reason why we should not gather the property of the country together just as easy as they did there; in fact, if we could have gold made the only legal tender, we would have a commencement and it would not take long to get up some scheme to have bonds issued. I think we can all agree upon this, that to make gold the only legal tender and measure of all values is the most important for a start, the opening wedge as you may say, and when you get this the other things will naturally follow. Now to effect this we must in some way destroy the paper money, or at least destroy its usefulness and I think that I have hit upon a plan."

"Good," said the other two, clapping their hands.

Mr. Baxter then continued: "My proposition would be to use strategy rather than force; it is always safest and more in keeping with the general working of the gold power. Our first object will be to destroy the usefulness of government money to make room for our gold to circulate.

"Under our present constitution and government policy, together with the satisfactory working of the same, it would be impossible to have this done by legislation as it was in the case of greenbacks in the United States. I would therefore suggest that we

adopt the same method used by the gold men of
Britain to destroy the continental money of the colo-
nies during the Revolutionary war.

"My plan would be this, take a copy of the great
register of each county, also a sample of the different
issues of money, go to London, obtain an interview
with some of the leading bankers, make a careful and
correct statement of the condition of things here; I
think perhaps it would be a good plan to go immediately after the shipment of gold by the Government,
that is if the shipment is made soon which it probably
will be. That they have these bills counterfeited in
the best possible manner, then send through the mails
from $100 to $500 of these counterfeit bills to each
voter. I tell you it will knock this money higher than
a kite. We must have a few of the leading journals
bought up—no matter what it costs—to raise the cry
of rag-baby, fiat money failure, honest dollar, sound
money and such gags as we may be able to invent
that will answer for a hobby. This plan to me looks
feasible and as a similar scheme proved a success in
the past so I have all confidence in it now."

It seemed to be the best plan yet offered and it was
therefore agreed that they should sell, then return to
Kiyongo. Then they talked the matter over as to how
they would manage with their gold; they had brought
it all with them to the mines, so they now had $300,000
in all, and since the immigration had come in they
hardly knew what to do with it. They were afraid to
sell it to the Government because they despised it,
besides would have to take the money they were trying
to destroy; $200,000 of their gold was in coin and if
sold was liable to betray them; so they had no end of
trouble. It was finally decided to box it up and remove
it to their building in Kiyongo and place it in the
vaults they had so carefully constructed some years
before.

In a few weeks after this they sold out the mines and
returned to their old home in Kiyongo. At the next
election the people decided by their vote that all gold

in the treasury be shipped to the United States and then converted into bonds or other securities.

This was considered a favorable time to carry out Mr. Baxter's proposition, so all things being arranged, he took passage for Liverpool, on board of one of the finest steamers that had been built at Summerville by the ship building company of that place, and now owned by the steam navigation company of the young Republic.

Although Mr. Baxter had been very quiet about his movements as will be seen, he had not been entirely unnoticed. Secretary Lincoln and President Bundy had long since filed with the Government detective organization, which had an agent in every town and county throughout the country, a written statement of all that was known about these men. The Department had therefore kept them under constant surveillance since the formation of the Government, and not one month had passed without a report of their movements. It was therefore not at all strange that three detectives took passage on the same steamer.

CHAPTER XXIII.

WE will now for a short time draw the attention of
the reader to the progress and prosperity of the
country during the next few years after the completion
of the road to the mines. Americans will remember
the wonderful degree of prosperity existing in the
United States after the late war, while greenbacks were
in circulation. How new railroads were built, new
counties settled; towns and settlements taking the
place of the Indian and buffalo.

Political tricksters and gold gambling statesmen
would, no doubt, attribute this to some peculiar effect
the war had upon the country; but we notice that in
all cases where money is turned loose among the people it makes lively times; for instance, the new discovery of rich placer mines or some great Government
swindle where immense tracts of land have been given
to private corporations, and to sugar-coat the dose and
make the transaction look plausible, large sums of
money have been turned loose through the building of
a railroad or other public works.

Those who recognize the fact that money is not a
commodity of value, like a book account, but is in
itself valueless; that it is only a means, a method, a
tool as it were, that has no value except where it can
be used in actual transactions of business or to accomplish the purpose for which it was designed; that as
you take the tool from the workman it makes him
helpless, so when you withdraw money from its usual
channels of circulation the people are paralyzed, small
enterprises are wrecked, panic ensues and millionaires
take to themselves the shattered fragments. Yes, those
who realize all these facts, and already know that this
young Republic recognized money, not as a thing of

intrinsic value but on the contrary only as a means, a
method, a tool and supplied it to the people through
a regular business system, that not only sent it out
among the people, but also brought it back into the
treasury, and as the heart circulates the blood through
the human system, so the treasury through its carefully
arranged business methods, forced the circulating
medium into every extremity, into every nook and
corner, there to do its work and in due time return
only to be sent out again. The great trouble with the
United States government is that its heart has been
dragged into Wall Street and sometimes fails to throb.
Again I repeat that those who recognize all these
things will not be surprised to learn of the improved
conditions among these people.

It will be remembered that, like the United States
our new Republic had a vast continent of farming land
as rich in quality as it was vast in extent. Thousands
of miles of mineral lands containing gold, silver, copper, lead, zinc, nickel, coal, iron and many other valuable minerals.

To go forth and subdue this great continent was the
mission of these people. The wealth of a great continent was spread out before them; cities, railroads,
bridges, wagon roads and homes were to be built and
these people would have it to do. "This country now,"
said one, "belongs to us all; shall it remain ours, shall
the improvements that are made belong to those who
make them, or shall they belong to an aristocracy of
idlers, that grow and fatten upon the body politic,
as vermin grow and fatten upon the unclean human
form?" These are illustrative facts that have been
proved for ages, while the human family groaned and
suffered under evils not by nature given, but by their
own ignorance. We are now brought face to face with
the great question and it must find a solution in our
new government. Immigration had been coming into
the country in one continual stream; the country
seemed to differ from the United States in but one
thing, its laws and business or financial management.

It had the same great rivers, the same great cotton

and fruit country, also its hog and corn country; the same great ranges, rich gold, silver and other mines; great forests, in fact it had all the resources necessary to maintain a great and powerful nation, without running in debt or selling their lands to foreign syndicates. All it lacked was men and money; these two obstacles were overcome by immigration and rational government.

During the time required to construct a road to the mines, immigration had been pouring in by ship loads; as was the case in the United States up to the time that great syndicates were formed and obtained control of the national finances, the immigration was of the most intelligent, honest and industrious classes.

When these people were once safely located beyond the reach of monetary oppression, they turned the searchlight of reason upon the science of government and soon discovered many a fact that our wise states-men had labored hard to cover up.

After great corporations had been formed in the United States they, in order to degrade labor, increase their own profits and establish an aristocracy, imported and encouraged the importation of Chinese and other laborers of the very lowest classes. What followed this wholesale importation of pauper labor, by these corporations is too well known to need comment. We are happy to record that the evils were of a character not known in our new Republic.

The immigrants to this new country were generally poor, so far as worldly goods were concerned, but they had a whole continent spread before them; they were rich in brains, muscles and determination, and came of their own accord; all they wanted was a favorable opportunity and it was to give them this that the Government was formed.

As money and men were the only things necessary in a country like this, to build cities, railroads, canals, bridges, wagon roads, in fact manufacture and raise everything that is necessary for man's comfort and happiness, it was decided to encourage immigration.

It is conceded by all that Government alone has the right to make money and the people, in forming this

new Government, having retained the right of legislation to themselves, it became a question to them as to
what substance should be used to make money of; they
had gold, silver, copper, iron, wood, leather and paper;
all of these had been used for money at different
periods and by different nations. All agreed that
paper, for all purposes, would be best, but some said
it should be based on something of value; others said
no; it was decided in the affirmative; some said let us
base it upon gold, others said gold was a commodity
which is liable to fluctuate in value. Its production
is liable to increase or fall off; its use in the arts may
diminish; the sinking of a ship between Liverpool and
New York might materially change its value; it was
therefore declared illogical to base upon gold.

Bundy said the bulk of gold was in the vaults of
the Bank of England and he would prefer having a
base for money nearer home. One said, as Government owned the land, and it was provided in the constitution that the title should ever remain with the
Government, the proper and sensible thing would be
to base our legal tender on land and general wealth of
the nation; let the amount in circulation be the measure
of value, that amount being regulated at so much per
capita and make it the business of the Government to
look constantly after the circulation, and regulate the
value of money by increasing or diminishing the
amount in use outside of the treasury.

The money would be good, because by common
consent a law had been passed which made it good;
because it was backed by the Government and based
upon real estate of twice its own value; because there
was no other money. By this plan the people went to
their own Government for money instead of going to
some foreign syndicate and inviting them to furnish
money to carry on their own great enterprises; thereby
obtaining title to every valuable franchise, every rich
mine and, in the end, an absolute control of the whole
industrial system.

It was agreed that no foreign capital was wanted;
that they did not recognize money as capital, but that

labor was capital and money only a means or method.

An abundance of money was furnished, as has been explained; it was turned over to corporations and they put it into circulation.

As all money was turned over to corporations in lieu of stock, so as the stock was sold the money came back into the treasury. This being the system, it follows, that whenever there was a railroad to build the money was always ready; if there were people in the country to make a railroad pay, there would always be spare labor enough to build it. The only thing necessary to set labor at work is money and it was therefore furnished in abundance.

Bundy said "there would be just as much sense in limiting the amount of tools to work with as there would be in limiting the amount of money to be used, which would certainly have the same effect, as money and labor were the requisites; Government furnished the money the people did the work and received the money." When it at last, passed into the hands of progressive persons it went back into the treasury, in exchange for stock in the road; thus foreign capital was not needed.

So it was with every branch of industry, from the building of a city to the opening of a mine. Wherever a project was to be carried out for the good of the people, which required a capital of over $100,000 it could be done on the joint-stock plan, hence no occasion for borrowing money.

The amount of capital required cut no figure, $100,-000 or $100,000,000, it was all the same. If there were people enough to do the work there would be people enough to buy the stock. If there were not citizens enough to do the work the work was then not needed.

"Work," said President Bundy, "that has to be done with imported labor had better go undone."

Under a system like this it is not at all surprising that this young Republic prospered; it could hardly do otherwise. There was no advertising for capital to come and take possession, scot free, of all the most valuable franchises in the country; no organizing companies and going to England to sell stock; all this was dispensed with.

In the territory of Arizona, U. S., there are some of the finest valleys the sun ever shone upon; no country was ever blest with a finer climate, but they had to have water to irrigate the land before it could be farmed successfully; to get water they had to construct ditches; there were plenty of men to do the work, but they had no money and instead of going to the government for it, as they did in this new Republic, and afterwards buying the stock as the country progressed, they were compelled to work under different methods. The people owned the lands and to make good homes and productive farms, they must have water; there was plenty of water in the river that belonged to the public but great canals had to be constructed to convey it to the land.

Under the system adopted in the New Republic, the people would have called a mass meeting, organized a company and applied to the chief of that department at Washington for a charter; when the charter had been granted the full amount of stock in $10 shares was also printed and together with money to the same amount would be sent to the sub-treasury, in Arizona; the money to be drawn upon from time to time as the work progressed; the stock to be kept for sale at its par value. The charter for a company, together with commission to officers would also be forwarded; these officers would receive a reasonable salary and hold their places until removed for cause; by this method the stock of these ditch companies would, in a few years, pass into the hands of the farmers and people, generally through their savings and the money back into the treasury.

Under American methods, some shrewd man, seeing the situation, calls a few friends to his assistance, organizes a company under the laws of the territory, secures a franchise and right to the water; these very valuable acquisitions cost the company nothing and have, by these transactions, been transferred from the people to the lawful possession of a soulless concern that often becomes so powerful as to defy all law.

Having been duly organized, they receive their franchise and water right, issue stock or bonds, sell a part of the same to some great syndicate for money to build the ditch with; the money thus received is used to set the people to work and they build a canal. For doing this work the good people receive wages enough to keep them alive until the canal is completed; when water is upon the land, they learn that a man owning 160 acres could not buy water, even for cash, until he had first bought a water right that would cost him from $500 to $2,000; this right simply guaranteed to him the privilege of buying water for his land by paying for it in advance; if he refused to buy the right, they would turn the water back into the river and starve him out. If he had no money to pay for a right, a bank was there that had plenty of government money they would lend him at a good round interest and take a mortgage on his land. So between interest, taxes, and a big price for water, the farmer soon goes to the wall, and in a very short time the moneyed men own the whole thing, while the farmer becomes a tenant on his own land.

The reader will of course suppose that this water right that cost the Arizona farmer from $500 to $2,000 gives him some kind of stock or share in the ditch, but in this he would find himself mistaken, as it only gives him the *privilege* of buying water when the company has it to sell. Nothing more, nothing less, and you can't buy water unless you own that right This is rather a hard story, but if any man doubts let him investigate. I call it plutocratic law, pure and simple.

It has been before explained that a steam navigation company had been organized at Summerville. This company had unlimited capital. Congress by special act had fixed fares and freights at such a figure as to make the business extremely profitable and arranged that its profit above 5 per cent be invested in other ships to that end that it would alone be able to do all the cargoing and passenger business of the country. One object in this act was to increase fares and keep out unwelcome immigration. Its capital stock could also be increased at any time that more vessels were found necessary. For a while this com. pany bought many ships abroad, but this was not destined to last long in a country where there was plenty of material of all kinds, plenty of skilled labor, plenty of money and a business system that gave every man an opportunity of becoming part owner in the company for which he toiled.

The ship building company that had been organized at Summerville, like all joint stock companies in the Republic, had unlimited capital, that is, it could increase its capital stock whenever the business required an increase, and receive money from the Government to balance the stock. Being fully alive to the growing necessities of commerce, this company was using every available means to get to the front rank as builders and were now constantly putting new vessels afloat, all of which were sold to the navigation company, except such as were disposed of to private individuals and firms for coast trade. There was another ship building company at Summerville but its entire force was used in constructing war vessels. The Government also had a school of experts in connection with this company, who were studying new plans and inventions thought to be useful in operating against and destroying iron vessels. This school received plans and inventions from all parts of the country, and it was believed that they had a vessel that would not only be proof against shot and shell but would be able to sink the heaviest armed battle ship by colotion. These boats, it was claimed, had greater speed than any war vessel afloat and was designed for coast and harbor defense.

The settlements were spreading in every direction; the cotton country was fast being converted into productive plantations and thrifty villages were springing up everywhere; the wheat and corn country was also rapidly being taken up, not by speculators, but by people who wanted homes. Railroads were being built everywhere, factories started and the great ship-loads of immigrants that were constantly arriving, would melt away into the busy throng without attracting the least attention, for all found something to do. They were from what is called the middle class, but composed of honest and intelligent people, who had lost their savings and their homes during the wealth-concentrating period that followed the passage of the contraction act in the United States. The simple fact that during the fifteen years following that event, there was not one financial act but was directly in the interest of bankers, gold-gamblers and their conspirators, enabling them the more successfully to fleece the people; and that business failures became the rule and not the exception, is quite enough to account for these men hunting new homes. As the United States had furnished homes for the homeless of Europe in by-gone days, so now the new Republic was called upon to furnish homes for those who had been made homeless in so short a time in America.

These people, like a large part of the immigrants who came to the United States, had more or less gold and silver, beside other goods of value; there was an import duty on gold because it was an article not needed in the Republic and this law, to some extent, helped to discourage its importation.

Those who brought gold or silver, after the duty was paid experienced no further inconvenience, as they could sell it to the treasury deparement at a small discount for National money which was a full legal-tender in all parts of the Republic, and with it their outfits could be purchased at the lowest figure. This constant stream of gold which was being dumped into the treasury by immigrants, in addition to the vast product of the mines, soon put the statesmen to their wits' end.

As every man in the country was, by their own peculiar government kept constantly employed, with an abundance of labor-saving machinery, there could be but one result, an over-production of everything, but no man, woman or child starved or went half clad in consequence of this over-production, but to the con-

trary. The surplus was bought up by a huge join'
stock company, that had its agents in all parts of the
world, and had complete control of all export and import trade. Owing to the peculiar methods by which
all joint-stock companies were formed and controlled,
this company worked in harmony with the steam
navigation company, and the result was, the citizens
of the Republic owning the stock in both companies,
received the benefit of all profit arising from their own
carrying trade or transportation.

All goods were kept constantly marketed by this
company, in such portions of the world as they were
most needed. With average production and an honest
deal, there could be no other result than an excess of
exports, and as the balance of trade in favor of the
Republic was paid in gold, which soon found its way
into the treasury in exchange for money, the gold
problem became more difficult of solution day by day.
To discontinue the purchase of gold would destroy the
mining industry; as gold was not needed in commerce,
no man wanted it; to let it accumulate in the treasury as
a useless surplus, with an imaginary value, was called
bad statesmanship.

At this critical moment, a wag suggested that they
follow the example of the United States and invest it
in the Bank-of-England confidence. "I would use the
gold," said he, "for money, withdraw the national
money by a contraction act and burn it up for fear the
people might call for it again, then coin the gold into
honest money; sell all the mines and railroad stock to
English syndicates for more gold to make more honest
money; then issue a lot of gold bonds, bearing a big,
gold interest, then a national banking system to control
the money. Do as I tell you and as sure as history
repeats itself, it will soon take all the surplus of the
mines, farm and factory to pay for confidence, and
interest on confidence to our syndicate millionaires."

Among the farmers who came there were some of
course who had little or no means; some of these
worked for others until they earned money for a start;
others took land near some of their friends or worked

among their neighbors who would return the compliment with their teams, and the crop was soon planted, and when harvested, seldom failed to sell for enough to buy teams and tools for the coming year. In this way the great farming-lands were being settled up by an intelligent and industrious class of people.

With plenty of rich soil, every man owning his own farm, an abundance of the most approved farm-machinery, no rent, no interest, mortgages, or taxes, it was found that every energetic farmer had a regular surplus to invest in railroad or other commercial stock.

While the farmers were prospering, it must not be supposed that, like the bankers of Christendom, they were robbing every other industry; on the contrary, we see manufactures springing up everywhere and thousands of men constantly employed in making such articles as found ready sale among these farmers.

In every city, town and county we see mechanics, tradesmen and manufacturers organizing companies, starting up business of all kinds, and the stock of all these companies going out through the sub-treasury as commercial stock, and being constantly absorbed by the savings of the country.

To those in the United States who have seen bankers, money-sharks and gold gamblers prosper and all others go to the wall or exist as auxiliaries, or at the pleasure of the great millionaire and syndicate, it will seem strange, of course, that one class of people can prosper without doing so at the expense of some other class; but such proves to be the case in our new Rebublic. In fact, so exactly to the reverse of this did things appear, that each industry was the life and support of every other class, and each being dependent upon all the others for a market, all worked in harmony.

The price of labor being regulated by the department of industry, in accordance with the price of commodities or of living, that question became obsolete and was unknown among the citizens of the new Republic. A workman would no more think of an increase of wages than would an American soldier, except it came through their own savings and investment in commercial stock, which made them recipients of the 50 per cent dividend on the same. As no decrease in wages could occur until preceded by a corresponding decrease in living commodities, no hardship was ever felt from this source and men found questions of greater interest to discuss than the vexed question of capital and labor as it exists in the United States.

When the system of government was formulated there was a great difference of opinion as to how the financial system would work. Some claimed that the gold should be run into money and sent out instead of paper money; others thought it should be kept in the treasury as a base for paper money; others again said that would be wrong, as it would limit the circulation of money and also tie up the gold so it could not be used as a commodity in exchange with foreign countries without decreasing the home circulation; some objected to the whole system, saying that the government in issuing such vast sums of money to build and run manufactures of all kinds, wholesale stores, erect large buildings in cities, put up buildings for schools, colleges and the use of science; build and run railroads, telegraphs, telephones and every other enterprise where large capital was required, would so inflate the currency as to make the money worthless; but it was found the savings of the country were as fast as possible converted into stock, and in this way an equilibrium was preserved between money and commodities.

As time rolled on all stock passed into the hands of the people through their savings, and the money of course was then all back in the treasury. Had not the Government sent this money out again stringency must have occurred; but to avoid this, Government was not only compelled to carry on great public work but also made large appropriation to each state to be used in building public roads through the farming region.

In the United States this money would have been turned over to a banking aristocracy, and they in turn would have loaned it to the people at a heavy interest, taking a mortgage on their homes. But these people had seen how the system worked, and as a burned child dreads the fire, they resolved to steer clear of banks.

In consequence of this plan of getting money into circulation by spending it in improvements, the roads throughout the country were nicely graded, bordered with grass and shade trees and soon became the pride of the nation.

After the business stock had passed into the hands of the people through their over-production or surplus of savings it was found that the two per cent on commercial stock, together with the revenue derived from the graduated tax on incomes, was so enormous that the money passed back into the treasury in one constant stream, similar to the manner in which it floods Wall Street in the United States, but after the money had lodged in these great money centers the method of getting it out and in circulation again was very different. Money once lodged in Wall Street remains there until business men are compelled to have it to carry on business or meet obligation. Then by force of necessity they are compelled to borrow it at enormous rates of interest; so the business man eventually does business at the mercy of the money lender.

In the Republic things are quite different.

When a surplus of money found its way into the treasury and in consequence less than $50 per capita was in circulation, it became the duty of the Treasurer, unless other provision by law had been made to meet the emergency, to portion the money among the different states, the same to be used in general improvement of the country at once, and in this way the money soon found its way back into the proper channel. Interest, discount, mortgages, honest dollars, parity, sound currency, gold standard, starvation wages, child labor, paupers, tramps and millionaires were terms never heard in the new Republic, though common in the United States.

The expense of running state and county government was not nearly so large as under the system in vogue in the United States. There was to commence with no bonded debt, hence no interest to be paid to foreign money lenders.

Then again, lawful possession and constant use was the only title known to land, consequently the expense of running that branch of the government was largely reduced. As there was plenty of money and work for all, with no saloons, crime disappeared to a remarkable extent. Taxes were promptly paid and business was never cramped as it often is where money is controlled by a few individuals and stringency occurs.

Americans who are accustomed to the good old way of striking two blows for the money changers or land speculators and one for themselves, will no doubt wonder how a state or county government could put up public buildings without issuing bonds to get the money; and in order that they may understand how this was done, I will explain:

When the organization of Government was perfected, thirteen states had been partially settled and had a population of from 50,000 to 100,000 each, making an entire population of 1,000,000; at $50 per capita, this would require a total circulation of $50,000,000. The Government had been issuing money for every business in the country on the joint-stock plan, and although there had been issued over $300,000,000, there was now less than $50,000,000 in circulation, the balance having come back into the treasury in exchange for stock.

As there had been no over-plentiful amount of money in circulation during the past, and as there were instances in history where nations had carried a circulation of $70 or $80 per capita successfully, it was decided that the amount of money in circulation be increased to $60 per capita, and that the extra $10 be given to each state for building purposes.

According to the arrangement a state having a population of over 100,000 would be entitled to one million dollars. This money was to be held in trust by the government subject to the order of each state when needed for the erection of public buildings, and as population increased this fund was also to be increased at the same rate of $10 apiece.

This money was to be like all national money—a full legal tender and forever remain in circulation. According to the American system this money would have been given to the banks and they would have loaned it to the states for bonds bearing large interest; thus interest and confidence would cost the people, in the course of events, more than their buildings (all for the benefit of the bank.)

In order to meet running expenses each state issued scrip in exchange, the same to be receivable for taxes and redeemable in National money when there was money in the treasury. In order to bring this scrip in on taxes, a 5 per cent premium was given for it when offered for that purpose.

As all buildings had to be paid for out of the Building fund there was no difficulty in raising, by direct tax, the amount of money necessary to redeem the scrip once a year. Thus the running expense of state and county government was always paid in scrip, nicely printed in from one to twenty dollar bills—duly protected against counterfeit. Having a 5 per cent premium when used in the payment of taxes, it was always desirable and constantly in demand at par.

It will be remembered that a building company was organized at Summerville for the purpose of constructing and renting such buildings as were needed and would cost over $100,000. As building companies, were organized under special laws and operated under a somewhat different plan from other joint companies, it will be necessary to explain: Wherever a town or city was being built a joint company could be formed by the people electing men to manage the business of same and making an application to government in regular form for a charter. The government in establishing the company, as in all other cases, would forward to the sub-treasury of the place money to the full amount of capital stock. The stock in ten dollar shares was also forwarded; the money to be held subject to order of the company as it was needed in actual business transactions and stock to be kept on sale, but to bear no dividend until the building it represented had been completed, after which its holder would be entitled to a 5 per cent annual dividend from the chief office of building department paid through the sub-treasury.

The profits of these companies being like all others limited to 7 per cent, the rents of buildings were so adjusted as to as nearly as possible bring that result. The government always received the full amount of profit and paid to the stockholders 5 per cent dividend per year.

As land was never sold its value was never taken into consideration in adjusting rents; in fact it had no monetary value any more than so much air or water, and was never taxed. The entire outlay of the company on a piece of land formed the base for assessing rents, but buildings in favorable locations were always assessed higher rents than those in unfavorable quarters, and in finding the company's profits the entire business transactions of the year were taken into account.

When it so happened in a city that a lot or square remained in the hands of parties with inferior buildings, an ordinance by some citizen was laid before the city council requiring that a certain kind of building be erected on said lot or square to correspond to other buildings on the same street. The ordinance would be voted on at the first election and if carried, became a law and the occupants were notified to commence work at a certain time; failing to do so, his building would be appraised; the building company were then notified to pay for the improvements, take possession of the property, remove the old building and erect a new one in compliance with the ordinances.

This would at first seem to be rather of an arbitrary plan and liable to work injustice to some, but as the land belonged to the government and the man had already received the use of it for several years without rent, it was generally conceded that he had but little right to complain, being paid for his old building. In fact most merchants preferred having their surplus

cash invested in stock at 5 per cent per annum to having it tied up in real estate, and it was noticed that
.he men owning the buildings were generally first to
suggest the plan for a new building that could be rented
so reasonably.

Their building called for insurance and in case of a
pinch was hard to convert into cash, while the stock
required no insurance and could be converted into cash
on presentation.

Some men of course who had been raised under the
old English land law, millionaire rule of the United
States, made a good deal of fuss and said that the
legislation was all against individuals who had been
frugal and accumulated wealth. They would sometimes
use the same old gag of dividing up all the property,
a thing that none but themselves ever thought of, but
all this was considered a kind of disease, the result of
having been raised under bad conditions among millionaires, and they were reminded that the land
belonged to the Government or people, and its increase
in value belonged to the people; that for any one man
to claim either the land or increase in value of the land,
further than its increased usefulness to himself as a
home, was to say the least, extremely selfish if not
dishonest.

This class of people was also reminded that the Government was of the people and for the people; the
greatest good to the greatest number. That in no case
should laws be made for the benefit of an individual.
The individuals should conform to the law but in no
case should the law be made to conform to the wishes
or interests of an individual, as that would certainly
be class legislation, and directly opposed to that already
well established rule, the greatest good to the greatest
number.

Mr. Bundy said that while it was important to the
people as a nation that every man should own his own
home, there was no good reason why a business man
should own the house he does business in. The home
was for the accommodations of the family and should
be owned by the family; the business house was for the

accommodation of the public and should be owned by the public.

As the rent of buildings was placed on their real cost and limited to 7 per cent, it was found that business men could generally make more on their money by using it in their business than they could to have it invested in buildings; while stock furnished a nice investment for such surplus as might arise.

These building companies were organized in all parts of the country; as a rule they constructed all state, national and county buildings. Having extensive and complete outfits and skilled workmen, they could, when a building was needed, carry on the work without hinderance or delay. Such work was all done by contract, and as work progressed they drew upon the state or county, $10 per capita, building fund, which was generally found to be more than sufficient, but when it ran short the Government issued the amount to meet the emergency and it went into circulation, to be kept out of such building fund as might accrue to the state in the future from the general Government as population increased, but in no case did snch fund or shortages bear interest.

In the building department there were two classes of companies formed; those just described were for the construction of public or business houses; the other companies constructed dwellings and were different from the first mentioned only in their peculiar method of renting their buildings.

CHAPTER XXIV.

THESE home coustruction companies, as they were called, were organized in every town and city in the country. They were joint stock companies and organized on the same plan as all other companies; a house that cost $1,000 would bear a rent under the 7 per cent law or rule of $70 a year; to cover wear, 10 per cent or $10 was added, making in all lawful rent to the amount of $80 per year; in addition to this, they charged a purchase rental of $74 per year, making in all $12 per month. Taking the price of other things into consideration, this was thought to be a reasonable rent. At the end of the first year, as $74 had been paid, 8 per cent on that amount was added to the $74 making his credit the second year $79.92. From this it will be seen that in the two years the renter would have placed to his credit $153.92, and in this way the credit would increase from year to year until the house was paid for. Then the renter would receive from the company a quit-claim deed to the property.

This system was adopted by the Government for the purpose of encouraging citizens to own their own homes. After a man had paid rent on a building until his credit amounted to $100 or over, he could transfer, for or without consideration, his right of possession, together with his credit on the company's book, to a third party; but that third party in order to derive any benefit from the credit, must use the house for his home and continue to pay rents. Any failure to do this forfeited both possession and credit.

There is no wonder that Mr. Goldburg was surprised when he learned from the newspapers that he could buy Government bonds bearing interest, a good, round sum, with his greenback, and while drawing on the bond have 90 per cent of his money given back to him to lend out among the people to take the place in circulation of greenbacks he had just paid to Government for bonds.

When he saw that by this very strange act of Con. gress, he was enabled to receive one interest on his money from the government, and another interest on the same money from the people, he knew for a certainty that the money power was framing the laws and that the idea of the government being of and for the people was an exploded theory, hence his surprise; but it was no greater than the surprise of these honest toilers to find that they were living under a Government which did actually recognize the rights of man to live and receive justice. While it was explained to them that the Government was losing nothing in the transaction, but on the contrary, both the Government and the company made a reasonable profit, they were highly elated and declared that if the system continued for fifteen years, every family would have a home to beautify, and this might truly be called a Government of and for the people—not the millionaires. It was also remarked that in the United States the wise statesmen who were memorized subjects under control of millionaires had talked so much about the sacred rights of property, that it seemed strange to see the rights of man recognized.

Mr. Bundy said: "This system is the outgrowth of advanced thought; so long as we, through our Government control money, also control the accumulation of property in the hands of individuals, by limiting inheritance and graduated income tax, just so long will we have a Government of and for the people. But whenever we limit ourselves as a Government in our accumulation to the actual expense of the Government and allow individual property to roll on from year to year, and age to age without check or limit, there can be but one result, the power of wealth in the hands of a few will become stronger than the Government, control legislation, monopolize machinery; labor will go unemployed, and crime increase, while chaos and confusion will reign."

Large newspapers were all run on the joint stock plan under the control of that department of Government; as with all other companies, the Government furnished the money and sold the stock. The 7 per cent rule, also, applied to them as to all other companies. From this it will be seen that the press was beyond the reach of subsidy and became the great guiding star of the Republic. As every man had a home, every man took a paper. As eight hours was the universal day's work, all had time to read and all did read—men, women and children.

As the forms of the Government were all simple, all understood them. They had no parity between the metals, gold and silver, to puzzle statesmen; these metals had been reduced to commodities and a boy ten years old could give you their exact value. Everybody knew that money was worth just what it would buy, and the figures on the bill told as plainly what that was as though it were stamped in gold. Everybody knew the money was good, because it was the pledge of the Government, and the Government owned all the land and controlled all the business of the country. The people who had the use of the money free of interest, also had the land free of rent.

Under such circumstances is it any wonder that the citizens of the new Republic prospered and needed no protective tariff?

Mr. Bundy said: "With the finest machinery in use, no rent, no interest, light taxes, every man owning his own home, they could compete with the slave or pauper labor of any or all other countries; beside, if all the other countries under the sun were blotted from existence, it would not seriously affect their industries; they would still have enough to eat, plenty to wear, plenty to do and plenty of money. These things are absolutely necessary to bring about prosperity."

In farming regions, people with old fashioned ideas were very much worked up by not being able to get a deed to their land. One man hearing that a Catholic explorer had landed on the coast of Africa some 16,000 years before the flood and had claimed the country, he believing this to be the oldest title that could be procured, wrote to the Pope, at Rome, and in consideration of his faith, piety and a few gold dollars, received a warrantee deed; that man thereafter, was the envy of the whole neighborhood, and was recognized as the only man in the country having a warrantee deed. As time rolled on, some lawless parties drove him from the land and themselves took possession; he applied to the authorities, who arrested the parties and reinstated the man. It then dawned upon the people, that land could only be held peacefully, under the protection of the Government; it also occurred to them that a Government could as easily protect a man's possessive right, as though he had an abstract title running back to the day of Constantine. They began to comprehend that absolute ownership of land had been one of the prime factors in enslaving mankind since time began.

The mines had been worked for years by private individuals; but as they grew deeper and surface mines were exhausted, they required more capital; to secure this they organized companies and took advantage of the joint-stock system.

It should be here explained that although mining companies were organized on the same general principles that other companies were, the stock was managed very differently; when sold it was never received back again into the treasury in exchange for money or otherwise, except on deposit. The dividends, instead of being limited to 5 per cent were paid upon the net productions. On being applied to for a charter on certain property, the Department sent experts, who were of high standing and employed by the year, to examine the mine, not only to report on its merit, but also to make an estimate of the cost of such work as would be necessary to put the property in a paying condition; attend also to the building of roads, buying machinery, putting it in place with all necessary buildings, tools, fixtures, in fact, everything necessary to

successful operation.   When this report was made fully
satisfactory a joint-stock company was formed by
appointing officers to run the concern; a charter was
then forwarded to the sub-treasury nearest the mine,
together with stock to the full amount of the cost of
the work as reported by the expert, and money was
sent to balance the stock, to be used as needed on the
work; one-fourth of the stock to be given to the owner
of the mines, the balance to be placed on sale at a
premium of 25 per cent.

Applications for stock were received for thirty days
before sale of stock commenced and then the orders
were filled by commencing with the smallest order,
then the next smallest and so on up to the greatest.
This was law.   After a thirty days' run had been made
the product was turned over to the Government, as
was the universal rule; its entire value was ascertained;
from this, 10 per cent was taken as royalty, then 10
per cent for a sinking fund, to be added to such money
as remained after the work of putting the mines in
order was completed; this 10 per cent sinking fund
was taken out and retained as long as the mine run,
unless the rule was suspended by the mining department.   It was held in trust by the Government to cover
contingencies and at last, when the mine was abandoned
if any remained unused to be paid out as a dividend
on stock.   After these sums had been subtracted from
the total product the balance was paid out as a dividend on stock.   When the first run had been made, if
any stock remained in the treasury, its price was fixed
in accordance with the production, but was not allowed
to be sold below 25 per cent premium; so that the
Government not only received 10 per cent royalty, but
they received such increase in value as might accrue
after thirty days' run; but it was found that under this
system, the stock was generally sold before the mine
started.

As a general rule, when a company was formed, every
man and woman, boy and girl in the neighborhood
who had ten dollars to spare, registered at the sub-
treasury for stock, and in a majority of cases there was

not stock enough to supply the demand. Of course many large fortunes were made in these mines, but foreign capital received no favor, because it was not needed and was prohibited by law.

Notwithstanding the production of these mines was much less than the mines of the United States, their working had a very different effect upon the country and people. As large capital was required to work the mines in the United States, for the want of money men were often forced to sell to foreign capitalists; thus many of the best mines passed into the hands of foreign syndicates for a nominal sum and their immense wealth was forever lost to the United States, for want of a system that would furnish money to the people, instead of the banker. Individuals too in the American mines often made millions; with this money they obtained vast possessions, monopolized railroads, real estate and other valuable property, finally becoming insane over the sudden acquisition of such wealth and power; others go to foreign countries and there court royalty, often ending by marrying a daughter to some titled pauper, who spends their wealth in a foreign land.

Thus the country which owned these greatest of producing mines known to man, receive little or no benefit from them; on the contrary, Americans risked their lives delving for gold which an idiot might squander in a foreign land. In fact, such has been the legislative management of the United States for the last twenty-five years, that while the gold and silver has been constantly going abroad, the surplus beef, pork, wheat, corn, cotton, rice, tobacco and many other commodities have to a great extent fed and clothed the civilized world; during that period the United States as a people, are said to have become the debtor-nation, not only of millions, but billions upon billions of dollars and are to-day paying tribute in the shape of interest to foreign syndicates, amounting to millions upon millions of dollars annually.

Can any American who loves his country, respects himself and his kindred, help feeling a sense of shame when he contemplates these things. Whether it comes from ignorance of legislators or unparalleled dishonesty, trickery and bribe taking, it matters not; it is robbery, nevertheless.

While this has been going on for years, the United States Senate has had the services of many able men, whose wisdom has been unquestioned, holding positions and receiving pay at the hands of the American people. But not one man has dared to grapple the plutocratic monster and oppose a system of class legislation that many of the ablest men in the nation foresaw and publicly proclaimed would bring about this slavish, inhuman result; but while many lent their silent consent, others in violation of all righteousness gave their intellect and best efforts toward the passage of acts that will forever stand in history as a monument to the debauchery of the men who voted for them. Shall we attribute all this to ignorance or dishonesty, or is it possible that there is no better way and that American liberty which once inspired the heart of our people has been smothered in debt and pauperism? Perhaps some of the gentlemen who have been in the United States Senate during this time and have become millionaires from a salary of $5,000 a year, could give us some light upon this subject.

When that patriotic, American statesman, Charles C. Pinckney, used these words: "Not one dollar for tribute but millions for defense" and found a responsive chord in every American heart, he little thought that in a few short years, from class legislation, his countrymen would not only be paying millions upon millions of tribute in the form of interest, rent and dividends, but that one-half of their number would be living in rented homes.

It seemed like a pity to spoil a good story by such an array of disagreeable facts, but in order to show clearly the beauties and advantages arising from the order of things existing in the new Republic, the contrast is important; besides it enables the writer to show the different effect of a Government run in the interest of the people and one run in the interest of bankers and millionaires.

When years rolled on the exports of the Republic became enormous.   As not one dollar of it went to pay interest, dividends or profits on foreign capital, and very little to be spent in worshiping a royal class that owed their station in life to birth, not to merit, the people of the Republic enjoyed a degree of prosperity unparalleled in ancient or modern times.   Their institutions of learning became the wonder of the world.   Owing to the improved condition of the country, travel became so cheap that space was in a manner overcome, and people living hundreds of miles apart, were often like next door neighbors.

Improved machinery released so many men from other departments that the railroad companies increased their construction and repairing force, until the road beds and bridges were made so perfect that with their universal double-tracks danger of travel was reduced to a minimum, collisions and other accidents being next to impossibilities.

The postal system became so perfect in its workings that farmers had their mail laid at their door every day. .

Newspapers were so far superior to the subsidized press of the United States, that a comparison would be odious.   One ever leading in a constant search for new truths.   The other constantly seeking new subterfuge to cover up the crimes of millionaires; the one the life of progress; the other the greatest known obstacle in its way; one a credit; the other a disgrace.

As cleanliness was said to be next to godliness, a huge joint-stock company was formed that did business in every city, town and county in the country.   Steam laundries were brought to such a high state of perfection and work was done so cheaply that they were patronized by even the poorest families; light wagons were constantly making their rounds gathering up the soiled clothes and returning them ready for use.

Churches, while grand in architecture, were modest and less pretentious in inside ornamentation.

In religious teachings they had kept pace with the general advance of intelligence; creeds and dogmas had in a great measure been abandoned and the brotherhood of man, as taught by Jesus Christ, was accepted in its simplicity. An endless, burning hell of fire and brimstone, with all teachings representing God as a brutal monster, were forever buried with the musty records of the past.

As limiting inheritance and a graduated income tax produced a more equal distribution of money and property, there were wealthy men and women by thousands in every county, town and city. In consequence of this when, from drouth, fire, flood or pestilence, assistance became necessary, many willing hearts and hands brought prompt relief.

Roads were hard, smooth and shady borders made them so delightful that bicycles took the place of horses to a great extent. Fruit, flowers and trees were so common that every house became an eden, every farm a paradise; people from the cities often sought the shady nooks and corners in the country for recreation and repose.

The only army found necessary was used in garrisoning the forts along the coast; some even considered these superfluous, claiming that the advanced condition of the people, intellectually, physically, socially and morally would make them capable of taking care of themselves against the combined world.

General Summerville being kept in command of the army, continued the use of natives and pronounced them the very best of soldiers; but he had another reason for not enlisting white men and that was, that times were so good outside of the army that none chose to enlist except in case of war, and there was no probability of that.

One of the most peculiar features of the new condition of society in the Republic was, while the cities were already assuming gigantic proportions, the manufacturers and farmers crowding their surplus or overproduction upon the market, the great steam navigation company was kept busy transporting it to all parts of the world, the people en masse receiving the dividends on stock that represented all the great corporations of the country; free schools and colleges running the year around without interruption. All this had been accomplished without the use of gold as money, without a national bank, without a foreign debt, and not the shadow of a millionaire, picture of a pauper, or a subsidized press.

Kiyongo had now become a populous city and it was American to the core. A society was formed there by such men as had been crowded out of business in the United States by the disastrous result of contraction and other acts of Congress. The object of the society was to keep in memory that sad event; it was ordained by this society that they would build a monument of a fine quality of building stone that had been found in the mountains; to be located on a beautiful knoll three miles east of the city of Kiyongo, the place being selected on account of being in plain view from both city and lake. It was erected in order to keep fresh that legislation in the United States known as the exception clause on greenbacks, gold interest on bonds, contraction, resumption, and demonetization of silver. It was claimed that the people of the United States, through this legislation, had been robbed, not only of millions upon millions, but even billions upon billions had been wrung from an industrious people and millions of men, women and children had lost their homes and had been reduced to a state of want and suffering to enrich a few individuals. It was also claimed that John Sherman had been the main party through whom this class legislation was secured; that the work had been done with eyes not blinded to the results that would follow, as was clearly shown by his former speeches; but that it was a plain case of corruption, and therefore his name, with that of Arnold, and Judas should be kept in memory as the three greatest traitors to human progress that the world has ever known and that a representative statue of each be placed upon the great monument, and a history of their diabolical work be traced in flaming letters on its sides.

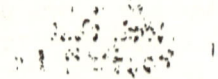

CHAPTER XXV.

WHILE Mr. Goldburg was in Boston, Rebecca wrote to one of the Professors of a seminary where she had formerly been a student asking for a situation as a teacher, and having been in high esteem in the school, she received a prompt reply offering her a place to commence at her earliest convenience. She put the letter where she could get it readily and made up her mind that if difference must come between her and her father she preferred being the aggressor. The second day after her father's return from Boston, he stopped in the sitting room for a few moments to look over the morning paper and Rebecca thinking it a good opportunity, took the letter and presented it for his approval. He read it with astonishment.

"Why is this?" he said, "that you are wanting to disgrace the family by going to work for a salary? Did your mother not tell you of the plan I have in view, of uniting the two great estates through your marriage with Mr. Goldaker?"

"Yes, father," said Rebecca, "but I do not like that man."

"No, you never like any man that is respectable; while I have been many years hard at work building up a fortune that can be left as a monument to myself and family, you absolutely refuse to marry where you can, by so doing, throw millions into my possession, and also start a family to inherit this vast estate, which will be equal to the largest in the United States and give your children a rank in the coming Nobility, which is already organized and fast developing into power."

"I am so sorry to oppose you, father; if you were in want I would do anything possible to comfort you."

"Want," said her father, in a mocking way, "do you suppose that with all my gold I could ever come to want? It is not want by which I am actuated, but it is business, purely business."

"True," said Rebecca, "it is business with you, but I am not property to be bartered off for gold; I am human and I'll die before I will marry a man I do not love."

The millionaire flushed at such insubordination and straightening himself up, said: "Call your mother."

Rebecca obeyed and was about to leave the room, when her father called her back. Addressing his wife, he then said: "I have watched for years this growing tendency to disregard my wishes. Rebecca has thrown me out of millions of dollars by her sympathy for poverty and her unpardonable contempt for power; while presidents and statesmen are subservient to my will, she alone stands out, as firm as the rock of Gibralter. You, I believe, have by your silence allowed this continual disobedience to go unchecked, and it is now my full determination to stop things where they are, therefore all you have to do is to state the amount you will require, and since our union has ceased to be of benefit the sooner we separate the better."

This was just what Mrs. Goldburg was expecting and she knew that talk would be futile. The father, she knew, would accept nothing on the part of Rebecca but unconditional subjection to his will; this she could not grant. She had long believed from the drift of things that she and her daughter would eventually have to become entirely subservient to the power of money which had so completely taken hold of her husband and held him in its deadly grasp, or a dissolution would naturally follow. She was therefore, in a manner, prepared to hear such a proposition, but to name an amount she had not considered. The estate was worth several millions of dollars and she did not care to answer without thinking over the matter. The millionaire however was too anxious to make the trade before some lawyer might interfere, and continued:

"You may have this property (meaning the old home) and the store that Col. Bundy is running, also the building the goods are in; I will also give you each a check for $100,000 now drawing interest in the bank. This is enough for anyone."

"Yes," said Mrs. Goldburg, "I have always claimed that all money and property above a competency is a curse to the possessor. I therefore should be satisfied."

Mr. Goldburg promptly drew two checks of $100,000 each, presented them and also drew up a paper for their signatures, releasing him from further claims. "This evening," said he, "you shall have your deeds;" and the business thus completed, he moved on into his office, apparently well satisfied.

There had been times in bygone days when a scene like this would have broken the hearts of both, but since gold and greed had turned the heart of the father and husband into a plutocratic, domineering boss, it was surely a relief to let him go.

On the next day Mr. Goldburg had the papers all made out, signed, and properly turned over to his wife and daughter; then proceeded to settle up his business affairs and went to Boston, where he afterwards married an actress; but continued business with Messrs. Goldaker & Son.

When he had gone Mrs. Goldburg and daughter proceeded to take stock and consider their great possessions. When comparing their large estate of about $270,000 to the millions of dollars that the father had kept to himself, Mrs. Goldburg said she never before comprehended so forcibly what an immense sum a million of dollars was, and what gigantic frauds must have been perpetrated in Congress in order to procure legislation that would enable men to build up such vast estates in so short a time. She declared that Mr. Goldburg had given nothing in return for the vast property that he now held, hence some one was surely robbed and that some one was the American people.

Now that all restraint had been set aside, the manner in which Col. Bundy had been robbed loomed up before Mrs. Goldburg as a monster swindle. Always, since the Colonel's failure, Mrs. Goldburg and Rebecca had felt as though by accompanying Mr. Goldburg to the farm when he induced the Colonel to go into business, they had indirectly assisted him and were in some degree responsible for the Colonel's misfortune.

Looking at the matter from this standpoint, a mutual feeling existed to do something for Col. Bundy and family. Mrs. Goldburg believed he was robbed, and in order to satisfy themselves they had the books brought from the store, and on examination found that the Colonel's losses commenced with the destruction of greenbacks. That as they continued to withdraw greenbacks from year to year, so his losses continued, and as Mr. Goldburg, with other bankers, had put up large sums of money to secure the passage of that act, and as many millions of dollars had been lost by others, all over the country during the same period, and that bankers all over the country had at the same time enjoyed unparalleled prosperity; they felt it was safe to conclude that the same law which had robbed the people from Maine to California and built up the banks, had also robbed the Colonel and built up Mr. Goldburg's bank.

It was agreed that they would make Mr. Bundy a present of the entire stock, and deed the building over to its proper owner, Mr. Stillwater, taking his note for a small sum. A few days after the transfer of the property, Mrs. Goldburg and Rebecca called on Mrs. Bundy, and before leaving, presented her with a bill of sale of the entire store. Mr. and Mrs. Bundy naturally declined the gift at first, but after an explanation that they only considered it a return of property stolen, she accepted it with many thanks.

After Mr. Goldburg's departure home affairs went on pretty much after the same old fashion. For years he had been from home so much, and was so selfish and so unsocial when at home that his absence was more of a relief than otherwise. Now that her father was gone Rebecca made every possible effort to increase her mother's happiness. The servants also enjoyed the change.

Since the Colonel failed the friendship between the Bundy and Goldburg families had not been of the most intimate character, but now the two families met as one. They were also on better terms with all their neighbors, and it was noticeable that affairs had been vastly improved in every respect.

Rebecca had always paid much attention to the flower garden, and now that she felt it really belonged to her, her interest increased and this pastime added largely to her happiness, as well as her correspondence with Minnie Sheppard.

After a few years spent in this pleasant, but aimless way, Rebecca received the following letter:

HOME IN IOWA,
Sept. 4, 18—

MY DEAR FRIEND: I had such a strange dream last night, if it was a dream. I seemed to awake in the night; a rich glow of golden light was spreading in gentle wavelets throughout the room. A small cloud from which the light emanated stood out before me and as it dispersed to mingle with golden light and add to it another charm, a form was revealed which filled my soul with joy, love and confidence, for I knew it was Jesus. The form addressed me, saying: "Behold thy Savior; see, if thou wilt, the nail holes and be convinced. I come to give you a mission; this has been my chosen people, but cruel hearted men have been installed in office; a golden money God has been set up for the worship of my people; my churches have been desecrated and turned into dens of thieves for money worship. Were I to-day to visit these plutocratic temples as I did long years ago in Judea, they would look at my raiment and cry out as of old, 'give us Barrabas.'

"While they profess to preach and worship in my name, they suffer my little children to starve while they hoard up wealth which they do not need; they suffer thousands of my good people to be in want. They buy up all the abundance which my Father has caused to grow and have it stored in great houses away from my people; they live in great castles, while many of my good people have no place to lay their heads.

"I say unto you, it will be more tolerable for the infidel and scoffer in the day of judgment, than for these hypocrites who pretend to worship in my name, but do not the things which I taught, and have become but a plutocratic hoarde.

"Since my people have made this land a land of gold worship, a land of millionaires and paupers, I will give them a little time to wax hot, then I will destroy their golden God and I will cleanse this land with fire.

"Before that time I will take many of my chosen ones into a land, even to Africa, where the power of gold has been destroyed; where man lives in harmony with his fellow men and gold is not hoarded; neither has it any value as money; where plutocrats are unknown and where man's productions are used for the benefit of man. To that land would I have you go."

"Therefore I say unto thee, take thyself and thy chosen friends, go unto that land where there are many pupils and few teachers; go, I say and I will put words in thy mouth and thou shalt become a power for good in the hands of thy God."

Here my vision ended and I slept sweetly till morning; but when I awoke my vision was on my mind and I could not forget it; so I wrote to the New York Ledger to find out if the new Republic would be a safe place in which to travel. You will see the answer in the last number of that paper.

I will not write any more for I am coming to see you. Good bye.

Yours affectionately,
MINNIE.

Rebecca read the letter to her mother, who laughingly said: "The girl is crazy."

But Rebecca replied: "It matters not, mother, when she is with us, she will get over it."

The subject was dropped. Mrs. Goldburg probably never gave the dream a second thought; but to Rebecca, it seemed to have a fascination.

She read the letter to the Bundys; they paid no particular attention to it. Mrs. Bundy said: "It was like her message; the minister had told her some very strange things did occur, but it was generally conceded to be the work of the devil and not safe to fool with."

Of course this did not concern Mrs. Bundy, but Rebecca took a different view of the matter. In her opinion, a message received from some unknown intelligence, through some law as yet not fully understood, it was hardly fair to give all·the credit to the devil; beside, she did not understand how the minister became convinced that it was through the devil; she was not altogether satisfied.

Another week elapsed and a telegram came announcing that Minnie would arrive on the next train. Had it been the Queen of Sheba, Rebecca and her mother could not have been more delighted to receive the visitor, and the meeting could not have been more joyful. The family reception over, the two girls went to their own room. Minnie hastened to give her plans; she said she could not drive the vision from her thoughts; it might be a dream; whether it was or not, she had been taught to believe the Bible to be true, and, said she: "I read in it that Jesus appeared to his disciples, and if he could appear to them, why could he not appear to me? I believe that Jesus spoke to me, and I believe him in preference to those who preach charity while practicing selfishness and dispense entirely with justice. If I find myself mistaken I may change my mind.

"One thing I do not understand; that is, that men who claim to be called of God to preach, always laugh and ridicule my story while a skeptic says, 'that is strange!' Be this a dream or be it fancy, it matters not; it is a new country and teachers are in demand. I want to go where religion is not a mockery and preachers deal more with justice; less with dogma, more for love and less for fame. The Ledger's answer to my question is that the Republic is considered quite safe to travel in, even for ladies, and that teachers are in demand. I am going, and you do not know how glad I will be to have your company. I have been kept· in idleness all my life, except while at school, and now I want to do something to show that I am an individual and not property."

"I rather like your wild scheme," said Rebecca, "may be we can start a seminary for girls."

"That's it," said Minnie, full of enthusiasm," but how do you think your mother will like the plan?"

"I can hardly say," said Rebecca, "she will laugh at us, but you know both of us can present the case, and she can't stand much coaxing; beside, she has for some time been talking about a sea voyage. I can see no harm in taking the trip, if we don't like the country, and if we do there is nothing I should like so well as to begin a school in a new country, where the young mind can escape the slavery of churches founded upon creeds which have been formulated in a semi-barbaric age. Only think of a man going round in a night-gown saying one thing over and over and putting wafers on the tongues of his dupes."

A few days passed pleasantly, the girls spending the most of their time in the flower garden, while they speculated on the prospect of an active life. They were agreed upon one thing, that any kind of a life of activity was better than this subordinate condition and constant inertia, in which woman's aspirations are restrained and her individuality, in a measure, lost.

If the hope of meeting in travel those from whom they had been so cruelly separated in former years found a place in their minds, that hope was so faint that neither considered it worth mentioning. The two girls, through sad disappointments, had reached that condition in life where desperation demanded a radical change. Had their teachings in early years enslaved their minds as do infallible dogmas and their secrets, in the hands of some powerful priest, they would, perhaps, have been an easy prey to superstition and might have fallen into the strong embrace of some nunnery, or some other female prison of the same char-acter; but such was not the case. Education and a free interchange of thought among the many students, teachers and associates of different beliefs, had turned their thinking faculties loose, and when the intellect is

once set free, its course is ever onward. They hoped
to be so situated as to be able to assist in spreading
the light of truth and to reach upward after that higher
knowledge for which the liberated intellect so sincerely yearns.

After talking over many different plans and discussing
the matter in every conceivable light, a plan was formulated and the two girls approached the mother. Minnie
was spokesman and the manner in which she presented
the subject would have done credit to even a Webster.
She first drew Mrs. Goldburg's attention to the
improvement in both health and spirits that would
naturally follow a sea-voyage, how the changed condition would relieve their minds and produce a good
effect generally; the scenery and travel in darker Africa
having been brought into full view and made accessi-
ble by the resistless hand of progress.

Mrs. Goldburg had been advised by her physician to
take a sea-voyage and had been thinking seriously of
doing so; the proposition was received favorably at
once, but the thought of going to Africa was one which
needed time for consideration.

Soon after, Mrs. Bundy dropped in, and being
informed of the plan, approved it at once; this might
be attributed in part, perhaps, to that hope which so
fondly clings to the mother's heart of finding her lost
boy, and seeing in this a possibility of realizing the
strange prophecy of the lady medium, she looked upon
it as a good omen and hoped, as mothers always hope,
when others all despair. A few weeks of discussion
now passed and it was decided to go; the word went
out and while preparations were going on the neighbors
kept dropping in, giving their opinions and wishing
them good luck. When nearly ready and the girls
were feeling that every obstacle had been overcome,
the most formidable difficulty of all was encountered.
A spinster in the neighborhood, conspicuous for long
prayers and earnest attention to the wants of her
neighbors, happened in at Col. Bundy's. In speaking
of the contemplated trip of the Goldburg family to
Africa, Mrs. Bundy remarked that she was glad they

wer: going for she now had a faint hope of realizing that ever present dream, awakened in her heart by the dream of a medium or fortune teller. This was enough to horrify the spinster; she told Mrs. Bundy that she considered it downright wicked to think of that message as being anything but the work of the Devil.

Mrs. Bundy saw at once that she had made a mistake but it was too late. That evening the spinster called upon the minister and finding him at home, sitting in his easy chair, thinking, no doubt, upon some deep subject, trying to solve the question as to how much more money a minister ought to get for sitting around in idleness half of his time during the week and doing a very moderate day's work on Sunday, than a laboring man could earn by working six days in the week from daylight till dark, with no time to cultivate his mind.

When the lady entered the presence of the Parson, it was evident that something of importance was about to be disclosed. She seated herself, and after taking breath and composing herself she began:

"What do you think? I've found out all about what is taking Mrs. Goldburg and the girls to Africa. When Parson Dingley had charge here, several years ago, Mrs. Bundy went to a medium and received a message telling her that her absent son was in Africa; of course everybody knew the message came from the Devil, but Mrs. Bundy believes in it, and Mrs. Goldburg and Rebecca are fairly bewitched with it yet; they have coaxed the other girl to go, and I think it is a real shame; people here should put some of them in the insane Asylum; there is plenty of evidence. I believe Mr. Goldburg had to leave his wife on account of her crazy notions, and the church lost one of its best paying members when he left; to be sure he did not give so very much money, but just see what his influence was worth. Every rich man in town wanted to belong to the same church with the banker. See how Mrs. Goldburg did about that property—gave it all to the Bundies and Mr. Stillwater; never gave the church anything. I think it a downright shame and the Devil is leading them into Africa to punish them for not giving all that property to the church. I think they ought to be stopped by law from fooling away their money, and the church ought to attend to it."

It was a matter of fact that the minister had been receiving very material aid from Mrs. Goldburg and Rebecca in the way of contributions, and anything which would detain them without making a rupture between them and the church would be greatly to his advantage; so he took it upon himself to visit the family and make a vigorous protest to their going; he was received with courtesy and so well did he present his objections to Mrs. Goldburg that for a time the girls were in despair; but at last he carried his objections too far for Rebecca's patience and when she took the case in hand it proved a very one-sided affair and the minister was soon vanquished.

CHAPTER XXVI.

IT WILL be remembered that in the close of a former chapter Mr. Baxter left the country for the ostensible purpose of forming a conspiracy with bankers of London to destroy the usefulness of the currency of the new Republic and thereby force the states to accept a gold standard, also the English banking system and land laws; that he was accompanied by two detectives, (we might here add) who shadowed him through the whole trip.

On arriving in London Mr. Baxter obtained an interview with some leading bankers; they took but little stock in his proposition, but finally consented to try the experiment.

The services of some of the very best artists in the country were secured and five hundred million dollars of the best counterfeit was struck off and the mails were loaded. So well had his actions been watched, the mail was examined before it was allowed to land, and all letters containing counterfeit money were taken to the treasury. This ended the job; no more letters came. After a few weeks Baxter returned, but for some reason best known to the officials was not arrested, and at once resumed business where he had left off. Times were good and he seemed to be making money, but the failure of the plot was in his mind; defeat rankled in his bosom and he kept his gold buried awaiting the time when it might once more be clothed with power.

Coy and Saunders remained at the Capitol and after the failure of this scheme, spent a great deal of their time in traveling through the country, watching the progress of things, trying to stir up discontent; talked constantly of money inflation, honest dollars, sound currency, etc.; but people were too busy to pay much attention, seeming only to listen; it reminded them of old times. However this did not discourage the gentlemen and they continued to lay plans for strangling the new Republic, by establishing a gold gambling banking system similar to that which had been used in robbing the American people and by this means build up an aristocracy in which they themselves would figure as leaders.

A few years of unparalleled advancement and prosperity passed; after which they felt that the time had come to act; the Government was evidently growing stronger, beside as people saw the great advantages which came to them through the absence of monetary power, vested in great syndicates and millionaires, and saw too, how completely these great dynasties were prevented from forming by the inheritance and income tax, they were becoming bitter in their denunciation of the old games of bankers who had impoverished them in days gone by. Others who were deeply grounded in the superstitious worship of gold, were beginning to forget the dogma, growing in grace and were also becoming reconciled to the changed condition.

Recognizing these facts, Coy and Saunders felt there would certainly be danger in delay, so the two managed to meet Mr. Baxter at Summerville; there, locked in private apartments, beyond the reach of listening ears a caucus was held.

Mr. Saunders was the first to explain; after referring to the progress of the country, he said there was something to work for. The property was now in sight and such a harvest for financiers had never before been heard of, except it might be in the United States, while working the rich gold and silver mines, and: "Look," said he, "at the men who made millions out of that; by a little nice financiering on the part of English bankers, when the richest mines were worked and the Bank of England had the gold, the Americans the experience, and had become the debtor nation; yes, with all their virgin soil, rich mines, immense productions of all kinds, they became the debtor nation; in less than twenty-five years after that man Seyd dropped in on Congress, button-holed the great Ohio statesman, and through him controlled the financial legislation of the country.

"I need hardly refer you to the gold interest on bonds, the exception clause on greenbacks, the strengthening act, or contraction, or redemption, or demonetization of silver; you both understand it all and know how it was done; one robbery after another and the American people stood it. These people are not a whit smarter than the Americans and they will stand it too; we only want to stand in or get the Bank of England at our backs, the machine in operation, and we will gather titles to property as easily as they did in the United States.

"But we must knock in the head this bloody Constitution and have gold used for money; we can corner it and people will be compelled to have it back to do business with; then we can dictate price and terms; but if we were to get this paper money all in the bank the Government would issue more and the business men would be independent of us, and we could not affect prices an iota, for there would still be plenty of money in circulation.

"We must have banks and banks are no good unless we can control the price of labor for that is the bottom of all value."

"What we want," said Baxter, "is clear enough, we all know how the thing was done in the United States; there is no doubt the same effect would follow the same kind of manipulation here if we had the same kind of government; but suppose you were to make a millionaire of one of these Senators as was done in the United States, what could he do? There is the referendnm in the way; to carry an election where there were regularly organized political parties was an easy matter, all that was necessary was to buy the leader; but here the candidates are all independent and stand upon their personal record, or merit; to say you had been a democrat or republican for forty years would be laughed at, The newspapers all have plenty

of backing and you can't buy them as you could in the
United States where they were all in debt to the
banks. The people here make their own laws; they
have become so accustomed to using paper money and
shipping their gold to foreign powers, when they either
get a big price for it in such things as they need or
exchange it for bonds that bring back a yearly interest.
I am afraid the old cry of sound currency, honest
dollar and such gags would have but little effect.
Why, I see from the last series of school books that
this great gold and banking swindle is so completely
exposed that twenty-five years from now a man would
hardly risk his reputation by advocating gold money
and national banks in this country; every school boy
would laugh at him."

"Yes," said Saunders, "we must modify this Consti-
tntion and change the whole system; the land must be
deeded over to the people, so we can get a chance at it;
we must have titles to the land, we must have gold money
and national banks, and we must also have the power
of the people, through their Government, to accumulate limited, and the power of individuals to accumulate
wealth, unlimited; then we can soon amass money
enough on the outside to be actually stronger than the
Government, and able to control it. This done, laws
can be passed in the interest of the men who have the
gold. Millionaires will then spring into existence
everywhere, the people will be impoverished and
become slaves.'

"The Government will become the dog of the plutocrats to take charge of the masses and furnish prisons
for those who have been robbed of their property and
complain of being out of work and are hungry. This
has all been accomplished in the United States, and
millionaires there to-day are enjoying every luxury that
wealth can give; if they do not wish to reside among
their slaves, they can move to a foreign land and leave
their dog, the people's Government, to watch and take
care of their sacred property rights. Now with gold
money, English land law, national banks and unlimited
inheritance, I believe we can, with the assistance of

English capital, put ourselves as absolutely in control of this people, as the millionaires are of the American people.   But we must have the entire system changed and the Constitution doctored or destroyed; to accomplish this it will be necessary to be rid of Bundy, Lincoln, Summerville and Jefferson.   If we were rid of these, we might control the executive and by not enforcing the laws get people so indignant that they would be finally led into revolution; then with a body of well organized men burn the Capitol and destroy all records; upon the heels of this call for volunteers, organize an army to protect the Government; then in rebuilding the Government use English money and get in your work; see to it that the new Constitution contains what we desire, and from that on we will have clear sailing.   People will be easily excited under such circumstances, and when a report is circulated that the Government is about to deed their land away to some great syndicate they will all demand a title and that will settle the land question, for when the land is once deeded we can issue bonds the same as they did in the United States.   Every man that has money to spare will invest it in these bonds; then when money becomes scarce the bonds will pass into the hands of moneyed men who will use them to bank on, and with a national banking law like that of the United States, will receive money from the Government at 1 per cent and loan it to the people at 8 per cent;   also take mortgages, but then, what is the use to talk, you both know just how it was done in the United States. "

Baxter, who, notwithstanding his long association with crime, still had a small degree of national pride, becoming slightly worried at hearing an Englishman refer so often to these disgraceful acts of robbery that had been forced through the American House by the terrible pressure of the money power, said:

"Well, what do you propose to do, have you any plan?"

"Yes," said Saunders, "but it will take time, Coy and myself have been talking the matter over for a long time; the bankers of the world have so much money invested in newspapers, and money loaned to others, and still others which they advertise in, it is safe to say, they control the press of civilization. This is a power to be both feared and respected. We believe that when rightly informed of the wealth and growing greatness of the Republic they can be easily enlisted in the cause and no stone will be left unturned to carry out our plans. Our first plan was to control the press of this country, but the objection to that is, the principal papers are owned by joint-stock companies and have an abundance of capital and good support; but being in good circumstances and working for a salary, they would be hard men to approach; even if you were to buy one or two the balance of the press of the country would be turned on them and the Department would be forced to remove them; in fact, public sentiment has been so thoroughly moulded in favor of the new system that even the press would be instantly antagonized by the people, if it failed to work in their interest."

"The principal objection that occurs to me," said Baxter, "is that the limit to inheritance has checked man's everlasting greed; put people more on a level. As the struggle for money has been modified among the rich, the struggle for a living among the poor has entirely ceased. To tell the truth, in traveling through the cities, towns and country, it seems to me there are no poor, at least every one has a home and I have never heard the word charity since I have been here, except in a religious sense."

"True," said Saunders, "this inheritance law has been one of the main obstacles in our way all along; then comes the income tax, national money, Government control of stock companies and sale of stock among the people; in fact, the whole system is negative to the formation of a favored class as in England, or the United States, and it must be destroyed, by fair means if we can, by foul means if we must.

"The plan that we have hit upon is that you take another trip to England. Of course it would hardly do for either of us to show ourselves in that country yet, but if these bankers see they can use us in destroying this system and founding a government here like the United States, based upon the English land laws, gold money and banking system, we will become millionaires as suddenly as John Sherman did with a $5,000 salary; so we must keep in the back ground until you have the business well under way; then they will need us, and the fact of our being able to get away with a pile of English, as well as American gold, will only be to our credit and they will recognize in us men worthy of becoming members of the great banking fraternity.

"This country to-day furnishes the world to a great extent with cotton, sugar, rice, tobacco, beef, bacon and flour; we are also shipping gold and silver in large quantities, and all this business is carried on without one dollar of foreign capital. In addition to this the iron, copper and lead mines are extensive, with an abundance of lead and coal; in consequence of this steel, car and locomotive works, also wagon and farm machinery works; they also have manufactories of every description.

"The bad feature seems to be from the banker's standpoint and is, that through the natural savings of the people, the stock which represents all this business has been absorbed; you can not monopolize it, for if you hold above a certain quantity the income tax takes your interest, and to save yourself you are forced to turn some of it back into the treasury, only to see a lot of old hay-seeds come along and buy it for their son, John or daughter, Jane. Bankers and money speculators you see are entirely shut out; this however will all be in our favor in getting backing from the money power."

"Speaking of this stock," said Coy, "reminds me of a very peculiar run that I noticed last winter. This stock, you see, all has coupons that fall due on the first of December; all through that month people of all shades and conditions could be seen going to the treasury to cash their coupons. If you interrogated them you would find that nine out of ten of them would use it in buying Christmas presents, and the whole people are learning to await Christmas as cattle look for the early coming of grass."

"Yes," said Saunders, "I have noticed that, and it looks to me like sheer nonsense to thus scatter money among the common people. I think we should make a note of all these things and reduce it to writing so that Mr. Baxter will miss nothing in making his statement to the bankers of London."

"It is quite clear to me," said Coy, "that unless some check is put to this Republic, in a few years it will be supplying the markets of the world with all kinds of goods and produce, barring every kind of competition.

"As it is, only their own surplus is shipped in their own vessels the price received will be of no great importance to a people who import little or nothing, sell all their gold and silver product, pay no tribute or interest and have unlimited capital of their own. Men of all trades can work cheaper here than in any other place in the known world, because every man owns his own home, pays no rent, no interest; but to the contrary receives a regular 5 per cent dividend on all his savings. Talk about pauper labor; there are no business men on earth, with pauper labor, who can pay taxes, rent and interest and compete with these people. These facts are already being noticed by the money power, and if all the facts in the case are properly presented, we will have the bankers of the world at our backs; if these fanatics think that the moneyed classes, who have reared their children in luxury for ages, will allow themselves to be robbed of their property rights, see the good things of life given up to the use and enjoyment of the common herd, either by legislation, or any other way, they are mistaken."

Without further discussion it was arranged that Baxter should go to England at once. In a few days, everything being in readiness, Baxter, armed with such papers as Coy and Saunders had carefully prepared, took a steamer for England. On reaching London he presented himself at once to Baron Rothschild; the cordiality of his reception was to him a great surprise.

They talked over the failure of the counterfeit scheme; the banker said since that time the banks had been reaping such a rich harvest in the United States that they had paid no further attention to African affairs. He was very glad Mr. Baxter and his friends had deemed it time to make another effort.

"We," said the Banker, "were considerably surprised the other day by a cablegram from America to the effect that an envoy from the new Republic had arrived in New York with an immense quantity of gold which they made an effort to exchange for Government bonds bearing interest; failing in this, they succeeded in exchanging for western State and County bonds. We cabled our agent in New York to offer them English bonds, but they declined, saying their first object was to dispose of their gold in such a manner as to be able to draw upon it in case of famine, or failure of crops, and as England could not produce enough for her own people, they could never count on assistance from that source; we look upon this as the best joke of the season.

"Upon receipt of this news I made up my mind that this new Republic should be looked after at once and am very glad you have taken the matter in hand; heretofore the Republic has been quite a relief to us, by draining the United States of its surplus labor that had been superseded by a cheaper class; it has also assisted us materially in securing title to lands (by attracting the owners), which will furnish a nice income in the shape of rent for all time to come. Of course we do not receive this rent direct; we have not come to that yet, but others do and that enables them to pay interest on bonds, bank stock, etc."

"I am very glad," said Mr. Baxter, "that your schemes in the United States have been a success, as you will be the more willing to give us your assistance."

"Exactly," said the Banker, "but large bodies move slowly and you must not be impatient of immediate results. At the close of the Revolutionary war we owned nothing in the United States; since then our efforts to control that country have been incessant;

to-day we own all their richest mines, a large share of all public works, such as railroads, telegraphs, city water works, etc.; in addition to this, all their vast product of gold and silver is carefully stored within our vaults. It is like the Veiled Prophet, the Americans never see it, and for this reason their worship of it is more intensified. Their manufacturers are protected by a heavy tariff, which enables them to form great pools and crush small enterprises. These pools borrow money from our banks which gives us quite a large tribute; we even own their business, and every man who drinks a glass of beer pays us tribute. When you take into consideration the fact that this has all been accomplished by careful financiering and that the civilized world has been largely fed and clothed from American products, during this same period, you can scarcely fail to see that we have a money system that is invincible. I also would call your attention to the fact, that while we have actually captured one-third of the property and business of the United States the English indebtedness to us has been largely increased, and there is not a civilized government on the face of the earth which does not pay tribute to the golden god we keep safely locked in our vaults. From this, no matter how slowly our work in the new Republic may appear to move, you will understand that the power of gold acting upon superstition is omnipotent, and you need not despair of the result."

Notwithstanding Mr. Baxter had been completely awe-struck in the presence of the great gold king, or monarch of monarchs, he here ventured to say that to him the worship of gold, supposed to be safely stored in vaults and actually had an existence, was more sensible than worshiping a God who seems to have no existence.

"That is true," said the great gold king. "I have heard good Christians, Mohammedans, and others calling upon their God day after day, week after week, month after month and year after year, and the only answer was the echo of their own faint voice; when I call upon my gold bags, I always meet with a quick response. I would not interfere with any man's belief, but gold is my god and I believe that more men worship gold than any other god."

The banker now set out a box of cigars, after which he dismissed Mr. Baxter with a promise that the papers should be examined at once; he also invited him to call at six in the evening.

Mr. Baxter retired to his apartments in the hotel where he was interviewed in the afternoon by a number of reporters; agents of brokers also dropped in, having seen his name quoted among the arrivals from the new Republic. They desired to purchase such an amount of national money of the Republic as he might happen to have, stating that it was in great demand among the merchants, as they could buy goods from the great shipping company of the Republic at 5 per cent less with that than with gold; this surprised Mr. Baxter, as he had always been taught when young by American statesmen, that money to be good in a foreign country had to be made of gold or silver; when he became a man he was told that money must be made of gold alone to be an honest dollar and good the world over; now he was confronted with a new problem. Here were men in London, wanting to buy paper money of the Republic and offering its face value, in small sums, or 1 per cent premium for large quantities; he could hardly comprehend how a piece of paper the size of a one dollar bill could be worth $101 in gold.

"Why," said he, "it is nothing but paper."

"Yes," said the banker, "and this coin is nothing but gold; the paper will buy more goods than the gold in the new Republic, and that is why we want it."

At twenty minutes past six Mr. Baxter once more started out to call upon the Banker; as he passed one of the great hotels, he stopped at a cigar store, ordered some cigars, and happening to have a $20 gold piece in his pocket, put it down; the shop man picked up the coin, examined it carefully, then said:

"This is an American coin."

"Yes, sir," said Baxter. He was then informed by

the shop-keeper that it would be necessary to take the coin to the Broker and exchange it for English coin; the fee for exchange would probably be twenty-five cents. Here again Mr. Baxter's early teaching in regard to honest dollars had been a myth and in a jocular manner he drew from his pocket a $20 bill from the new Republic. Throwing it upon the counter he sarcastically said: "How do you like that kind of money?"

The shop-keeper examined it and asked Mr. Baxter if he was from the new Republic. Being answered in the affirmative, and also informed that he arrived on the steamer Queen of the Seas, the day before at Liverpool. Asking his name, the shop-keeper picked up a paper announcing the arrival of the steamer, and finding Mr. Baxter's name among the list of passengers concluded the bill was all right.

While the two were engaged in further conversation a boy took the bill into the next door, which was the office of a wholesale cigar store, where it was cashed, returned, and Mr. Baxter given the change in clear English coin.

"How is this?" said Baxter, "that you take paper money from the Republic in preference to American gold?"

"Because," said the shop man, "there is a large company in the Republic which has complete control of the trade between that country and this; I am told they have an office in every important shipping port throughout the world; their business is carried on like machinery; they ship all their goods on their own vessels and everything is conducted with system and true business principle of justice to all and favor to none; they buy and sell on so large a scale that competition is out of the question. Of course they take our money but never send it out of the country; on the contrary they turn it into goods and ship the goods; they always sell goods at 5 per cent less when it is paid in money from the Republic, or in other words, pay a 5 per cent premium on money of the Republic;

this is what makes their money worth more than gold the world over.

"I am told that they have such fine government and business methods at home that no time is lost on the part of the toilers; they all have an opportunity of investing their savings in the stock of the company for which they work and the dividend on their stock soon becomes an important factor in life. In consequence of this many of our best tradesmen in every branch of industry have emigrated to that country and send back glowing accounts. They say they have the finest machinery in the world and make it themselves; work eight hours per day and every man is kept constantly employed; as a result of this, their exports largely exceed their imports, and it is only by accident that we get hold of any of their money in buying it from travelers here at the hotels, the brokers occasionally make a little money."

It would naturally be supposed that such talk as this would set Baxter to thinking and turn him from his course. It will be remembered, however, that he had already cast his lot with the money power; he was already committed to the gold standard; he dare not falter, he dare not stop. The gold power had in a measure controlled the world for ages and it was stronger to-day than it had ever been. It had captured the great American states, why should he doubt of its ultimate success in crushing this new system? Notwithstanding he found many reasons for continuing in the course already mapped out, when his mind took in the old cry of honest money and sound currency, raised by the wise statesman, and contrasted that with his late experience, he could not help saying: "What a set of donkeys these American statesmen are."

On reaching the Banker's office he found the millionaire in the very best humor and after a little desultory conversation the Banker informed Baxter that he had examined the papers and partly agreed with them; that he felt the time had come when the gold power should assert its rights; this cancer upon the body politic of the world must be removed; that he had called a convention of bankers for Monday next. "The bankers of Germany and France," said he, "will be represented and I am confident some step will be taken; what, I cannot tell, but think we will likely send a committee back with you to feel of the Government and suggest plans."

This gave Baxter an opportunity of visiting different parts of the city, and he declared to a companion that the city was actually barbarous in comparison with Summerville, Kiyongo or the other great cities of the Republic. Monday at last arrived, and Baxter found himself once more among the bankers. The meeting was a large one; over fifty men present; all bankers and millionaires. After the meeting came to order the paper was read which had been so carefully prepared by Saunders and Coy, in which they gave a detailed account of property which had sprung into existence as if by magic; gave a careful description of their form of Government; how completely it operated to throttle capital and destroy the power of gold. In terse words it was declared that the new methods of business and government were, to concentrated wealth, as fatal as machinery and imported workers had been to labor in the United States; that unless checked the Republic would ship their vast product of gold to other countries, and so inflate the money of the world as to materially decrease its value, positively refusing to use the article themselves, for any purpose, except for filling teeth.

After the reading was concluded, Mr. Baxter was introduced. He stated that he and his associates, Saunders and Coy, had owned mines in the Republic; they had made quite a sum of money, but finding themselves limited by the inheritance law, they sold out their mines and since that time had been "lying on their oars," awaiting an opportunity to secure favorable legislation. "But," said he, "the Republic is constantly growing stronger; it has not only destroyed banking, and in fact all monetary control at home, but from its present growth there were good reasons for grave apprehension on the part of the money power of the world. Having watched the thing for years, he declared it to be his belief that further delay was dangerous; sure as the world moves, if this new Republic continues its growth for twenty years, it will show a front worthy the steel of any power."

It was plain to Baxter that his talk had its weight; the faces around him were long as the moral law and he began to realize the fact that he had found the place where the money laws of the world were made. It also occurred to him that this was the place from which some of the great American statesmen and financiers received their inspiration, and this accounted to some extent for a United States Senator becoming a millionaire off an annual salary of $5,000.

When Mr. Baxter had finished, he was put upon the witness stand and questions came thick and fast from all directions. The first interrogation was, quite naturally, in regard to the extent and richness of the gold mines. Mr. Baxter informed them that as yet there were vast regions of unexplored country; that the gold fields already developed, were probably equal in richness and extent to those of California and were already yielding large quantities of gold; whether the unexplored country would prove equal in richness and extent to Montana, Idaho, Dakota, Colorado and other gold producing states and territories of the United States remained to be seen. It was evident that under the present form of government they would not be developed for years to come, for the simple reason that the Government so completely and systematically controls the business of the country, backing every enterprise with all the money necessary to the end that every man in the country should have constant employment.

"There, statesmen argue," said Baxter, "that where all are kept constantly employed, where transportation and commerce are honestly and systematically carried on, there can be but one result, an excess of exports and home prosperity among the masses.

"While this is the case few men will abandon society, home and friends to hunt for gold. Having lived from youth to maturity on the fat of the land, producing nothing themselves, but consuming in luxury the productions of their fellow men and women, through the power of gold, acting upon superstition, it could hardly be considered strange that not one of these financiers entertained a doubt as to their ability, through the power of gold to crush, if need be, the new Republic."

Without noticing that matter they proceeded to discuss the advisability of opening these rich gold mines. One said that there was gold enough now. Their vaults were full; besides, what matters it as to the size of the pile, when all values are measured by it, all money based upon it?

"As the business of the world is done on credit and all dues are made payable in gold, and having the bulk of the metal in our possession we can fix its price and that price we will have, for there is no other source from which gold can be obained. Then why not secure a title to the land and put a wall around these mines? It will be worth as much in the ground as in our vaults and should give greater confidence, for people will know we can't spend or fool it away. We can estimate the amount of gold by what has been taken out of the mines in the United States and Australia. If we can build a wall, succeed in keeping it beyond the reach of the common herd, we can issue gold certificates to the full value of the gold."

"What will you do with the gold certificates?" asked a voice. "That is plain," said the learned financier, "we can loan them to the United States to be used as gold money." "How will you redeem them?" asked another.

"I would have our Secretary write at once to John Sherman, Grover Cleveland, Carlisle, McKinley, Harrison, Vorhees and others of our members in the United States, have them demonetize silver and secure a large issue of bonds; then we will buy the bonds with these certificates; they will be good of course, because they represent gold."

"In redeeming them how would you proceed?" was asked by another voice.

"That is easy," said the financier. "Suppose the

bonds run forty years, the interest at 3 per cent; they will pay the certificates all back to us as interest long before the bonds are due, then they will have to borrow them again to pay the bonds with. Of course the next thing will be to issue more bonds, which we will again buy, thus keeping the certificates in circulation. I have studied finance for over forty years and I have noticed that the gold always lays in the vaults and the business of the world is largely done with paper representing gold; this being the case, it has long since occurred to me that a vast amount of labor might be saved by this method. Why go to this great expense of taking the gold from one hiding place and putting it in another? Why take it from the earth and put it in a vault? I tell you, gentlemen, this redeeming money is all nonsense; as long as people live they will want money, and as long as they want it there is no necessity for its redemption. If we can get control of the legislation in this new Republic, as we did in the United States, we can own the whole country, people and all, inside of twenty years; and I would suggest that the first thing to be done is to issue an immense quantity of paper money, get it into circulation by building a wall to protect the gold mines, keep a few trusty experts busy exploring the mines, and through the associated press and our gigantic dailies, keep the people of the world well posted in regard to the vast quantities of gold we possess; call every man a crank who dares to dispute it. We can then furnish the world with money and stop this everlasting talk about gold being scarce."

As no one seemed inclined to oppose this plan, the subject was dropped for the time.

Another gentleman whose build was somewhat after the Cleveland style of architecture, with a very large body and very small brains, rose to his feet and said he had been keeping an eye on this new Republic for some time; he was taking several papers from there did not read very much himself, had strained his judgment when young in figuring on the problem of squaring a circle, which he finally accomplished by driving a harrow tooth into a rat-hole. In consequence of this early strain upon his reasoning faculties, he had always made a practice of hiring his reading done by his private Secretary who had been keeping himself posted thoroughly and would now make a statement.

The private Secretary was then put upon the stand and told what he knew, after which a learned discussion took place. One of the most intelligent bankers said for a long time he had been troubled with corns and dyspepsia, in consequence he had read but very little, his private Secretary would therefore speak for him; he would however say this much, that he was in favor of the plan to issue gold certificates to be used for money, the world over, and buy American bonds as already suggested. He then took his seat amid a storm of applause.

The private Secretary then stated that Bundy, Lincoln and Jefferson seemed to be leading men in the Republic. "All bad names," said the chairman, and an audible "yes" came from the audience.

At this juncture some one called for Mr. Baxter to state the amount he thought would be necessary for the control of the men. The sound of his name brought Mr. Baxter to himself. The thought of being surrounded by so many millionaires and such a display of ignorance on the part of the owners, and cunning on the part of the secretaries, had completely hypnotized him and thrown him into a magnetic sleep in which he had seen all kinds of devils; the room was full of them. Even these great financiers seemed to have cloven hoofs, horns and tails; there were little devils and big devils; old devils and young devils; devils with horns and devils with tails. Lucifer himself could hardly have turned out a more interesting set of devils, and each had his hands full of gold certificates, and was watching the United States and the new Republic. Rothschild seemed to be the prince of all the devils and he read a letter from John Sherman, a great American financier, who had made several millions of dollars from a salary of $5,000 in the United State Senate.

A large, ugly looking devil then came in staggering under a load of United States bonds. After dumping them at the feet of the Prince of the gold power, he straightened up and the Prince of devils said: "This is Grover, the stuffed prophet; for this service I appoint him first in my cabinet." Baxter then looked and it was Grover, sure enough, with his well-known, besotted look. Like the others he had cloven hoofs, short horns, and a tail of wondrous length; he smelled fishy, and the buzzards had been roosting in his hair. The Prince patted him on the head and he danced in ecstacy, then waltzed and waltzed until he became entangled in his own tail; while in this laughable situation, the sound of Baxter's name awoke him from his trance to a realization of the fact that he was among bankers. He sprang to his feet, a picture of confusion; wiping the cold sweat from his face, he collected his thoughts and proceeded to inform the millionaire bankers that he did not think Bundy, Lincoln and Jefferson could be bought; at this he saw a smile of derision light up the face of all, and the Prince of bankers said: "Not so, my man, we have proved this thing to be a truth, that all men have their price."

Mr. Baxter was then asked if he was personally acquainted with any of the Senators; he answered in the affirmative, stating that he had been quite intimate with Senator Sherman.

"Senator Sherman?" inquired the Prince of bankers, "have you a man there by that name?"

"Yes, sir," said Baxter, feeling his own insignificance more and more, among the bankers."

"Is he any relation to the Ohio Senator?"

"He says not," Baxter replied. "No matter," said the Prince, "I rather like the name, that is, if there is no Billy mixed up in it." "There is not."

After further discussion it was decided to send a committee of one to report plans for establishing a National Banking system in the new Republic; also a gold standard. It was suggested that a man by the name of Lord Dead Ernest Seyd had been quite successful in dealing with American Senators and Congressmen, and he was therefore selected for the mission.

He was sent with instructions to spend $10,000,000 if necessary to secure the recognition of gold as money; also secure some change in the laws concerning the great newspapers.

"It is important," said the Prince of bankers, "that we control these papers; if the present ones cannot be controlled, we can afford to start and run larger ones and circulate them at ten cents a year for the next ten years, in order to control votes, and I would advise that you pay particular attention to this matter. The manner in which we control the vote of the United States through the great dailies is quite sufficient to convince you of its importance.

"If legislation fails, look after their defenses; feel of the people. If the Government cannot be controlled it must be overthrown by inciting insurrection. I am told they have no saloon, nor political parties; this is all wrong for they all form a part of our methods. If all else fails, as a last resort, you know the English Bank and syndicates own Great Britain, and we will fix up a claim to that part of Africa and send around a lot of iron-clads, which will probably have a very salutary effect."

In regard to this matter the Prince of bankers said to Mr. Baxter: "Holding a debt against the English Government of more than she can pay, and our own vaults filled with gold and full control of all the banks of England and the United States, you will not for a moment doubt our power to do this."

CHAPTER XXVII.

IN a former chapter we left Mrs. Goldburg and the two girls busily engaged in preparing for a trip to Africa, with the purpose in view, on the part of Mrs. Goldburg, of seeing the country; with the girls, however, another object was prominent, that of founding a College in which they could find use for the intellectual culture they had gained in years of careful study; both felt that under the system in vogue in the United States, there was but small chance for ladies to distinguish themselves They had seen cultured and brainy women in the United States too often held up to ridicule by a subsidized servile and insolent press, while using freely both talent and money for the upbuilding of society and amelioration of mankind, to even for a moment, think of subjecting themselves to such a terrible ordeal.

As teachers were in demand in the new Republic, they hoped that the conditions there would be more favorable and woman's influence recognized as a necessary element in maintaining an equilibrium in both government business and society, and that her place, as toy and slave, would be filled by animals, if filled at all.

Preparations for the trip being completed and a farewell taken of loving friends and old neighbors, they were soon standing upon the deck of one of the great ocean steamers of the new Republic, watching the city and American coast as it faded fast from view.

The voyage passed without incident and when they landed at Summerville, each was enjoying the best of health and spirits; they took rooms at the Palace Hotel where they found every comfort and convenience possible and far beyond their expectations. They rested quietly until the next Monday, then took a trip about the city. The hotel was fortunate in having as housekeeper and hostess a young lady, Miss Colvil, by name, who was a person of superior attainments; in her kind, affable way she had shown the ladies every attention and thus made them feel perfectly at home; she also accompanied them as a guide in viewing the points of interest in the city.

At nine o'clock the party took seats in a fine carriage drawn by a span of black horses which they were informed were shipped from New York. They rolled almost noiselessly over smoothly paved streets, 'mid tall, magnificent structures of granite; through the business streets the buildings were of stone and one of the most charming features was the superior style of architecture, each entire block seemed to have been designed on one common plan, both for usefulness and beauty. Business seemed to be conducted on a grand scale, for it was not uncommon to see a whole block occupied by one company, as, for instance, a wholesale boot and shoe company occupied one whole block, supposed to have been built fire-proof, and especially designed for the business. This place received their goods from many different manufactories, as the company could increase its capital stock when necessary by application to the head of the department; they were enabled at all times to pay cash, which enabled manufacturers to do the same, and the credit system had entirely passed out of use. As the company, like all others, was limited to a 7 per cent dividend, there was seldom any marked change in prices, which greatly simplified business, and as the profits of the concern were never invested in the business but paid out regularly once a year on dividends, there was seldom any necessity for change in the arrangements. All wholesale business was carried on in the same way and under the same general rule, so that competition was unknown and thousands of dollars saved, which might have been wasted in advertising.

If an overproduction of a manufactured article occurred, manufacturer's prices remained the same, but they were not allowed to increase their work until the demand had become equal to the supply, and it was sometimes found necessary to change the same labor from the manufacture of one article, but under no circumstances was a company allowed to diminish the number of its employes.

The surplus which fell upon the commercial companies was either held for future consumption or shipped to foreign countries and exchanged for something of value; if it happened that nothing of value could be obtained that was needed at home gold, silver or money was taken and exchanged for securities. Gold was never shipped home for as it was only used in the arts there was always an over-production coming in from the mines; the commercial companies therefore, held it in their foreign offices until such time as it could be disposed of.

All other branches of business, such as dry goods, clothing, hats, caps, notions, hardware, etc., were conducted on the same general plan, each occupying one or more blocks and were entirely separated from other business. The buildings were of uniform height and each seemed to be constructed with reference to preserving the symmetry and beautifying the whole street.

For an hour or more they continued their drive through this grand emporium, when suddenly the scene changed and they found themselves in the residence portion of the city; on all sides they were greeted by tasteful homes, situated on spacious grounds and surrounded by flowers in profusion and ornamental trees in great variety.

The buildings were artistic and beautiful, the streets were wide, having two street-car tracks, with wide drive-ways on either side, and kept in complete order. "I cannot understand," said Mrs. Goldburg, "how the city can afford to keep such a continuation of streets in such perfect order; we have been driving for hours and still everything looks as it did in the most aristocratic part of the city. It looks as though this was a city of wealthy people."

"Indeed it is," said the hostess, "we have more wealthy people than any other city on earth and yet we have not fifty men in the city who have reached half a million and there is not a millionaire in the whole country. Our city is not. aristocratic but it is social and stylish to an extreme; since under our new methods all have become useful, so all have become wealthy, independent and prosperous, each in his own line. Everything is done on so grand a scale that the very best results are attained; profits, too, are small and labor is well paid; with no loss of time, no strikes or lockouts, a good investment for their savings and no monopoly of land, we find that all are fully able to live according to their tastes, and the very fact that there is a limit put upon inheritance seems to stop that everlasting grabbing after all that is in sight.

I remember of hearing an old veteran say, that in the war of the great Rebellion, while they were in the South, poor men who had never owned a slave and never could own one under any ordinary course of events, would come into camp and ask: 'Why do you-uns come down here to free our slaves?' I suppose that human nature is the same the world over and as these people were afraid of losing the slaves they never owned or had the slightest chance of owning, so many of our people who have not the slightest chance of climbing for wealth one-fourth of the way to the limit of inheritance, have already begun to lose their hoggish grasping, money-worshiping notions, through a fear that Government might inherit their wealth. Thus selfishness begets righteousness and as it is man's destiny to follow his ambition after an ideal, on seeing the way to millions obstructed, he soon finds his course of progress turned into another channel.

"Having once seen the goal of happiness, great wealth, far in the future he now beholds a world of comfort near by and that goal transferred from accumulated wealth to a higher state of civilization, of better living, greater enjoyments and more intelligence. Under this condition of things, his ambition to excel leads him to build beautiful cottages and make flowery homes.

"As incentives to his becoming a millionaire have been removed, man, true to his nature, follows another incentive to excel in such attributes as will be most appreciated by his fellows, thus gaining their admiration and applause."

"In our whole trip," said Mrs. Goldburg, "I have seen no indication of a saloon; is it possible that your people have been able to do away with the use of intoxicating drinks?"

"The habit, fashion or custom," said the lady, "whichever you please to call it, of dram drinking, is only an effect; the result of a condition. When we removed the cause the custom disappeared. It is claimed by our teachers that, as the Sunday School is the nursery of the Church, so the saloon is the nursery of hell; as the free school is the fore runner of knowledge, so the fashionable saloon is the educator of drunkards, cause of much misery and fore runner of crime, debauchery and a multitude of sins. We have no saloons, but we have their counterpart, halls of pleasure, where everything is found which is calculated to please and attract; all visit and enjoy these places, old and young, ladies and gentlemen, alike attend to spend their leisure in social conversation, in singing, dancing, eating, speechmaking, debate and in many other ways, all calculated to amuse, entertain and instruct. Many refreshing beverages are served, but none that will intoxicate; they are kept open at all times, and as reading rooms are attached, they become a place of leisure for all ladies and gentlemen, though entire strangers are always welcome. Millions of dollars are invested in the furniture, fixtures and paraphernalia of these great halls; large sums of money are being constantly spent in securing the very richest display of art and on account of the thousands of halls, it has created a demand for fine art in painting, sculpturing and filigree work, as to set in motion the wheels of evolution in that direction.

"In consequence of this, schools of this kind have been established from one end of the country to the other, and it is believed that the day is not far distant when our people will lead the world in art.

"It has been our aim to treat the liquor question, as

all others, in a rational manner. Used properly, it is considered valuable, but dram drinking is considered a curse and saloons are believed to be institutions calculated to foster and perpetuate that curse; therefore they are dispensed with, by placing the sale of liquor in the hands of an immense joint stock company, that has an office in every town and city, where the very best liquors are kept on sale by the quart or gallon only, and it is under no circumstances to be drank upon the premises. The very cheapness of it is said to have a tendency to make it unpopular; beside, our people are all educated and in our ethical teaching, to drink is disgraceful."

After passing that part of the city where wholesale trade was carried on, they came to the streets occupied by retailers; here the sight could hardly have been surpassed and on inquiry the ladies were informed that nearly all of the retail business was done by individuals; draying, teaming, repair shops of all kinds were also done by individual enterprise; but the hatred usually engendered by unbridled competition is not present; it is generally believed the principal reason is in consequence of the inheritance laws and graduated income tax. "None seem anxious," said she, "to accumulate wealth to be inherited by the Government, which would put it right back among the people again, through public institutions of learning or public work, while the great business done by our joint companies promotes pride and patriotism.

"As the labor of the country is largely done by machinery, there are a great many men who would find no employment were it not provided by the Government; therefore the cities, counties, states and Republic, each have a regular system of improvements where every idle man may find work. This is why you see the streets and walks so invariably fine."

Mrs. Goldburg spoke of the spacious building lots and the lady guide said: "Our street car lines are so perfect, and being run by a company whose profits are limited to 7 per cent, car fare is so remarkably low that distance is considered of but little consequence and many of the shop men ride four and even five miles to work; so you see there is no necessity for crowding buildings together."

The party put up for dinner at an inn on the out-skirts of the city. The building was home-like but a magnificent piece of architecture; it was surrounded by a flower garden with its fountains and statuary; the ladies had never seen anything so beautiful.

"From what country do you get all your works of art?" asked Rebecca

"This," said the guide, "is all the product of our own institutions, many of which have been running for several years; in consequence of the extensive use of labor-saving machinery, a system of government, too, that gives every man employment and encourages industry by just legislation, so there is no loss from conflicting interest; we find there is an abundance of spare help which gives every man having a taste for art or science, an opportunity to gratify that taste; their productions are fully appreciated by those other-wise engaged; it is claimed by our economists that with our improved tools and farm machinery one man will produce an abundance of food for twenty-five persons; that our manufacturers can do ten times that amount; as a very large portion of our population are farmers, you will see at a glance that after taking out all our middle-men, such as merchants, draymen, mechanics, railroad men and others beside women, children and students, we still have abundance of help to spare. Government, therefore, encourages every branch of industry and learning by liberal appropriations; our surplus wealth, you understand is handled by the Government to improve the race, while in other coun-tries it passes, through legislation, into the hands of millionaires and is used to enslave the race or is hoarded beyond the reach of those who need."

The grounds were beautifully laid off with walks, shady nooks and rustic seats for the comfort and con-venience of the public. The party rested for a while after dinner and again took up their journey. By a circuitous route they returned to the Hotel through a country, as Rebecca expressed it, that looked like a picture of continual prosperity, happy homes, beautiful grounds, playing children and warbling birds; not the slightest evidence of a pauper or a millionaire had met their view. While they had seen many magnificent carriages, they were not attended by footmen dressed in livery, indeed they were told that such attendants, in that country, would be called slaves and the man thus attended, a snob and both would be ostracised from society. On reaching their apartments at the Hotel the guests were left to entertain themselves, which they did in looking over the evening papers and recounting the events of the day. They all agreed that the whole appearance of the place was charming.

Miss Colvil joined them in the parlor after supper and found the ladies in excellent spirits and not in the least fatigued but delighted with their experience.

Minnie, too, enjoyed everything she had seen but the ride had set her to thinking; everything was so different from what she had seen before. Said she: "If anyone had told me that a city of this size could exist without its horde of paupers, and that such an extensive business could be conducted without banks and millionaires to furnish money, I would have thought them insane."

"True," said the hostess, "I too have always been accustomed to seeing money controlled by the banks and it seems strange to me; but when you understand our system, which is so very simple and works so perfectly, you will wonder how the people of the United States have allowed themselves to be robbed by the bankers so long and so completely. In other countries governments make the money and give it to the bankers to speculate on; with this control of the money they soon own a large share of the property. When the plant is thus started, through rent and interest, it is like the rolling of a great snowball and gathers to itself, as time rolls on, until it becomes more powerful than the government. As it grows rich year by year, the people must of necessity grow poor; it could not be otherwise.' If a man dies, it matters not, the estate rolls on, collecting rents and interest, robbing the poor and building up an aristocracy.

"Here these vast estates are not allowed to exist; no one man or woman can inherit more than $100,000. Of course the property ls here as in all other countries, but there has never been any difficulty in finding persons willing to own it; we find that it is not necessary that bankers and millionaires should own our property; the large business enterprises are owned by joint stock companies, as in the United States, but our people seem perfectly willing to own the stock and as bankers and millionaires do nothing but own property, we think we can do without them, at any rate so long as men and women come nobly to the front and each own their share. We are determined at all events, that if bankers and millionaires can do without us, we will make an effort to do without them; if they want all the gold in the United States and England, we are glad of it; it will give us a good market for the production of our mines; we don't want it, we find paper money is better for us."

"O yes," said Minnie, "nobody will deny but what paper money is more convenient than gold. We use it in the United States, but we have gold in the treasury to redeem it with and of course that makes it good. While I do not wish to be understood as criticising your Government, I would like to ask how you expect to redeem your paper money after you have disposed of all your gold?"

Minnie said this with a degree of hesitancy which showed that she felt keenly the awkward position Miss Colvil would be in at having such an unanswerable question propounded; on the contrary the young lady felt quite at ease as she said: "I suppose, Miss Minnie, you noticed some of our business institutions when we were driving, yesterday?"

"O yes," said Minnie, "they were grand."

"What did you think of their permanency?"

"Why," said Minnie, a little surprised at such a question, "permanency seems to be one of their strongest features; the buildings are of the most solid material possible."

"How long do you suppose the people will continue to do business in this city?"

Minnie, a little puzzled, answered: "Always for anything we know now."

"Then," said the hostess, "will you please to tell me at what time and for what cause these people will discontinue the use of money?"

Minnie now began to see the point, but she was honest and always willing to learn and she answered promptly: "I suppose so long as they do business they will need money."

"Then how could Government redeem this money without putting out other money to take its place? When a bill becomes worn it is redeemed with a new one and gold cuts no figure in the case, simply because it is not recognized. Your Government, the United States, has had $100,000,000 laying idle in her vaults for the last twenty years for the ostensible purpose of redeeming the greenback, which has not been redeemed yet and probably never will be; during that time the Government has paid over $75,000,000 interest on bonds that could have been paid with that gold. Would it not have been the wiser policy to have waited till they wanted the greenback redeemed, before borrowing the money, and thus save to the people that enormous sum of $75,000,000 interest. We propose to loan all our gold to the United States; we are glad they want it; we can loan them $100,000,000; in thirty-four years they will have paid the gold all back to us and will still owe us the full amount. Is it any wonder the Americans are a debtor nation?"

Minnie was overwhelmed by the peculiar turn which things had taken; she said not one word, but Rebecca soon broke the silence by saying, in a jesting way: "Minnie, we must remember that things often look differently from different standpoints."

"Yes," said Miss Colvil, from the bankers' standpoint their gold system is all right; fortunately we are entirely rid of that class of society which is composed of bankers and millionaires only; getting rid of them, we consider a wonderful step in human progress."

After a short silence Minnie asked if there were any places of amusement.

"O Yes," said the hostess, "these halls of pleasure are always open; they take the place of saloons and are a great place to spend leisure moments. I was just about to suggest that we visit one of them to-night."

"Do ladies visit such places," asked Minnie in a doubtful manner.

O yes, you will see as many ladies as gentlemen there and I know you will enjoy the evening."

"We will go," said Minnie, looking at Mrs. Goldburg, as if still doubtful as to the propriety of such a step. "Why," said Mrs. Goldburg, "Miss Colvil has been a very good guide so far, and I think we may safely follow her now."

"O," said the hostess, "you may rest assured you will see or hear nothing but what would be admissible in any drawing room. It is very different here from what it is in the United States; here the gentlemen all have ladies of their own to look after and we shall hardly be noticed.

"You see the methods of business here are so thoroughly based upon principles of justice that every man has an opportunity not only to make a living, but also to have a good time, enjoy life, and lay by money for old age. If a man rents a house and pays his rent regularly for a few years, he finds himself sole owner of the property. Americans would laugh at such a proposition, yet when you examine the plan it is absolutely just, and in consequence of this, there are few bachelors and old maids; all have good homes and are surrounded by good influences; consequently crime has almost disappeared and our many criminal laws have become obsolete. In fact the business of the country has been so thoroughly systematized and is so absolutely just, that law has, in a wonderful degree, become unnecessary, and there is not one lawyer here where there are ten in the United States; you will find as you proceed through our country that there is a vast, difference between a Government in the interest of the people and one run in the interests of a class of aristocrats."

After Miss Colvil's reassurance that it would be perfectly safe for ladies to go upon the streets unattended, they were soon ready to go, and Miss Colvil and Rebecca took the lead; a short walk took them in front of one of the finest blocks in the city. The doors were standing wide open and a throng of people were coming and going. There were no screens before the door and Rebecca mentioned this fact to Miss Colvil who remarked: "People controlled by honorable motives require no screens; even in the United States they are only used in saloons and banks and their only object is to hide dishonorable methods."

They passed through the vestibule when they emerged into a grand and magnificent hall, brilliantly lighted; it was about 125 feet long and had a double row of billiard tables running the whole length of the hall. "This," said Miss Colvil, pointing to the billiard tables, "is our national game." Every table was in use; at some of the tables ladies were playing, at others gentlemen, and at others ladies and gentlemen were playing together. Along each side of the hall in front, was a magnificent bar and the wall back of it was one solid mirror; in front of it was a shelf of onyx resting upon cabinet work of a superior order; at intervals along this shelf stood large globular jars of pure water in which different varieties of the finny tribe were sporting in the perfect artificial light of the hall.

The water was kept pure by connection of silver tubes which kept a tiny stream filtering through the jars; these tubes wound around and assumed fantastic shapes as they led from jar to jar, while resting upon filigree work of the rarest kind, formed principally from silver, gold and precious stones. "This," said Miss Colvil, pointing to this wonderful display, "is the way we use our silver and gold."

Vases of silver containing beautiful boquets occupied places in every part of the hall, while growing plants and blooming flowers were also there. Cages hung from the ceiling containing birds of beauty and song which were adding much to the grandeur of the occasion. As the ladies stood before this wonderful display and beheld it so charmingly reproduced in the great mirror, they regarded it as a sight long to be remembered; turning from this magnificent scene, they feasted their eyes upon the busy throng of players with happy but earnest faces, listened to the click of ivory balls and watched the faces of the players as they changed from smiles of satisfaction to looks of perplexity. Rebecca remarked the perfect order which reigned supreme and contrasted it with the whiskey saloons of the United States where drunkenness and disorder prevail to such an extent as to make woman's presence inadmissible, and even men prefer a screen to hide them from the accidental glance of some respected friend.

After passing the bar, which was about forty feet long, small tables filled the space along the side of the room, where spectators were seated, eating, drinking and looking at the play. The walls of the hall were adorned with paintings rare and costly; passing down the aisle midway, they stepped into an elevator and in another moment the scene changed; they were in a hall with galleries and a stage; the chairs on this floor could be moved, thus converting it into a huge dance hall. Here they listened for an hour to charming music, both vocal and instrumental. Miss Colvil explained that this part of the establishment was under the management of a musical and literary club, consisting of several hundred members; from this club, talent is chosen to furnish entertainments, consisting of vocal and instrumental music, elocution, dramas and comedies.

The club was organized for the double purpose of enjoyment and instruction; the performers received no pay and therefore, there was an opportunity for all to learn, and the very best theatrical talent was developed.

The regular admission fee to these entertainments was ten cents, but nightly tickets could be purchased for $1.00 a month; this money went to the landlord, who was expected to keep the room in order and furnish scenery and paraphernalia.

Ranged along by the side of this great hall was a series of rooms nicely furnished and carpeted, provided with chairs and tables where ice cream and fruits could be served to four, six or eight persons. In front of this was another long hall fitted up and used as a free reading room.

After having visited every part of these great halls, the ladies returned to the hotel thoroughly satisfied with their evening's enjoyment.

"Are there many such halls?" said Minnie, as they were once more quietly seated in the parlor of the hotel?

"O, yes," said Miss Colvil, "they take the place of the saloon; as the saloon was designed by the Devil to give every young man a fine start for hell, so these halls have been designed by Christians, in accordance with the Christ-principle, to give the young a start toward a better state of existence; as the saloons have been abolished, a number of these halls have been substituted to accommodate the people, for all like to enjoy life. As our industries are based upon true business principles, owned at home, run constantly, and profits scattered among the people, so all have money, and you would be surprised to see how universally these halls are patronized."

"It must take a great many Police," said Rebecca, "to keep order and protect the women and children from insult."

"Woman requires no protection from man," said Miss Colvil, "she is an even match for him under all circumstances; it is only brutes she fears, and when men are transformed into brutes by the use of alcohol, woman trembles; here we have no drunkards because we have no saloon system to teach men to drink. We have hundreds of these great halls in this city, some of them more extensive than the one we were in, others not so large, all run on the same general principle, varying only in accordance with the ideas of the managers. They all keep open on Sundays and in the club room or hall a minister of the gospel is employed, at the expense of the house to deliver three religious non-sectarian sermons or lectures. You would think this would interfere with the churches; it does in some particulars but not in attendance or support. It holds them to the test of common sense and does away with bigotry to some extent. When men of brains become ministers, they advance intellectually more rapidly than their followers and are obliged to put on the brakes. These halls give the people so much wholesome instruction, that the ministers feel at liberty to turn loose their best thoughts, thus the effect is a salutary one.

It was growing late, so Miss Colvil took her leave and the ladies retired to dream of their wonderful experience and the peculiar fashion, new methods and ideas.

The next morning at nine o'clock, having breakfasted and returned to their apartments, Miss Colvil entered and they arranged to take a ride on the street cars to Lake Park. On entering the car they found that neither pains nor money had been spared to make it both comfortable and beautiful. Rebecca spoke of this and Miss Colvil said: "Did you ever notice in the United States that whatever was done by the Government was always done lavishly? It is the same here in all business, where comfort and convenience can be taken into consideration; our business is done by large companies under the absolute control of Government; as individual greed has no part in the affair, work is never slighted to save money, nor is anything ever spoiled by cheap making to gratify a stingy owner."

The streets traversed that day were similar to those visited on their previous ride; beautiful buildings, comfortable, home-like and tasty, with indications of happiness and prosperity everywhere. On returning to the hotel it was agreed that nothing could have been nicer. "Yes," said Miss Colvil, "if you go through our markets and stores, you will find it of rare occurrence that anything is exhibited for sale, not produced at home; in fact our people are such great producers that we have over-production, and the over-production is greater than our imports; consequently we have no foreign debt."

"What is the reason," said Rebecca, "that the United States which is also a Republic, is equally rich in land, timber, mines, navigable rivers, with equal chances is largely in debt to foreign powers and a large part of their property and business is already owned by foreign syndicates?"

"The trouble is," said Miss Colvil, "the American people borrow money to do business with, from English banks; the interest is eating up the country and eventually will take everything."

"The people who come to this country," said Rebecca, "must all have been rich." "Not as you understand riches," was the reply; "we call labor, capital."

"Our people were intelligent and all the trades were represented; they had nothing but could make everything and the first thing they made was money; they had some gold but they exchanged it for tools to work with and made their money of paper."

"But is paper money good?" said Rebecca.

"I guess it is," said the girl, "there seems to be no trouble to get rid of it. Our Government makes the money; there is no bank, but a law prohibiting the taking of interest, consequently we have no debtor or poor class. We have little law, but the finest business methods in the world; our business system is so perfect that there is no want but can be supplied without recourse to dishonest methods."

"Why do you object to interest?" was asked.

"Simply because a man who pays interest cannot afford to pay his help what is their due; and if a man cannot loan his money on interest he will use it himself and be compelled by the law of supply and demand to pay his help, the same as others. If he has bonds or notes bearing interest, he at once becomes a parasite. One of the fundamental principles of our law is, that no man shall have something for nothing; if a man invests his money in business stock he is supposed to become a part of the concern and is held to be justly entitled to his share of profits; this in the nearest

our Government comes to allowing interest. We have
a great continent; our mineral and agricultural productions are only limited by the amount of work that is
done. Our Government keeps enough money in circulation so that no enterprise suffers for want of it, and
all have constant employment; as labor is the pro-
ducer of wealth, we are fast becoming wealthy people.

"The American Government, as has been shown,
makes both bonds and money and gives them to the
banks. Through bad, if not dishonest legislation, the
banks loan the money to the people and get a big
interest on it; the Government pays interest on the
bonds; thus the banks, which are only parasites at best,
grow in power until they are able to corner money;
then industries suffer, men cease to labor, the production of wealth is discontinued and the banks or
syndicates who have cornered the money, soon own all
the property that has been produced; classes are formed,
want and misery reign with some, while waste, luxury
and extravagance is the rule among others. They all
want honest money, but we want honest men; honest
money and honest hammer with us would have the
same meaning, which would simply be an article which
honestly filled the bill for which it was intended;
nothing less, nothing more."

The subject was dropped and after a short pause
Miss Colvil said: "If you are not too much fatigued,
let us visit the Senate to-night. I know you will like
it; the hall is one of the largest and finest in the
country. It was built by the Government and is now
under the control of a reform society; It is a govern-
mental concern and the society receives its authority
to operate, under certain regulations from the Government. The subjects discussed generally pertain to the
science of government. There you will hear every
system of government discussed, from socialism to
absolute monarchy."

"Who are your speakers?" asked Minnie.

"O they come from all parts of the country; there is
not a prominent man in the Republic but at some time
takes a part in the discussion Once a year they hold

a Congress in which every noted speaker is invited to take part and they are glad to do so as it brings them prominently before the public. In this Congress they discuss all questions pertaining to government; such as money, gambling, gold, faro banks, national banks, lotteries, saloons, whiskey traffic, taxes, tariff, transportation, commerce, crime—how to prevent and how to punish."

"Ahem," said Minnie, "I would like to know what gambling, banks and lotteries, and such things have to do with Government?"

"There is not a Government on earth," said Miss Colvil, "except our new Republic, but are absolutely controlled or intimately connected with gold-gambling, while national banks are a part of the gambling machinery in the United States; while whiskey and saloons cut a prominent figure in controlling the vote. In this Congress every gentleman and lady are supposed to speak their true sentiments, and if ever they become candidates for office the sentiments there expressed will be held up before the people as their platform or political faith.

"This we are told, is to encourage men to be honorable and weigh their opinions carefully; as our papers are run on the investment of the people, they are under obligations to no one but the people; therefore if a man goes back on his record as made in this Congress, they show him up at once; as there are no political parties to back him up, he must be careful and make a record that will stand the test of criticism. It is said that from the records of this Congress have been obtained some of our best laws, and through it some of our best men have been introduced to the public; the reports of this free, unpaid and unlimited Congress, on all subjects pertaining to Government are published, not only by every newspaper in the country, but they are also put into book form and extensively sold at cost of publication.

"By this method we not only bring the best talent to the front, but it comes pure and beyond the debasngi influence of monetary power. The reports have such a general circulation there is not a reading man through the country, no matter what his occupation, who is not better posted than ninety per cent of your Americans, on all matters of Government. I do not even except your Congressmen. When a law is referred by our Congress to the people, they generally know how to vote; as a result, what few laws we have are very good ones. This Congressional session commences each year on the 10th of No/ember and adjourns before the Holidays; during the other months a variety of subjects is discussed both by home and visiting talent. One night in the week is set aside for students, another for amateur speakers; sometimes rival societies choose speakers and have joint discussions and it becomes . very interesting. All public lecturers use this hall."

The interest of the ladies was so much aroused, that the decision was made that the following night they would visit the Senate. The evening passed very pleasantly in receiving callers who were introduced by Miss Colvil, and the next evening found them all on their way to the Senate.

The entrance was through a large Reception Hall in which were placed tables and chairs, and these were occupied by little groups of persons, some merry-making, others getting ready for debate. The subject for that night was one of general interest and as good talent had been procured the crowd of people gathering into the great hall was immense; the ladies took a seat at a side table and ordered some glasses of cotch, a new beverage, which they found to be both delicious and refreshing.

While thus seated Minnie picked up a paper and read aloud the subject for discussion that evening, as follows: Resolved, that National Banks and Bankers during their reign have committed and caused to be committed more crime and caused more suffering than all other thieves, robbers, murderers and criminals combined,

These ladies had seen some of the power wielded by these banks in the United States and long since regarded the growing power of the institution as dan-

gerous to man's liberty; but to have them boldly pro-
claim it the giant cause of more crime and suffering
than all others combined was entirely beyond their
comprehension; it was with no small interest that they
looked forward to the discussion. As they looked
about the great hall, everyone seemed to be busy;
some were gathered in groups chatting with friends
they had chanced to meet, others promenading up and
down the hall; all were richly dressed and everything
seemed to have the appearance of a gala day. A band
was playing sweet strains of music. On either side of
the hall were tastefully arranged tables for the sale of
nuts, fruits, ice-cream and drinks of many varieties,
but nothing that would intoxicate.

Passing on the ladies found seats in the great auditorium; a small circular was placed in the hands of
each, from which they learned that the discussion
would be opened by Prof. Charles D. La Rue, who had
just completed an examination of the subject in question, as chairman of a committee appointed by the
Government to investigate the following subjects:
Banks, their methods and effect upon Government,
commerce and society; the use of gold as money, its
effect, and where and how the superstition originated.

Prof. Charles D. La Rue had served three years as
chairman of this committee of five and their investiga-
tions had been thorough and complete. Having turned
the results over to the Government and been discharged,
he was now at liberty and would lead in the discussion
in the affirmative. The work of the committee was
afterward published and was pronounced the greatest
monetary history extant.

The great hall and its galleries were packed and the
ladies remarked upon the intelligence and attention of
the audience.

"The fastest horse is always the nicest looking," said
Miss Colvil: "it is so with people; the better their
condition and the more intelligent they become the
better they look. Good opportunities make thrifty
people; under our home-made laws and perfect business
methods, our people are not only happy but they are

fast becoming the most intelligent people on the globe; the ladies in particular are fast coming to the front in all public affairs."

Prof. Charles D. La Rue was now introduced and proved himself, not only a fine orator but seemed to have the history of banks and of money at his tongue's end; he boldly charged the banking system and individual control of money, with all the poverty and three-fourths of the crime in England, France, Germany and the United States; he showed conclusively that the banking system, from first to last, was the foundation of a giant conspiracy against the Government and the people in all countries where it exists; that bankers were never satisfied to let the representatives of the people make the laws, but were constantly interfering with legislation and when once fairly established in a country they expected the legislators to consult them on all financial questions; that their advice under such circumstances is always in their own favor is only natural.

He referred to instances in the United States where in order to carry through Congress such bills in their interest, this great banking class or conspiracy, would hold meetings all over the country and in the name of the great people whom they assumed to represent, demand the repeal of certain laws, or the passage of acts which were altogether in their own interests and detrimental to the interests of the people. He showed further that wherever the system had been suffered to exist, it never failed to become stronger than the Government and control legislation in its own behalf; that their wealth, also was accumulated in so systematic a manner, or method of robbing others, through the manipulation of gold and carefully prepared banking schemes, that the very people who had been robbed often considered the bank had been showing them favor.

He also showed in a clear and comprehensive manner the many gambling games and the machinery invented for the purpose of robbing the masses; among others which he named and described were the wheels of fortune, faro bank, state bank, national bank, and

lotteries of every description. "They differ," said he,
"only in method, the principle is the same and the
result is to enrich the gambler at the expense of the
masses; the existence of such a system was only made
possible by the ancient, superstitious worship of gold,
which still clings to the human race." He showed that
the principle upon which these games are run is percentage, and percentage taken by a national bank of
the United States on the Bank of England, only differed
from the faro bank in the amount taken and the
manner of taking

"The percentage of a faro bank is called "splits;" you
lay your money on a card; if the card wins you are
paid in full; if it loses they take your money; but if
it splits, which really is a stand-off or a draw, then
they take half your money. This is their percentage,
and if a dozen men play all night, it is safe to calcu-
late that the bank will have more money than all of
them put together in the morning. It is taken so
gradually that no one misses it; it is the same with all
gambling games. The national banks have their discount, commission and interest. The only way it
differs materially from the other gambling games, is
that through their system they control legislation and
compel every man who uses money in any way to pay
a certain part of their percentage; while in the other
game there is no compulsion, if you don't play, you
don't pay.

"Of course it is difficult to understand just how this
is done; our statesmen are forced to confess they do
not understand the money question; to save their lives,
they cannot solve the problem of banking or money.
When we consider that these are picked representatives from a nation of people whose common country
school teacher is supposed to be able to solve any and
all mathematical problems, based on reason and true
principles of philosophy, we can readily see how carefully this great gold game is guarded. The people will
probably never understand the game, but I fully believe
they will get tired of its bad effects and eventually
destroy it, root and branch.

I once saw a machine for the manufacture of envelopes; the paper was put into the machine between two rollers which cut the paper in proper shape for envelopes, folded, pasted, counted and dropped them out in packs of twenty-four. I looked at the work in wonder and astonishment; I could not understand the inside working of it, but I could see the result. The Bank of England in the first place is not a bank owned by that Government, as its name would indicate, but is nothing more nor less than a private corporation to which the Government grants many privileges. It was started less than 200 years ago on a very modest capital; since that time it has loaned the English Government so vast a sum of money that the hope of ever paying it has long since vanished and the great English statesmen now advocate the doctrine that a government debt is a government blessing. As the wealthy class own the bank, and also Government debt, which has been largely received through the bank, the interest on that debt must be paid by taxing in some way the labor of the people. The debt certainly is a blessing to the rich, and if the rich are the Government then this obnoxious doctrine must be true, but if the people are the Government, the proposition is absolutely false. This same great bank has not confined its money-making schemes to Great Britain, but it should be borne in mind that while the American people in the last quarter of a century have produced material to, in a great measure, feed and clothe the world, have worked the richest mines on earth, under the mysterious working of this English banking system, these same people have seen their products go abroad and property fall into the hands of English syndicates.

"My countrymen," said the Professor, "I can no more understand the secret workings of this great gold and silver banking business, than I can understand the envelope or any other nice piece of machinery which is all boxed up. But I can see its deadly work; I can easily see the United States has had a dozen different great states and territories, producing millions of dollars' worth of gold and, to-day, there is not gold enough in the country to pay off the British syndicates. Where has this gold all gone? To satisfy the balance of trade? No, for the balance of trade has been in favor of the United States.

"It is like irrigating a field; a man turns a great stream of water into a large field; the fish run down into the field and collect in the low places; they see the water taken up by the loose soil; they watch it disappear; it is really fascinating; they are optimists and when one hole gets full, they hunt for another. That worked all right as long as there was plenty of water in the reservoir which fed the stream, but when the water runs low the stream decreases but absorption continues. The poor fish are first left in a pond, then in a puddle, but at last in the mud. While the American people had a great continent loaded with wealth, right from the hands of the Creator, they were happy, contented and prosperous; but in an evil hour the bank of England got in its work and established its machinery in every city, town and village. The absorption of wealth at once commenced; when men lost their homes they moved west and took Government land; they hunted new places and made new discoveries; the continent was one immense pile of wealth, but it could not last always; the absorption was too great. The people saw millionaires springing up everywhere; thousands upon thousands of dollars bet upon prize fights. They saw palaces, palace cars and yachts; it was fascinating, but at last the rich mines of gold had been exhausted, the Government land had all been taken, everywhere valuable franchise had passed from the control of the people; even their homes had become the property of syndicates. The people are now in the pond; how far, O how far away may be the time before they reach the mud.

"Is it any wonder that the wise statesmen of the United States are so often compelled to confess ignorance on a simple question of dollars and cents? I shall never blame any man for not understanding interest, discount and commission. I think these words should be expunged from the English language. I would vote for such a law. The proudest act of my life is that of casting my first vote for our glorious constitution that demonetizes gold, does away with the intrinsic value of money, prohibits taking or paying interest, limits inheritance and gives to woman equal rights with man. It is with a touch of embarrassment that I come before an audience of the size and intelligence of this to speak on an ordinary subject, but upon this great question, embodied in our Constitution, and others of a similar nature, I feel that I could defend the cause before the arch-angels and the bar of God, feeling myself fortified by the everlasting rock of truth."

The speaker continued by exposing the crooked ways of gold-gamblers and bankers, generally, and showed conclusively that the secret working of the great banking conspirators had, without doubt, caused more poverty and suffering than all other causes combined. It is not our purpose, however, to allow the Professor's speech to interfere with our story; suffice it to say, it was quite in line with the general thought and observation of the ladies and they returned to the Hotel feeling that they had not only been very highly entertained, but that the lecture had been highly instructive.

The hours had passed so pleasantly and the new developments had been so wonderful, that the ladies retired that night with the feeling that they were still in a land of civilization and that the grand principle of truth was still at the bottom of all things; they also felt that the power of superfluous wealth and superstition, urged on by greed, would become so great that its self-destruction would be inevitable, then Truth and Justice would come to the front.

With harmonious feelings like these, they were soon wrapped in such restful slumber as comes to those who live and are at peace with all the world, forgetting self, in the welfare of the great brotherhood of man.

Rebecca had informed Miss Colvil of their intention of founding an institution of learning, for young ladies, somewhere in the New Republic, and she had communicated the same to some of the members of the Ladies' Society of Progress and Advancement; the result was that on the following day they received a call from a number of ladies belonging to that society. If Rebecca had been both astonished and gratified at the manifestation of honesty, brotherly love, and charity for other's faults, which she had seen on every hand, it remained for these ladies to fill her cup of joy to overflowing.

To behold the spiritual development of these ladies and note the harmony existing, which could only be accounted for as the natural condition resulting from changed methods and new ideas, carried Rebecca into an ecstacy of delight; to be present at a gathering of ladies where they were discussing methods and means for the advancement and general good of others, each unmindful of self, acting harmoniously and searching far into the realm of thought, after new plans for the destruction of man's greatest enemy, ignorance and superstition; all this without, apparently, a thought of the expense that might be incurred, with a knowledge that these ladies represented the wealthiest families in the place; finding how completely their ideas, thoughts and desires harmonized with her own, her heart was too full for utterance; excusing herself, and leaving the ladies to be entertained by her mother and Minnie, she went to her room that she might regain composure; it is not to be wondered at that all which had transpired during the last few days had wrought upon her nervous temperament and she needed solitude and perhaps the relief which comes from weeping to restore her equilibrium. She soon returned with complete control of her feelings and prepared to discuss any subject which might be introduced. The conference lasted for several hours and before its adjournment, Rebecca had been chosen to deliver a lecture before the society the following Saturday evening. After arranging preliminaries they adjourned.

To one of the ladies Rebecca expressed herself as having noticed a singular peculiarity which she had met—the utter disregard of any expense which might

be necessary in carrying out their plans. To this the
lady replied that such a condition was due to the fact
that all property above $100,000 to each heir, goes to
the Government and then finds its way back among the
people through public works.

"There is probably not a family represented here
to-day," said the lady, "that is not already far beyond
the limits; consequently we are handling our surplus
money which we really have no use for, in other
words, we are handling Government money, and do
you not remember how lavish your people are when
they handle Government funds? But another thing has
a good deal to do with the liberality of our people,
and that is, if either a lady or gentleman has business
qualifications, an opportunity to make money is always
open. All our extensive business is done by joint-
stock companies; this makes a demand for business
men, and no matter what a man's peculiar calling may
be a place is always found to suit him, and when it is
known that chances are always open for all, even their
own sons and daughters, they can afford to be liberal.

"All people love to excel and thus receive the
applause of mankind; in the United States all applaud
wealth. The approach of a palace car or the yacht of
a millionaire is always heralded by every newspaper in
the land and attention is called to it by conspicuous
head-lines; people with hungry children, worship
wealth; it is a sign of superior financial ability; honor
counts for nothing unless backed by money; intellect
counts for nothing unless you use it for money getting.
All the selfish qualities of men are brought to the front
in the reckless scramble for gold. The biggest hog
gets the biggest pile of the necessaries of life and
locks it up; the others go ragged and hungry but call
him great.

"With us things are quite the reverse; by experiment and careful calculation, we have demonstrated the
fact that with our improved machinery, which we make
ourselves, one man's labor is quite equal to the support of many others beside himself; where no robbery
is going on and there is no waste of time or product,

the good things of life become so common and easily obtained that man, to excel, must explore other fields than wealth. This gives intellectual advancement new impetus; here the historian, humanitarian, philosopher, scientist, moralist, religionist, artist, sculptor, author, journalist and tradesman all find their admirers. Music, too, is cultivated to the very highest degree and receives its share of patronage. It is those who excel in these things who gain the admiration of our people. Our rich men are so plentiful and have so little power, that they attract but little attention.

"The American hog is of two varieties, the quadruped and biped; the one is fattened and killed; the other, too, is being fattened but for what purpose is not so clear. Should history repeat itself, as it is said to do, their chances seem fairly good to meet the same fate as the other hogs.

"We have discarded both varieties and neither fatten the one nor the other, nor do we allow them to control our money or make our laws. Our changed conditions make different people; there is no occasion to be selfish for all have everything in abundance and some to spare. "

Rebecca listened to all this with great interest; it seemed so entirely in keeping with, and explanatory of her general surroundings. She was fast opening her eyes to the real cause that had brought such a happy state of affairs among these people. It was with light hearts and kindly feeling that the ladies separated, after this long and interesting visit; in fact so marked was this feeling of harmony and good cheer, that Mrs. Goldburg remarked after the departure of the ladies, that such an absence of all selfish motives was truly wonderful. "Such a meeting," said she, "would be impossible in a country where a conspiracy of bankers and gold-gamblers, not only rob industry of half its earnings, but destroy the means of production by controlling money and withholding it from the producers when most needed.

CHAPTER XXVIII.

WHILE Baxter was visiting bankers in England, Coy and Saunders had not been idle. After returning to their place in Kiyongo, they made it a point to become more intimate with John Benedict Sherman. This Mr. Sherman was a man of fair ability but was without honest motive. Naturally he was a traitor at heart, was not ostentatious but loved money; with him it seemed to be a mania. He was willing to enter into any plot to impoverish others, in order to increase the size of his own useless pile of gold; not because he needed it but because he wanted it. When he had succeeded in robbing others, he did not hide his face for shame, but stood boldly up and made long arguments, full of subterfuge and point-blank lies, to cover up his work and make black look white.

He had one very peculiar trait of character and that was to buy American gold coin with every dollar he had to spare. The Coin being at a discount, as Mexican silver is in the United States. In buying it he would increase his number of dollars and would rake it in from the treasurer's counter with a chuckle which indicated an idiosyncrasy representing gold-worship, probably inherited from some of his ancestors far in the past. He had a building of his own, with an under-ground vault where he kept his gold coin; he would often go into it, and by the light of a candle count it over and over again, sometimes for hours. He was getting old and had no children to inherit his wealth; but like the common wood-rat of the Rocky Mountains he semed to possess a mania for increasing his pile, without any visible reason for so doing.

Messrs. Saunders and Coy were not slow in discovering this peculiar trait in the man's character. It appeared that a brother of his, being a man of noble character, had in the past done some great service to the people and being now dead, this man, John Benedict Sherman, in consequence of his brother's noble deeds, had the full confidence of the people, and great influence. It was therefore decided to court his friendship and have him ready for use; from that time he was feasted on every occasion.

For a long time they had been acquainted with a couple of fast young men, or rather rough gentry as they supposed—Jack Pixley and Tim Bowen. These two men claimed to be doctors, but it was evident they had but little practice, for to all appearance they were always at leisure; the two became acquainted with each other through Saunders and Coy. After this the four gentlemen often took oysters together and frequently met at the halls. They had given hints to Coy and Saunders, that they were first-class crooks, had plenty of money, but were always ready to make an honest dollar. They had both been anarchists—one in New York, the other in Chicago—but both were now at leisure. It occurred to Coy and Saunders that the services of these men might be of importance; they invited them to their rooms which were furnished in fine style; the house, too, was not without its well-stocked liquor and card room; here the gentlemen spent many a lively night in playing that favorite American game called poker.

The game was very limited for all agreed it was only a friendly game with money enough on the board to make it interesting; some nights cards were dispensed with and the whole evening was given up to revelry. On one of these occasions, when all had become quite lively, Mr. Pixley said he had been a confidence man in New York, and in consequence of a little killing he had to get out. Since he had been here he had robbed several men, but his experience had been that the sub-treasury system was so complete that every man in the country carries a check book, the money stays in the treasury and these checks do the business of the

country, so if you rob a man you get nothing and it
don't pay. Saunders then took him into his confidence and told him that he had a little job on hand
that there would probably be lots of money in, but it
was likely to require a little blood-letting.

"O that's all right," said Pixley, "I am an American of the late pattern and anything for money is my
motto." "Correct," said Saunders.

While this conversation was going on Coy and Bowen
were in another room making up a fresh lot of hot stuff
and as they returned the conversation was dropped.
The glasses were filled and Coy offered the following
toast: "The United States and honest money."
Pixley now became eloquent and delivered a tirade
upon the new Republic, denounced its rag-baby money
system and finally wound up his remarks with eulogies
on John Sherman and the Stuffed-Prophet, both of
honest money and sound currency fame in the United
States. This speech met with hearty approval and all
drank to the Stuffed-Prophet. When the night was
well spent in drunken revels the party separated, to
all appearance with the very best of feeling. When
Pixley and Bowen took their leave, Saunders and Coy
agreed that the two men were bricks. Saunders said
that he believed that man Pixley would think no more
of killing a man, than he would of killing a fly.

The next day Saunders and Pixley met by chance
and went to a private room in a hotel where they took
several drinks out of Saunders' bottle. After a little
more talk as to the prospect of something exciting in
the near future, where all would have an opportunity
to distinguish themselves and make a few honest dollars, it was arranged that Pixley should make it a
point to meet Bowen and feel of him gently to see if
it would be advisable to let him in to any of their plans.

After a few days Pixley again met Saunders, gave
him the substance of two or three conversations with
Bowen and wound up by saying, he believed that all
that would be necessary would be for them to approach
him carefully and convince him there was money in it;
Saunders was of the same opinion, so it was arranged

that Pixley and Bowen should come around and spend an evening occasionally until further developments. After this Pixley and Bowen might often have been seen engaged in frivolous conversation, making their way at early evening to the rooms of Saunders and Coy, where they would spend long hours in gambling and drinking; the plot still remained in embryo. After several weeks had passed, Baxter appeared on the scene; on telling his experience, Coy and Saunders were impatient for some move toward the accomplishment of their hearts' desire, that of overthrowing in some way the present money and property system and establishing the gold base and English land-law system. But the money lord had decided to travel over the country before seeing them, but at last he entered the city, quite unnoticed. True, his name had been taken from the hotel register by the evening paper, but there were no millionaires to hob-nob with him, nor did Senators and Congressmen seek his advice, for the referendum put a quietus on them.

Mr. Baxter met him at the hotel and afterward escorted him to the private rooms of Saunders and Coy; the four had a pleasant chat and it was remarked that the great money-lord loved champagne as well as a common man loves whiskey; in fact, he finally threw off his mask and called for whiskey straight and all acknowledged after he was gone, that a money-lord is very much like other people, when robbed of the power of gold. Saunders said that no man of any distinction cound command the respect that is due him, in a country where the common herd are fed on the fat of the land. Said he: "Had we received the Lord in style due to his rank, driven him about the city in a coach and four, and foot-men in livery, as they would do in Washington, every paper in the country would have made its grand effort to get out a cartoon which should be more ridiculous than all others; as the papers are daily visitors to every family circle, the affair would meet with ridicule from one end of the country to the other, and thus a man of wealth loses prestige.

As this was the first time that the Lord had found an opportunity to take a social glass with kindred spirits since he had been in the Republic, it is not surprising that he got a little too full and the whole night was given up to bacchanalian orgies, or what is called by common people, a regular old drunk.

The next night the Lord of money again dropped in; this time without Baxter. After a few drinks, he proceeded to business. The Lord was given a complete history of the growth of the new Republic and a full explanation of its peculiar laws; several plans were suggested but nothing was agreed upon; it was finally agreed that they would meet in secret at least once a week, and that they would have a regular meeting every Saturday night to which Baxter would be admitted. They dare not trust him in all their plans, but needed his services too much to be willing to lay him one side entirely.

It was further arranged that the Lord should make the acquaintance of some of the Senators; to accomplish this, the Senator, John Benedict Sherman would be used. A few nights later they again met and getting filled up on hot whiskey the Lord gave as his opinion that nothing short of revolution would accomlish anything. Sherman, he said, seemed to be the only man that could be handled; beside, said he: "The Senators have no power; under their peculiar business system there are so few conflicting interests that law is made, in a great measure, unnecessary and the Referendum works to a charm. Public sentiment makes the law and as there are no political parties, no saloons and the newspapers are run by stock companies with plenty of money, and are limited in their profits, I see but one way and that is to overthrow the Government; in organizing a new one, get in our gold bank and land-laws; this done the remainder of the work will be easy."

After a long and earnest council it was conceded that the most plausible plan was to secure the original copy of the Constitution and rights of man, have them doctored so as to make gold the money of the country;

if this could be accomplished through Senator Sherman, they could then organize a conspiracy, employ roughs, have Lincoln, Bundy, Jefferson and Summerville assassinated, and burn the Capitol; then in organizing a new Government the new copies of the Constitution would recognize gold and in the excitement it would be passed over unnoticed, as was the demonetizing of silver in the United States in 1873. This done, they believed they could get gold in circulation and of course, national banks would soon follow. "This done," said the money Lord, "it will be only a question of time."

"I think it will work all right," said Saunders, "if we can get rid of these few men." "I, too," said Coy.

After draining their glasses once more, the money Lord said: "We will continue our social meetings and obtain all the information possible; further than this we can do nothing until I hear from my people."

Thus saying, he took his departure.

Immediately after this, the following letter was sent to a friend at home.

CITY OF KIYONGO, CENTRAL AFRICA, August 20th.

To the Earl of Tuxbury;

My Dear Sir: I have delayed writing from week to week and from day to day, hoping that something favorable would result, but as yet am completely nonplussed. I find things very different here from the United States. There they fall over one another to do honor to a man of wealth; the newspapers herald his approach and political tricksters are after him for bids; you can buy the leaders of the great parties and they, with the help of the saloons, control the vote. The banks too are always with you in financial legislation; here there are no banks nor saloons and no political parties; the great corporations, instead of being for you, are against you. There gold and silver have always been their money; here it has never been used; here their whole financial system is founded upon this general principle, that gold and silver are productions of the earth, consequently have a value as bullion which must change as do all other commodities, according to its production and use.

That money is created by the Government in order to facilitate book-keeping and enable parties to make exchange of commodities, that like a note or order, a bill payable or a bill receivable, its values should never change; therefore it is claimed that money made of gold has two values, one a bullion value which is always changing, another a money value which should never change; to harmonize the two is simply impossible. They should therefore be kept forever separate.

Finance is taught here in all the schools and this is the fundamental principle; the old theory of giving money an intrinsic value, has been so scoffed at and ridiculed here, that I am fully convinced that legislation in favor of metal money is entirely out of the question for the present.

In approaching any public men here in regard to the use of gold, they say at once, they have gold enough in their mountains to supply the world with money. They also say they don't need the gold and they have no men to spare to dig it; that while other nations are producing gold, they will be found busy producing something of more value to man; this is the way they talk. Only yesterday a man said to me: "My kind sir, do you know that we have extensive treasury vaults full of gold and silver bars which are the products of our mines? That the immigrants bring millions of dollars of American, English and German gold coins to our country? These being at a discount here soon find their way into the Government vaults. That we have plenty of national money in circulation to keep all business active and every man in the country employed? We manufacture everything and import but very little. As we have the most improved machinery in the world and no interruption of business in consequence of breaking banks or want of confidence, our own productions are simply enormous, and as our own vessels keep the surplus production constantly dumped upon foreign markets to sell for what it is worth there, we are often forced to take gold and silver in exchange. It has become a rule with our foreign trade to exchange all our gold accumulation for interest bearing bonds or other securities; but when this is sometimes found impossible, the gold is shipped home to the already bursting vaults, and thus, from so many sources the great pile of gold continues to increase its bulk.

"Our methods differ materially from the Americans; they exchange their surplus productions for confidence and interest; we exchange for such articles of commerce as we need and when we can get nothing else we take gold. Our paper money is worth more than gold, simply because merchants can buy more of our goods with it than they can with gold. What do you suppose we care about an International Conference? Our people have all the mechanical arts and sciences known to man and if other nations were to use all the gold they have to make a golden calf and all fall down and worship it, our system would not be changed a particle. We only want the rest of the world to consume our products; we have enough and some to spare and we don't care what kind of money other people use. If they were to push their golden calf into the ocean and through their blind, superstitious worship of gold, follow it in, the loss of the gold would not affect us in the least, but the loss of the people would. If all the gold on earth were sunk to the bottom of the sea, does any one suppose the world would be materially affected? It would only be a blow to superstition."

This is the way these people talk. It is claimed by some of our most successful financiers, that to work a man successfully, you must bring a pressure of some kind to bear, then you can get his attention and in some way control him. The business system and peculiar laws here, make every man so completely independent there is no chance for a deal; public sentiment is free, it is not controlled by monetary pressure; hence men fear public sentiment. In the

United States, public sentiment is controlled by the money power, through the use of national banks, news-papers, the associated press, whiskey and saloons; hence men say: "Public sentiment be damned, all I want is money."

The press here is perfectly at ease; there are ten newspapers here to one in the United States and they are said to be well supported. All large papers are run by companies controlled by the Government, the people owning the stock. The editors of that class of papers work for a salary and while, in a great measure, they control public sentiment, it is only an intellectual control; its force and power consists in being right. If wrong, public sentiment soon finds a way to make itself felt, to that extent that it can be consistently said: "Public sentiment controls these large papers." The smaller papers are run by private enterprise and probably in their way, do as much toward moulding, as do the large ones. If one of these editors goes crooked the others would burn him up and if it were possible to buy every paper in the country, public sentiment would start new ones; beside, even if it could be done, it would cost much for the risk. From this you will see what a difficult matter it will be to do anything in this direction.

I have examined their coast defenses and am sur-prised to find every point fortified, and the only army they have is drilling on these batteries; they have extensive ship-building works and have constructed a cigar-shaped vessel for the purpose of smoking our battle-ships; its purpose is to collide with our vessels. It carries no guns and no shot can affect it; it requires but six men to manage it, and they have a safety apparatus by which the crew escapes if the boat goes down in colliding; it is built for a speed that will overhaul our vessels, and they claim to have enough of these turtle-backed monsters to sink one-half of the English navy, with no particular risk to themselves. They are designed for harbor defense, and after seeing one, I am convinced it will do all they claim.

If they sink in colliding, they say the loss is small

in comparison to the damage that might be done by one of our great ships. Their manufacture of firearms is not to be excelled, and it is claimed that they could, if necessary, put a large army in the field in a few days; still they have not the expense which other countries incur in keeping a regular standing army; even their police force has very little to do, and all things considered, it seems to me like a very dangerous project to urge a war with these people.

They are all soldiers at will, and statesmen from necessity; having no political parties to guide them, vote from principle; they pay no fancy prices for public service, and there is no country in the world which exacts more from its public servants. They are not man-worshipers and it is said, that if a president die, there is hardly a school district but can furnish a man to fill his place.

Their manufacturing establishments are a marvel of perfection and they have established this fact beyond controversy that labor, money and system are the three requisites in production; they have a maxim: "That nature produces men, Government makes money and system is the outgrowth of constant effort to overcome obstacles." I believe if we were to send a half dozen battle-ships here to force an issue of any kind, there would be a gala day in the cities, while the monsters which are impervious to shot and shell would send them to the bottom.

After a careful study of this matter, my conclusions are that there is but one method by which we may hope for a reasonable degree of success in securing the control of money here, and I have formed my plans to that end. I have some good men as helpers—Messrs. Coy, Saunders and Baxter are all staunch men and can be depended upon. I have also made the acquaintance of a man by the name of John Benedict Sherman, a member of the Senate, in high standing, principally in consequence of some noble deeds of his brother; his price is rather extravagant, I think, but without doubt, he can be bought to do whatever is necessary. Our plan is to organize a band of staunch men, secure

possession of the original Constitution and rights of
man, and have them so changed by an expert penman,
as to abridge some of the radical points; this done,
we will probably have to resort to very extreme measures before accomplishing much in the way of legislation; therefore should you hear of anything startling,
you must consider that it was unavoidable; the fact is,
this paper money system must be destroyed or it will
destroy all our gold interests throughout the civilized
world. They are even now talking about making
another large shipment of gold to the United States to
be exchanged for securities; it is not their production
of gold that we need to fear, but it is their example in
their use of paper money and the sub-treasury plan,
which will sooner of later take the place of our gold
and national banks, and this would be the downfall of
class supremacy.

Should you still desire that I should make an effort
to crush the monster, you will please send at once the
best expert penman you can command; have him bring
such chemicals as will be necessary to remove ink and
doctor the Constitution. I shall make no report until
I have accomplished something, but will write you an
occasional private letter.

Very truly and respectfully yours,
DEAD EARNEST SEYD.
(Lord Luxenburg.)

After this letter was written the parties already
named continued to hold their secret meetings in which
plans were formulated. The money Lord, Coy and
Saunders had a secret plan which they dare not lay
before Baxter or Sherman; this was, that after the
Constitution had been doctored, Lincoln, Bundy and
Summerville were to be assassinated; having learned
that Jefferson was about to return to the United States
his name was not taken into account; then the public
buildings were to be burned and all books destroyed,
except the original copy of the Constitution, which was
to be doctored.

It was believed that this general destruction would

be followed by placing Senator Sherman in the Presidential Chair, and once there he could be depended upon to do anything for gold; all agreed that to pile up gold was the height of his ambition. The money Lord could afford to make him a millionaire twice over to get legislation in favor of gold.

Coy suggested that arrangements should be at once made with Sherman to have Saunders put in charge of the police on Sherman's coming into power, and that salaries of these men be largely increased.

"That is right," said the money Lord, "if we can control the police and sheriff, we can enforce such laws as are to our liking and nulify the others; if the people make too much noise the number of police can be increased; when we get control of the public crib, we can afford to pay these fellows well."

"The salaries of all officers," said Saunders, "should be doubled at once. In this way we will secure their confidence. See how they increase the salaries in the United States and mark the effect. It became a panic and extended from president to constable."

They had already secured the services of Pixley and Bowen to do the killing, for which service they were to receive from the money Lord $100,000 each.

Time passed slowly and meetings were discontinued for a time in order to avoid suspicion, but each man was busily engaged in getting better acquainted with the officials. After a long and anxious waiting, a man arrived from England, prepared to change the Constitution. The money Lord, Sherman, Saunders Baxter, Coy and the expert penman at once held a meeting; their plan was outlined by the money Lord, as follows: Sherman was to secure the original copy of the Constitution and bring it to their place of meeting on the following night at half past seven, when they would all be together; the work of changing the Constitution would begin at once. "That done," said the Lord, "we will lay on our oars and see what we can do toward having a law paased in favor of gold."

They then separated in different directions, but in accordance with previous arrangements, the money

Lord, Saunders and Coy met again at the same place an hour later. After quietly enjoying their whiskey toddy and cigars, the discussion began; all agreed that favorable legislation would be impossible until they were rid of the objectionable parties; the money Lord said that as soon as these men were out of the way and the excitement of the affair had subsided, he thought there would be but little difficulty in getting gold made the money of the country. "Then," said he, "we will have a power by which future legislation can be controlled. The next step will be a national bank, and then the thing will run itself."

He referred to the manner in which silver had been demonetized in the United States by a mere trick; neither the men who voted for the bill nor the President who signed it, knew that it demonetized silver, and yet it became a law and millions upon millions of money passed into the hands of the money class from its enforcement. "While this was being done," said he, "the people were kept quiet by strong, silver coinage planks in all political parties, and that is one thing we must attend to here; we must never miss an opportunity to raise political strife that will be likely to lead to the organization of parties. It will be much easier to buy the leaders than the voters; the referendum, too, must be repealed or nulified; this Government control of whiskey must also be broken up, and the right to run saloons restored to the people, for that is a very prominent part of our system."

Pausing for a moment while all hands took another drink, the money Lord proceeded to discuss at length the working of the gold game. "National banks," said he, "are the machines which do the work; as attachments, we have the broker's office, clearing house, saloons, trusts, lotteries, gambling houses and bucket shops; as supports we have the two great political parties, board of trade, subsidized newspapers and associated press; as methods we have the control of money, bonds, mortgages, interest, discount, confidence and money panics; as arguments we have sound currency, honest dollars, rag-baby, reform, protection, over-production, parity, and a Government debt is a Government blessing.

The system has been planted in the United States, and its successful working there has been too great to admit of a doubt, but immediately on making gold the money of this country, our success is assured, and the desired results will follow, as a matter of course."

The others coincided, so they took another drink; all smiled, then laughed, then smiled again and took another drink; this time all hands clicked glasses to the health of Johnnie Bull and the national banks; a ha ha ha, followed this and all lit fresh cigars.

By this time all had become quite well enthused and Saunders explained that Pixley and Bowen could be depended on to do the killing of at least two; that he would take care of the others, and all that was necessary was the fixing of the Constitution, and by the snap of his finger he could send the fanatics to hell.

"Don't talk so loud," said Coy, feeling alarmed at the simple utterance of such words.

"Why," said Saunders, "have these walls ears, or has the earth become a telephone that I should fear to speak? I tell you, gentlemen, I knew full well some years ago that this would come about, and I did not build these walls so loose and thin that the vulgar horde might list to what I say; no, no, not I, they are two feet thick or more. The very floor is stuffed and air-tight overhead, beside the room above is where I sleep and is always under lock and key. Here, far beyond the reach of human ear, is where I come to think and drink, and drink and think and lay my plans; and now that it will soon be mine 'to beard the Lion in his den,' I feel quite brave. Long years have they my efforts all despised; debased my gold and made of me a laughing-stock; ha ha, these knaves: their time is short for power will soon be mine, and when I wield the scepter my ambition shall be satisfied. Gold, gold will be the power with which I'll crush these toiling hordes that fatten at the cost of Government employ, while men with gold, pass by unnoticed and without due respect.

"Hate, hate, yes, cruel hate shall be the watch-word of my heart's desire, until I quench with deadly fire, the life of these my mortal foes.

"Buried down beneath the floor I have the glittering gold on which I'll found this nation's bank and on that base I'll furnish money for this land; they have what they call money now, but I do not; 'tis trash, green-back would be a better name, and when these fanatical knaves are gone and Sherman in the chair, we soon will have contraction, and then it is I'll make my power felt.

"When words of want, consternation,. misery and woe come forth as from a burning hell; alms-houses, prisons, jails all full, Soldiers' Homes for many thousands more; other millions tramping for a job and soup-houses everywhere; then it is, and not till then, they will come to me for help. I'll give it, not in gold, but paper money, based on gold, honest money, sound currency."

Once more the glasses clicked and the Stuffed Prophet received their compliments. Soon the party retired; the Lord, Chief Counselor, Financier and Banker, Dead Earnest Seyd, to his hotel, Coy to his private home and Saunders to his room above, all to meet the following night to doctor the Constitution.

CHAPTER XXIX

WE must now return to the hotel in the city of Summerville and continue to record the travels and experiences of Mrs. Goldburg, Rebecca and Minnie. In a former chapter it will be remembered that Rebecca had accepted a proposition to address one of the leading Progressive Societies of the place. Several days elapsed before the appointed time, during which the ladies made the acquaintance of a family at the hotel, by the name of Gardner; the family consisted of Mr. and Mrs. Gardner and four children, only one of whom, a daughter, was at present at the hotel. The eldest was a son, Charles by name; then Mary, Jennie and Theodore. They lived on a farm in the interior, nearly one hundred miles from Summerville, and sixty miles from Kiyongo.

On this occasion Mr. Gardner had come to the city in a light carriage, accompanied by his wife and eldest daughter, Mary. As their route was through a beautiful farming country, thickly settled, and the roads being fine, they had preferred coming this way in order to visit friends along the route. Mr. Gardner was a very unassuming man, but the essence of politeness.

Rebecca was greatly attracted by this family and found Mr. and Mrs. Gardner to be persons of deep thought, who had ascended to intellectual heights where superstition seemed a pigmy, far below. Mary, too, was a bright girl and at once became the favorite of these ladies. Her disposition was so innocent and confiding, that Rebecca and Minnie took her to their hearts and she became their constant companion; Mrs. Gardner and Mrs. Goldburg also became fast friends, and as the family were to return home in a few days, they insisted that Mrs. Goldburg and the two young ladies should accompany them. It would give them an opportunity to see something of the interior of the country, and also to make new acquaintances.

Their carriage had three seats, and the roads being smooth, all could ride comfortably, and as they were desirous of seeing the country as far as possible, they decided to go.

Before they left the hotel, Mrs. Goldburg was not only surprised, but felt highly complimented, at receiving from the Street Car company, a pass over their line while they remained in the city; taking into consideration the wonderful cheapness of this way of travel, it did not amount to much in a money point of view.

The reader will naturally wonder that Rebecca was able to prepare for her lecture on such short notice, but it must be remembered that while she was at home, she had long weeks, months and even years of leisure, all of which she had devoted to self-improvement. She had not only read, but had written a great deal; among these writings were lectures, leisurely and carefully prepared; some of them, even, committed to memory and rehearsed before her mother and Colonel Bundy's family. The subject of the lecture she had chosen for this occasion was, "Crime, Its Causes and Its Cure."

The subject being an important one, the Lecture was the result of much careful study, and to say that its rendition was a success, would be tame language. She had expected to address a small audience of only the members of the Society, and when she learned that she was to appear before an audience of five or six thousand she was somewhat abashed; she possessed great determination, however, and accepted the situation; she had often been upon the rostrum before.

On this occasion she went upon the platform and in a calm, clear and earnest voice, dealt with facts in so forcible a manner as to win the confidence, admiration and love of that great audience. As a result of the appreciation of her efforts, the ladies were tendered a banquet before they left the city.

Three days after the lecture they took their depature

but the time was so occupied in receiving calls, that they were obliged to give up for the present, all further explorations of the city.

From information gained through interviews the ladies were of one opinion, that the improved conditions were only made possible by the limit of the accumulation of wealth in the hands of individuals. All conceded that the establishment of great monetary dynasties to roll on down the ages, and become a power in the hands of a few to interfere with the honest working of Government, trade and commerce, to the injury of the masses, long after the man who first made the accumulation is dead, and gone to that place where no man goes until he has surrendered the last farthing, is wrong. That it is a custom dangerous to good government, to liberty and civilization; that it is a custom that comes down to us from semi-barbaric age; that it belongs to hereditary Kingship and should be expunged from all Republics where people aspire to a higher state of civilization.

The days passed quickly amid such enlivening experiences, and the morning for their anticipated trip came. The start, which is always regarded as the most difficult part of a journey, had been made without incident. The day was all that could be desired, the roads smooth and their route took them past many a comfortable home, situated on a forty-acre tract of land, and occupied by people both intelligent and prosperous; the land all seemed to be surveyed in long, narrow strips running back form the road.

The houses were not large but artistically built and in various styles; one thing was noticeable, all were surrounded by trees both ornamental and shade, and shrubbery and flowers abounded; neither was there a neglect of fruits and vegetables; indeed, Mrs. Gardner remarked that their tables were largely supplied the year 'round from their own gardens and orchards; not only that, but the cellars were well filled with canned fruits and vegetables which they prepared by a method of their own, to keep indefinitely; each family had a small pasture where a few Jersey cows and a few horses and sheep were kept—the American hog being dispensed with. Another habit of these people which Mrs. Gardner mentioned, is that they are adopting an almost exclusive vegetable and fruit diet, combined with milk, and for this reason they prefer the Jersey to any other kind. They believe such food more conducive to health and longevity, beside being more easily produced than a diet which includes meat.

"Don't you find it difficult to supply the table with a sufficient variety of dishes to satisfy the taste, without meat?" asked Mrs. Goldburg.

"Not at all," was the quick reply. "On the contrary, I have found that we live better now than when we used more meat; then we too often thought that if we had meat alone, that was sufficient, while now we take greater pains to have vegetables well seasoned with butter or cream; in addition to this, we are never without some kind of fruit. When we get to Uncle Ben's to-night, you will see what a really good country meal is, and I doubt if you would eat meat if they had it. I believe the day will come when people will look back upon this generation of meat-eaters with the same feeling of disgust which we have for cannibals."

It was now near noon. They had been constantly meeting farm-wagons going to the city, laden with products of the garden, farm and orchard; each wagon was driven by a citizen; good, honest and intelligent; not a Chinaman or a dago was seen. The thought that each of these men had a home, a wife and innocent children, and that these homes were made secure by a Government for the people, and protected from every species of invasion, was food for reflection. Mrs. Goldburg called the attention of Mr. Gardner to the absence of all low and ignorant classes of foreigners, such as are often seen in the United States.

"This," said he, "is easily accounted for; the United States corporations run the country and control the legislation; their first move is to secure a high tariff on imports; this shuts out foreign competition. The next step is to pool all interests and put wages as low as possible, and to secure plenty of help in case of strikes they import paupers by millions, and they become useful to the money power in controlling the price of labor. Here we have no money power, no pools, no monopolies. No man comes to our country except of his own free will and pays his own expenses. True, we have extensive emigrant societies, but they are like Missionaries and work for the good of the country; their office is to go among the most intelligent classes of the foreigners, circulate literature giving all facts necessary to secure a good class of emigration."

At noon they drove up before a farm-house standing nearer the road than was common. The Gardners had stopped at this same house on their way to the city. Seeing them the lady at once recognized Mr. and Mrs. Gardner, and coming to the carriage, invited them to stop for dinner, an invitation they very willingly accepted. The husband of the lady, just then coming from the field, assisted Mr. Gardner in putting up his team while the ladies passed into the house and the gentlemen soon joined them. While dinner was being prepared by the lady of the house and her two daughters, the party took seats upon the porch.

It was evident that the travelers were fully alive to the changed condition. They had noticed that nearly the whole population was American and yet they were so much more liberal and sociable than people at home; on mentioning this, the stranger said: "It was the confidence people had in their ability to live upon their own earnings and there was no way in which others could build up monetary dynasties that would eventually rob them of their homes and means of living. When we feel secure in all these things, why should we not be sociable? We have all the comforts of life and save money every year; a millionaire can have no more." "In what way do the people generally invest their earnings?" said Mrs. Goldburg.

"We have so far invested them in stock, but the last year or two stock has been very hard to get; the only way we can get it now is to leave our money at the treasury and make an application for stock; then you are entitled to the first that is on the market in your

town, according to date of deposit. In addition to
this, as an investment, we are constantly improving
our lands, thus making homes for our children; others
spend all their surplus or over-production in enabling
their children to come to the front, intellectually; while
some spend all their surplus in frivolous enjoyment
and high-living.

"Instead of one man, like Astor, owning his $100,-
000,000, we have 1,000 persons with $100,000 each;
these 1,000 persons spend a great deal more in luxury
than the one millionaire, and this all helps to keep
our money in circulation."

"In case of war," said Mrs. Goldburg, "can your
Government issue bonds?" "Certainly not," said the
gentleman, "we would only continue to issue money
to meet all demands."

"But would not that produce inflation?" said Mrs.
Goldburg. "To some extent, probably, and prices of
everything would advance in proportion. The price
of labor and all that labor produces would be increased.
Money would be plentiful and business active. Government then having power to control all corporations
and regulate the profit on business done by these great
corporations to the needs of the government, would
raise the price of freight, fares, and in fact, everything,
until the profit of the business of the country would
keep the circulating medium within bounds.

"Congress you will understand has power in time of
war to suspend the payment of the five per cent dividend on stock until the war has been closed, and by so
doing could prolong a war indefinitely."

"But," said Mrs. Goldburg, "will not money then
become so plentiful as to lose its value?"

"We think not," said the gentleman, "in fact I see
no reason why it should. Our Government is the
people and the people are the Government; in it every
individual is represented. All lands belong to the
people or Government; individuals having only possessory title to small tracts of land so long as they
keep the same in use. Our money in based upon this
land and cannot depreciate in value, unless the land

also depreciates. As money becomes more plentiful, land, with all other property, appreciates and preserves an equilibrium. The stability or value of the land as a surety depends upon the ability of the Government to defend its title, and its ability to defend the title depends upon the patriotism of the people. History records no instance where an intelligent people have been called upon to defend their homes and did not respond. It is only bankers who hold back under such circumstances for the sake of speculation.

"The title to land may be considered good, hence its value as a surety cannot be questioned, and money is also good. If our people were conquered, and our land confiscated by the conquerors, our money would be an entire loss. When a country has its money based on gold and is conquered, and the people lose their homes by confiscation, they lose nothing on gold from the fact that the bankers ship it all out of the country, often before the first gun is fired, all for the sake of the 'dear people;' I will let you decide which is best."

"Another question, Mr. Gardner. As the law prevents the collection of interest-bearing debts, what will citizens do with money which collects in their hands during flush times?"

"When your bankers," said the gentleman, "have more gold coin than they can loan to advantage, they store it away in vaults until such time as it is needed; here we have no bankers, consequently the people have the money and they do with it just the same as your bankers; they lay it away or deposit it in sub-treasury vaults until it can be used to advantage; you see it is like a postage stamp, always good.

"There is one more thing that our Government offers to individuals as security for our money. You are already aware that we, as a Government, own a share in the profits of all the business done by these great joint stock companies, and they are as numerous as the Government is large; even without taking our land into consideration, this alone would make our money

good as wheat, and far better than gold, a thing which
you can neither eat, drink nor wear.

"As another resource in time of war is that our Government, in order to protect its mines, buys all gold,
silver, lead and copper products. The surplus of
metals is carefully stored in great vaults, where it will
be safe in time of war; some of this gold has long
since been converted into United States bonds, but it
comes right back into our treasury again, as interest,
in a very short time and we still retain the bonds.
As the United States is a producing country, these
bonds would be a resource in time of war.

"The gold and silver bullion which is constantly
piling up in our vaults would be another resource; by
its shipment we could keep the balance of trade in our
favor through a long and tiresome war; our lead and
copper surplus would also be a resource. We believe
that by being well prepared for war, will save us probably, from ever having one; in fact, there is a belief
that the time is not far distant when Justice will be
enthroned the world over; then war will be unnecessary, a thing of the past and known only in history."

"If you will excuse my inquisitiveness," said Mrs.
Goldburg, "I would like to ask who built all these
fine roads?"

"Certainly," said the gentleman, "we are proud of
our country and like to talk about it. Our Government controls all the corporations and retains from
their profit 2 per cent per annum for the entire capital
stock. This profit is so enormous that the money of
the country flows to the treasury, as it does to the
banks or to Wall Street in your country. It Government did not in some way get it in circulation again,
we would be subject to the same panicky conditions
that are so often felt in the United States and Great
Britain and would soon have starvation, tramps and
soup-houses right in the midst of abundant crops.

"To prevent contraction our Government once a year
makes an appropriation for public improvement to
cover all surplus funds on hand, and with a view to
keeping from $50 to $75 per capita of money in circu-

lation; if money is destroyed or placed on deposit by the people and thus kept from circulation, more is issued by the Government to preserve an equilibrium between money and its uses. This accounts for our turnpike and gravel roads."

Dinner was now announced and the travellers were not only agreeably surprised, but their requirements were fully satisfied by an array of good things, even though there was an absence of meat. Dinner was followed by an hour's pleasant chat, after which the guests continued their journey, feeling as if they were parting from old friends instead of acquaintances of but a few hours. They were obliged to decline a pressing invitation to remain over night. The drive during the afternoon was past a continuation of pleasant homes where prosperity was indicated everywhere. They continued to meet loads of produce being taken to the city. To gratify the ladies, Mr. Gardner often stopped and made inquiries as to crops and other matters calculated to give information to the strangers as to the true condition of affairs; to the surprise of the ladies, the old story of hard times and scarcity of money, showing distress in financial affairs so often heard at home, was here unknown. The only thing mentioned as being scarce was help; "the people have plenty of land, and plenty of stock; they raise an abundance and have enough to sell, and if help were more plenty would have a still larger surplus; our farms are not large and no one wants to hire more than one or two men; unless they can find men who have been well raised, who can be taken into the family and treated as such, they prefer doing without help. We can get negroes, but they are disliked as a rule, and with our good machinery, work is easy and we have a surplus from our labor."

As they progressed on their journey it was noticed that the farms were larger, many of them containing eighty acres. Mr. Gardner explained that the farms were surveyed in smaller lots, near to the cities, in order to secure an abundance of fruit, vegetables and eggs convenient to market.

They had just passed a beautiful farm when Rebecca remarked to her mother: "Can you tell me why we have not met one man in all this time carrying his blankets? These people must have beds for their men." This excited Mr. Gardner's curiosity and Mrs. Goldburg explained: "That in California, she had heard it said, it was customary for workingmen to carry their own blankets to be used as beds; they were not furnished by their employers with so much as a wind-break, farther than what a wire fence might give."

"Is it possible," said Mr. Gardner, "that free, independent American citizens can be brought down to so degraded a condition?"

Long before night they reached Uncle Ben's. The whole family were all on the lookout, Uncle Ben, Aunt Lizzie and the children, beginning with a young man nineteen years of age, down to a little girl of five, were anxious to give them a cordial greeting. They were all musicians, and had two violins, guitar and bones, beside a fine organ and plenty of hands to play all; they had been under the tutelege of a fine Master and had become very proficient; in addition to the instrumental music, they were gifted with fine voices and entertained our friends with such soul-stirring strains. as carried them away to that realm where human thought seems to communicate with angels.

Minnie was a lover of music and to her this was a feast. In her ecstacy she exclaimed to Mrs. Goldburg: "Why, oh why will Americans deprive themselves of happy homes and joys like these, only to allow a few men the privilege of satisfying a chronic, greedy appetite, more the result of habit and education than of natural law. O, will people ever learn to listen to the words of Jesus, lay aside greedy desires and work for the good of all?"

"It would seem," said Mrs. Goldburg, "that these people have pretty thoroughly solved the question by establishing a Government of the people, and for the people; Justice crowned, and money-Kings destroyed."

After dinner the following day, our travellers tore themselves away from this happy family, with a feeling of gratification at the kind treatment they had received and all agreed that it was folly to be encumbered with wealth, when such comfort and happiness could be found in country homes. A competency was to their minds a surer passport to happiness than a surplus of wealth.

"The greatest sin," said Rebecca, "if such a thing as sin exists, is for a set of men to organize themselves into a conspiracy to rob such people as these of their little homes, with their luxuries and comforts and means of enjoyment, through a carefully prepared system of banks, interest, mortgages and control of money; if the people of the United States do not rise in their might and overthrow the monster, the system from its own vile wickedness will destroy itself."

"I wish we could visit those people again," said Minnie, as they drove away. "I shall never forget them," said Rebecca, "and I mean to write to them."

"Mother," said Rebecca, after a few moments of silence, "do you know this makes my heart ache for the people at home?"

"Why so?" said her mother.

"Why, mother, only think of the contrast; while these people are free, happy and contented, with a surplus of everything; the finest free school system in the world, no foreign capital, no foreign credit, no foreign debt, no bank, no millionaires and no paupers; our people have a similar country to this; good credit abroad, large national debt, one-third of the business owned by foreign syndicates, biggest crop of mushroom millionaires the world has ever seen; paupers, tramps, soup houses everywhere; with all this they are not happy, contented nor satisfied, but are still found voting for more.

"In this land we hear no cry of distress. Every farmer owns his own home; no rent, no taxes; with good tools, improved machinery, and all at work, each produces a surplus, and it is because they are not robbed by a National banking system, that they are all able to enjoy life. When the farmer and laboring masses prosper, trade is always good with merchants;

in fact everybody has a little money and something to do, consequently everybody feels good. When surplus goods are shipped away, there comes something in return to contribute to man's happiness. In our country, statesmen say that over-production brings want with starvation; surely they are honorable men.

"While they are sending great ship-loads of wheat, beef, pork cotton, rice and many other things abroad to pay for the use of gold, the people whose labor produced these things are crying for bread, and still they vote yes, blindly, blindly vote. I fear our people are not capable of self government. Here we read no accounts of the Treasurer of State conferring with a council of bankers to devise means to relieve the wants of the dear people, simply because there are no banks, no bankers nor any people in want."

"There is one thing," said Mr. Gardner, "before it slips my memory. In your country an unprincipled man, by the accidental discovery of a mine or by getting to the bottom of some great swindle, founds a great estate; nature has decreed that his time of rascality and oppression shall be short and death cuts him off; your laws, instead of placing the property at his death among the people who rightfully own it, and from whom it has been drawn, either by chance or rascality, actually preserve it as a power to roll on down the ages and crush and grind the unfortunate people who come in contact with it, just in proportion to the good or bad disposition of the man under whose management it happens to fall."

"That is true," said Rebecca, "and it would certainly seem right to let a man's power to oppress end with his death, and your inheritance law seems to accomplish this admirably."

We will not attempt to follow the party through their long journey, but simply state that the remainder of the trip was similar to that already described, one continuous scene of prosperity, happiness and good cheer. On arriving at the home of Mr. Gardner, which was a most delightful one, they found that the boys had been left in charge outside, while an aged aunt had been their housekeeper.

As in Uncle Ben's family, the children were all musical. They had instruments and knew how to play them. It was understood by the children that the ladies were to remain a week, and they were anticipating a fine time. They had ample time before night to explore the flower garden, and Mary took great pleasure in showing its beauties to Minnie and Rebecca; Mary noted with delight the development of her favorite plants and was rejoiced to find everything in such splendid condition.

Mrs. Gardner thought Minnie was a little hasty in asking the young ladies to go out before giving them a chance to even rid themselves of dust, but they were as eager to go as Mary was to have them and returned to the house feeling repaid for such a variety of shrubs and flowers they had never seen before; indeed, Rebecca was so fond of flowers that she listened with as much eagerness to their childish glee in telling who each plant belonged to and who it was from, as she would have done to a discourse from Henry Ward Beecher. After thoroughly inspecting the flower garden, Mary took them to the pasture to see "old Bloss," their old family cow; then they must go down the lane to see "old Beck's," new calf, which Jennie said was the "sweetest calf" she ever saw. The young ladies felt a deep interest in the happiness of their little companion, and enjoying the healthful exercise of following her through a narrow walk with shade trees on either side, which combined use as well as beauty in yielding a bountiful crop of nuts.

On they went down the long lane, only stopping to admire the rich plumage of some feathered songster or listen to its sweet warblings. At last the gate was reached and passing through they found the cows standing quietly in the shade; the cows seemed to recognize the fact that Mary had returned and submitted willingly to the caresses the little ones bestowed upon them. Then the colts came in for a share of attention and each was admired in turn and its history given in full.

During this ramble Rebecca's thoughts were not idle she was contrasting this happy, contented home-life here, with home-life in the United States, where a few were struggling to get everything and place it beyond the reach of the masses, while the masses in turn were s'ruggling to keep what they have for their children or subsist on a crust while their principal crop goes to pay the interest on a mortgage which was given for greenbacks that had already been paid as interest; still the principal now demands gold, which is worth more than twice as much as the greenback was; all this to keep up a splendid banking system.

After supper, which was thoroughly enjoyed, each one attended to his own particular duties about; the place, and Mrs. Goldburg and Rebecca retired to the parlor, while Minnie lent her assistance to Mrs. Gardner in the dining room.

As soon as the lamps were lighted all gathered in the parlor where a pleasant evening was passed in conversation and music; a number of the young people of the neighborhood happened in and each contributed to the musical part of the entertainment, so that Mrs. Goldburg remarked upon the fact, and Mr. Gardner proceeded to say: "My dear lady, music is not only taught in all our schools, but teachers are employed in nearly every family, so if you were to travel from one part of this country to the other, you would find music everywhere." When this musical treat was ended, the older ones withdrew to another room, leaving the young people to enjoy themselves to their own tastes.

Mrs. Goldburg began the conversation by saying: "In looking over your paper I see that your mines of gold, silver, lead, copper and iron, also your manufacturing industries and transportation are all carried on upon the grandest scale; your iron and steel works are almost equal to those in the United States, and still you say there is no foreign capital invested in the whole country?"

"O no," said Mr. Gardner, our financial system is

the secret of our success. In your country, when they want to build a railroad, or erect some great manufacturing work, that will cost, say $100,000,000, a company is organized and issues $100,000,000 stock. Then a couple of men are posted off to New York Boston, and finally to England and sell the stock at a big discount; then they build the road; if the money runs short, they issue bonds (mortgage) for more money which also goes to England in exchange for gold.

"When the road is completed, they charge such enormous freight rates and fares that it becomes necessary, in order to have their profits look reasonable, to call the road that cost $100,000,000 worth twice that amount; this they call capitalizing. Honest men and people who pay fare and freight are not supposed to understand the full meaning of this word, it belongs only to financiers. To common people, it seems to have a double meaning; in fare and freight terms it means much, more or all; in tax times it means right the reverse; little, least, nothing.

"The result of this system is, that the English syndicate soon gets the gold back and still owns the road. In this country our people framed a constitution treating gold and silver as commodities; it was provided that it be held in vaults to be used as bullion in satisfying the balance of trade with foreign countries. It was agreed that our money, like checks or drafts, belongs to the book-keeping, exchange or business department of the country and is simply a tool, a means, a convenience to enable citizens to exchange labor and the products of labor and carry out business methods. Its value, like any other tool, consists in the many uses to which it can be employed. That our people will need this money as long as they continue to do business; for the next thousand years. Money made of gold, if kept in actual circulation would, it was believed, in one hundred years lose from wear one-fourth of its original weight and to preserve its similarity to other coins it would not only require re-coinage but would also require a large purchase of gold. To avoid this constant expense, it was agreed to use gold only as a commodity in bullion. Government made money of a less expensive material and one that could be renewed at a small cost. The value thereof was to be regulated by keeping as nearly as possible from $50 to $70 per capita in circulation; the money to be made a full legal tender for all debts, both public and private.

"To satisfy a few old moss-backs who believed that money could have no value unless some arrangement were made for its redemption with something having intrinsic value, like gold or silver, it was ordained that after the expiration of one thousand years, if the people found no further use for money, they could then borrow gold on bonds to redeem it with; just as well as for us to be running in debt to keep up the interest and wear of gold through all that time. By this arrangement it was claimed that the people one thousand years hence would not only have the satisfaction of gathering all the gold in the country to take the place of money, but they could also issue bonds, establish a national blessing, and their children will inherit the blessed privilege of paying the interest for all time to come.

"Our Government not only made and furnished money for all these great enterprises, but the stock representing all these vast sums of money has been reserved for our own people, just the same as they reserve the land, only the use of the land is given to citizens and their heirs free of rent or taxes, forever. or as long as they keep it in use as a home, and the stock furnishes them an investment for their savings.

"As the inheritance law prevents its being monopolized, you will find it now scattered among the people and does away with the necessity of a savings bank."

Rebecca and the two youngest children, becoming tired of play, had joined the circle; Mr. Gardner, after pausing a few moments turned to his wife and said: "Mother, won't you show Mrs. Goldburg our stock?" In response, Mrs. Gardner turned to the bureau and proceeded to open a drawer; it was plain to Rebecca that some new treasure was about to be disclosed for she had noticed that the children had been very much

interested while the father was talking about stock.
In another moment Mrs. Gardner returned and placed
upon the stand in front of Mrs. Goldburg a beautifully
ornamented treasure-box, and on opening it four large
envelopes were taken out. On each was printed in
beautiful type the name and address of each of the
children; Jennie and Theodore each took their envelope and showed their stock to the ladies; it amounted
in all to several hundred dollars. Jennie explained
that their father gave it to them and they were to keep
it, principal and dividend, until they were married,
then they could use it as they pleased.

"The pleasures, joys and comforts arising from the
vast amount of money that is paid out each year,"
said Mr. Gardner, "among the people as dividend on
this stock, could never be counted in dollars and cents.
It bears its good fruit everywhere."

"Yes, sir," said Mrs. Goldburg, "but can it last?
My observation is that laws so absolutely just are generally evaded in some way or not enforced, and my fear
is that the money power of the earth will finally com-
bine and bring to bear a pressure that will destroy the
system; it occurs to me that you will need many safeguards to maintain it, for you see that it destroys
plutocracy absolutely."

"Just so," said Mr. Gardner, "and the safeguards
that we depend upon are our free schools which teach
business and finance to the end that every scholar of
eighteen is well posted on the way the world has been
robbed by the gold banking frauds. The protective
tariff and land frauds of the United States are also
thoroughly exposed in our school histories; next to our
schools is the initiative or referendum which brings
every change in statute law before the people; the
absolute prohibition of all political parties; we also
have another, which I believe should be classed second
to none, and that is universal suffrage. We find that
ladies will vote invariably for what they believe will be
for the good of their children, and no amount of bribe
money or false logic will turn them; men are careless
with their votes, women are careful."

"Suppose foreign nations refuse to take your money?" said Rebecca. "That is just it," said Mr. Gardner, "that is just what we want; money that is perfectly good at home but cannot be used in foreign countries. We require a certain amount of money to conduct business; when that money is withdrawn, business suffers; so long as it remains in circulation at home, it is where we want it, right where it can be used.

"When you started for this country, you exchanged your national bank currency for gold coin; when you got here that gold coin was not money and you had to go to our national treasury and sell it; you did this to get money to pay your expenses while here. As gold is used as money in the United States the business of that country has suffered a loss of just that much of this money; should you continue your journey to England, you would have to do the same thing there—go to a Broker or Bank and sell your American coin for just what the gold is worth as bullion; if your coin is worn and falls short in weight, they give you only its bullion value. Suppose one of our people go to England or France—he goes to the Treasury here where he buys gold bullion for 50 per cent less than it is worth in London; when he gets to France or England he sells his gold bullion just the same as you sell your American coin, only he gets 50 per cent more than he paid.

"The talk that you hear from your great statesmen in the United States, 'we want a dollar that is good the world over,' is either sophistry made to deceive the confiding people they are so systematically robbing, or it is the voice of ignorance; like an echo, repeating a shallow sound."

"If," said Rebecca, "you are selling gold from your treasury for 50 per cent less than it is worth in London, why don't London bankers come here and buy it? That, it seems to me, would be a good profit on gold."

"It certainly would," said Mr. Gardner, "but how will they get the money to buy it with? They can't come here and buy our gold with English or American money, because foreign gold coin is worth 50 per cent less here than our national money; so after a banker pays 50 per cent premium for our money to buy gold with, he would have his trouble for his pains.

"The fact is, that so long as we keep our people all employed with our abundant capital to carry out so many enterprises, our fine machinery to work with and an abundance of rich soil, we will continue to have over-production; in consequence of this, our exports for all time to come, will exceed our imports; hence, gold bullion will continue in the future as in the past to flow into our treasury. There it will pile up and represent our over-production. In your country over-production is a ghost from whose spectral form many a half-starved family shrinks; its ghastly presence is felt in every convention, stands guard at every ballot box, stalks abroad among the troubled masses and cries aloud, 'I am the winter of thy discontent.' We have the advantage of every country on earth, except the United States, in amount of superior farming land, rich mines; of timber, of water-power, and we fully believe that a little, unproducing island, like Britain, will never be able to compete with us in the markets of the world. We have the advantage of the United States in this; they pay so much for confidence and credit abroad, that the people are impoverished and not able to increase the irproductive powers."

"This looks all right," said Rebecca, "but how about inflation?"

"Inflation," said Mr. Gardner, "is another English ghost that escaped from the island and has found a home among American statesmen. Its warning cry has been heard in every part of that great country; it is strictly a political ghost and makes its home among bankers. Its mission is to frighten the victims of plutocracy and keep them in the rank of ignorance. Inflation is a myth; a gold-monger's hobby; the law says just how much money shall be put in circulation and no more. When people have free coinage of gold, inflation might be brought about by the discovery of rich gold mines, then additional legislation would be necessary; it is the same way with our money; if new mines of great richness were discovered, their large products would increase the volume of money, but as the taking of interest is not allowed, those who had more money than they could use, would lay it aside until the Government's share of profits on the business of the country would reduce the circulation. Our greatest trouble has been to keep the money in circulation; the tendency has been toward contraction, by the money flowing back into the treasury."

"How do you levy State taxes?" said Rebecca.

"Taxes," said Mr. Gardner, "is a word that is almost obsolete among us and would probably be expunged from our books of learning, were it not for its use in limiting incomes. The expense of Government is quite small. We have no land disputes but can be settled before a Justice of the Peace; we have no lawsuits with corporations or between corporations. All these thousand-and-one laws growing out of unlimited competition of unbridled wealth, have been unnecessary by our improved business system. In order to protect our elections against fraud, we put the salary of officials at what is supposed to be the average pay for the same class of work in private life. We therefore pay no fancy prices, and men cannot afford to pay much money to get an office. We pay no interest on bonds; our criminals have been the most important item of expense, but even that is light in comparison to your country and is gradually growing less.

"The Government's share of the profit on the business of the country, and a revenue derived from a graduated income tax is so enormous that it has been found necessary, in order to keep the money in circulation, to make annual appropriations to each State of so much money per capita; this has been found sufficient to pay the entire expense of State Government, including schools.

"The cities have a license system which seems to work very nicely; as the cities are supported by the trade of the people, this license is supposed to affect all alike."

"You spoke of criminals," said Mrs. Goldburg, "if

your criminal code is as different from ours as your other laws it would be interesting to hear something of it, if not asking too much."

"Not at all," said that gentleman, "our treatment of criminals, I assure you, is very different from that in vogue in any other country. We start out on the broad ground that to punish crime with a view to avenging the wrong done, is a crime itself. It is claimed by our Law-giver that when a crime has been committed and the fact fully established, the Court has two duties; first, to the people, they being the injured parties, and that duty is to prevent a repetition of the crime; this is done by confining the criminal. It is claimed that crime is simply an effect. Its causes are an unbalanced mind, bad education, surroundings or conditions. Therefore the duty of Government toward this man or woman is to improve the surroundings, enlighten his understanding, and doctor and improve his mental condition. To accomplish this, our Penitentiaries are like small cities thoroughly walled in.

"Life prisoners have a department to themselves; they are given their choice, hard work or an education; to avoid hard work they commonly begin studying very diligently and finally take up reading as a pastime. Their sanitary regulations are of the best character and they are furnished billiard tables for exercise and amusement. Those who need discipline are carefully managed, but those who are industrious are allowed to choose their own hours for study, reading and recreation; if a prisoner's wife wishes to follow him into prison, she is allowed to do so and provision is made for her comfort; but she is required to attend the class with her husband and advance with him intellectually.

"Prisoners for smaller crimes are allowed four hours for work, two hours each day for recreation, four hours for study; they can learn any trade they choose, and the product of their labor is kept and given them when they are discharged. We also have a Humane Society whose business it is to provide places of employment for these unfortunates when they are discharged; imprisonment here is not attended with disgrace; on the contrary, it is considered a very good school and I have known a number of cases where men went right from the prison to the pulpit. There have been but few cases where men have not come out thoroughly reformed."

"Does not their work come in competition with honest labor?" said Mrs. Goldburg.

"There," said Mr. Gardner, "is another absurdity of bad Government; the very idea of complaining of a man because he works. If your American friends would adopt an Industrial system that is founded upon Justice, strip the money lords of their control of money, quit tramping, go to work and improve the country, they would soon find that the more work every man did, the better it would be for all, Our prisons are schools run at the expense of Government and we visit, take an interest in, and are as proud of them as we are of our free school system."

"One thing more I would like to ask," said Rebecca. How much stock are you allowed to buy?"

"All you have money to pay for, if you are a citizen; but the law absolutely prohibits the Government from paying dividends to foreigners."

"Will you not then have millionaires?"

"O no; it would be a difficult matter for a man to become one under our form of government. You can own only what land you can cultivate; you only hold that by right of possession; therefore there is no mak-ing millions out of land speculation. In mercantile or manufacturing business, you would come in competition with these great joint stock companies, and they do business on so small a margin you would be a long time reaching the million mark."

"Well," said Rebecca, "suppose a young man were to inherit $100,000, invested it in stock, compounded it for a lifetime, would he not be pretty rich?"

"If he did this," said the gentleman, "he would have to earn his living at the same time, so he would become a useful citizen, and when he died, all his surplus wealth would be inherited by the Government and go right back into circulation through its liberal appropriations; beside, we have a tax on all incomes above $10,000, levied with a view only to preventing an aggregation of wealth."

"Then you really think your Government has done away with rich men altogether?" Rebecca said.

"Not at all," said Mr. Gardner, "on the contrary, suppose Gould, Vanderbilt and Astor to be worth $300,000,000; in place of these three rich men we would have 6,000 men with $50,000 each, and in this country everything is produced so cheaply, in consequence of keeping our people constantly employed, with the very best of machinery, that $50,000 is quite sufficient to keep a man and his family with all the comforts and luxuries that even a millionaire's wealth can provide; and I might say more, for in consequence of all our people being employed, our brightest minds find time to study such branches of the sciences and of art as will produce luxuries that your millionaires never dreamed of. So you see that we have hundreds of rich men where you have but one. It has not been the purpose of our Government to do away with rich men, but to make conditions such that all who are inclined to work and economize, would not only be able to live in comfort, but also to accumulate something for their children; also bring about a condition of affairs that would develop the latent powers in man's nature, that the world might receive the benefit of them.

"Our system encourages the bettering of man's condition by every honorable method; but forever puts the veto on any man, by chance or rascality, establishing a monetary system that will continue to grow until it becomes a factor in Government. The question that we propose to solve is, shall wealth rule and govern the people or the people control and govern wealth."

"What do you think of the theories of Government put forth by Socialists?" asked Rebecca.

"I hardly like to say," said Mr. Gardner, "Socialists are a people who have my warmest sympathy: I believe they are honest in trying to better man's conditition, but their system looks to me like taking a step backward. The Roman church is socialism; the Mormon church is socialism. I have read Bellamy's book— Looking Backward—then I have an article here giving Anna Regent's views of a social Government. To me it looks more like the picture of a self-supporting poor house, where a few direct and others do the work.

"The greatest boon to life, is liberty; liberty to lay plans for your own welfare and to advance your own interests in your own particular way. All any man wants is a chance to work out his own destiny independent of Prince, Potentate and Priest. The family is by nature a social, independent government and any law, religious or political, that mixes up the interests of one family with those of another family, is wrong and not in accordance with natural laws. As an individual, all any man should ask is justice; as a member of a government a man has a right to ask justice and protection against combined powers such as the power of crime, the power of combined or aggregated wealth, the power of organized bodies such as churches, mobs, and parties.

"We hold that a church as a monetary power is wrong and to be feared; that all churches as religious gatherings for honest worship are right and should be encouraged; that a mass meeting for the purpose of discussion or getting an expression of the people is good; but if that mass meeting continue an organization from year to year for the purpose of influencing legislation or the vote of the people in their own favor, it becomes a conspiracy and should be prohibited.

"With us political parties are prohibited, in fact all national organizations are prohibited; five or more persons in any neighborhood can organize for any legitimate purpose and secure a charter, then ground will be furnished them for a building; but they state positively in their articles of incorporation that they are not connected with any similar organization, either financially or in a business way; that they pay no tithing or money in any way to any other institution; that they acknowledge no allegiance to any man in any way outside their own organization or to any power except the Republic."

"I should think that would be a blow at religion," said Mrs. Goldburg.

"It don't seem to be," said Mr. Gardner, "you see fine churches everywhere and our ministers are never forced to the sad extremity of preaching to empty benches. The fact is, they did not like the idea at first, but one after another called their little crowd together and organized a church. It was soon found that they were so much more liberal than when under church discipline that the plan fairly captured the public and we have a regular boom all over the country in church building and church going. It has interfered with the church of Rome more than any other, and we consider that, not as a church, but rather a monetary, political despotism, based upon superstition and maintained by a rigid church discipline, centered in an infallible Pope. Its mission is to rule through ignorance and money. Since these people through compulsion of law have been forced to abandon the Pope, like other creed-bound souls, they are coming to recognize the true teaching of Christ, the Universal brotherhood of man, and are fast growing out of their former slavish condition."

The ladies remained a few days longer during which they took many delightful drives; in answer to the question as to how their magnificent roads were built, Mr. Gardner said: "Government furnishes the money; sometimes farmers take the contract, but usually it is done by contractors from the city; they always have one year to do it in, so they can take a dull time and thus keep their men constantly employed. In this way our country saves millions of days' work that in your country would be spent in tramping, hunting for work."

CHAPTER XXX.

WE WILL now look after the money men. In a former chapter arrangements had been made for the purpose of doctoring the Constitution. They met on the night appointed. The Lord Earl Chancellor and Dead Earnest Seyd, accompanied by the Expert bookkeeper and penman, in the room of Saunders and Coy and were soon joined by Baxter, Bowen and Pixley. Drinks were served; the money Lord and Saunders then passed into another room for a moment and held a short conversation in a very low whisper.

On returning to the room the money Lord placed a sack of gold on the table, then quietly took his seat; Saunders then stepped forward, took the sack and scattered its glittering contents on the cloth, then said: "Gentlemen, here is the cash that moves the world; with it you are respectable in every land and clime; its possession makes reliable critics of knaves and fools; it possesses power that no man can stay; without it even Kingdoms crumble and decay; with it Rothschild is a monarch in his peculiar way. He rules, not one, but all the clans on earth; with his golden sceptre he stands behind the throne and dictates terms of peace and war. He has the power to crush, he has the power to build; before this man all nations bow and act upon his will. But still, it is not the man they fear, it is the power of gold and here it is; plenty and to spare and every man who does his part will get a splendid share.

"Our cause is just. These people here are drunk upon the paper stuff they call cash, but it is not, it has no worth, it is only paper trash. Their Government has usurped the right of ruining all the banks and robbing wealthy men of that which they accumulate; in the name of God it must be said, they rob the living and the dead by what they call law, inheritance and income tax; they say it is right, but we do not; we call it rot, and wrong, and robbery of that noble class of men who purchase land and rent it to the poor for homes; then feed the worthless mob on soup when panics come and all are out of work. Fanatics here are leading on toward calamities untold; no nation has ever lived without the help of gold.

"When over-production and inflation overtake the foolish crew, they will die like rotten sheep, beyond the care of the noble few who own the gold.

"Now," said he, in a mild and confidential way, "it is to avoid this calamity that Sherman has agreed to interfere in behalf of the dear people and you, brave, noble-hearted men who stay with us through each and every move will get your gold; you will also be made members of a class of money lords who know no such thing as fail. Here now is a little gold my Lord has asked that I should give to you, that you might know we mean just what we say."

Then giving part to each, the glasses were filled up and from the sparkling cup all drank long life to the bank that has the gold. Soon after this a knock was heard and in a moment more John Benedict Sherman entered. "How now my noble Lord?" said John.

"Quite well," replied the money Lord, "and how art thou, old friend and nearest to my heart of all this noble band?" "Quite well," said John. "And how about thy most important enterprise? Hast thou the Constitution?" "I have, my Lord," said John, pulling from his breast the document which he had stolen from the room containing archives of which he was custodian.

"Bravo," said every man as Mr. Sherman handed the coveted prize to the money Lord, who quickly placed it in the hands of the expert; this man examined the document for half an hour, then asked if it could be left over for half a day. After considering the matter for a time, Sherman consented to an arrangement of this kind. Mr. Saunders then showed the expert to a room where he could work without interruption.

This done, the money Lord addressed his little band as follows: "Mr. Sherman, my brave men, has done a noble deed." "You," said he turning to the Senator, have taken the first grand step toward placing gold where it rightfully belongs. There is no nation on earth but acknowledges the superior rights and privileges of that class who own the gold. Its rights and properties as money have been acknowledged since civilization began and must not be interfered with now. In behalf of the gold banking power of the world, allow me, in presence of these gentlemen to present to you, Senator Sherman, as part compensation for the noble service you just rendered, this paper which entitles you to stock in the Bank of England to the amount of $1,000,000. You are now a millionaire; it is our wish that you remain in this country in the interest of the bank. While it will be necessary for you to remain a citizen of the Republic, we shall expect you to visit us in England, now and then, and I am authorized to say to you that upon your first visit, you will be made Knight of the Garter and your picture shall adorn our walls."

Glasses and bottles were now brought out and all drank the health of Rothschild. The Money Lord in order to impress upon his hearers the power there is in gold, explained at great length how the English syndicates and bankers had controlled legislation in their own favor in the United States since 1862. The exception clause on greenbacks, the bond issue with gold bearing interest, banking act contraction, resumption, demonetization of silver and many other base frauds were referred to, showing conclusively that not one financial act had been passed in all that time that was not directly in the interest of the money power.

"In a few years," said he, "we have reduced the common horde of America to their proper place and classes have been formed and money rules the American to-day more completely than it does the English; by the national banking system we actually get money from the Government for one per cent and loan it back to the people, their own money, on good security at 8, 9 and even 10 per cent." ·

At this all gave an approving laugh, except Baxter, who seemed a little nettled at having the weakness of his own people exposed; the talk was soon interrupted for a moment by Saunders ordering drinks. After partaking freely a box of cigars went round. Then the money Lord continued addressing Sherman. "It would take too long my dear Senator to explain all the details of how we captured that country, but in short, you will find that history records the fact that while the United States has been working the richest gold and silver mines the world has ever produced, has been raising provisions to feed the world and cotton to clothe them, their indebtedness to us has constantly increased.

"Their great gold production is all safely stored away in our vaults, the silver in theirs; and mark me well, Senator, the time is not far distant when we will have them demonetize their own silver and borrow our gold for which we will demand interest bearing bonds. Of course we have had many good, true Americans helping us, but they have all been well paid and have become millionaires; in fact, we now have an organization of monied men all over the business world, and in it millionaires from America figure very conspicuously; this organization will eventually extend throughout the earth and the gold power will elect presidents and control legislation, make kings and depose them when they fail to carry out the mandates of our order.

"As the great wealthy classes have ruled the world in past ages through the power of superstition centered in a Pope, we propose to rule the world through the unlimited power of gold; but its central office will be in London, not in Rome. The business of the world will soon be done by joint stock companies; the money or gold power will own the stock and through it receive all the profits of business and individual effort.

"The New Republic of Bundy, Lincoln, Jefferson and Summerville has already been neglected too long, but the war has commenced; the power of concentrated wealth will soon be felt; this fanatical system must be destroyed and the power of gold restored.

"If we can do this by controlling legislation, we will prevent the shedding of blood and reap eternal blessings from the powers on high.   I tell you, Senator Sherman, if our efforts should entirely fail, there will be a pressure brought to bear upon these people that will leave them rotting by the roadside; when the scourge has been removed, classes will be formed; the toiling masses will then be taught not to get above their occupation; that it is a mistake for them to abandon their own sphere and infringe on the rights of nobility."

It was now suggested that drinking time had come again and soon the corks began to pop; this time they drank success to the money Lord.

This finished, the Lord took a dignified position and with the air of one who held supreme authority, also considered himself complete master of the situation, he inquired of Sherman if he knew any member of the lower House who could be considered worthy to become one of their associates. After thinking a while the Senator said he "thought he could name a man who, by money, could be induced to associate himself with us; his name is Benedict Arnold and I take him to be one of our kind."

"Would it be possible to see him and bring him here this very night?" said the Lord.

After consulting his watch, Sherman said: "Should I find him without delay, it would be barely possible."

"Will you do this little favor," said the Lord; "then bring him to me at once; make known that this is a matter of honor; our office is one of charity. What we wish to do may not be exactly right, but we do it to avoid something in the future that we believe would be still worse; be sure, my dear Senator, and impress upon his mind the fact that money will be no object if our ends can be attained."

The Senator now took his departure; the Lord politely escorted him to the door and by way of caution, said: "It will perhaps be well, Senator, to have the man commit himself; here is $100 in gold, see that he accept the same as bonus before he comes; should we fail to agree on general terms, this will pay him for the trouble we have given him. We represent a noble class, have an important work to do, wish to be strictly honorable in all our methods and liberal with our friends."

The Senator took the money, passed into a dark alley, followed that to one of the back streets; after a brisk walk he reached a main thoroughfare where he stepped upon a street car and in a few moments was at the hotel where he found Mr. Arnold quietly reading the evening news. As the Senator approached Mr. Arnold recognized him, arose and extended his hand; a few low words passed and the two retired to a private room; after being in deep conversation for some time, they again came forth and as they did so, Sherman dropped some pieces of gold into the hand of the Congressman which he quietly slipped into his pocket; soon after this the Lord and his companion heard a low knock at the door and Saunders received the two gentlemen and they were ushered into the presence of the money Lord. Mr. Arnold was introduced in due form, after which a few common-place remarks passed between them, drinks were served and for a time all went merry; at last when things had quieted down the man of gold addressed Mr. Arnold as follows:

"You are a member of Congress?" "Yes, sir."

"Have you considered the financial situation?"

"As a special subject," said the Congressman, "I can hardly say that I have. Our financial system is so simple that it seems to require no particular study; it is a mere matter of dollars and cents and we have none of those difficult problems arising from giving money two values; one a bullion value which is constantly changing, the other a money value which should never change."

"True, true," said the money Lord, "there are many knotty questions, but it is through an understanding of this problem that we make our money; we understand it but the common people don't; do you see?"

After quietly knocking the ashes from his cigar and taking another puff, the money Lord continued:

"Mr. Arnold, has it never occurred to you that it is humiliating for a great Republic like this to be tying themselves to the rag-baby make-shift for money, instead of using the clear quill?"

"I hardly know how to answer that question," said the Congressman, feeling his own insignificance in the presence of this money Lord who wore diamonds and had millions at his back. He then proceeded in regular school boy style, as follows: "I was raised a Republican in the United States and was taught that paper money had no value unless based on gold; when I first came here I talked a great deal about the evils that would arise from a paper currency. I called it rag-baby and such other names as the bankers gave it where I was raised. When I saw our Government issuing money to the great companies by millions, enough to run every conceivable enterprise and give work to every one that wanted to work, I said now we will have inflation; but the people kept buying up the stock and the money kept going back into the treasury, the same as it goes into the banks at home. My prophecies of inflation all failed; times, too, have been so wonderfully good and growing better all the time, it actually looks as if the people of this Government had all gone into partnership on the joint stock plan and are doing so much work that they will soon, with their fine machinery, be able to feed and clothe the entire globe. In this reckless push of all kinds of business, they seem to have forgotten all about gold and lost respect for it; in fact, things have assumed such a shape through our extensive exports that gold is worth absolutely nothing. The agents of these great companies have had so much trouble abroad in exchanging gold for interest bearing securities that I supposed it was getting to be a drug on the markets of the world."

"That you see is where the trouble comes from," said the Lord, "your people are constantly taking out gold and shipping it to us; we cannot buy it for they will not take our money and the exchange of goods is all in their favor. We can hardly afford to give them bonds for that is our stock in trade, beside we do not need the gold. You see a little gold does us as well as more would, for the fact is, we don't use it as money very much, because paper is so much handier; but gold is made the base; we keep it in our vaults; that makes our paper good. There is where confidence comes in. We get gold base, and confidence, and parity, and honest dollars all mixed up until none but a financier can understand it, and that is the way we make our money. We have millions of money laying idle in our vaults; all we ask is for all the Governments on earth to make gold the only legal tender; then, as we have pretty much all the gold and people compelled to have it to pay debts with, we can fix the price, and the less we have the more we can ask for it. As long as the United States can get gold from this Republic, they will not come to us. If your country will use their own gold for money, their circulation is so great that they, too, like the United States, would soon have to come to us for money and you who assist in securing this end will fare as sumptuously as have the bankers of the United States.

"I should think," said Arnold, that when the people of the United States see their property slipping away from them, the masses growing poorer, the bankers richer, they would change their policy."

"Yes, you would think so," said the Lord, "but they don't; the fact is they are proud of their millionaires and the poorer they get the better we can manage them. We have banks in the United States and a bank in England; when we want to force Congress to pass a law in our favor, we ship the gold to Britain, the associated press sends out the report for news; we get up a big scare, the banks quit loaning money, a panic ensues, business firms collapse, men are thrown out of employment, soup houses started; then through our great dailies we raise a cry for whatever law we want passed, as a means to restore confidence and make good times.

"Shysters who expect favors from the moneyed men or from banks, take up the cry and if any man dare to oppose it, they call him crank, calamity-howler or anarchist; confusion prevails. We tip the great states-men and remind them that it takes money to run the great political machine; then they make long speeches, full of sophistry, arguing from false stand-points and finding no solution, until the people conclude that the truth is like the way of the Lord, past finding out, and they become disgusted, quit reading the papers and turn their attention to rustling for something to eat; then mid the cry of distress, the law is passed, banks again loan money and the starving get something to do at the lowest possible prices.

"Time rolls on and we have an election and a land-slide, that is, the voters slide out of one party into another. Then we repeat the dose and make another haul. A robber stops the train and robs the safe of a few hundred dollars. they shoot him down on sight; we get the company in a pinch, take the whole road and they call us great.

"Since · time immemorial there has been a wealthy class. There has been a poor class and there always will be. Some men are born to be rich, some are born to be poor. Right now, there is a chance for you to get on the winning side, and what I want is your assistance in getting a law through Congress to bring about free coinage of gold; that will be pretty good for the present; but we will try to get a law through' the next · Congress to withdraw the present money and issue bonds in its place; also establish national banks, based on bonds. The banks can loan national money based on the bonds, that will supply business with the means of continuing, and we, as bankers, will get interest from the Government on the bonds and interest on the money from the people. This will be millions of dollars in our pockets each year, and you will soon see millionaires coming to the front here as rapidly as they did in the United States after we got control of their money."

"Do you suppose," said Arnold, "that our legislators

could be induced to withdraw from circulation all our paper money, which amounts to millions upon millions of dollars, and put out bonds, thereby actually create a debt where none exists, the interest of which would in twenty-five or thirty years amount to more than the face of the bonds? Besides this, compel the people to borrow money to take its place. The interest on the money, even, without the interest on the bonds, would impoverish the people."

"Never mind the people," said the money Lord, "we must look after our own business and let the people look after theirs. I will make it of interest for you to be with us."

"But," said the Congressman, "it is a bare-faced swindle. Our people would never stand it."

"My dear sir," said the Lord, "there is where you are mistaken; you understand we are not going blind; we have a precedent. In the United States after the civil war, there were millions upon millions of dollars of money in circulation, enough to satisfy every demand and make business lively; the people were drunk with prosperity, just as they are here to day. They went to their work joyously singing, 'Uncle Sam is rich enough to give us all a farm,' and right amid these lively times we forced a bill through Congress similar to the one I have just proposed. Bonds with gold interest were exchanged for national money and the money was destroyed; then through the national banking act, we deposited the bonds with the Government and they gave us 90 per cent of our money back and we loaned that to the people to take the place of the old-fashioned greenback. So you see this plan is no new thing. The American people stood it and your people are not one whit smarter than they were. Of course the same causes will produce the same effect here. As to the part you are to play in this affair, in making up your mind, you should consider former examples.

"In the United States, General Weaver fought the scheme in Congress where he was antagonized by Mr. Garfield, who afterward jumped from almost obscurity to the Presidential chair; while General Weaver, who remained true to the people, has never received an office since and has spent thousands of dollars advocating the people's cause. If you look the matter up, my dear Mr. Arnold, you will find that those who supported our scheme in the United States have all been well paid; they are millionares to-day and hold the destiny of the nation in their hands."

The money Lord now, by a peculiar motion of his hand, which is only practiced and understood in that high order of society to which he belonged, suggested drinks; toasts went round and merry-making became general. When, after many drinks it subsided, the money Lord continued: "I am fully authorized, Mr. Arnold, to push the work and the money at my command is unlimited; every man who assists me in the scheme will be promptly and liberally paid; in the end will become a millionaire and one of us.

"In the United States there are more millionaires than in Great Britain and they are to-day members of our noble order and are of our making; for without our careful engineering the United States would to-day be plodding along with her greenback money, and there would be hardly a man in the whole country wealthy enough to command the respect of his fellows. Now if you are willing to assist us in this matter, and link your destiny with ours, braving every disappointment, I will make you one of us, and to make my word emphatic, what say you to a cool $100,000 in gold?"

"Gold," said Arnold, "has little value in this country; you see, my Lord," and the Congressman came near choking, for he had never said, "my Lord" to a man in his life before; he had been taught by a kind and loving mother, that Lord meant God and there were not many gods, but One; but the smiling face of the money Lord reassured him and he went on: "Our foreign trade is conducted by probably the greatest joint-stock company in the world, and our exports so far exceed our imports that the gold in our vaults is piling up continually and to check the accumulation, our Government has refused to buy gold, except the production of our mines. If I am to remain in this country a life-time $100,000 in gold would be a good deal like a white elephant, good for a show, only; I could neither sell it nor use it for money. If you could give me $100,000 in our money, I could invest it at once where it would produce an income; there are always chances to become a partner in some business that will pay; I would then have something to work on with some hope of success; but gold in this country is a drug."

"That is all very true, but it is impossible," said the money Lord, "to get that kind of money. Gold will not buy it; but what we want is a law for the free coinage of gold and you will see how quick our gold will show its power. First, the law makes money of gold, then money makes law to sustain gold and increase its value. With your assistance I think we can pass a law this very year that will place gold in power."

"I doubt that," said Arnold, "there is Lincoln, Bundy and Summerville; these men are high in authority and always on the alert. I have locked horns with them before and they are a power, beside, there is the Constitution in the way."

The money Lord gave a knowing look to Saunders, then said: "What care we for the Constitution; if we get gold made the money of the country, we will put so much of it in the hands of officials here that we can trample the Constitution under foot; and as for Lincoln, Bundy and Summerville; all along the page of history, from time immemorial, you will see such men have always died at the hands of those they tried to protect. The people are ignorant and ungrateful; money men are wise, educated and pay their helpers well. What we want now is work; I present you with a check for $100,000 in British gold. If we succeed, you will be a nobleman of wealth and a power in the Government. Should we fail, you can exchange with some man who is going from here to some of the gold-base countries; but we belong to a class that know no such thing as fail."

Mr. Arnold took the proffered check, put it carefully

away and drinks were once more served; several glasses were emptied in quick succession. All became quite well enthused and with a shake all around, agreed to meet on the following evening when unfinished business would be taken up.

As the party passed into the back yard, Sherman staid behind and the Lord instructed him to post Mr. Arnold, according to his own discretion, on the contemplated change of Constitution, then accompany him back on the following evening.

Mr. Arnold was not really a bad man. Being a lawyer, he accepted the first $100 more as a retaining fee than as a bribe. He knew Mr. Sherman as a prominent statesman and had no reason to believe him dishonest. He stood high as an authority and had the confidence of the people. When he found himself in the presence of the money Lord, he was over-awed; that gentleman's superior manner, backed by unlimited capital, made our Congressman's personality fade into insignificance. Persons of modest means who have been thrown into company with millionaires, will recognize the disadvantage under which Mr. Arnold was placed. Mr. Sherman was in a position far his superior and was undoubtedly working for the money men, then why should he refuse? He had always considered himself a very ordinary man; the people had elected him to Congress, then called him honorable; he had never believed himself better than his neighbors, but in this he must have been mistaken, else these money kings would not be taking him into their confidence and giving him more wealth than he could accumulate in a life time. The money Lord's arguments were good. He knew what had been done in the United States. If he kept the check and the scheme failed he would be a rich man. If they captured the new Republic as they had the United States, he would become a millionaire and a place in the Senate would be secured to him for all time to come. Thus Arnold soliloquized.

On the following night the parties again met at the private room of Saunders in accordance with their previous understanding. The first thing in order was drinks; long life to the money power, was the sentiment expressed. The expert then produced his work upon the Constitution. All agreed the job was complete. The Inheritance clause had been so changed that it could easily be evaded. The effectiveness of the Money clause had also been destroyed, and still there was not the least evidence of the Instrument having been tampered with.

The Money Lord said it was a marvelous work and equal to the demonetization of silver in the United States in 1873. Mr. Sherman explained that it was not exactly what he wanted, but he was willing to accept it in order, as he believed, to prevent something worse. Unless something was done he feared the people would continue to prosper until they became so drunk on worthless money, big wages, fair prices and plenty of work that they would demand free coinage of silver and that would be disastrous. "Too much money," said he, "makes men reckless and extravagant." He thought common farmers and toilers expected to live as well as the wealthy classes and he feared to contemplate the end of a system that encouraged such extravagance. Drinks were now called. All drank success to the new enterprise, and while Saunders was on one of his political flights, in which he extolled plutocracy, a heavy jar or blow burst in the outside door and footsteps were heard along the narrow approach to this room. All noise was hushed; tramp, tramp, tramp came the unwelcome sounds.

"What means all this?" said Saunders. "I see, we are betrayed. Baxter, give me the key, I'll meet them in the hall, and e'er they burst another door, I'll bathe this blade in human gore."

"Brave Saunders," said the money Lord, "hold, hold, thou art too bold. We'll let the knaves come in, then buy them with a little gold and make them part of us. They, possibly, are the kind of stuff that we most need."

Then Saunders turned and said: "My Lord, these men are knaves, but I feel sure they never will sell.

I'd rather put my trust in hell, than in these men." Then, turning to the little band, said: "Who is the traitor that would give us up to death?"

"Look," said Pixley, "see in me one of the common horde, a spy, detective, police; all that you men most despise."

"Thou art the traitor, then," said Saunders, "and die thou shalt," and brandishing his blade he made a move, but Pixley, brave as he, with gun in hand, said, "stand!" At this, from heavy blows, the door gave way and a dozen men, or more, all in uniform, marched in.

"In the name of the Republic, I command you to surrender," said the Chief.

"Ha ha ha," said the money Lord, "have seats, gentlemen, and let us talk the matter up."

"Not so," said the Chief, "we came here not to talk."

"One moment with thee, then," said the money Lord, and the two with Saunders stepped into a side room. "Be seated," said the Lord.

"No, no, you must be brief," said the honest Chief, "I cannot dally here for idle words."

Then said the Lord: "Now is you time to make a raise and secure a place in society seldom reached by ordinary men. We have a scheme in view for legislation here. We want your help. I mean just what I say. I represent the banking business of the world. There is no limit to my cash. Say now that you will work for us and a million dollars in gold in England's bank is yours."

The Chief in anger, said: "Dost thou take me for a knave, to offer me a bribe?"

"Not so, not so," said the Lord, it is only like the finding of a mine to you and such a chance will not come to you every day."

The Chief, in an irritated air, said: "What care I for your gold? It is trash and does not weigh when honor is in the scale."

"Honor," said the Lord, "is measured up by gold; with it man is honorable everywhere; without it he is never heard. The world at large honors the man of gold; the man without it has nothing and knows nothing; he dares not say his soul is his own, and now I bid thee take this check and we will make thee one us."

"Sir," said the Chief, in earnest tones, "my duty is first to my country and to God. This talk is all to no effect. Were you to give me all the gold on earth it would not cure a solitary pain nor would it buy one pure, angelic thought. Had gold been clothed with the same power in the new Republic that it is in other countries, few men, perhaps, would have refused a bribe like this, but gold being debased, Justice reigned and in its course the people's cause sustained." ·

After this positive refusal, the Chief stepped to the door and said; "Come on," and passing to the other room the men could only follow. When all had returned, he said: "Gentlemen, my duty is impera-tive and in consequence of the enormity of the crime of which you are charged, I shall be compelled to put all in irons."

"I protest," said Saunders, "against this foul act. We are all honorable men of fortune. Fix your bonds, sir, and we can give you all you dare to ask."

"Bonds," said the Chief, "do you not know that in this land, liberty cannot be bought with gold? We take no bonds; the rich and poor are responsible alike for their crimes."

"Then I protest," said Sherman, "against the usurpation and ungentlemanly procedure. I am a Senator of this Republic and there is no precedence for such arbitrary and inhuman conduct toward a gen-tleman of official standing. I will give you my honor, sir, to report at court to-morrow and will be responsi-ble for all of my associates, but I deny your authority to arrest either me or my associates."

"I, sir," said the Lord, "am an English citizen and will claim the protection of the British flag."

_ "Put these men in irons," said the Chief, and his orders were quickly carried out.

This being done, the room was searched for papers and the Constitution found among some books where it had been laid during the hilarity of the evening.

All were then taken to jail. As court was in session, they were tried in a very few days, found guilty, and the Judge, in sentencing them to be hung for conspiracy and treason, calling their attention to the enormity of the crime, said: "There was but little doubt that the main body of conspirators were in the United States and England. If he had them all, he could hang a traitor to human liberty on every telegraph pole from one side of the continent to the other."

CHAPTER XXXI.

WE will now return to the quiet farm of Mr. Gardner. It was situated not many miles from the city of South Bend; the ladies had several times been driven to the city and had been interested in seeing its large factories and smaller concerns, running in full blast. The retail stores were first class and well supplied with goods, and were the only establishments run by private enterprise, in the same way as they are run in the United States, except that there is no such thing as having credit; there was no necessity for that.

"Persons who are well can always find work," Mr. Gardner explained to them, "and if one person meets with misfortune, assistance is furnished by neighbors, all being well off. Before the national banking system and gold-gamblers had sway in the United States, the same condition existed there, but now there seems to be a reign of selfishness and terror.

"A gentleman came here five years ago from Indiana, by the name of Grimes, and started a carriage and wagon shop on a small scale; being a good mechanic his neighbors induced him to organize a joint-stock company with a capital stock of $300,000 to carry on the manufacture of carriages and wagons. After organizing in due form, we sent our papers on, the plan was approved, a charter granted and the stock and money sent to our sub treasury; officers were appointed. and Mr. Grimes made superintendent. It is a much simpler method than selling the bonds to foreign syndicates.

"On receipt of the money business commenced and the factory has ever since furnished constant employ-. ment for many men, made a market for timber, also for such other articles as are consumed by the work-.

men and their families. Two-thirds of the stock is now owned by those who work for the company; the remainder is scattered among the people, and the factory, with an abundance of capital, is shipping its vehicles to all parts of the country. In the Republic we have several such establishments, but their profits being limited, they do not come in competition.

"These other large manufacturing establishments were started on the same plan; the stock is now owned by our citizens, not one dollar of it having gone out of our own county, while the money that started the institutions has all gone back into the treasury from whence it came. From this you can see the beauties of our system; there is nothing useful to man, outside of natural productions of the earth in a wild state, but is the product of brain and muscle; the people have that, but it is worthless without means; money is the means by which men are set to work; their work soon earns money which, finding no better investment, goes back to the Government in exchange for stock. You see the result; we have no place, nor use for foreign capital, while we hold that it is the duty of Government to keep the land for the use of the people, we also hold it to be the duty of Government to keep all commercial stock for the purpose of securing, so far as possible, a safe investment for the savings of the people and to prevent its being monopolized. Our inheritance law has served a very good purpose."

"I am told," said Mrs. Goldburg, "you have many great ships; how do you manage to build them?"

"In exactly the same way, only the stock is portioned out to the different sub-treasuries, according to population; this is done with a view to giving all our people an opportunity to invest their savings."

During their stay an election was to take place; the ladies, knowing that universal suffrage was the rule and that no proposition could become law until voted on by the people, thus making themselves their own legislators, had a desire to learn something of their peculiar methods; therefore when an opportunity presented itself, Mrs. Goldburg said to Mr. Gardner:

"I would like to know something concerning your elections. It occurs to me from what I have heard, that a polling place is about the last place that a modest woman would like to be seen in."

"Modesty," said he "should prevent no one from going where duty calls. We are taught that there exists in man's nature, two controlling elements, one for good and the other for evil. The one is constantly leading upward toward God, the other farther away from truth, justice and light. It is claimed that where the elements for good predominate in an assembly, woman's safety and protection are secured and her presence is always desirable; if the proper place for woman is not at the polls, it is the best evidence in the world that the people have surrendered their right to self-government and allowed bad influences to come in and dominate elections.

"Show me the place where the presence of a man's wife, mother and sister is not admissible and I will show you a splendid place for him to avoid. While our elections are so pure that our women and children can be present, we have no fear of the vote being influenced by bankers or any other conspiracy against the best interests of the people, through the use of money, whiskey or dishonest methods."

After a moment's pause, he continued: "To-morrow we are to have an election and if you will, we would be glad to have you all go and see for yourselves how our elections are conducted."

Two miles from the farm was a prominent cross-road and a central point in the neighborhood. Government had reserved two acres of land on each corner for public uses; on one corner a magnificent church had been erected, the combined effort of the entire religious element. It was owned in common by a society organized for the purpose, whose charter stipulated at what time each denomination should have its use.

On the same lot was a small building designed for small gatherings, such as primaries, literary or other societies. In this building the election was held. On the other corners stood a public school building, a

residence near by for the use of teachers, and opposite
a repair shop and a store.

On the day of election the ladies went to the place
for voting, in Mr. Gardner's carriage; they found
many other ladies already there, and having been
introduced to several prominent people, they took seats
and became interested spectators of the scenes about
them. Everything was quiet and orderly; a majority
had brought their ballots from home already prepared,
and these were standing about in groups engaged in
pleasant conversation, in so low a tone as not to disturb others; in the back of the room stood a table and
around it were sitting the board of electors consisting
of five persons, three of whom were ladies.

Public sentiment here being opposed to the use of
even the mildest form of whiskey at the polls, it was
not tolerated; consequently there was an absence of
bottles. Mr. Gardner remarked, "that they would as
soon think of allowing a lunatic to vote, as a drunken
man. Money-sharks were conspicuously absent; men
here receive office more as a matter of honor than for
profit, the salaries being gagued by the general price
paid for the same kind of work outside thus no one
could afford to pay for position except by good works."

That evening, Rebecca received through the mail, a
letter from a member of an Ethical society in Kiyougo,
asking her to deliver a course of lectures before their
society. She returned an answer to the effect that she
would do so and allowed them to make their own
appointment as to the time.

During Rebecca's visit at this delightful home, she
had informed herself through the papers of the trial of
the conspirators and of the dreadful sentence. She was,
under all circumstances, opposed to capital punish-
ment and determined, if her lecture was a success, to
risk everything in the effort to secure the release of the
men. She had learned something of President Bundy's
character but nothing of his previous history and dared
not hope that the honest, innocent, simple-minded
youth who had occupied so prominent a place in her
thoughts and affections, and had gone to California

while yet a boy, was now the President of a great
Republic. She dared not mention to her mother or
Minnie, the possibility of such a thing, nor was she
willing to allow herself the comfort of such a hope;
still the name was constantly presenting itself and she
found herself often thinking of her early love.

The society at Kiyongo had given out the appointment
and in order to meet it, it was necessary for the ladies to
take the morning train, which they did after saying good
bye to this kind family. On arriving in the city, they
were met by members of the society and escorted in a
carriage to the hotel where the committee arranged to
meet them later and withdrew.

That evening President Bundy was looking over his
evening paper, when General Summerville, who had
just returned from a trip to the coast, came. While
conversing, a hand-bill announcing the lecture was
thrown in; the name, Rebecca Goldburg, at once
attracted the attention of the President. For a time
he was completely lost in thought and so oblivious to
his surroundings that it required persistent entreaty
on the part of his companion to elicit this explanation:
"I once knew a girl by the same name; I learned that
she was married to a millionaire in Boston; but this
announcement leads me to think I may have been
misinformed."

"Oh, yes," said the General, "I remember seeing
that name written on waste paper on your desk, about
a thousand times. I am not surprised at your being
interested."

"What do you say to our going," said the President
and the two friends soon found themselves occupying a
box in the great hall.

"The seats filled up rapidly and the President asked:
"Do you know where the lady is from?"

"I do not," said the other, "she delivered a lecture
at Summerville not long ago and I was told by a friend
of mine that she made a decided hit; he called her a
regular star."

They had not long to wait; the seats were nearly
full and the band had just ceased playing an American

national air, in honor of the fair lecturess, when Rebecca stepped upon the stage, was duly introduced and greeted with a round of applause.

To Frank, for it was Frank Bundy, now, pure and simple, it was like an apparition. There before him, stood the fair form of his early love; was it all a dream? No, it was too real.

He sat as one entranced, and when her clear, calm voice, unfaltering in its accent, penetrated the atmosphere of that great hall and touched the hearts of all, its effect was like the balm of love or zephyrs laden with rich perfume.

All seemed deeply interested, and every word was distinctly heard in that vast auditorium.

The lecture was a brilliant satire on man's inconsistencies, but had, from beginning to end, an underlying principle of love and wisdom that carried men's souls upward and onward.

Frank sat leaning forward, catching every accent, his whole soul filled with his boyish love, and to him, Rebecca's voice was to his love-thirsty soul, like nectar to the lips of the famished traveller.

The subject of the lecture was "Progress," and as it has been the design of this work to show, in as simple a manner as possible, the false teaching of gold-gamblers, no effort will be made to reproduce Rebecca's words, except so far as they were related to evils resulting from the superstitious use of gold as money.

Going back into remote periods, she pictured man in his barbaric state; first, in families wandering through the forests and along the streams, sleeping in caves and cozy nooks in nature's wilds; they lived upon fruits, leaves, grasses, barks, herbs and insects. When they were scarce, they hunted game and lived upon meat; as time rolled on, in favored regions, mankind became more numerous. It was then decreed in nature that man should go forth and subdue the earth; by the natural course of evolution, from necessity and inborn desire to progress, he began to cultivate the soil and soon found himself, as farmers and toilers always do, (if not robbed) with plenty and to spare.

Then, guided by brutal instinct and void of reason, others came in larger numbers and robbed them of their crops; this forced those who toiled into small communities for protection; there progress continued and animals were domesticated. Those who lived on high and barren lands raised goats, while those who occupied the fertile bottom lands, raised corn.

Those on the high lands, as stockmen always do, found that nature had supplied them with more than they could use; when a man in the valley had a surplus of corn, he was often willing to take a goat in exchange for a bushel. At last it came to pass that the herdsmen wanted ten bushels of corn; but the farmer said, "I have no place to keep the goats." Then the herdsman proposed to give ten pieces of leather of a peculiar kind, made only by himself and said to the farmer: "This is my money, each piece represents a goat; I will give them to you for corn." The farmer took the money; the next day a man came to work for the farmer and was to have one bushel of corn for each day's work. The farmer wanted twenty days' work, but the man wanted only ten bushels of corn. Then said the farmer: "What do you want?" "I want goats " "All right," said the farmer, "I will give you ten pieces of money and you can buy goats. The man did the work and took the money and it so happened that he wanted pottery from another neighbor, but the man said, "I do not want your work, I want corn and goats." "All right," said the man, "I will give you money and you can buy corn and goats." He then took the pottery and gave him six pieces of money and kept four for his own use.

"This," said the fair lecturer, "was money in every sense of the word; it did everything that money can do for man's benefit, assisted in the exchange of product and labor. An ax has its use and its benefits to mankind are incalculable, and yet men have been known to kill others with an ax; so it is with money, it has been used to rob and oppress mankind since earliest history and will continue to do so until the people learn the difference between money for the benefit of mankind and money for the benefit of a few and oppression of the many."

As time rolled on the robbers of the forest, being no longer able to seize upon their crops by main force, brought in nuts, dried-fruits, skins and other things to barter off for corn; thus trade began; the robber chief kept trading until his place was called a store. As men multiplied, crops increased; other stores were started and a Government formed under a King. This King had a council of wise men, similar to the House of Lords, or the United States Senate, and these wise men formed the laws and made money of leather. The country prospered, the King had castles built, roads made, the country improved; had a great many men employed and there was plenty of money in circulation, and everything was life.

Then gold was found by the robber bands in the mountains and was brought to the stores, but no one wanted it; at last, when all the gold had been gathered that could be found, each store had some. It had cost them nothing but the finding; they wanted to trade it for corn and for work, but the people did not want it. They then called a meeting of the other robber chiefs and assumed the name of bankers. This was the work of a conspiracy against the people. They had a few bright coins made of gold; those coins weighed one ounce each and were marked twenty dollars. To each of the wise statesmen they gave five of these coins, then said to them: "Ye are great; ye are the King's council; make us money of this, we pray, and demonetize all other money." Then these robber chiefs, merchants or bankers set up a cry for honest money; they said unto the wise men or King's council: "See, you all have coins; they are worthless now, but make them lawful money and you can buy corn with them to last a year." "These bankers argue well," said one, and made haste to pass a few coinage bills and demonetize all other money; then the bankers went to the Government and had their gold coined into money free. The people must have money to pay debts and do business with. The bankers then said: "As we have all the gold, our note is good; the people, to have prosperity, must have confidence;" so they issued money-notes and bought up all the large holdings of corn. After a few months, when corn became scarce, they said to the laborer: "Give me my price or starve;" and the laborers were forced to work all the time for what they could eat. The men who owned the gold, had great ware-houses full of corn; the people were many of them starving. As was natural, the farmers asked "how it was that they had produced all the corn and still must go hungry, while those who had raised nothing had more than they could use." To settle the vexed question an extra session of the wise men was called and after debating the question for several weeks, decided it was all on account of over-production and inflation and extravagance on the part of the people. It was ordained that the farmer might have the privilege of borrowing honest money from these bankers at a reasonable interest and give a mortgage on their homes; the reasonable interest, however, was to be whatever the gold-men chose to ask.

The vexed question was settled for that time. "From that day to this," said the fair Lecturer, "the same question has been settled in the same way, every few years. All the time the people grew poorer and the robbers grew fatter; the King and his council became willing tools to the money power; at last the people rose in arms, cut off the heads of the King and his wise men; the bankers gather up their gold and fly to some other country; the people war with one another in their starving condition and thousands are slain."

Thus progress is overcome.

Since those days, time after time, civilization has been hurled back into a state of semi-barbarism by this same power of gold in the hands of greed; but the principle of love and of honor has been found underlying these disasters, and upon these our progress has been based. At each successive rise, our civilization reaches a higher plane. In this, our present, the mortal mind seems to have tapped a boundless ocean of thought, and men and women are to-day, thinking

as they never thought before. Greeds are being
shaken with internal strife; the pulpit is sometimes
invaded with original and independent thought, and
our intellectual giants have turned the search-light of
reason on an endless, burning hell and proved it to be
a myth. Kingdoms are crumbling and the labor
problem is coming to the front; the invention of labor-
saving machinery has been the giant of our modern
times. By these great machines which are bought
up by money Lords, thousands of men have been displaced. The machinery is doing the work the men
were wont to do; by the present reign of things, these
men have lost their usefulness, and from the standpoint of a demagogue might well be called an over-
production. But honest, intelligent men will look for
facts and find that while commerce, manufacture, and
industry have undergone an entire change through the
use of these wonderful inventions, the science of Government, dominated by the gold power, has not advanced
an iota; therefore the whole system is out of balance,
and in order to bring about an equilibrium in our
social affairs, it is now time to call a halt. Let the
gold power be overthrown and the same great mass of
intellect that has invented so much machinery, turn
their attention to the science of Government, and when
that science shall have reached the same degree of
perfection that other things have attained, man will
surely have reached a higher plane of civilization.

"It would seem from what I have seen in the last
month," said the lecturer, "that here in this great
Republic, wonders have been already accomplished in
that direction. From the great structure of your
Government the light of reason, truth and justice seems
to radiate like the glow of a brilliant sun.

"In your system you seem to know no such thing as
over-production, but over-accumulation is nicely cared
for by being inherited by the Government and gradually finding its way back among the people who
produced it. The adoption of this law may be
regarded as the grandest step in the reform of Government ever taken since time began, and from it will

spring all the rules and regulations necessary for man's comfort and happiness.

"As sensible laws have been adopted by your people want, extravagance and crime have in a great measure disappeared. That crime will eventually, entirely disappear, is hardly an unreasonable hope; as it disappears progress will crown your efforts with her smiles; love be enthroned in every family; harmony exist and who shall say that some day our people will not be brought in juxtaposition with friends in immortal spheres. As intellectual development has already produced an instrument with which the very heavens have been pierced and planetary systems, with their orbits, mapped, who will say that a farther intellectual development will not produce an instrument that will invade the realm of our future hope, and there disclose our loved ones gone before, carefully preparing a place for our reception and enjoyment in that house of many mansions. Then will death surely have lost its sting and the grave been swallowed up in victory; but shall progress cease? Not while mortal or immortal man exists. Not while one star of this great universe continues to shed its lustre upon its fellow, will progress cease. Never falter, never fear, onward, upward; remove by thy harmonious, intellectual power the veil that separates us from the great angelic hosts and there behold our loved ones, fathers, mothers, sisters, brothers; all in harmony, plucking the sweets of everlasting joy and love, and weaving wreaths by which we may be crowned according to the good they find in us.

"Progress cease? Not while eternal, everlasting and unbounded space remains. Onward, upward, through countless ages, learning, improving, developing, unfolding, step by step, slowly but surely, ever onward; through realms of boundless light till we creative powers attain; then onward to the borders of our universe and add to nature's store another world, another sun, another planetary system. Then shall progress cease? Not while eternity remains."

In closing her lecture, Rebecca said: "As I close my eyes and look into a wilderness of thought, I see before me the happiest and most intellectual people on this broad earth; no cry of hunger, want or woe is heard, but all is peace and love; and yet methinks I hear the clank of iron chains upon the limbs of men, and in their iron cells I see wretched men condemned to death. O horror of horrors! Will the flames of everlasting hell be never quenched and superstition never lose its hold upon our minds? Is there no power in prayer? Let us rise and invoke the favor and guidance of angel friends, and greatest of all Him who rules through the power of love and justice."

At this juncture, while the audience, as by an inspiration, rose to their feet, Frank quietly left his box and in one moment stood behind the scenes, beyond the view of the audience, but within a few feet of the long-lost treasure. When the audience became quiet once more, Rebecca moved a little forward, as if to come in better touch with their feelings, then began: "O Father of mercy, Thou who rulest all things by Thy great love and wisdom, in this, the mistake of a million souls give us counsel, give us strength, give us of Thy great wisdom that we may not mistake a heartless cruelty for law and justice. Let us not reproduce those brutal scenes handed down to us from a barbaric age, through our lingering superstition; send to us, O Father, Thy great angelic hosts, that we may of them take counsel and in thy presence, let us wash our hands of the blood of these men and invoke the source of power to turn them loose, but send them from this land."

Seating the audience, she said: "This night, before I close my eyes in sleep, I will pray that these poor souls be sent back to the land of their birth and that instead of destroying men, the power of this great Republic may be used in destroying the conditions which make the production of such men possible. Is there one in this great audience who will say amen to a prayer like this?"

Quick in response, from that great audience, came one stentorian, "Yes."

Rebecca bowed herself from the audience and as she turned half round to leave the stage, their eyes met;

she recognized her Frank and as he approached her rapidly, with one wild scream of joy, she sprang into his arms. Full of excitement, General Summervllle rushed to the stage to congratulate his friend. Mrs. Goldburg and Minnie fully realizing the situation, moved quickly forward; as Minnie and the General met, the recognition was mutual and Minnie saw in him the realization of her early love; while he, too full for utterance, clasped her to his heart.

This was a scene where it might well have been said: "The angels wept for joy." Had there been a Shakespeare, a Burns, or a Bacon as a witness, the world would perhaps have been furnished with a literary treat. But no poets nigh, the writer must needs draw the veil and leave these fond hearts to re-plight those vows so often made in youth; after so cruelly broken; and loved ones separated through the power of gold, now reunited where gold had lost its power.

We will only add that the sympathies of the people were brought to bear so powerfully upon the court and executive, from that time forward, that the sentence was remitted and the prisoners with their great box of gold were banished for life.

A Great Vote Maker!

"The Grandest Work that Ever Came Before the People!"

WHITHER

ARE WE

DRIFTING

AS A NATION?

WENDELL PHILLIPS said: "It is able, profound, interesting and sure to have a wide and deep influence.'

"Whither Are We Drifting," is a Book of over **700** Pages. Price, postpaid: Cloth, $1.00; Paper, 50 Cents. Order from The Chicago Express, P. O. Box 369. Published by L. D. RAYNOLDS, 267 South Lincoln Street, Chicago, Illinois.

⇌A COMPLETE⇌
HANDBOOK of FINANCE.

COINS
AND
CURRENCY

BY C. B. FENTON.

A work that should be in the hands of every Reformer.
Nothing better for general circulation.   Makes
the Finance question as plain as a b c.

It Contains Quotations from Leading Speakers and
Statesmen.   Price, 25 cents.

ORDER FROM

THE CHICAGO EXPRESS, P. O. BOX 369.

Published by L. D. Raynolds, 267 South Lincoln St.
CHICAGO, ILL.

BREAKERS AHEAD!

A Startling Array of Facts!

This Book, by Edward Irving, is a candid
discussion of the Great Questions of the day; a con-
vincing work and should be given the widest
possible circulation.

Paul Van Dervoort calls it: "A Striking Presentation
of Facts."

A NEW EDITION FOR THE 1896 CAMPAIGN

and the Price Reduced to 10 Cents.

ORDER FROM

THE CHICAGO EXPRESS, P. O. Box 369,

Published by L. D. RAYNOLDS, 267, South Lincoln St.,

CHICAGO, ILL.

Get It At Once!

WHAT?

WHY, THE

FARMERS TRIBUNE.

No true Reformer should be without it.

It is in the fight to stay and is one of the ablest exponents of the rights of the people. It is a large eight-page, printed in nice clear type and is full of hot shot at the enemy every issue. It keeps up with the times and merits the support of all.

Price $1.00 per year. Order it at once if you are not already a subscriber. You are sure to be pleased.

Sample copies sent on application, but don't wait for samples, send your subscription and save a stamp.

Address: FARMERS TRIBUNE,

Des Moines, Iowa.

Unique and Interesting

STORY of the BUTTONS

OR

THE MAN
WHO OWNED
THE EARTH.

By PROF. A. J. CHITTENDEN.

A Poem that cannot fail to awaken thought on the
Leading Questions of the day. Written in that
pleasing style so characteristic of its
author, it is sure to have an
immense sale.

"The chance may never come again;
But it may be well for boys and men
To take the story for what it is worth
And learn the trick of owning the earth."

This book, when
once commenced, will be read
to the end and he who reads cannot
fail to think. The Usury Question is made as
clear as day and the evils of a contracted currency are
vividly portrayed. PRICE, 10 CENTS.

ORDER FROM
THE CHICAGO EXPRESS, P. O. Box 369.
Published by L. D. RAYNOLDS, 267 South Lincoln St.,
CHICAGO' ILL. .

MONEY FOUND

Shows how money would become plenty when put into circulation through confidence in government banks.

By Thomas E. Hill.

In 1890, Hon. Thomas E. Hill, the well known author of "Hill's Manual" and other standard educational works, proposed through the press a vital and far reaching reform in the monetary system of the United States, by the establishment of government banks, in fact, government ownership and control of the entire banking business of the country.

Mr. Hill's system met with instant approval from many of the clearest thinkers of the country and it has been already endorsed by many local conventions of the People's Party.

In response to many requests Mr. Hill elaborated his system in the book, "Money Found," in which he points out that the business depressions which periodically afflict the country are largely due to the people's lack of confidence in the banks.

"MONEY FOUND" explains how the United States might open a bank in every important town and pay a low rate of interest on long time deposits, make loans on a reasonable rate to borrowers who had adequate security, and instead of the business being an expense to the government, it would yield a net revenue of millions of dollars.

The latest edition of this work contains important statistical tables, shows the rates of interest in the several states; amount of gold, silver and paper money in the principal countries of the world and a review of the financial legislation of the United States.

This appendix alone is worth many times the cost of the book.

Price: Paper 25c; Cloth 75c; Morocco $1.00.

ORDER FROM

THE CHICAGO EXPRESS, P. O. Box 369.

Published by L. D. RAYNOLDS, 267 South Lincoln St.

CHICAGO, ILL.